Praise for

Named one of the best book

Autostraddle

GOOD MORNING AMERICA BUZZ PICK

Marie Claire Book Club Pick

"Maybe it's because we're coming out of a year of isolation, or maybe it's because I've spent far too much time extremely plugged into social media, or maybe it's simply because I'm a Gemini, but sometimes, I wake up and crave chaos. I (truly, emphatically, unconditionally) don't want to be a part of the drama—but I do want to read about something so outrageous, so unexpected, so out of pocket, that I feel as if I am buzzing and I can't help texting my friends to gossip about it. How lucky I am, then, to have read Mia McKenzie's hilarious, electric novel, *Skye Falling*." —*The New York Times*

"This endearing and hilarious book is an ode to chosen family, soft Philly pretzels, and the people who make us feel at home." —*BuzzFeed*

"One of the truest depictions of modern queer life I've read in a while." —*BookRiot*

"A disenchanted protagonist for the ages." —*Bitch Media*

"You can't escape your past. It's one of the oldest literary motifs around, yet it feels fresh in Mia McKenzie's *Skye Falling*. The novel explores how dealing with painful memories and embracing anger can unlock a freer future—but only if you're brave enough to try. . . . *Skye Falling* is multilayered in the best way as it explores Skye's character growth. McKenzie weaves together several themes—gentrification, racism, child abuse, grief—and each topic carries equal weight. For a novel that addresses many serious subjects, the story never feels heavy. That's a credit to Skye's narrative voice, which McKenzie infuses with both a sense of humor and strong opinions." —*Bookpage*

"Razor-sharp and outrageously funny, *Skye Falling* is an absolute winner. Mia McKenzie has created a one-in-a-million heroine in Skye Ellison and has crafted an entirely fresh story about love that charms with curmudgeonly wit and a tender heart."

—TAYLOR JENKINS REID, author of *Malibu Rising*

"I can't remember the last time a book made me laugh, cry, and reflect as thoroughly as *Skye Falling*. Mia McKenzie has written the kind of story I've been searching for, and maybe even gave up on as a possibility, and now, suddenly, it's here. This is a narrative about family, responsibility, and home. It's a new kind of love story, the best kind, and you'll be turning the pages just as quickly as I did."

—ASHLEY C. FORD, author of *Somebody's Daughter*

"Mia McKenzie is a writer who can move from heartbreak to laughter in a single paragraph, while brilliantly reinventing queer family and friendship and the ways in which we get stuck and unstuck along the way. When I could manage to put this book down, I looked up from its pages to a world charged with new potential."

—TORREY PETERS, author of *Detransition, Baby*

"What if your most wounded, immature, rude, self-destructive, and antisocial habits were forgotten when a twelve-year-old walked into your life, saying 'Love me'? This page-turner had me laughing out loud at Skye's acid tongue and thoughts, and yet without abandoning the barbs it unearths—and earns—something like grace. Full of vivid women, each complex and funny as hell, *Skye Falling* reads like a hot summer jam, and it adds up to a lively, full meal."

—QUIARA ALEGRÍA HUDES, author of *My Broken Language*

By Mia McKenzie

The Summer We Got Free

Skye Falling

Skye Falling

A NOVEL

Mia McKenzie

RANDOM HOUSE | NEW YORK

Skye Falling is a work of fiction. Names, characters, places, and incidents either are the product of the author's imagination or are used fictitiously. Any resemblance to actual persons, living or dead, events, or locales is entirely coincidental.

2022 Random House Trade Paperback Edition

Copyright © 2021 by Mia McKenzie

All rights reserved.

Published in the United States by Random House, an imprint and division of Penguin Random House LLC, New York.

RANDOM HOUSE and the HOUSE colophon are registered trademarks of Penguin Random House LLC.

Originally published in hardcover in the United States by Random House, an imprint and division of Penguin Random House LLC, in 2021.

LIBRARY OF CONGRESS CATALOGING-IN-PUBLICATION DATA
Names: McKenzie, Mia, author.
Title: Skye falling: a novel / Mia McKenzie.
Description: First edition. | New York: Random House, [2021]
Identifiers: LCCN 2020052393 (print) | LCCN 2020052394 (ebook) |
ISBN 9781984801623 (trade paper; acid-free paper) |
ISBN 9781984801616 (ebook)
Classification: LCC PS3613.C55665 S58 2021 (print) |
LCC PS3613.C55665 (ebook) | DDC 813/.6—dc23
LC record available at https://lccn.loc.gov/2020052393
LC ebook record available at https://lccn.loc.gov/2020052394

Printed in the United States of America on acid-free paper

randomhousebooks.com

1st Printing

Book design by Susan Turner

*To my mother, who worked on a novel at
the dining room table while we played*

Skye Falling

1

I'M LYING VERY STILL ON TOP OF A HOTEL BED'S RUMPLED SHEETS. My mouth is slack. My eyes are open. My stare is cold and lifeless. If anyone looked down on me from overhead right now, they'd think I'm dead. And it probably wouldn't be a huge shock. I'm pretty sure no one who knows me would be like: *Wow, I never imagined her life would end like this! I always thought she'd die at a ripe old age, surrounded by seventeen great-grandchildren!* Because no one thinks that. I don't even think that myself. I've never really been the *surrounded by seventeen great-grandchildren* type. In junior high, my classmates voted me "Most Likely to Be Single." Which, like, what even is that? I spent all of recess sulking in the library, feeling deeply misunderstood. It didn't help that I *hadn't* been voted:

1. Most Liked
2. Most Ride-or-Die Homie
3. Most Likely to Marry the Cute One from Color Me Badd

And while being voted "Most Likely to Be Single" at twelve years old isn't necessarily an early indicator that one might die alone in a hotel bed many years later, it's not hard to imagine it as part of the same narrative, right? Not that you'd *expect* it, but if you heard about it, you'd be like: *Uh-huh, okay, I can see that.* So, yeah. Nobody would be super surprised. Is what I'm saying.

Plot twist: I'm not dead, I'm just really hungover.

I snort and sit up straight in the bed. The sudden movement sends a wave of nausea through me and I close my eyes and take a long, deep breath, trying not to puke. When it passes, I squint hazily around the room. It's a nice room, in a nice little bed-and-breakfast called Narradora. The niceness of it is somewhat diminished, though, by the greasy, crumpled take-out bags I keep forgetting to throw in the trash and the suitcases open on the floor, spilling out dirty socks and underwear. In my defense, I just got done leading a two-week-long group trip to southern Africa for Black travelers for We Outchea, the company I own. The trip back to Philly from Zimbabwe was twenty-three hours long and I've been recovering from the flights for a week and three days, during which time I couldn't possibly have been expected to clean up after myself. A purple thong hangs out of a carry-on, crotch-side up. I squint at it through eyes that are blurry both because I'm not wearing my glasses and because they're burning in my head like little balls of fire. I rub them with my fists, like a sleepy kid.

There's movement beside me, and I jump a little. There's a naked man lying next to me, sleeping with a smile on his face. I try to remember who he is but, after a few moments of racking my brain, I give up. I decide I will never drink again probably.

There's a knock on the door. I look over at the sleeping man. "You expecting someone?" The man, who is light brown and has a muscular ass, doesn't answer. I look around for my glasses, don't see them, give up, get out of bed, feel another intense wave of nausea, stumble, trip over a suitcase, and fall face-first onto the floor.

Mother. Fucker.

I get to the door and squint through the peephole, which is point-less, since I can't see shit.

"Skye. It's Viva."

Viva Robinson is a friend of mine from high school who also owns this nice B and B. Because I'm bad at keeping in touch, she's one of the few friends I still have in Philly.

I'm about to open the door when I remember there's a naked dude in the bed. I grab the sheet and cover him from head to toe. Maybe she won't notice.

"Veev," I say as I open the door, "I can't find my glasses."

"Ajá, no estás vestida," she says.

This is when I realize I answered the door in a camisole and a thong. I'm not embarrassed; I don't have many bits that Viva hasn't already seen. But her tone suggests there's something I'm supposed to be dressed *for* and I have no idea what that is. I guess my cluelessness shows on my face because she says, "Art sale."

"Oh, sí." It's all coming back to me now. A year ago, one of our other high school friends, Naima, quit her bookkeeping job to do art full-time. Which I only know because Viva told me. She's still friends with some of the people we kicked it with in high school. Like, actual friends, not just social media friends. I haven't seen Naima, or almost anyone we went to high school with, since graduation, except in pass-ing. But for some reason I can't recall now, when Viva asked me to go to Naima's art sale with her, I said I would.

"It's at eleven," Viva says. "Remember?"

"Of course I do." Nah, I don't. "I just need, like, ten to get ready. Fifteen tops."

I move toward the bathroom as Viva comes farther inside the room. I catch her eyeing my mess. "Have you thought about getting an apartment?"

I turn to look at her. I'm only in Philly for a couple of weeks every few months, between trips, which I guess makes it my base, but getting a whole-ass apartment feels more permanent than I'd like. "Is this your way of telling me I've worn out my welcome?"

Viva shakes her head. "Claro que no."

Good. Because I love this place. The theme of the bed-and-breakfast is famous Black and Puerto Rican women writers and the six rooms here are styled after the works of Zora Neale Hurston, Lola Rodríguez de Tió, Lorraine Hansberry, Julia de Burgos, Gwendolyn Brooks, and Gloria Naylor. My current room, the Zora Neale Hurston, has a late-1930s chaise made of ebony and upholstered in deep pink velvet; a tall, narrow, dark-finished oak armoire that reminds me of playing hide-and-seek as a child; framed book covers from *Jonah's Gourd Vine*, *Their Eyes Were Watching God*, and *Moses, Man of the Mountain* hanging on the walls; and a painting of Zora herself, grinning in a feathered hat and fur-collared coat. I love being here, surrounded by all this. Plus, Viva and her husband, Jason, who helps manage the place, let me stay for mad cheap.

"I just don't know how you survive on French fries for two weeks at a stretch," she continues, pointing to a particularly greasy bag.

"The potato is a vegetable. I'm pretty sure."

"I worry about you sometimes," she says.

"Ew. You sound like somebody's mother. Not mine, you understand. But somebody's."

She laughs. "Well, you are almost forty, chica. And you don't even have a toaster."

I shrug. "Luckily, it's the twenty-first century and I can procure crunchy bread at any number of establishments throughout the city. Also—and this is really important, Viva—I'm thirty-eight and three-quarters, not *almost fucking forty*." And with that, I take my ass to the shower.

I'm in there, trying not to throw up, when I hear a scream of surprise and I figure Viva and the naked guy are making each other's acquaintance.

* * *

VIVA AND I WALK TOGETHER from the bed-and-breakfast to Naima's art studio, straight down Fifty-first Street, past large, wide-porched row houses lined up like heavy books on shelves. It's sunny and warm out, unseasonal for early April in Philly, and I say a little prayer to the global-warming gods for their generosity. I'm kidding; I know climate change is bad. Hip-hop songs spill out from open car windows, battling for attention with the loud sighs of city buses. The air smells like garbage and then not garbage and then garbage again. Which doesn't help with the nausea, tbh.

The art studio is in a little storefront on Baltimore Avenue, a busy-ish commercial strip lined with take-out joints, small grocers, and the occasional artsy-fartsy shop. Inside, the large windows throw daylight into every corner. The exposed brick walls—some of which are crumbling here and there but in a very artsy way, somehow—are hung with paintings and prints, most of them depicting Black women and girls with Afros or cornrows riding tractors or motorcycles or, in one instance, a rhinoceros. Or maybe it's a dinosaur of some sort. Either way, it sounds dumb, right? But it's actually kind of cool.

There are more people here than I expected for this early on a Saturday, at least a couple dozen folks staring at the walls and sifting through large bins full of neatly arranged prints. Some people have even brought their kids, which means Naima must be pretty good because, the way I figure it, you have to really be committed to showing up somewhere if you're willing to drag a kid along to do it. There's a tween girl standing near the door, staring at a print of two women scissoring. It's mostly shadows and suggestion but . . . still. I worry it's not really child-appropriate. But then I'm like: Whatever, it ain't my kid.

My phone buzzes in my back pocket and when I check it there's a text from my brother.

U in town???

I text back: *No. In Zimbabwe.*

Marv just called me. He saw u on Baltimore Ave a few minutes ago.

Wasn't me. Marvin's prob smoking that shit again.
U know that nigga ain't reliable.

Are you coming by to see Mom?

I just said I'm in Zimbabwe, WTF?

I stuff the phone back in my pocket.

From across the room, Naima waves and bounces toward Viva and me. She's wearing a yellow Kangol and turquoise lipstick. It's the most Black Philly look you've ever seen. "You made it!"

"¡Seguro que yes!" Viva says, hugging her. "We wouldn't have missed it."

"Skye," says Naima when they part, "it's so good to see you."

"Okay," I say, realizing a second too late that THAT'S NOT A NORMAL RESPONSE. Ugh. I wish I was better at this. And by "this" I mean any sort of social interaction with another human being.

Naima laughs. "Well, you haven't changed, have you?" Which is possibly an insult? I don't have time to decide before a little bit of bourbon-flavored vomit creeps up into my throat and I have to concentrate hard to swallow it.

"I was actually just thinking about you the other day, Skye," Naima says. "I saw the photos you posted of your group in Zimbabwe. So amazing!"

"Yup."

"I need to get it together and sign up for a trip. Where are you going next?"

"Brazil next week. Then Cuba."

She sighs. "I'm so jealous. I would travel all the time if I could."

I hear that a lot. And, as someone who actually travels all the time, I'm not sure I believe it. Nonstop travel isn't as romantic as it sounds. A lot of it is hard and lonely and complicated and infuriating and I don't think most people imagine it that way.

"We have to get dinner sometime and talk about all the places you've been," Naima says.

I nod. "Cool." There's no way I'm doing that.

"Selfie for the event page?" Naima asks, taking out her phone.

"Sí," says Viva.

I hold up a hand in protest. "Um, can we not?"

Look: I know photos of happy people smiling at your events are good social capital and I'm not trying to be unhelpful. I swear. I just have a rule that I never let my picture be taken by anyone I'm not sleeping with. It's been my experience that if you're performing cunnilingus on someone on a regular basis, they tend to care how you look in photos, because of their own ego. People you're *not* regularly going down on, however, care less about catching your good side or making sure your hair's not doing anything weird. They'll legit have you looking busted, with one eye closed and food in your teeth and then tag you so everyone can see. Also, I'm not super photogenic to begin with. Most of my facial features are twice as large as they functionally need to be. My face somehow works fine in real life, but *pictures* of me have startled babies. Like, made actual babies cry and throw food. I'm not making that up.

"Oh," Naima says. "Okay. No problem. Maybe just Viva and me, then?"

Viva and Naima take a few smiling selfies while I stand there looking uncooperative. When they're done, Naima posts the photos, then waves at some people coming in.

"I'm going to go say hello. We have refreshments set up right over there," she says, pointing to a table where plates of crackers and cheese, bottles of fancy Italian soda, and those little clear plastic cups

have been arranged, "so help yourselves. I'll come back to chat later."
She bounces away.

Viva gives me a look.

"What? I wasn't trying to be difficult, I swear."

"And yet, you succeeded anyway, antipática," she says, laughing
and shaking her head.

My phone buzzes in my pocket again. I ignore it.

"There's Tasha," Viva says.

"Tasha? Ugh, what's she doing here?"

Tasha Mosley is an ex-girlfriend of Viva's and an ex-friend of mine.
We used to be homies of the highest degree, from second grade
through high school. We had a pact to go to the same college, but
then Tasha decided to go way out of state. At first, I was devastated.
Then, when she didn't even bother to keep in touch, I was pissed.
When I ran into her in Philly the next summer, she was all, *hey girl*,
and I was like, *nah*. Eventually—I'm talking years later—we started
saying hi again when we saw each other out at the club or wherever
but dassit. I haven't seen her in years now.

Viva looks at me. "What do you mean? This is Tasha's art sale."

"This is *Naima's* art sale."

"No," she says. "Naima shares the space with Tasha and they both
planned the event. Pero it's Tasha's art sale."

"You didn't tell me that!"

"It was right there on the event page."

I barely even looked at the event page. I only hastily RSVP'd
"maybe" so people would see it and think I'm a very busy, popular
person, which I'm not.

"I thought you two are okay now?" Viva asks.

I shrug. "I never see her. Which is what I prefer."

Viva frowns. "We can leave if you want."

"Viva!" It's Tasha. She's spotted us and is heading in our direction.
GREAT.

I stand there while Viva and Tasha hug. It's a long hug. Longer than necessary, in my opinion. When it's over, Tasha sort of half-smiles at me. She looks taller than I remember and there's some gray in her hair, which is cut in a tight fade. She's wearing a button-down with a bow tie, neat slacks, and wing tips, which is to say: She looks gay as hell, as per always. "Oh, hey, Skye," she says. "I didn't know you were back in Philly."

Why would she? We're not friends. She needn't be privy to my comings and goings.

"When did you get back?" she asks.

"Week ago."

"Cool. How was . . . Africa, right?"

"Yeah. Hot."

She looks at me for a few seconds, like she's waiting for me to say more. I don't. I suppose I could make more of an effort, but I find small talk to be a kind of torture on par with waterboarding, and doubly so with people I don't even like. *Triply* so with people I once trusted who, as it turned out, couldn't actually be counted on.

"Okay, then," she says, rolling her eyes. She looks at Viva. "I saved that print for you. It's in the back."

Viva looks at me. "Are you okay on your own for a minute?" she asks, as if I'm completely socially inept.

"Of course," I say, muchly offended, as they walk off.

So now I'm standing there alone, and I suddenly feel eyes on me. I get super self-conscious and can't figure out what to do with my hands, so I put them in my pockets, all casual, like *hey whatevs*. But that feels awkward, so I stop and take out my cellphone to text someone. I can't think of anyone I actually want to text, though, so I put my phone back in my pocket, as another wave of nausea rolls through me. I decide to look for a bathroom in which to puke.

Down a narrow hallway, I find one. I try to vomit, but nothing comes up. So, I pee and then head back. As I'm re-entering the room,

I see my brother standing at the refreshments table, stuffing cheese in his mouth. I back out, quickly, before he sees me, pressing myself against a wall.

I can't believe this nigga came to find me. He's annoying but he's also lazy and rarely has the follow-through to finish an anecdote, let alone orchestrate an ambush. I'm halfway impressed, to be honest. But also I'm searching for an exit.

There's no door I can get to without my brother seeing me but there is a window down the hall in the direction I just came from. I head straight for it. It's kind of high off the ground, but I think I can hoist myself up if I use my core like they made me do that one time I tried yoga.

"Excuse me."

I glance over my shoulder. Standing there is the very serious-looking kid I saw viewing adult content earlier. She has braces, and hair done up in plump, shiny cornrows that curl under where they touch her shoulders, and curious, russet-brown eyes.

"Are you Skye Ellison?"

"Nah."

She frowns at me. "Yes, you are."

I glance toward the studio, out of which my brother is probably going to emerge any second, see me, and start bitching about how I never visit our disabled mother, how I suck at family and, really, at relationships of all varieties.

The kid is still staring at me.

Maybe she's right about me being Skye. After all, I *am* considering jumping out of a window to escape a pretty standard family obligation. Plus, my mouth tastes like sweat and rancid bourbon and . . . well, balls, frankly. I'm probably gonna hurl any second. All of that sounds a lot like Skye.

"Okay, yeah," I tell her. "Fine. Who are you?"

A look passes across the kid's face, part *I knew it* and part *oh shit* and then she says, "Okay. Well. I'm Vicky. I used to be your egg."

2

I WAS TWENTY-SIX. I HAD JUST RETURNED TO PHILLY AFTER A COU-
ple of weeks in London. I was standing in line at Saad's, probably trying to decide between falafel and lamb shawarma, when I felt a hand
on my shoulder. Assuming it was Some Nigga™, I turned around,
ready to give him my best *the fuck you want?* look, and saw Cynthia.

Cynthia had been my best friend at summer camp. It was a day
camp, run from the basement of Holy Sanctuary Church of God,
which was my family's church, and I attended from the age of five until
the age of thirteen. On the first day of camp in the summer of 1989,
when I was newly nine, Cynthia came and sat down next to me at the
long breakfast table and whispered, "I hope they don't make us read
Revelations in Bible study. I read some of it this summer. It's scary. I
don't think fourth-graders can handle it."

"Are you in this group?" I asked her.

She nodded, her pink barrettes bouncing at the ends of her plaits.

"So, aren't you in fourth grade?"

"Yeah," she said, "but I'm more of a fifth-grader, emotionally."

I didn't know what that meant. But it sounded cool and I was nervous about not making friends that summer. My regular bestie, Tasha,

always spent summers at her grandparents' house in Wilmington, and my usual camp bestie, Adina, who I'd rolled with every summer since we were five, hadn't shown up that year. So, I decided right then and there to claim Cynthia as my own. I nodded and said, "I'm pretty much a sophomore, emotional-wise."

She laughed, and I laughed, too, even though I wasn't entirely sure what the joke was.

We were lightning-fast friends. The kind of homies who held hands while jumping into the deep end of the public pool, who sat together at every single camp activity, and who sometimes called each other first thing in the morning to coordinate matching outfits. We had a lot in common. We were both dark-skinned girls who got teased for it. We were both honor roll students who could memorize long Bible verses with ease. We both liked listening to really sad love songs and making ourselves cry as hard as we could.

Like many kids who showed up for camp there, Cynthia's family didn't go to our church. She didn't go to my school or live within walking distance. Because of this, I only ever saw her at camp. After a few years, she stopped coming to camp and I lost touch with her. I hadn't seen her in fifteen years before that day in Saad's. Still, somehow, I recognized her instantly.

"Hey, Cynthia."

"Skye! Oh my God, girl!"

She asked me how life was, what I was up to. I told her I'd just got back from abroad and she reminded me how I'd always talked about wanting to travel a lot when we were kids. Instead of taking our food to go, like we'd both planned to, we sat together at a booth and spent an hour catching up.

"Do you have a significant other?" she asked me, which I took to mean that my recently shaved head and new septum piercing were making me look exactly as gay as I was going for, otherwise she probably would've just said "husband" or "boyfriend" like most straights do.

I told her no.

"Kids?"

Oh God, no.

She was on her second husband, she said. I thought back to camp, when she'd agreed to go steady with this dark-skinned boy whose name I don't remember, fifteen minutes after breaking up with this light-skinned boy whose name I don't remember.

She said she didn't have kids but that she wanted them "very, very much."

Once we were all caught up, and had spent a little while reminiscing, she had to get back to work. It was Saturday, but she said she rarely took a whole weekend off.

"Let's get together sometime," she said.

I figured she meant it in a polite, *we're not really going to do that though* way, so I said sure and we exchanged numbers.

A week later, she called and invited me out for coffee. This time there was no summer camp nostalgia. She got straight to the point. She said she had been diagnosed as infertile, after several years of trying to get pregnant. She said her eggs were no good and that she was looking for an egg donor. She wondered if I might be interested in being that.

I wasn't planning to have kids of my own. I'd decided at age six, when my Penny Pee-Pee doll whizzed on my favorite Wonder Woman T-shirt, causing me to fly into a rage, twist off her head, and throw it out a window, that babies weren't for me. Thus, I did not feel very attached to my ova. She told me she could pay me five thousand dollars. Which: Um, yes, please. I'd been dreaming of a trip to sub-Saharan Africa, where I'd never been, and five grand would make it possible. I couldn't think of a reason not to do it. But I did hesitate for a second.

"Why me?"

"You're intelligent," she said. "And funny."

ALL TRUE.

"And we have some of the same features, physically. One thing, though. Do you have any cancer in your family? Parents, aunts or uncles, or grandparents, especially?"

I shook my head. "No. None of those people. And no one else as far as I know."

She smiled. "Good. So, what do you say?"

I said yes. Obviously.

I STARE AT THE KID as the ghost of bourbons past wails in my belly. I close my eyes, willing it to stay down. It's not going to. I cover my mouth and sprint to the bathroom.

I'm throwing up stuff I don't remember eating and between heaves, out of the corner of my eye, I see the kid standing there, watching me. I forgot to close the stall door and I feel grateful to the kid for not looking disgusted or horrified, but instead curious, border-line amused even. I stop upchucking for a sec.

"You're really my egg?"

The kid nods.

"Well, then, do me a favor and hold back my hair."

The kid comes into the stall, grabs my locs on either side of my head and holds them back, and my vomiting resumes.

After a minute or two, the bathroom door opens and I hear a young woman's voice. "Vicky, are you okay?"

"Yeah," the kid says, sounding totally sincere. "I'm good."

HALF AN HOUR LATER, THE kid and I are sitting in a booth in a fancy hot dog shop, which is apparently a thing. Thanks, hipsters. The kid has a hot dog loaded with relish and mustard and she's eating it from the middle out, instead of end to end, which I have never seen any-body do, and I wonder if I'm dreaming this whole day while still passed out. If I am, I just hope someone turns me on my side so I don't drown in my own vomit like Hendrix.

The young woman from the bathroom is sitting at a table nearby, drinking a soda and keeping an eye on us.

"Who's that?" I ask the kid, sipping seltzer. "Your babysitter?"

"Babysitter," she says, "b-a-b-y-s-i-t-t-e-r." Then she shakes her head no. "That's my stepsister."

"Oh. So, your parents got divorced?"

"Yeah."

"And now Cynthia's remarried?" That would put her on her third husband, which is 1980s-*Dynasty* levels of husbands.

"No. My dad's remarried. My mom died."

At first, the words don't really register. I spend at least a couple of seconds staring blankly at the kid. Then I'm like: "Cynthia . . . died?"

She nods. "Yeah."

"Wow," I say. Which is probably not the proper response. I honestly don't know what to say, though. No one I was friends with as a kid has ever died, at least no one that I know about. I think of Cynthia, holding my hand as we ventured out into the deep end. I feel sad. But also . . . I don't know . . . disturbed? Cynthia was only nine months older than me. Also, in addition to sad and disturbed, I'm a little bit nauseated still. And now I start to worry that the look of sympathy I'm trying to give the kid resembles my *I'm about to puke* face. I force the corners of my mouth down as hard as I can, trying to unambiguously convey sadness instead of queasiness. But I guess it doesn't work because the kid looks at me like she's afraid I'm having a stroke.

"What's wrong with your face?"

"Nothing. I'm just really sad for you about your mother."

"Oh," she says. "It's okay. It was, like, two years ago almost."

I relax the corners of my mouth a little. I sort of want to ask how Cynthia died. But I don't know if you're supposed to ask kids questions like that.

"You were friends with her?"

I nod. "We went to the same day camp for a few summers. Once we got too old to go anymore, we lost touch."

The kid takes another bite of her hot dog and is quiet for a moment while she chews, then she says, "So, you got paid to do it?"

"That's right."

She nods, like she knew that. "How much?"

"I don't remember exactly," I tell her. It's a lie but it feels like the right thing to say.

"Did you ever think about it?" she asks. "I mean, about me? Like, afterward?"

"Sure. But in all my imaginings, it never once occurred to me that you might be a person who would eat a hot dog from the middle out instead of end to end."

She looks down at the hot dog. "This way is better, though."

I shake my head. "Can't be."

"The way I do it," she says, "the meat stays even in the bun, so when you get to the last bite, it's equal. It's, like, meat-bun balanced. But when *you* get to the last bite, there's always more bun left than meat. Don't you hate that?"

Holy shit, I do hate that! I've hated that my entire life! "Wow," I say. "My egg growed up to be a genius." Possibly only about hot-dog-related things, but I think we can all agree that's not nothing.

"Genius. G-e-n-i-u-s."

I want to ask why she's spelling things, but I'm worried that she already told me and in my haziness I've forgotten. I must look confused, though, because she says, "I'm practicing for the spelling bee. I'm West Philly Montessori seventh-grade champ." She sips her soda.

"That's impressive."

She shrugs. "There's not that many good spellers in my grade."

"Oh." Well, there's still the hot dog thing, I guess.

"Where did you go?" she asks me.

"To school?"

She nods.

"Hamilton, for middle school," I tell her.

"You're from West Philly?"

"Fifty-seventh and Larchwood."

"You still live there?"

"I left the day I turned eighteen. But I still stay in West Philly when I'm in town. My friend owns a bed-and-breakfast not that far from here."

She's watching me intently now and I'm sure she's trying to read me. I don't like it. Most people can't get a read on me but I worry that if this kid really wanted to, she could, like a genetic knowing, passed to her through my DNA or some shit. Then she says, "Why'd you do it, though? Just for money or, like, other reasons, too?"

I can see the kid is getting at something. I guess this is why she came: to know the reasons she exists. That feels heavy and I wish this conversation wasn't happening.

"How'd you find me?" I ask her, mostly to deflect.

"Google."

"You searched 'where is my egg donor' and that led you right to me? Wow, technology really is on some next-level shit."

She laughs a little, and I like the sound of it more than I could have anticipated. "No, not like that," she says. "I saw your name on these papers. I guess they were my mom's. Then I looked you up on Facebook and saw you might be at that art thing today."

"Ah."

"So, why'd you give your eggs to some girl you only knew at camp?"

"Jesus Christ, kid," I say, because she's legit relentless. "That's a really heavy question."

"Sorry," she says. "I'm a lot sometimes. People say that about me."

Same.

"It was a long time ago," I tell her. "I don't really remember all the reasons. But probably some part of my twenty-six-year-old self thought it would be cool to help make a kid I could maybe someday meet but not have to, you know, support financially. Speaking of which, you know we're going dutch here, right?"

She laughs again. The sound gets up under my ribs in this weird way, like a vibration. And then, out of nowhere, this thought occurs to me: *I have never seen such a perfect human being.*

"Excuse me for a second," I say. "I need to, um, vomit." I get up and walk toward the bathroom. When I'm out of sight of the kid, I change course and head straight for the exit. I stop. The stepsister is right there by the door. Shit. I head for the bathroom instead.

I'm halfway out the window when the door opens and the kid enters. She sees me making a break for it and *now* she looks horrified. Not curious. Not amused. Horrified. I knew we'd get there eventually.

"You're sneaking out?"

"No!" I look down at myself, one leg already out the window, the other foot dangling above the sink. "Well, yes."

"Why?"

Trouble is, I don't really know why. Not entirely. I mean, obviously I can't handle this. But going out a window to escape my brother is one thing. Going out a window to ditch a twelve-year-old girl seems extreme even to me. "Look. You seem like a nice kid. But I'm not really . . . you know . . . motherly."

"Yeah, that's kinda obvious," she says. "Good thing I don't need a mother."

I'm not sure I believe her. People can be tricky when they're trying to get something from you, especially if that something is love.

The kid shakes her head. "Fine. Whatever. Just go."

I feel shame blossoming in my chest and I don't like it. Maybe it would be better if I came back inside. Maybe the kid really isn't looking for another mother. I mean, how many mothers does one girl need in a lifetime? I have one and, frankly, it's too many! And even if she is . . . well . . . maybe I *could* be that. I mean, I might not make the best mother, but I probably wouldn't be the worst. I could maybe pull off second mom in a pinch. I look at the kid. Take a deep breath. And climb a little farther out the window.

"You're still going?!"

"What? You just said I could go!"

Exasperated, the kid turns and storms out of the bathroom.

This is the part where I'm supposed to go after her. But I don't. I just sit there, half in, half out of the window, until some old lady comes in to pee, sees me, and frowns, all judgy, like she thinks I'm trying to dine and dash or some shit.

"This isn't how it looks," I tell her.

She smirks like, *if you say so*, and goes into a stall.

When I get back to our table, the kid and her stepsister are gone. The word "dutch" has been scrawled on the check and there's cash for one hot dog beside it.

IT'S MID-AFTERNOON AND EVEN WARMER and sunnier than it was this morning, the sky a stunningly clear, almost glassy, blue. I walk the eight blocks back to the bed-and-breakfast because I think the air will help clear my head. It sorta does and it sorta doesn't. I'm less queasy, but the last couple of hours feel like a weird dream.

When I get back to my room, I'm thrilled to find it clean and completely free of naked strangers. I put the DO NOT DISTURB sign on the door, strip down to my underwear, then go into the bathroom and throw up one more time for good measure. My phone buzzes. It's Viva. I ignore it. I get in bed and close my eyes. My phone buzzes again. It's my brother. I put it on silent and pull the covers up over my head. At least the kid doesn't have my number.

3

I SLEEP FOR FIFTEEN HOURS STRAIGHT. WHEN I FINALLY EMERGE FROM under the covers, my body is stiff and sore and the morning light streaming through the windows hurts my eyes. I stretch, hearing things crack in various parts of my thirty-eight-and-three-quarters-old body, then pop a pod in the Keurig and drag myself to the shower.

It's Monday, which means I have a ten o'clock staff meeting with my single employee: my assistant, Toni.

"You look tired," she says, peering out at me from the video chat screen.

Considering I just slept for fifteen hours, and even bothered to put on mascara, I feel pretty insulted.

We dot i's and cross t's for our upcoming trip to Brazil, which kicks off in São Paulo in six days, with twelve Black American travelers in tow. Toni, who's in charge of making sure passports and vaccines are current, assures me that everything is on track.

After we hang up, I spend a couple of hours answering emails from our travelers, and then, when my stomach starts to growl, I decide to head out for food. I'm walking past Viva's office when I hear her call my name and it's only then I remember that I bailed on her at the art show yesterday.

"What the hell happened to you?" she asks me from behind her desk.

I don't really want to tell her about the kid. But I can't think of a quick lie that's good enough to justify ditching her without a word. So, I opt for the truth. I tell her all of it—from day camp and Cynthia to how the kid held my hair back while I ralphed. When I'm done, she's staring at me in wide-eyed disbelief.

"¿Una *nena*? An actual human child?"

"I was pretty hungover," I tell her. "But half human, at least."

"Wow," she says, shaking her head in amazement. She leans back in her chair. "So? ¿Ahora qué?"

I shrug. "¿Qué quieres decir?"

"Well, you're going to see her again, right?"

I shrug.

"But she's . . . sort of your kid?"

Skreech. Nope. Nuh-uh. "She's not. At all. Not even a little bit. That was the deal when I gave Cynthia my eggs and she gave me thousands of dollars."

"O sea, full," Viva says, nodding. "I get that's how it works, pero you must feel *something* for the kid, right?"

I almost shrug again, but then it occurs to me that if I keep shrugging, I'll look like a sociopath. Because what level of fucked up would you have to be to feel nothing for a kid who

1. got half her genes from you;
2. is a genius about hot-dog-related things; and
3. is a better speller than several other kids who aren't very good spellers?

I'm not sure I'm okay with being that level of fucked up. So, I hedge.

"Even if I wanted to see the kid again," I tell Viva, "I don't know how. Unfortunately, she didn't leave me any contact info." I don't mention that we never got around to that because when last we talked I was halfway out a bathroom window.

"There's probably a way to track her down," Viva says. "How did she find you?"

"She saw my name on some egg donor papers, I guess, and then googled me."

"Well, you could try that. Kids don't always have digital trails, pero maybe. ¿Cuál es su nombre?"

"¿Qué?"

"¿Su nombre?"

"Huh?"

Viva frowns. "Girl. You don't know her name?"

I think about it. "I wanna say it's . . . Charmaine?"

"You *wanna say* it's Charmaine? Or it's actually Charmaine?"

"It's Charmaine," I say, nodding.

"Well, there's probably not a lot of twelve-year-olds named Charmaine running around. ¿Cuál es su apellido?"

"No sé. Lucas, maybe? That was Cynthia's last name. But the kid might have her father's name, right? Because patriarchy and such?"

Viva nods. "Maybe. What about her neighborhood? Did she mention where she lives?"

Okay, this has turned into Sherlock Hermana and the Case of the Egg Donor super fucking fast and now I regret telling Viva about the damn kid.

"No, Veev. She didn't say anything like that."

". . . or where she goes to school . . ."

Okay, wait. Now I can feel my brain trying to reach back and grab something. The spelling bee. At West Philly Montessori. Holy shit. "She goes to West Philly Montessori."

"Chévere," Viva says. "So, you *do* know how to find her."

I nod. "Yeah, I guess I do."

"I can go with you if you want," she says. "I could use a break from bookkeeping."

Wayment. "Go? Where?"

She checks her watch. "Most middle schools let out at two-fifty. You can catch her leaving."

I start to say no way, like how did we even end up here? I WAS ON MY WAY TO GET FRIES. But Viva's looking at me expectantly and if I protest, she might decide I've become a jaded loner who no longer cares enough about anyone to put in some extra effort. I don't want her to think that. Even though it's probably true.

WHEN WE GET TO West Philly Montessori, it's only two-thirty. I don't feel like sitting in Viva's tiny electric car for twenty minutes, so I suggest we take a walk to a nearby record store I like. Viva's down, so we cross Spruce Street and turn down Fifty-second and in half a block we're at Gus Brown's Records. It's a small store that's been here as long as I've been alive and I don't really understand how it's still in business. Gotta be a front for a drug operation, but whatever, the records are mostly good. The inside smells like old carpet and sometimes body odor, but today just old carpet. Gus is reading a book behind the counter and he looks up when I enter, squinting at me over his glasses. "Ain't seen you in a minute," he says.

"I just got back from . . . Mozambique . . . ?"

"You telling or asking?"

I'm not altogether sure, so I just shrug and head to the blues section, while Viva heads for hip-hop.

Blues sections of record stores are where I feel the most calm. There's something about being surrounded by old, blackity-Black music that settles my nerves. I can feel my shoulders relaxing as I pick up a John Lee Hooker *Never Get Out of These Blues Alive* LP. The cover is worn, which is how you know somebody loved listening to it. I move my fingers over it, remembering how, when I was a depressed teenager, I blasted the title song on repeat while holed up in my room. On rare occasions, my mother, who didn't know I was alive most of the time, poked her head in to tell me I had no idea about being "doomed" with the blues and that I should stop being so dramatic.

At the end of the aisle, there's a small glass case with a record on display inside. It's a vintage Etta James "If I Can't Have You" live jawn, in perfect condition from the looks of it. There's a woman standing on the other side of the case, peering in. She's thick-thighed and dark-skinned, with a pile of dense, kinky hair that's pinned up on top of her head in a way that somehow looks both neat and excitingly precarious. She's wearing glasses on a delicate chain around her neck—like your third-grade teacher—and knee-high leather boots—not *at all* like your third-grade teacher. We lock eyes for a second and then she starts looking around for Gus. I look for him, too, but he's left his spot at the counter. She smiles at me.

"I've been trying to get my hands on this recording for ages," she says, in a West Philly–accented voice that's a little bit deep and raspy.

"Yeah, me too," I tell her, which isn't true.

"I'm buying it for my grandmother," she says. "It's the first song she and my grandfather danced to. He passed a few months ago."

"Oh, that's so sad."

She nods like, *isn't it?* and then looks around for Gus again.

"But, actually, I'm buying it for my grandmother, too," I say. "You're not going to believe this, it's such a crazy coincidence, but it was also the first song she and *my* grandfather danced to. We called him Pee Paw. He also died. Yesterday."

I should mention here that I don't believe a word of her sad grandma story. I'm good at knowing when other people are full of shit, maybe because I'm so full of shit myself. But I realize I'm taking a pretty big risk here. If she's the bullshit liar I suspect she is, this move is gold and I'm proud of it. If she's not lying, I'm officially the worst person on earth or, at the very least, the worst person in this record store right now.

For a second, she just stares at me, her mouth open a little, like she can't believe what is happening. Then she blinks a couple of times and says, "You can't do that."

And I'm like, "Huh? Do what?"

"You can't just steal my story."

"But it's such a good story," I tell her. "It has everything. Romance. Family. Grief. It's perfect. Bullshit, but perfect."

"But it's *my* bullshit story," she says. (I knew it!) "You can't just repeat it back to me."

"I didn't. I made Pee Paw's death much more recent. Makes the pain more visceral and immediate, amirite?"

The woman is looking at me like she can't decide whether I'm batshit crazy or a genius. It's a look I'm super familiar with. "Okay, so"—she flashes her palms toward the ceiling—"what now? What's fair? We flip a coin? Draw straws? Rock, Paper, Scissors?"

What's fair? What a naïve way to look at the world. I want to say to her that there is no fair. One of us just has to want the record more than she wants to be liked by a stranger. Also, I always lose at Rock, Paper, Scissors because I always do rock and the other person, no matter who they are, always does paper. I mean *always*. Like, *one hundred percent of the time*. I've tried to not do rock, but at the last moment I just can't stop myself. It's a compulsion. I have no explanation for why the other person always does paper. That's just how my life is.

"I'll make you a deal," I say. "I'll take the record but I'll buy you dinner to make up for it." The suggestion catches even me off guard. But I was right about her being a liar, so I feel confident I'm also right about her being queer. It's not something I picked up on at first, but as the exchange has progressed I've noticed that she holds eye contact for long periods of time. Most straight women don't do that. Most *people* don't do it unless they're attracted to the person they're talking to, even if only subconsciously.

I should say here that I'm not a woman who picks up other women. I used to be, in my aggressive femme lesbian youth, when I had a kind of awkward-girl game that women found irresistible. But somewhere in my thirties, I lost my game and my nerve. What has gotten into me on this particular afternoon, I can't really say for sure. Maybe everything that's happened in the last twenty-four hours has pushed me to the brink of emotional overwhelm, the inevitable outcome of which is me hurling myself into some sort of emotional kamikaze mission. Maybe. Whatever it is, it feels like it's happening almost outside my control. Also: She seems like a woman who takes up space and I've always been attracted to that kind of woman.

I've rendered her momentarily speechless for the third time in the span of three minutes and that makes me feel like I'm winning, although I haven't decided at what.

"I think I'd rather just have the record," she says.

I chuckle. It's a more awkward chuckle than you could possibly imagine.

"I guess I'm flattered, despite this being the strangest conversation I've ever had. But I'm not—"

"You're not queer?" I ask. "Shit. Are you sure? Because you seem really queer to me."

"I'm . . . not really sure what you mean by that. But I was going to say I'm not single."

"Oh," I say, chuckling again. WHY DO I KEEP CHUCKLING? "Okay, then. It's cool. I mean, whatever."

Mercifully, Gus has reappeared and she waves him over. She doesn't look at me again and I know she's decided she'd rather have the record than be liked by a stranger, which makes me feel kinda proud of her.

WHEN VIVA AND I GET back to the school, tweens are pouring out of it. We stand a little distance from the exit while I look for the kid in the crowd. Part of me is worried that I don't remember what she looks like. I know that if I walk up to a kid who turns out not to be her, Viva will think I'm a horrible monster and I'll probably agree. But then I see a girl bouncing down the steps in fatigue cargo pants, her unzipped jacket revealing a pink T-shirt with Grace Jones emblazoned on it, her shiny cornrows held at the ends with colorful rubber bands, and there's no doubt in my mind it's her. I see hints of my girlhood self: same walk, same tilt of the head as she looks around for her ride.

"That's her," I tell Viva.

The kid spots us super quick and I think she frowns when she sees me. I give a little wave, like, *Hi, remember me? I'm that dipshit who helped make you and who also tried to climb out of a window while you were eating a hot dog in a really weird way.* A little surprisingly, the kid runs toward me instead of away. When she's about three feet from us, she stops and looks uncertainly at me.

"Oh, hey, Charmaine," I say, smiling, trying to seem real casual and shit.

She looks confused, like, *Who the hell is Charmaine?* "My name is Vicky."

Fuuuuuuck. "Right!" I say. "I knew it started with a consonant!"

The kid looks at me like I'm the worst person she's ever met. I want to tell her that I'm not, that I'm just bad at human-on-human relationships. Instead, I say, "Look, I know you're probably still pissed about the window thing—"

A car horn honks loudly and the kid turns to look. Then, without another word or even a glance back at me, she walks away. I watch her head toward a silver SUV that's double-parked halfway down the block. Once she's inside the car, it U-turns and drives off.

"What window thing?" Viva asks.

I shrug. "Fuck if I know."

"Pero *you're* the one who said it."

I turn to look at her. "Why did you force me to come here? The kid didn't even want to see me!"

"Force? ¿Como que *force*? You said you wanted to come."

I shake my head. "Whatever."

I turn and start down the street away from her.

"The car is over here," she calls after me.

"I'll walk!"

While I'm waiting for the light to turn, my phone rings. It's my brother. "For fuck's sake," I say out loud to nobody. I open my airline app and in a few swipes I change my plane ticket so I can depart for Miami tonight, then head to São Paulo early. As soon as I get back to my room, I start packing.

4

I'M STUFFING UNDERWEAR INTO MY CARRY-ON WHEN I HEAR A TAP-ping at my window. I'm on the second floor, so I don't know what the hell is going on. I try to ignore it, but it's relentless. Tap. Tap. Tap. Finally, I go over to the window and look down. Standing on the sidewalk below is my stupid-ass brother. I try to duck back real quick, but he sees me and yells my name. "Skye!"

Shit.

"I see you! Don't be an asshole!"

I open the window and lean out, frowning at him as hard as I can. Like, my face actually hurts, I'm frowning so hard. "What are you doing here, Slade?"

He shakes his head, like it's a stupid question. "You thought I was just gon' go away?"

Um, yeah, that's what I was hoping. By the time I finished vomiting, he'd left the art fair and I let myself believe he wouldn't just show up again.

"How did you even know where I was?" I yell down at him.

"Where else would you be?"

"How did you know what room?"

"I didn't. I been throwing jelly beans at every window I could see," he says, opening his hand and revealing a palm-full of assorted colors. "Let me up."

"Viva's here," I tell him, thinking this will stop him in his tracks.

"No, she's not," he says. "I waited until I saw her leave."

"Ugh! Coward!" I shake my head. "Fine. You're not coming up, though. I'm coming down." I shut the window, zip my suitcase, check to make sure I've got everything I need, then call a cab.

When I open the door, Slade is leaning against the porch railing, smoking a cigarette. He looks skinny, for him, and his shoes look a little worn, but his hair and goatee are freshly cut, so I know he has a job, or at least a pretty good hustle. He eyes my suitcase but doesn't say anything.

"You can't smoke in here," I tell him, rolling my bags out onto the porch.

"I'm not in there," he says, and takes another drag.

"Oh, here comes Viva!" I say, looking down the block.

"Shit!" He drops his cigarette and looks like he's legit about to jump over the railing and sprint down the street. Then he sees the lie in my face and looks angry and embarrassed. "Why you gotta be such a jerk?"

Across the street, I can see Miss Newsome—an old lady who sits on her porch all day, smoking and listening to the gospel station on a boom box, while watching everyone come and go—leaning over her own porch railing, peering at us. She probably saw Slade throwing jelly beans at the windows and is trying to decide if he's a gentleman caller or a quirky drug dealer.

"What do you want, Slade?" I'm not usually this direct with him, but I don't have time for his bullshit right now.

"You coming to visit your disabled mother or not?"

Well, shit, I guess we're all being direct today.

"I kind of have a lot going on."

He frowns. "Like what?"

"Well, for one thing, I'm flying to Miami in like an hour and a half."

"So, you're just leaving? Without even coming by?" he asks, sounding sort of sad, which isn't what I'd expect from him. "When will you be back?"

"End of June."

"That's three months from now." He sighs and shakes his head.

I don't know why he cares so much all of a sudden. For the last six years, I've been coming back to Philly for two-week breaks, every three months. During those breaks, I rarely visit our mother, or see my brother, who still lives with her. Slade never went to any trouble to get me to see either of them, even after our mother fell and hit her head on the sidewalk a year and a half ago. But for the last few weeks he's been all the way up my ass about it. I guess I could ask him why. But I'm not sure I actually want to know.

"Did you hear Cynthia died?" I ask instead.

He stares at me, confused. "Cynthia who?"

"From camp."

"Oh," he says. "Actually, yeah, I did hear that. Marcus told me."

Marcus is one of Slade's friends who started going with Cynthia the summer we were eleven and he was fifteen. Which, at the time, seemed dangerous in a cool way and now seems dangerous in a dangerous way.

"Why didn't you tell me?" I ask Slade.

His face hardens. "When was I supposed to do that? You don't even answer my calls."

"How'd she die?" I ask. "Did Marcus tell you?"

"She had some kind of cancer, I think. It was pretty tragic, actually."

"Why? I mean, besides the usual reasons?"

"Because she didn't have any family or friends around," he says. "She didn't even really have but one or two visitors, even near the end. Except for her kid."

"That's awful." I feel a kind of twisting in my gut.

"What does this have to do with Mom?" my brother asks me.

"Nothing."

He takes a deep breath, like he's trying not to lose his shit. Then, after a moment, he says, "I read somewhere that girls come back to take care of their parents when they get old. I guess you tryna be different, like always, right?"

I don't say anything because I don't know what to say. The truth is, I didn't like our mother before her accident and I haven't been able to muster much energy to pretend to like her now. Maybe that makes me a bad daughter but, in my defense, she doesn't give a shit about me, either. She never has.

"She keeps asking about you," Slade says.

"No, she doesn't."

He frowns. "Why would I say that if it wasn't true?"

"I called her the last time I was in town," I remind him.

"That was what? Three or four months ago? And you know that's not the same as showing up in person anyway!"

"I have to get to the airport. My cab is coming in a minute. So, like . . . can you go?"

He gets up off the railing. "Fine. Forget it. I don't even know why I'm trying with you."

I shrug.

He walks off up the block and around the corner without looking back at me.

I peer up and down the street for my cab, but it's nowhere in sight. I sit on the front steps and try to think about São Paulo. I try to feel excited like I usually do when I'm gearing up for a trip. But now I'm all emotionally discombobulated, overwhelmed by a number of sensations I can't exactly identify. I take a series of long, deep breaths to center myself. When that doesn't work, I get up and start pacing the porch. Miss Newsome is watching, as usual, and I almost yell at her to mind her old-ass business. I'm still pacing when Viva comes up the steps.

She eyes my suitcase. "Are you leaving?"

I nod. "Heading out to Miami tonight."

"You're supposed to be here another week."

"Change of plans," I tell her. "Things here are getting a little bit . . . much."

She nods slowly. "Okay," she says, but she keeps standing there, watching me pace back and forth. It's mad uncomfortable. After like a minute, she asks, "Are you waiting for a ride?"

"Yes." I check the time on my phone. "And it's late."

She watches me make another lap across the porch and back. "Chica, you look stressed. Even more than earlier. ¿Qué pasó?"

"Slade came by."

She purses her lips, frowns, and I think she might ask what the hell Slade was doing on her property, but she doesn't. Instead she holds up a large, greasy brown bag she's carrying. "I have shrimp. Come conmigo. Then I'll drive you to the airport."

I look at her. "You will?"

"Of course."

Now I feel a little bit guilty for walking away from her at the school. "Okay. But let's eat quick."

EVEN THOUGH I HARDLY EVER go in there, the kitchen is my favorite room at the bed-and-breakfast, because it always smells like oregano and basil and cilantro. There are glass double doors at the back and they open out onto a yard that, in spring and summer, is bright and flower-filled, bursting in yellows and pinks like a kid's coloring book. Now, in early April, it's mostly bare out there, plant-wise, but the wooden benches look freshly sanded and stained and the brick walkway is swept of dead leaves, so the space still looks inviting in the late-day sun, which floods the kitchen in soft orangey light.

Viva takes the shrimp out of the bag, along with French fries and coleslaw, and arranges it all on the counter like a feast. She goes into the pantry off the kitchen and comes out with a bottle of wine. She pours two glasses and holds one out to me.

"No, thanks."

She looks super surprised, as if I've never turned down alcohol before, which I totally have probably. She puts the wineglasses down on the table and sits. She's quiet for a moment, and then she takes a breath and says, "Do you remember when we were fifteen and we trusted each other with everything?"

"Not everything," I say. "You didn't tell me you were a girl."

She nods. "Okay, well, almost everything, then."

I nod. "Yeah, kind of." But I don't "kind of" remember; I totally remember. Viva was Tasha's boyfriend during our sophomore year of high school. For a while, the three of us were inseparable. Tasha and Viva were the first people I came out to, at fifteen. They both followed suit in a matter of months, though Viva came out as gay then, not trans. The next summer, I fell in love for the first time and subsequently got my heart ripped from my chest by Rashida Jordan. Tasha was in Wilmington with her grandparents for a month, so it was up to Viva to listen to me cry for an hour at a stretch, and make sure I ate, and generally keep me from hurling myself in front of a bus. Which she did without a single complaint. Now she's looking at me patiently. So, I start talking.

"My brother just told me Cynthia died of cancer."

"Vicky's mother?"

"Yes."

"That's very sad," she says. "I'm so sorry."

"That could be me, Viva."

"What do you mean? Is there even any cancer in your family?"

"I mean, I could end up like her. I don't talk to my family much. I don't have a partner."

"Do you want a partner?"

"No. But who's going to take care of me if I get sick?"

"You have friends," Viva says. "I'm sure plenty of people would show up for you—"

"Would you? Would you drop everything to take care of me if I got sick?"

"Of course."

But I know she wouldn't. Not because she isn't a good person, but because no one does that. People take care of their parents, partners, and kids, and that's it.

"Dying without anybody around who gives a shit is the worst thing that can happen to a person, isn't it?"

Viva sighs. "Didn't you once tell me you expect to die drunk and alone in a hotel room somewhere far away?"

"Probably. But I was what, nineteen? Maybe I thought it sounded cool. It's possible I've just never checked in with myself to ascertain whether or not it *still* sounds cool two decades later. Like, 'Hey thirty-eight-and-three-quarters self, are you still planning on dying alone or is that actually a horrible idea?' "

"Okay," Viva says. "Fine. So, what then? I'm not saying I think you're right, or even that I fully understand this conversation, but for the sake of argument. Let's say you're on the road to dying alone and that's not something you feel okay about anymore. What are you going to do about it?"

"What do you mean, '*do about it*'?"

"I mean: What actions are you going to take to stop it from happening?"

I think about it for a moment, then shake my head. "I have no idea."

Viva frowns, and I think she feels sorry for me. I feel pretty damn sorry for myself.

Then I remember what Slade said, about how girls come back to take care of their parents when they get old, and I say to Viva, "Well, maybe I do have an idea."

HALF AN HOUR LATER, I roll my suitcase back to my room. I call Toni and tell her that I need to stay in Philly for a little while; that I'd like her to lead the Brazil and Cuba trips, plus the Argentina trip in May, and the Nicaragua and Costa Rica trips in June; that I'll call her again tomorrow to discuss further. In a few clicks, I cancel my flights to Miami and São Paulo.

This night, I lie awake for hours. I think about Cynthia. About youth. About death. Around one in the morning, I finally drift off. I dream about the giant anteaters of Brazil, laying chicken eggs.

5

NEXT AFTERNOON, I TAKE A LYFT FROM THE B AND B TO WEST Philadephia Montessori. "Picking up your kid?" the driver, a middle-aged Dominican, asks me when we're almost there.

"Not exactly," I tell him. "I mean . . . something like that. Kind of. But not really. No."

He glances at me in the rearview mirror. "You sure?"

"I'm not really sure of anything, sir."

He nods, like he understands exactly what I mean.

It's chilly out, typical of early April. The air is more than crisp today; it's borderline crunchy. The sort of air that has its own smell and, if you stick your tongue out in it, its own taste. From the back of the car, I watch Philadelphians trudging along in puffy jackets, my own down vest buttoned to my chin, and I try not to think too hard about the weather in São Paulo.

My phone buzzes in my back pocket. I almost don't even look at it. But then I do and it's Slade and I wish I hadn't. He's been texting all morning and I've managed to not read a single one. This time, I see the beginning of the text in the banner (*Call me right away*) and don't even open it to see the rest. I'm en route to Brazil as far as my brother and mother are concerned. I put the phone back in my pocket.

When we pull up to the curb outside the school, the bell has already rung and kids are everywhere. I see Vicky walk right by the Lyft and I scramble to get out of my seatbelt while opening the door at the same time. I'm not coordinated enough to do these two things at once, though, so I stumble out of the car, trip on the curb, and almost fall down on the sidewalk, which earns me a snicker from a bespectacled middle-schooler. I walk faster to catch up to Vicky, grabbing her shoulder from behind. When she turns and sees it's me, she looks annoyed.

"Leave me alone," she says. "I'm over it." And she keeps walking.

My instinct is to do what she says: to leave her alone. If she's over it, then she's over it. I don't need to chase the kid. But then I don't leave her alone. I follow her. "You're still mad about the window situation, right?"

She shrugs, doesn't stop walking or even turn around.

"It was a dick move," I say. "But I don't usually act like that. I swear. It was just a weird day. I was really hungover."

The kid stops, turns, and looks at me. "You were?"

"Um . . . yes."

"From what?"

"From drinking the night before."

"I know what hungover means," she says. "I'm not a fourth-grader. I mean, *what* did you drink?"

"Bourbon."

She nods. Then, after a few seconds, "My mom liked whiskey. That's the same as bourbon?"

"Bourbon is a kind of whiskey."

"She let me have a sip once. It tasted gross."

"Well, not every girl is a brown liquor girl," I say. "Also, you're what? Twelve?"

"Aunt Faye doesn't let me."

"Drink?" I ask. "That's probably wise."

"*Taste,*" she says. "Just a sip. Like, for fun. French kids drink wine. Did you know that?"

"Maybe . . . ? Wait, why are we talking about booze?"

She shrugs, then turns and walks away again.

"Let me make it up to you, okay?" I say, following her and thinking about what I'd want if someone let me down, what would make me feel the most better. "I can give you money." I reach into my pocket and pull out my wallet. "I have thirty dollars," I tell her, holding it out. I really have sixty, but that seems like a lot.

She stops and looks at the money. Her eyebrows are drawn close together and it occurs to me that this is a horrible misstep because kids don't want money, they want love. But then she shrugs and pockets the cash. "So, what now?" she asks.

I honestly have no idea.

"Vicky!"

I turn around and there's a woman standing on the curb, looking concerned. Her face is mad familiar, but I can't immediately place her.

"What are you doing?" she asks the kid. "Who is this?"

I look at Vicky, whose eyes are all shifty, like she's trying to think up a quick lie.

"Hold on," the woman, who I'm guessing is the aforementioned Aunt Faye, says. "You're that woman from Gus Brown's."

It clicks. I nod slowly, remembering the Etta James record, Pee Paw, and the whole rejection thing that happened. For some reason, I laugh really loud then, causing them both to look startled. "Ha! Yeah, that was me. Wow. How weird is that?"

She doesn't laugh. Instead, she gets between me and the kid. "Vicky, get in the car."

"But—"

"Are you some kind of stalker?"

Wait, what?

"Have you been following us?"

"What? No. I'm not stalk—"

"Did I just see you give my child money?"

"Well, yeah," I say. "But not in a creepy way."

"Vicky, get in the car," she says again. "I'm pretty sure this crazy woman is trying to kidnap you."

Fuuuuuck me.

"No, she's not!" Vicky says.

"Trust me. I had a conversation with her that no sane person would have thought was normal."

Wow, okay.

"Aunt Faye—"

"Vicky Valentine! I told you to get in the car! Get. In. The. Car. Now!"

An angry look crosses the kid's face and for a second I think she's going to yell right back at her aunt. But then she doesn't. Instead, she gets into an SUV that's double-parked nearby and rolls down the window, as her aunt rummages around in her purse, probably looking for her phone.

What the hell? I mouth at the kid.

Sorry, she mouths back.

Sorry. Great. That's mad helpful.

Don't tell, she mouths.

Don't tell? Seriously? Don't tell and just let myself be arrested for kidnapping? What kind of messed-up request?

Pleeeeease. The anger is gone from her face and she looks on the verge of tears.

Now I have like half a second to decide whether to keep the kid's secret that I didn't even know was a secret, and let her aunt call the cops on me, or rat this little motherfucker out and remain unarrested. At first, it doesn't seem like a hard choice. I mean, it's not my job to keep secrets for tweens, especially ones that are going to land me in handcuffs. But the kid looks so damn desperate. Desperate like only a kid that age can look, like the whole world is falling down around her and there's nothing she can do about it because she's twelve. I remember that feeling. I can't dwell on it, though, because Aunt Faye has located her phone and is now dialing what I can only assume is 911.

I frown at the kid one last time, then take off running down the street.

Make no mistake: I have found myself in some pretty horrible and humiliating situations over the course of my adulthood. I once licked shit off a baby because I thought it was cake batter. A peacock once chased me around in circles at the zoo while a hundred kids laughed hysterically. And they were Black kids. Black kids don't just laugh at you. They let their bodies go limp and fall on one another and on the ground because what is happening to you is so uproarious it atrophies their muscles on the spot. But let's be clear: Running down the sidewalk to escape a woman who thinks I just tried to abduct her kid may be the most horrible and humiliating thing I have ever experienced, due in no small part to the fact that I. Suck. At. Running. I was born with janky knees. I had to wear braces on my legs when I first started to walk and it helped some, but I'm still an extremely busted runner. When I run, I look like a giant toddler who you just know is about to fall face-first into the coffee table and fracture its skull. I'm also pretty sure I'm not running very fast. Sure enough, when I look behind me, Vicky's aunt is right there. She's only jogging but is easily keeping up with me. When she reaches out to grab my shoulder, I somehow find the leg strength to run harder, putting several yards between us. I round a corner and toddle-run another half-block and when I look back again, she's not there. I keep running. I'm on a street lined with pizza shops and burger places, and some of the people coming out of them watch curiously as I pass. Some smart-ass yells, "Run, Forrest, run!" I keep going until I'm sure the kid's aunt is no longer chasing me and it's only when I stop that I realize my lungs are on fire. I double over, sucking in air as hard as I can, trying not to die.

"Hey!"

Oh, no. Oh God, no. I'm still doubled over, so all I can see is her feet—in those same perfect leather boots—when she catches up with me. I can't possibly run anymore, so I just hold up my hand and, to my surprise, she stops a few feet away. When I catch my breath, I look up at her and my first thought is how goddamn much I like her face. Her eyes are super dark and intense and she has, like, a *presence* that fills the room even though we're not actually *in* a room. Also, somehow, she looks perfectly put together, even though she just chased a child-abduction suspect three whole city blocks.

I try to speak and a wheeze escapes me. She frowns, like she's starting to realize I'm either really bad at kidnapping children or possibly not a kidnapper of children at all. I hold up one finger in an attempt to communicate that there's an explanation coming any minute now. "I'm the . . . [wheeze] . . . I'm the egg . . . [wheeze] . . ."

Vicky runs up behind her aunt. "Skye, are you okay?"

Her aunt looks at her like, *Why do you know this slow-running kidnapper's name?*

"I'm the egg donor," I wheeze.

She looks at me. "What?"

That's right! Who looks like the crazy person now? is something I consider saying but I'm worried that, objectively speaking, I'm still the one who looks like the crazy person. So instead I just kind of shrug and nod and continue to clutch my burning chest.

She stares at the kid, who stares back at her with that angry look again. Aunt Faye opens her mouth like she's going to say something, only no words come out. We all stand there for a few seconds, frozen and silent except for my wheezing. Then Aunt Faye grabs the kid's hand, turns, and walks away with her. I watch them until they're out of sight.

My phone buzzes again. I forget to ignore it. It's Slade *again*. This time the text banner reads: *Mom in hospital. Stroke.*

Shit.

6

MY MOTHER IS SITTING UP IN HER HOSPITAL BED, WATCHING THE local news, when I arrive. She's wearing a hospital gown and a once-fuzzy pink bathrobe she's had for at least ten years. Her eyeglasses are perched on the end of her nose and she's peering over them at the TV. She looks totally fine, like she might as well be at home watching soaps in her bedroom. I know people can have little strokes and seem normal the next day. Nevertheless, I'm suspicious. My brother is slumped in the chair beside the bed, dozing, his snores louder than the weatherman.

"Skye Beam?" my mother asks when she sees me in the doorway.

"Hey, Mom," I say, coming into the room, which is small and cramped and smells like my brother's cologne.

"I didn't know you were in town," she says. "When'd you get back?"

"Yesterday," I lie.

The sound of our voices wakes Slade. When he sees me, he laughs a little and shakes his head. "You got here fast from Miami."

I throw him my meanest sneer. He shakes his head again but shuts up.

"How are you feeling?" I ask my mother.

"I'm doing alright," she says, "as far as I know."

"Well, you look great," I tell her. "Especially considering the stroke and all."

She looks confused for a second. "Did I have a stroke?"

Slade shakes his head. "No, Mom. Skye's just playing around."

Ugh, I knew it!

My mother pushes her glasses up on her nose and eyes me. "You look skinny. You working?"

You working? is a question my mother asks every time I see her. The answer has never been *no* but she still asks. I'm pretty sure this is a question all Black moms ask of children they don't see or talk to every day. *You working?* is basically the Black mom version of *How have you been?*

"Yes," I tell her. "I'm working."

"Where?"

"I work for myself, Mom. Group travel, remember?"

"Oh," says my mother. "You still doing that?"

To be clear: The "that" my mother is referring to is *owning and running a successful company that allows me to travel the world.*

"Yes. I'm still doing that."

"Must not pay much," she says, looking me over again. "You don't look like you're eating enough."

"I'm eating great," I tell her, which isn't objectively true.

"Well, you always had a fast metabolism," my mother says. "When you were a teenager, you used to sometimes eat half a box of Apple Smacks in one sitting."

"That was Slade."

"Oh, that's right!" she says, laughing. She looks at Slade. "You almost ate me out of house and home."

Slade shrugs. "Skye ate all the yogurt, though. Remember?"

My mother looks at me, and I can tell she's trying to recall it. "I do," she says finally, nodding. "You got that from your father. He always loved yogurt."

I feel a twitch at the corners of my mouth. I hate it when my mother starts talking about my father without warning. I've made it a habit to never think about that dude and I don't like it when other people break my habits for me.

"You always ate up all the ice cream, though," my mother says to Slade. "Especially cookies and cream. You could scarf down a whole gallon of that in a couple of days."

Slade laughs and my mother laughs, too. I'm thrilled as fuck they're having such a good time.

The sound of the local news in the background is suddenly distracting to me, like a mosquito buzzing near my ear, and I want to swat it away.

"I have to get going," I say, fake-checking the time on my phone.

"You literally just walked in the door," my brother says.

I frown at him. "Slade, lemme talk to you out here for a second." I walk out into the hallway and he follows.

"What is your problem?" I ask him. "You told me she had a stroke just to get me here?"

"I wasn't trying to get you here. I thought you left town last night. I was just trying to make you feel guilty enough to call."

"I hate you. Do you know that?"

He nods. "It's pretty obvious. One day you should tell me *why* you hate me so much, since I've never done shit to you."

"Whatever. Just tell me what *actually* happened."

"She said she felt dizzy, so I brought her here. They did a C-scan but it looked fine. They kept her overnight for observation, though," he says, then he starts to move past me down the hall.

"Where are you going?"

"Coffee," he says.

"You can't leave. *I'm* leaving."

"I'll be right back," he says, and keeps walking, disappearing around a corner.

For a second, I consider leaving anyway. I'm annoyed that Slade got me here by lying through his teeth. This never could have happened if I was on my way to São Paulo right now like I'm supposed to be. I *wish* I was there now. I wish I was anywhere other than this goddamn hospital.

"Skye Beam?" my mother calls.

Somehow, I resist the urge to scream until my throat is bloody and instead poke my head back into the room. "Yes?"

"I thought that was you," she says, as if I just got here. "I didn't know you were in town. When did you get back?"

I take a long, deep breath and go back inside. I sit down in the chair Slade vacated. "I got back yesterday."

"Oh," she says. "You working?"

"Yes, Mom."

"Where?"

"JetBlue. I'm flying planes now. Slade didn't tell you?"

She looks confused and for a second I feel bad for messing with her. Then she frowns and says, "Well, they must not be paying you much, 'cause you don't look like you're eating."

Ba dum tss.

A nurse enters. She's youngish and blondish and bubblyish. "How are we doing, Miss Mary?" she asks.

"Fine," my mother says, frowning a little.

"Let's get those vitals, okay?" She fiddles with her blood pressure machine and smiles at me. "Are you a relative?"

"I'm her daughter."

"I didn't know you had a daughter," she says to my mother. Then to me, "I'm Elizabeth. I've been taking care of Miss Mary today."

"Miss Mary?"

"Oh, that's what I call her," she says. "I can't pronounce . . . what is it? Amara-liss?"

"It's Amaryllis," I tell her.

"That's a mouthful," she says, giggling, waving her hand. "I just call her Miss Mary."

I look at my mother. "Did you tell her she could call you Mary?"

"I don't think so."

"Her name's not Mary," I say to the nurse. "No one calls her that. Her name is Amaryllis. You should call her Amaryllis."

The nurse acts like she didn't hear me.

"One thirty over ninety," she says of my mother's blood pressure. "A little high but not too bad. And your oxygen looks just fine."

"Excuse me, Emily?" I say.

"Elizabeth," she corrects me.

"Yeah, I hear you. But, honestly, I'm not in love with that name, so I'ma just call you Emily. Cool?"

She stares at me like she's trying to decide how serious I am.

"Is there a good bar around here, Emily?"

"I . . . um . . . I'm not sure," she says. "I don't really drink."

"Ah," I say, nodding.

She turns back to my mother. "Your vitals look great, Miss Ama . . ."

"Amaryllis," my mother and I say in unison.

"Am-a-ryl-lis," says Emily/Elizabeth suuuuuuuper slowly. "The doctor already put in your discharge order, so you should be out of here within the hour. Call me if you need anything in the meantime." She walks out without looking at me again.

"You believe that shit?" I ask my mother when she's gone.

My mother shakes her head. Then, after a few seconds, she says, "Where's Slade?"

Right. Of course. Slade. "He went to get coffee."

"Oh," she says, sounding disappointed.

Familiar theme music plays as the news comes back from commercial. A memory flashes in my mind, of me at twelve, watching the backs of my parents' heads through a closet keyhole as they watched the local news. My father had locked me in the closet because I'd talked back to him. My mother hadn't stopped him, hadn't defended me at all. She'd just sat there watching the news, like she is now. The memory fills me with a sudden sense of anger and panic. My heart pounds. I take a deep breath to calm myself.

"Listen, Mom," I say, "I have to go. Slade will be back soon, though."

"Alright," she says. "It was good seeing you."

I head for the elevators, walking fast. I see Slade coming toward me down the hall.

"You're already leaving?"

"Eat a dick, Slade," I say, not stopping.

When I get inside the elevator and the doors slide shut, I feel suddenly overcome. With what exactly, I'm not sure. But the elevator feels too small, like the walls are closing in on me. When the doors open into the lobby, I hurry out, almost running to the exit.

7

WHEN I GET BACK TO THE BED-AND-BREAKFAST, IT'S ONLY AROUND six o'clock. Nevertheless, I go straight to my room, strip, pull on a raggedy T-shirt, and collapse on the bed. I feel exhausted, the way I always do after seeing my mother, and also probably from being chased down the street like a robber in a cartoon. I fall asleep for what seems like hours and am awakened by the sound of knocking on my door. I turn over and try to go back to sleep, but the knocking persists. "Go away!"

"Skye, it's Viva. Tienes visita."

I get up and open the door. "¿Visita? It's the middle of the night."

"It's seven-thirty," says Viva.

"Who is it?"

"Dice que se llama Faye."

"Vicky's aunt?"

"All I know is she called for you earlier. I put her through but you didn't pick up."

I sort of remember ignoring the faraway sound of a phone ringing.

"She's waiting for you in the parlor," Viva says. "You might want to put on pants. Or at least underwear."

When I get downstairs, Vicky's aunt is kneeling in front of the wood-burning stove, staring through the glass door at the flames. Her brow is tightly drawn, as if she's trying to solve a problem that exists deep in the flicker of the dying fire. I watch her for a few seconds, until it starts to feel weird and lurky, then clear my throat. She looks up at me but doesn't say anything. Her brow is still furrowed. Finally, she sighs and says, "Your fire's going out. The back log isn't catching."

I shrug. "It's not really *my* fire, per se."

Ignoring my indifference, she removes an iron poker from the rack of fireplace tools and opens the glass door. "Sorry for showing up on your doorstep unannounced," she says, not looking at me. "I tried calling."

"I was working," I tell her. "On some super important stuff."

She nods and reaches the poker into the fire. "Once I talked to Vicky and sorted out what happened, I felt bad. I wanted to apologize."

"Okay," I say. I take a seat on the arm of a nearby chair and watch as she uses the little hook on the poker to try to drag one of the logs in the back to the front, where there's still flame for it to catch.

"My sister didn't want anyone to know about the eggs," she says, still looking at the fire, not at me. "She kept it a secret from everybody but her husband. She probably would've kept it from him if she could have. I didn't know about it until after she died."

"Wait. You're *Cynthia's* sister?"

"Yes."

I don't know why I assumed she was Vicky's paternal aunt. I do recall Cynthia having a sister a couple of years older, though I don't remember ever seeing her during my three summers with Cynthia at camp. She doesn't look much like her sister, who had a round face and wide, curious, friendly eyes. Faye is all cheekbones, heavy lashes, and intensity.

The poker's not accomplishing the task of moving the log where she wants it, so she puts it down and picks up some large iron tongs.

She uses both hands to work the tongs, grabbing the log between them and lifting it up, as embers pop and spark.

"Why didn't she want anyone to know?" I ask.

"Cynthia always wanted children. Even when we were just little girls ourselves. Maybe having to use someone else's eggs made her feel she'd failed in some way."

The fire suddenly gets bigger, the rogue log finally catching the flames, and we both watch it for a few moments in silence. I steal glances at her profile, see the reflection of firelight in her silver hoop earrings.

"That's my best guess. I could be all wrong. It's not something she would've talked to me about."

"You weren't close?"

She shakes her head, no. A thick twist of hair falls in front of her eyes. She grasps it between her thumb and forefinger and tucks it behind her ear, super tenderly, like she's trying to be extra gentle with herself. It's the most graceful of movements.

"Was she close to other people?" I ask.

She looks right at me now, surprised by the question. "Other people?"

"I mean, did she have close friends? Other close family? I didn't spend much time with her as an adult. I'm curious who she grew up to be."

She sighs and puts down the fireplace tongs. "She worked a lot. Other than Vicky, I don't think people were of much interest to her."

"Did *you* like her?" It's maybe an intrusive question but considering she showed up at my place of sleep with no warning, I feel pretty okay about being intrusive.

For a few seconds, she stares at me with the same look she had at the record store when I told her about poor Pee Paw: half disbelief, half caught. Then she says matter-of-factly, "I liked her when we were kids. As adults . . . I liked her sometimes. Which is probably more often than she liked me."

"Why?"

Now she looks uncomfortable. "Our grandmother used to say sisters are natural enemies. She had seven and despised every one."

Granny sounds nice.

"I wouldn't know about it," I tell her. "All I have is a really obnoxious brother. I don't even like him *sometimes*."

"Well," she says. "Let's save acrimonious kinship as a topic for another day."

Acrimonious kinship? Who even is this woman?

"For now, I apologize for just walking off the way I did. It was rude."

"Okay," I say. "I mean, I guess."

She frowns, ever so slightly. "You sound hesitant."

"Well, you did call me crazy and chase me down the street."

She purses her lips. "You don't accept my apology, then?"

"Well, *technically*, you didn't apologize for any of that."

The fire pops and little red embers explode inside the stove.

"I was trying to protect my niece," she says. "I had no idea she'd contacted you. How was I supposed to know you *weren't* just some crazy person?"

I shrug. "Maybe ask?"

She laughs, but less in a *this is funny* way and more in a *no this bitch did not* way. Maybe I shouldn't be giving her a hard time. It's true she didn't know who I was when she chased me down the street. But it's also true that SHE CHASED ME DOWN THE STREET. I toddle-ran for like three entire blocks! I could have died somehow! I just feel like we should all be on the same page about what exactly went down and who traumatized who by calling 911 on whom. Knowing what she knows now, she should apologize, regardless of what she did or did not know then. But she's looking at me like there's no way in hell she's going to do that.

"So, you came all the way over here to half-apologize?" I ask her. "You could've just left a voicemail."

"It's not that far. And, like I said, I felt bad."

Not bad enough, apparently.

"How did you know where to find me?" I ask, realizing she's the third person to track me down this week, a fact that low-key concerns me, considering

1. I pride myself on being hard to catch up with;
2. unexpected guests fill me with anxiety; and
3. I've given roughly three percent of the male population of Philly a fake number at some point and one or more of their ugly asses might show up on my doorstep at any moment looking for an explanation.

"I asked around," she says.

" 'Asked around'? What does that even mean?"

"Vicky told me you were staying at a bed-and-breakfast around here. There aren't many. Most of them are more like rooming houses."

So, she came to see how I live. The whole "apology" thing was just a ruse. Mkay.

"It turns out, I have a neighbor whose aunt lives right across the street," she says, gesturing toward the front window. "She knows everyone who lives on this block, including you."

"Miss Newsome?"

Faye nods. "The very same."

No wonder Viva calls her Miss Meddlesome.

"Although, according to her," Faye says, "you don't actually live on this block, you just—how'd she put it?—'show up every few months looking lost.' "

"How could I get lost going to a place I show up at every few months?"

"I don't think that's the kind of 'lost' she means."

"Ah, okay. I didn't realize Miss Nosy had a psych degree. But good for her. Are you done apologizing or is there more?"

She purses her lips again. I think she does this when she's holding her tongue. "If you'd like to see Vicky," she finally says, "you can."

"Oh. She's not grounded or something?"

"Why should she be?"

"She shouldn't. But you strike me as someone who likes to ground people. No offense. Also, you and your homie Miss Newsome don't seem to approve of me."

"Well," she says, "Vicky's been having a hard time and I don't want to be overly strict with her right now."

"Hard time with what?"

"With everything that's happened since her mother died," she says, taking out her phone. "So, if you give me your number, I'll pass it on to her." She taps the screen a few times, then looks at me, waiting.

I give her my number.

She thanks me, quite curtly, and bounces, leaving the fire to crackle in her stead.

8

THAT WEEKEND, ON SUNDAY, I WALK FROM THE B AND B TO THE KID'S house, six blocks away. It's crazy that she lives so close to Viva's and I wonder if we've crossed paths before, without knowing it. At the corner of Viva's block, I turn right so I can take Fifty-third down to Cedar Ave. It's another nice day, warmish and super sunny. The weather has brought everybody and their mom out of doors, and the neighborhood is vibrating with activity. People are turning over soil in their front yards or sweeping their sidewalks. Kids are popping wheelies in the middle of the street. Lots of folks are hanging out on their porches, blasting music from Bluetooth speakers and old-school boom boxes. It's all so familiar, so loaded with the heavy scent of nostalgia. And the occasional waft from a sewer.

Vicky lives on a narrow street tucked between two wider ones, quieter and quainter than many of the blocks surrounding it. As I start looking for house number nineteen, I hear yelling from up near the next corner, and when I look, I can see a group of people gathered on the sidewalk. There are nine or ten of them, mostly older folks, from what I can make out, all Black except for the white man who is doing the yelling. I spot Faye in the mix. She and an older Black woman are standing closest to the white man. Their body language suggests something may be about to pop off. When I get closer, I can see they're both frowning, the older woman shaking her head, her arms folded tightly across her chest. Faye keeps sighing and looking heavenward as the white man continues to yell.

"We've been through this, what? Half a dozen times already? How much plainer can I make it? My. Baby. Is. Trying. To. Sleep." He says the last part super slow, as if Faye and the older woman are small children or just really stupid adults. "If you don't stop, I'm going to call the police."

"I've been living on this block forty-odd years," the older woman says. "I've been leading church service in the basement for the last ten. How long have you been here? Six months? And been complaining since you got here."

The white man looks like he's getting angrier; his reddening face is pinched. "You're just not going to listen, are you? You're determined not to listen. Fine." He reaches into his back pocket and pulls out his phone. "I didn't want to have to—"

Faye gently places a hand on the man's wrist. "Calling the police is only going to make all of this worse."

"I'm not making it worse!" the white man says. "I'm not making it *anything*. She's the one breaking the rules!"

"Rules?" the older woman asks. "What rules? The ones you just made up when you moved here?"

"Go back to Roxborough or wherever!" someone yells. When I look, I see it's Vicky. She's standing next to a tall teenage girl in an ASSATA TAUGHT ME T-shirt. They're the only young ones in the crowd.

Faye throws Vicky a look like, *You're not helping.* Then she turns back to the white man. "Sunday service is over, Ethan," she says, glancing at the elderly woman for confirmation. "Isn't that right, Reverend Seymour?"

Reverend Seymour nods. "That's right."

"So, why don't we all just go home, enjoy what's left of the weekend, and discuss the matter when emotions are a little less high?"

Reverend Seymour nods again. "Fine with me."

Faye smiles at her and then looks at Ethan.

"I'm not obligated to 'discuss' it at all," he says. "I'm in the right. Next time, I'm calling the police." He tucks the cellphone back into his pocket. "Now I have to go and help my wife, who is probably still trying to get my baby back to sleep." He turns on his hiking-sandaled heels and stomps off to a house a few doors down, up the front steps, disappearing inside.

Everyone who was hanging back is now encircling Faye and the reverend, shaking their heads and grumbling about *that disrespectful-ass white fool*. Vicky moves to stand at Faye's side. This is when she notices me and smiles a little bit and waves. Faye sees me, and I think she frowns the tiniest bit before turning back to the group.

"This is the second time he's threatened to call the police," she says. "Next time, he's probably going to do it. I think we—those of us who live on the block—should keep an eye out. Get over here quick if that happens."

"And bring your phones," the teenager in the cool T-shirt says. "To record the cops."

"That's smart thinking, Keisha," the reverend says.

"Thanks, Grandma."

An elderly woman in dark glasses and a circa 1998 Mary J. Blige pixie wig nods. "I can do that."

"Me, too!" Vicky says, shooting her hand up in the air like Hermione in potions class. The reverend smiles at her.

"I don't know how to work the camera on my phone," says an old man with a cane, stepping forward. "But I can get my grandson to show me again. I can also holler for the rest of y'all if I see anything going down."

"Thank you, Brother Mitch," says the reverend, putting her hand on his. She smiles at Mary J. Blige. "And you, Sister Vena. And all of you."

"If Ethan does anything crazy," Faye says, "call me. I don't want you getting into anything with him. You hear me, Reverend?"

"I hear you, Faye. And I know you're right. It just makes me mad as heck."

"I know. Me, too. But I want you to promise."

"I promise to call you."

Faye gives her hand a squeeze and the reverend turns and walks up onto her porch.

Vicky bounces over to me. She's wearing her Grace Jones T-shirt again; I can see it peeking out from under her jacket. Her hair's different today, her cornrows replaced by two large Afro puffs separated by a part down the middle of her head. Her pecan-colored skin looks shiny in the sunlight. She seems cooler than I was at her age and I wonder if she's one of those kids who doesn't get teased, one of those girls who belongs. "White dudes are cray," she says, shaking her head.

Faye comes over and gives me a strained smile. "Hello, Skye."

"Hey."

Then we just stand there like that. It's awkward, y'all.

"Um . . . so . . . what was all that?" I ask, even though I got the gist of it from listening in.

"This house belongs to Reverend Seymour," Faye says. "She's been here since 1977. She raised six sons here. She used to be a preacher in a big church, but after she retired about ten years ago, she started running a little church service out of the basement. I guess she still wants to be able to connect with the people, you know?"

"Sure," I say. "If that's your thing."

"It's just an hour service Sunday morning, and another on Wednesday evenings. A few dozen people show up."

"Much to the dismay of this Ethan person?"

Faye nods. "He started complaining about the services as soon as his family moved in. He says it's too loud. He shouts about zoning ordinances and noise violations and all of that. The last time, he threatened to call the police, and now again. It's infuriating."

As Faye talks, I look around, trying to get a sense of the level of gentrification on this block. Most of the people out and about are Black, but there are a couple of white faces and another couple of faces that could be Middle Eastern or maybe South Asian. A few blocks down, closer to the University of Pennsylvania, there are white people everywhere, but they mostly haven't stretched out this far west yet.

Faye sighs. "Anyway," she says, looking from me to Vicky. "I have work. So, I'll leave you to it." She waves, crosses the street, and disappears into house number nineteen.

"You live with your aunt?"

"Yup."

I don't ask why she doesn't live with her father. Partly because I don't want to accidentally bring up a touchy subject and partly because living with one's father isn't something I value, considering mine was a dick.

"So, what should we do?" I ask the kid, realizing I probably should've already made a plan. But Philly's a big city, so there must be lots of kid-friendly shit to do here, right? There's definitely a zoo. "How about the zoo?"

"I don't like the zoo. The animals always look so mad. Like if they could get past the barrier, they'd totally kill you for letting them suffer. I don't like it when animals look at me like that, it gives me bad dreams."

I think about the peacock that chased me around the zoo that time. It did seem kinda pissed. "Have you eaten lunch?" I ask her.

"Nope."

"Wanna go get a pizza?"

ONE OF MY FAVE PIZZA spots is only a couple of blocks away. We walk back the way I came, back down Cedar Avenue, toward Fifty-second.

"How long have you lived around here?" I ask Vicky.

"Since the middle of sixth grade."

"Is that when your mom . . ." I hesitate. Maybe she doesn't like to be reminded.

"I lived with my dad and my step-monster for a while at first," she says. "They live in Bala Cynwyd. But I didn't like it there. I hate my step-monster. And Bala Cynwyd is the worst. It's all rich white people. I hated my school."

"You like the Montessori better?"

She thinks about it. "I like the kids better. I have a new bestie. Her name's Jasmine."

"Congratulations."

"It's still wack, though."

"What's wack about it?"

"The teachers. The principal. The vice principal. The guidance counselor. The nurse."

I laugh. "Even the *nurse* is wack?"

"Yup. Like, one time I was waiting to see the principal and I heard the nurse talking about me to the secretary. This was right after I cut off all my hair. 'Trying to look like a boy.' That's what she said."

"Hmm."

"It's anti-feminist or whatever, right?"

"Sure. Why were you in the principal's office?"

She thinks about it a second, then shrugs. "I don't r-e-m-e-m-b-e-r."

Well, shit. Now I want to ask how often she's in the principal's office, but I don't want to sound like the feds, so instead, I say, "You cut off all your hair? When was this?"

"Last January. On my birthday. I cut my relaxer out. It was like my present to myself."

"That's pretty bold," I tell her. "I was a senior in college before I got the nerve."

"Everybody went cray about it," she says.

I bet.

"I thought my step-monster was going to poop her pants. White people get nervous around kinky hair. My dad almost *cried*. Isn't that stupid?"

"Yes."

"But Jaz was like, 'it's *your* hair.' I was like, 'word.' "

I'm impressed. Both because she chopped her hair at eleven and because kids still say "word."

"So, your birthday is in January?" I ask. "What day?"

"The twenty-seventh."

This makes her an Aquarius. I like Aquarians. They're visionaries. They always want to change the world. I'm a Gemini. We're too inconsistent for world-changing. But I still admire that quality in others.

"When's yours?" she asks.

"June eighth."

Her eyes widen. "That's the same day as Jaz! That's crazy!"

It's not crazy for two people to have the same birthday. But I guess things like that seem cosmic when you're twelve.

We're stopped at the corner, waiting for the light to change.

"Who's your bestie?" the kid asks me.

I think about it for a second, which I guess is too long, because she decides I need her to be more specific. "Like, who's the person you hang with the most? Tell stuff to?"

"I know what a bestie is. I'm not a fourth-grader."

She smiles.

"I guess I don't really have one."

She stares at me like I just grew a titty out of the middle of my forehead. "You *don't have* a best friend?"

"Not really. Not in the way you have best friends when you're twelve, anyway. I just have regular friends."

She gives me a look like she feels bad for me. "Me and Jaz talk like a hundred times a day. If I didn't have her to talk to, I would probably just, like, die or something."

I remember this level of emotional dependence on another girl. "But it's different when you're a kid."

"My aunt Faye talks to her best friend every day and they're like fifty."

I sort of want to ask who her aunt's best friend is, but I don't want to seem too interested, so instead I say, "Perhaps your aunt has more social needs than I do."

"What's that mean? Like, you don't need people?"

"Everyone needs people. I guess I just need them less. Or maybe I just like to tell myself I do."

"How come?"

The question catches me off guard. While most adults shy away from potentially awkward inquiries, children will take any opportunity to get up in your business, and I don't spend enough time around them to remember that until it's too late. In lieu of the emotional maturity required to answer such a question, I just chuckle and shrug and say, "I don't know, kid." But for a second, before I can push her image back out of my brain the way it came, I think about Tasha and the emotional dependence we shared at twelve, light-years before I stopped needing people.

WHEN WE GET TO Bianchi's House of Pizza, which is smallish and decorated almost exclusively with art prints of classic Italian motorcycles, we find it bustling with lunchtime activity. It's a seat yourself deal, so we grab a couple of menus from a stack at the front and find a little table near a window.

"What do you feel like?" I ask the kid. "Hawaiian, maybe?"

She makes a face. "Pepperoni. Fruit on pizza is an abomination."

"Wow. Harsh much?"

She shrugs. "My mom used to say that."

I don't want to criticize her deceased mother's shitty opinions about pizza toppings, so I just make a noncommittal face and scan the menu. "I was strictly pepperoni when I was your age. My brother used to give me a hard time about it. He only liked sausage."

"Slade?" she asks.

"How do you know his name?"

"From your Facebook page."

I think about all the personal info we casually reveal on social media. It's really no wonder there's so much identity theft. This kid could probably buy a car in my name if she wanted to.

"*Slade*," she says again, giggling. "It sounds like a vampire from the Stone Age."

I laugh, too, because it kind of does.

"What else did you find out from my Facebook page? Besides my ridiculous brother's name."

She thinks about it. "You don't like your mom. And you don't like to stay in one place."

"I'm staying in one place right now," I tell her. "I'm missing a trip to be here."

"Oh," she says. "I'm right about your mom, though. Every time you talk about her on there, it's something bad."

"That's probably not true." It is, though. I rarely mention my mother on social media, but when I do, it's always in response to someone else's post about their own shitty parents, e.g.: *your mom sounds almost as half-assed as mine* or *so your mother fucked you up, too, huh?*

"How come you don't like her?" Vicky asks me.

I shrug. "Does any normal person like their mom?"

Okay, pause. Really? Who says that to a twelve-year-old who lost her mother? Jesus. Draymond. Christ. And it's not even true! Most *normal* people like their mothers. It's us *abnormals*—us emotionally damaged mofos—who don't. Before I can take it back, Vicky says, "I liked mine. She was fun."

"Of course you liked her," I say, wishing *I* were dead. "And you're totally normal. I was trying to be funny and it went left. Sorry."

A waiter comes over and takes our order: a half-pepperoni, half-Hawaiian pizza and two root beers.

"So, you and Cynthia were pretty close, huh?" I ask Vicky, once the waiter's gone.

"Yup. We did a lot of stuff together."

"Like what?"

"Like play basketball. Watch movies. Practice spelling. She used to do bees when she was a kid, too. She won like four trophies."

A memory scratches at the back of my brain, of Cynthia spelling out words from the Bible, like "hearken."

"She was helping me study for my first bee when she got sick," Vicky says. "She used to quiz me with words from her law books sometimes. Those were so hard! If she was at work, she would call me and give me a word over the phone."

"That does sound fun." It doesn't sound fun. But it sounds like the two of them got a kick out of it and that's what matters, right? "See, you're totes normal."

"I'm not that normal," she says matter-of-factly. "I have to go to therapy every week."

"Oh. Well, that's . . . pretty normal these days, right?"

"You go to therapy?" she asks.

"Not currently. But I did for a while in college."

"How come?"

Wow, kids really have trash boundaries, don't they? "I guess I was trying to sort out some things. About myself."

"Like being a lesbian?"

"Sure. But also family stuff." As soon as I say it, I wish I hadn't. I shift in my seat, suddenly anxious, and hope the kid doesn't press me. I don't like to talk about "family stuff."

The waiter places two fountain root beers on the table.

"Did it help?" Vicky asks when he's gone.

"What? Therapy?"

She nods.

I shake my head. "No. My therapist was a skinny, white grad student. I only went four times."

She sips her soda. "School said I had to go. 'Cause I used to get really mad."

"About your mom?"

"Yeah," she says. "I punched the wall one time."

"They sent you to therapy just for punching the wall?"

"Some other stuff happened, too. But it was a while ago," she says, shrugging. "I still have to go every week. I guess until they decide I'm not going to beat anybody up."

"Any*body*? I thought you just punched the wall."

"That time, yeah," she says. "This other time, I got really mad and punched this boy, Malik. But only because he said something bad about my mom."

"Hmm."

"I guess I was madder at cancer than him, though. That's what Vanessa said. She's my therapist. I guess if cancer was a person, I could've beat it up instead of Malik."

"Punch cancer in the stomach?"

"Yup."

"Scratch its eyes out?"

"Uh-huh." She sips her soda.

"Kick it in the dick?"

She bursts into hysterical laughter and soda comes out of her nose. I laugh, too, partly because I love my own jokes but also because her laughter is loud and boundless and I like being part of it. I think about myself at her age, angry, too, but with no clue how to deal with it, holding it in until it eventually morphed into depression. Maybe I should've just beat somebody up. I had a Malik in my seventh-grade class, too, but he'd been held back twice and was the size of a high school junior, so probably not him.

"What'd this little Malik bastard say about your mom?" I ask Vicky.

"He said that his mom said my mom was a stuck-up B."

Sounds like Malik's mama should've been the one to get clocked. "You told the principal that's why you hit him?"

"Yeah, but he didn't listen. Most grown-ups don't."

"What about your aunt?"

She shrugs. "Sometimes she does. Way more than my dad. Way, way more than his stupid wife. But not like my mom. She *always* listened to me."

That must have been nice.

Vicky takes another sip of soda. "Nobody loves you like your mom. You know?"

I laugh. An actual, factual out-loud chuckle. It's not the response of a well-adjusted person.

The kid looks at me, like she did that day in the hot dog shop, like she's trying to see inside me. I try not to let that happen, mostly by looking everywhere but directly at her. Finally, she sips her soda again and says, "Maybe you should go back to therapy."

"Well, shit."

"I'm not saying that to be mean. I just think it kinda helps."

"Is it helping you?"

"Yup."

"You don't get angry anymore?"

"Yeah, but about other stuff."

"For instance?"

She thinks about it. "Police brutality. The police in general, actually. Anti-Black racism. That's a big one. Slut-shaming."

"Slut-shaming?"

"Yeah! It's really messed up how girls get treated if some boy says they're a ho."

"You're in seventh grade."

She looks at me like, *Why would that matter?* I think back on seventh grade and see her point.

"Okay. What else?"

"The school-to-prison pipeline! I hate that!" She bangs her fist on the table and some soda sloshes out of my glass. "Sorry," she says, grabbing a handful of napkins and mopping it up.

"Where'd you learn about all this? Your mom?"

"Aunt Faye, mostly. And my friend Keisha. She lives on my block. She's in high school. My stepsister tells me stuff sometimes, too."

"If you and your aunt are anti-cops," I say, "why'd she almost call them on me the other day?"

Vicky shakes her head. "She wouldn't do that. Unless you were, like, murdering somebody maybe. We believe in community alternatives to police," she says, sounding like one of those tween activists you sometimes see on the news, holding up signs at marches that read: DONALD DUCK WOULD MAKE A BETTER PRESIDENT. It's adorbs.

I don't remember thinking much about important socio-political issues when I was twelve. I was too busy trying to catch a glimpse of a titty on the scrambled porn channel. Sure, I learned about the Civil Rights Movement in fourth grade but it was mostly Martin Luther King and Rosa Parks. They definitely didn't teach us about Malcolm X or Angela Davis. I never even heard of Ericka Huggins until college, when I joined the Black Student Alliance and we invited her to speak at a rally against campus police harassment of Black students. I was *twenty*. So, yeah. I definitely didn't know shit about "community alternatives to police" in seventh freaking grade. I think it's pretty cool that Vicky does, though.

"She was probably just calling Uncle Nick," Vicky says.

"Who's that?"

"Her boyfriend. Or fiancé, I guess."

"Wait," I say. "Someone is *marrying* your mean auntie?"

"She's not mean, usually," Vicky says. "She just doesn't like you, I guess."

Tuh! "Well, I don't like her, either. So we're on the same page. About that. About not liking each other. Equally."

The kid looks like she doesn't know what to say to that perfectly mature response.

The waiter brings our food and, as I stuff my face with it, I think about how wrong Cynthia was about fruit on pizza and then catch myself wondering if her mean sister likes Hawaiian or not.

9

DAY ONE OF MY TRIP TO BRAZIL IS GOING SPLENDIDLY WITHOUT me, according to Toni, who already looks sun-kissed and only a little bit stressed out on our video call the next morning. "There's been a couple of tiny hiccups, but nothing serious enough to bother you with," she says. "Our interns have been great. Our travelers are happy."

I feel pangs of envy and regret at not being there, especially because Toni is telling me all this while sitting in front of a window through which I can see the sand and surf of Maresias.

"And did you see?" she asks. "The June Bali-Sydney trip is almost completely booked already. You'll be back by then, right?"

"Definitely." Two and a half months is more than enough time to build a lifelong relationship, right?

I decide to stop feeling envious and regretful, and instead celebrate the first day of the Brazil trip by patronizing my regular bar—a little jawn not far from the B and B that has all my favorite bourbons. I'm sitting there, drinking a Knob Creek, thinking about sunny beaches, and generally minding my own business, when this ugly man comes and sits down beside me. There are four other empty chairs at the bar, but he sits right next to me. I hate it when men do this. "How you doin' today, sis?" he asks.

I don't answer. I just stare at him blankly, eyes wide, for, like, fifteen straight seconds, hoping he'll get freaked out and leave me alone.

"I said how you doin'?" he says again, leaning a little closer to me, like maybe I didn't hear him the first time. He has a gold tooth and it catches the light from one of the ceiling lamps over the bar. "What, you can't even speak?" he asks. "You one of them conceited chicks, huh?"

The blank stare isn't working, so it's on to plan B. *I'm sorry, I can't hear you, I'm deaf,* I sign. My sign language is a little bit rusty, so it's possible I'm not getting it exactly right, but I'm pretty sure this dude isn't going to know.

He blinks a few times and his eyebrows draw together. "You deaf?"

I stare at him.

"Shit, I ain't never met no deaf jawn. That's wild."

It's occurred to me before that pretending to be deaf in order to avoid harassment from ugly men might be kinda messed up. I mean, I like to think Deaf women would understand, but maybe not. Maybe if a Deaf woman saw me doing this, she'd be like, *How dare you, hearing-ass bitch?* Which is probably fair. But on the other hand: I really don't want to talk to this fugly-ass dude.

You're not even a little bit handsome, I sign. *Not. Even. A. Little. Bit.*

He looks from my hands to my face. Blinks a few more times. "What you drinking? Lemme buy you a round."

Oh, for Christ's sake. *You. Are. Mad. Ugly. Bro.* I sign it vigorously, with as much flourish as I can manage.

He looks around, in case there's someone close by who can help him figure out how to go about picking up a Deaf woman. A little farther down the bar, a man who has been watching us stifles a laugh. My suitor calls out to him. "You know deaf language, my nigga?"

He shakes his head. "Nah. Sorry, man."

He sits there a little while longer, saying things like, "Where you stay at?" and "You fine for a deaf chick" and "You only date deaf dudes or you like niggas that can hear?" I just stare at him the whole time, feigning a look of utter confusion. Finally, he shakes his head, mutters something under his breath that sounds like, "This really some wild shit," picks up his drink, and leaves. Not just leaves the seat, but leaves the entire bar, drink in hand. What the hell? But also: Thank God.

"That was amazing," says the man farther down the bar.

I ignore him.

My phone buzzes. It's a text from Viva.

You around?

> At the Swank.

Just got back from yoga. Mind if I join?

> Sounds good.

The guy down the bar asks, "Where'd you learn to sign?"

I catch the bartender's eye, point to my empty bourbon glass, and he pours me another.

"I know you can hear me," says the guy. "I know you're not deaf, Skye."

I look at him. He looks kind of familiar, but I can't place him.

"Shit, you already forgot me? That's cold-blooded."

"That's cold-blooded" is a thing only *old* Black men say. This guy looks too young to be saying it. That thought feels like déjà vu and then it clicks. I talked to this guy a few nights ago. More than talked, I guess, considering I woke up next to him the following morning.

"Oh. Hey."

He grins. "Hey."

I go back to my bourbon.

After about half a minute, he says, "So? Where *did* you learn how to sign?"

I'm never going to fuck you ever again, is what I want to say. But I'm trying not to be extra. So instead, I say, "Look, can we just forget what happened?"

He purses his lips, thinks about it for a second. "Maybe you can. I probably can't."

"Okay, then I will."

"Just like that, huh? You must have strange men dancing naked in your hotel room a lot if you can just forget it that easily."

"You danced . . . ?"

He grins again. "Oh, so you *already* forgot what happened. Well, you had a lot to drink, so I'm not surprised."

I sip my bourbon. "Well, I'm not drinking today, so don't get any ideas."

He looks from me to the bourbon. "You literally took a drink while you were saying that."

"I mean I'm not getting drunk," I tell him. "I'm just having this one drink and that's it."

"That's already your second drink."

"Jesus, who are you, my great-granddad? I coulda sworn Nana killed you and buried you under the azaleas in, like, 1983."

He holds up both hands. "Okay. Sorry." Then he says, "You know we didn't sleep together that night? I mean, we made out pretty heavily—"

Ew.

"And we did technically sleep in the same bed. But we didn't . . . y'know."

"Of course I know that." Okay, this is an enormous relief. I only dabble in dick, like one penis per decade, and I'm pretty selective. This guy's not bad-looking in a bug-eyed, young James Baldwin kind of way, but his is not a dick I would have selected under more sober circumstances. So, this is heartening news. It also explains why *I* didn't wake up naked that morning, a fact that is only just now occurring to me.

"Well, then," he says, "hopefully things don't have to be awkward. I really like this bar and I'd hate to have to stop coming here."

I shrug. "It's not awkward for me," I tell him. It's hella awkward, though, and he should definitely stop coming here.

He smiles, nods, throws some cash up on the bar. "Aight," he says, getting up to go. "I'll see you around, then, Skye."

"Cool beans, bruh." Ugh, why.

As he's leaving, Viva's entering and I watch him watch her ass as she goes by. Creep.

"¿Qué estás bebiendo?" Viva asks, sitting down next to me. "Bourbon?"

"Knob. ¿Quieres?"

"Chica. You know I can't handle brown liquor." She makes a face like she's having nasty bourbon-related flashbacks. Then she orders a White Russian.

My phone buzzes on the bar and I glance at it. "It's Slade again."

Viva frowns. "¿Por qué tanto Slade últimamente?"

"He's been nagging me about going to see my mother," I say. "He's never cared before. But the other day he made up a stroke to get me to visit her in the hospital."

"She's in the hospital again?" Viva asks, looking concerned.

"She's fine. She just got dizzy. I'm sure she's back home now."

I silence the phone and finish my bourbon. When it's gone, I stare into the empty glass.

"Another drink?" Viva asks me as the bartender brings hers.

"Actually, I haven't visited my mother much at all in the . . . What is it now? Two years since her accident?"

"Define 'much at all.'"

"Including the hospital a few days ago? I've seen her three or four times."

"Three? Or four?"

"Two." I signal for the bartender, point to my empty glass. "I haven't been a good daughter in twenty years," I tell Viva. "Maybe I never was one. Why start now, right?"

"I'm not judging you," she says. "I know your relationship with your mother is . . . complicada. You call, though, don't you?"

"I call. Sometimes," I say. "It's not that I don't feel sympathy for her. I do. So much of who she was is just . . . gone. She can't work. She hardly even makes it to church anymore because she can't remember to get dressed in time. She can't even go pee without being reminded."

Viva nods. "It's awful."

"And all she has is Slade to take care of her. Can you imagine? Slade's never properly cared for anybody in his life."

"Lo sé," Viva says. "From experience."

"And even recognizing that, I still don't go over there. I hardly even call. I feel sort of shitty about it, but at the same time . . ."

"¿Ajá?"

The bartender pours more bourbon into my empty glass. I feel like downing it but I don't. "I gave up on my mother a really long time ago. Maybe something should've changed after her fall. Maybe I'm supposed to want to try again. But I don't."

Viva reaches over and puts her hand on mine, squeezes. It feels nice and I let myself like it but then I feel a tingling at the back of my throat like I might cry or some shit, so I take my hand away.

"Vicky's mean aunt is engaged," I say to change the subject.

Viva raises an eyebrow. "The one who came by?"

"Mmm-hmm."

"Does that bother you?" she asks.

"No," I tell her. "Maybe?"

"Because you're attracted to her?"

"No! She's the worst."

"Then why do you care about her relationship status?"

"Because marriage is an institution concocted by the patriarchy to oppress women. Obviously."

She laughs and sips her drink.

"Okay, maybe I'm attracted to her," I say.

"I thought you didn't do relationships nunca más."

I shrug. "Who said anything about a relationship?"

"So, you just want to sleep with her?"

"Sí. But that's messy, right?"

"¿Por qué?"

"Porque she's the sister of the friend I gave my eggs to? Who she didn't even like? Who subsequently died? And whose kid she's now raising? Who is the product of one of the aforementioned eggs?"

Viva nods. "Well, maybe it's a little bit messy. Is she into you?"

A long sigh escapes me, made of sexual frustration, probs. "I thought she was when we first met. But she doesn't like me at all now." I shake my head. "Whatever. It doesn't matter. I kicked it with Vicky yesterday."

"Oh, sí?" she asks, raising her eyebrows again. "How'd that go?"

"Bien. I think we're bonding, maybe."

She smiles at me. "You don't bond easily, chica, so that's good news."

10

A COUPLE OF DAYS LATER, I PICK UP VICKY AFTER SPELLING CLUB, which is apparently a thing, and we go get soft pretzels. I'm squeezing mustard onto mine when I realize I haven't had one in almost twenty years. "I practically lived on these when I was a kid," I tell Vicky. "They used to sell them in school. A lady with a cart came around at recess. They were fifteen cents apiece. Two for a quarter."

"They still do that," she says. "But it's fifty cents for one now."

We sit on a sunny bench in Malcolm X Park and eat our pretzels. Vicky tells me about her life before Cynthia died. Like how they used to watch old movies together. Really old movies. Those black-and-white jawns.

"My mom liked Greta Garbo, so we watched her movies a bunch. My fave is *Ninotchka*. She plays this Russian who goes to Paris for work and falls in love with this dude who's supposed to be Parisian but doesn't have a French accent. It's so funny."

She tells me about life after her mother got diagnosed with breast cancer. About how, during treatment, Cynthia had to advocate for herself to receive more pain medication, on several occasions, because she wasn't being given enough.

"She told me Black patients get less 'cause white people don't think we feel pain the same as they do. It made me so mad. I still think about it a lot. Aunt Faye calls it my 'radicalizing moment.'"

Later in the week, I pick her up from school again and we walk down Fifty-second Street to the library, so the kid can check out books about hoodoo, Santería, and witchcraft.

"This is for an assignment?" I ask, watching her stack volumes on a table. "I thought Montessoris didn't have homework."

She shakes her head. "I just want to get some ideas."

"You trying to put a spell on somebody?"

She shrugs.

"It's not me, is it?"

"Nope."

"Okay, cool."

When I'm not kicking it with Vicky, I'm planning We Outchea's June trip, to Bali for the annual arts festival and then to Sydney for the Australian International Music Festival. With Toni leading the group in Brazil, most of her usual administrative tasks fall to me. Some days I make a dozen phone calls and write twice as many emails and it reminds me of the days before I had an assistant, when it was just me doing all of it, from trying to get deals on hotels to buying metro cards to making sure my travelers knew in advance not to venture out alone—or sometimes even in twos—in certain places. It was a lot of work. It still is. I'm up late on a Friday-night phone meeting with a club owner in Bali, tryna set up some VIP shit, and don't get to bed until three.

I don't wake up until after noon on Saturday. From under my covers, I can hear music and laughter coming from downstairs and, at first, I decide to avoid whatever that is. But then I get hungry and realize music and laughter probably also mean food, so I brush my teeth, throw on some clean-ish clothes, and head down.

The music and laughter is coming from the courtyard, where several dozen people are gathered, sipping drinks and eating off small plates. Many of them I've never seen before, but there are also familiar faces from the block, including Miss Newsome, who's standing near the DJ, dancing by herself with a beer in her hand. I spot Viva, smiling and laughing and being her generally charming self. I wave to her and then head for the spread, loading up my own small plate with cheese, olives, tomatoes, and crusty bread. I'm devouring it when Viva comes over.

"Hey. What's all this?" I ask her, through a mouthful of olives.

"My spring garden party," she says.

"Oh, right."

Every year, usually in April as long as winter doesn't hold on too long, Viva throws a party in the courtyard of the bed-and-breakfast to welcome spring. I'm almost never in the country when it happens. In fact, the last time I was in attendance was four years ago. I remember it because the flowers in the courtyard were so big and bright that they attracted hella bees and a bitch got stung, twice. To help with the pain, Viva made me a special drink, a bourbon jawn with caramelized pears, served up with a twist, and I had enough of those chumpies that I don't remember anything else about the party.

Viva is giving me a strange look.

"What? I got cheese on my face?"

"Sí," she says. "Pero that's not the problem."

"There's a problem?"

She nods. "Tasha's here."

Fuck. Me.

"Where?" I ask, my eyes darting around the courtyard.

Tasha's not hard to spot, walking into the party in a bright orange jacket and bow tie.

"Jesus, Viva! I told you I don't talk to Tasha. Why would you invite both of us?"

"I *didn't* invite you, Skye."

Oh.

"You were supposed to be in Brazil, remember?"

"Okay," I say, "but it's almost two weeks since I changed my plans. Why didn't you make an adjustment?"

She makes a face, like, *Bitch, are you serious?* "Contrary to what you seem to think, I have other things to do besides accommodate you. I have a business. A marriage. Familia. Otras amigas. Lo siento si all that got in the way of making sure you didn't end up within twenty-five feet of Tasha."

The implication here is that I'm being self-centered and immature. It's an implication I find offensive, frankly.

"Is it really that big of a deal?" Viva asks me.

"Yes."

"You can't put your feelings about her aside for one afternoon?"

"No."

She frowns and throws her hands up, exasperated. I don't know why she's being so dramatic.

"Hey, Viva," Tasha says, coming right over to us as if it's no big deal, violating—for the second time in two weeks—our unspoken rule of avoiding all avoidable interactions with each other. She kisses Viva on the cheek and then looks at me. "You're still in Philly, huh?"

"I seem to be."

"You're leaving again soon, though, right?" she asks, in this tone that's half innocent-conversation-making, half *this isn't your city anymore, so why are you still here?*

"Skye's not going to be leaving for a couple more months," Viva says. "Which is good for me, because the garden needs replanting and I can use an extra pair of hands."

This is the first time she's mentioned this to me. I shake my head at her. "You know I can't stand dirt under my fingernails."

"I know," she says. "That's what garden gloves are for, chica."

Tasha is looking curiously at us.

"¿Qué?" Viva asks.

"Nothing," Tasha says. "I just can't believe you two are still friends."

I frown. "Why wouldn't we be?"

She shrugs.

"¿Qué tal unos drinks?" Viva asks a little nervously, and starts to walk past Tasha toward the bar.

Tasha hesitates, like she really wants to say something else to me. Then she turns and follows Viva.

I should just take my plate of munchies and go back upstairs. But, guess what? I don't. I follow them both to the bar, which is just a tall table, from behind which Viva's husband, Jason, is serving drinks.

"Bourbon for Skye, babe," Viva says to him, putting a hand on his arm.

They're a weird-looking couple. Still. Even after four years. Viva's all cocoa skin, shiny hair, and legs for millennia, wrapped up in fashionable outfits and oozing charm. Jason Schneider is a straight-up goober. The type of white dude who wears khaki cargo shorts and Speedo slides with socks, and says "bro" with a hard O. Plus, Viva was never into white men before she met him. He's a strange choice for a starter white boy. My first white boy was Italian. Dark hair, dark eyes. His skin—and perhaps most important, his dick—was tan, which I think made for an easier transition. Viva made the switch to pink dick in one fell swoop. It had to have been jarring. All that said, though, Jason is attentive and sweet and, according to Viva, he lays impressive pipe. Plus, he always has her back.

"What are you drinking, mami?" Viva asks Tasha.

Tasha thinks about it, then says, "I'll take whatever good beer you have."

A memory flashes in my mind. Senior year of high school. Me, Tasha, Viva, and a couple of other girls getting sloshed in Tasha's basement off some pissy malt liquor we talked some old head who was loitering outside the state store into buying for us. The basement was recently finished but had no furniture yet, so we sat on pillows, taking turns chugging, and laughing about everything. When it got dark, we went out into the tiny backyard and lay together in the grass, holding hands and linking arms and crossing our legs together, a mass of brown limbs, beginning and ending nowhere.

"What are *you* drinking?" Tasha asks Viva, bringing me back to the present.

Viva shakes her head. "Nothing. I've had a few too many White Russians lately. They're going straight to my ass."

"Good," Tasha says. "Because your ass is perfect. It always has been. The *only* way it could be better is if there was more of it."

"Ay, gracias," Viva says, smiling and sticking out her butt a little.

Tasha reaches over and smacks Viva's ass. Viva laughs. It's all pretty disgusting.

"Should we leave?" I ask, indicating Jason and myself. "Do you guys wanna be alone?"

Jason puts his hands up, like his name is Bennett.

"I guess since you're not friends with any of your exes," Tasha says, "this seems weird to you."

Okay, listen:

1. smacking your friend's ass is weird, whether or not you used to date, so don't try to tell me it isn't;
2. a "perfect" ass cannot be made better, that's not how perfection works; and
3. how the hell does she know who I am or am not friends with?

"That's not even true," I say.

"Oh, my bad," she replies, all fake-apologetic. "Which exes are you friends with, again?"

"Ones that you don't even know about."

"Like . . . ?"

"Like . . ." Come on, brain, don't fail me now. There are so many women's names you can come up with on the spot. Andrea. Karen. Felicia. "Tif . . . onica." Damn it!

She laughs. "Tifonica? Really?"

"Yes!"

"That's a made-up name."

"Pssh. No, it's not."

Tasha looks at Viva. "You heard of this Tifonica person?"

Without skipping a beat, Viva says, "Sí. She's this Dominican girl Skye used to go out with."

"See! You don't know everybody I've dated, Tasha."

She shrugs. "Maybe I don't. But lesbian communities are small. Even when they're big."

"What does that even mean?"

"It means, women talk. Some of them talk about you."

"Who talks about me?"

She shrugs again, like she doesn't want to say. Which: Why are you bringing it up, then?

I decide she's just trying to mess with me. I mean, maybe a couple of my exes talk about me. I've had bad breakups like everyone else. But I'm not one of those lesbians with a trail of angry women in her wake. I've never had trouble moving on when something felt done. Most of my relationships have ended without a ton of drama. I'm not one of those *notorious* dykes. At least, I don't think I am.

Jason hands me my bourbon. I drink it in one shot and hand him back the tumbler, wait for him to refill it, then down that one, too. When I'm done, I say to Viva, "I'm going to my room."

"You don't have to," she says. "You can stay and enjoy the party. You don't have to skulk off by yourself."

"I'm not skulking. And I like being by myself."

Tasha laughs.

"What's funny?" I ask her, because I'm already feeling the bourbon and now I don't give a shit.

"I just can't believe you two are still friends."

"You said that already. If you have something else to say," I tell her, "just say it."

She puts her drink down. "You're probably not ready to hear it."

Probably not. "Try me."

"I guess I'm just surprised you haven't deemed Viva unworthy yet," Tasha says. "Like you usually do with people."

"What are you talking about?"

"You know," she says, "how you test people to see if they really care about you? Except they don't know they're even being tested? So then when they fail, you deem them unworthy and cut them off? Like you did me?"

"Like I did you?" I ask her. "When? When did I do you like that?"

"When we went away to college," she says.

"You're the one who didn't keep in touch," I tell her. "Seriously, are you drunk right now? Did you get hammered before you came here?"

"Is that how you're choosing to remember it?" Tasha asks me. "Damn, Skye, are you really that lacking in self-reflection? Still? At your age?"

"Chicas," Viva says. "Can we not, por favor?"

Naima comes over. "Hey, Viva? Is four-twenty allowed at this party or no?"

"No," Viva and Jason say in unison.

"I'm gonna go," I tell Viva. I don't say shit else to Tasha. I bounce before either of them can say anything else to me.

I'm all the way up the back stairs and halfway down the hall to my room before Viva catches up to me.

"Skye," she says, grabbing my wrist, "are you okay?"

"I'm fine, Viva. You don't have to take care of me. Go be with your friends."

"*You're* my friend. Dios mío."

"Tasha was just messing with me, right?" I ask. "When she said women talk about me."

Viva sighs. "No sé, Skye."

"Tú sí sabes. I can see it in your face."

At first, she just shakes her head. Then she says, "Well, you do have a . . . reputación."

Oh? "For what?" I ask as incredulously as I can manage.

"For leaving," she says, "as soon as anything goes wrong."

"That's bullshit. Who said I do that? Joy?"

"No," Viva says.

"Alana?"

She shakes her head, no.

"Serena?"

"No. But the fact that you just named *tres mujeres* who might have said it is maybe telling?"

"Really, Viva?"

"I'm just saying—"

"What? What are you just saying?"

"'Between stimulus and response there is a space. In that space is our power to choose our response. In our response lies our growth and our freedom.' Viktor Frankl said that."

"Who?" I must be tipsy now because I do not remember this Viktor nigga at all.

"It doesn't matter. The point is, you can just react to what Tasha said, like you're doing right now, or you can take some time to think about it."

"There's nothing to think about," I tell her. "Tasha's just wrong."

She sighs. "Bueno, Skye. Whatever." And she walks away.

My phone buzzes in my pocket. It's a text: *Spelling bee! U coming???*

11

THE GOOD NEWS IS, I'M NOT DRUNK. THE BAD NEWS IS, I'M NOT sober, either. I'd say I'm a little past buzzed but not all the way to tipsy. I'm bipsy. Which sounds too cute to be bad, right? Considering I'm cute and bipsy, I decide there's really no reason for me to miss the bee.

When I get to West Philly Montessori, the competition is already under way. The auditorium smells exactly like the school auditoriums of my childhood—like sweat and bologna. It causes a wave of nausea to roll through my bourbon-ated belly. I breathe out through my mouth, swallow hard, and say out loud to myself, "You're not drunk, you're just bipsy, so act normal, girl."

The auditorium is packed with students, staff, and parents. The stage is set up with maybe twenty folding chairs, half of which are filled by kids. I assume these are the ones who haven't been knocked out of the competition already. Vicky is one of them. She sees me and smiles. I smile back, trying to look as non-bipsy as possible.

"Brandon," says the only adult on the stage, the moderator.

A chubby kid stands up.

"Your word is 'vaporize.'"

I'm looking around for an empty seat when I spot Faye in the third row. I haven't seen much of her since that first day I kicked it with Vicky, when I watched Faye mediate between their neighbors. Whenever I drop Vicky off after we hang, Faye waves from the front door, but she never tries to talk to me and never invites me inside. Which: whatever. I don't even care.

There's an empty seat beside her. There are also plenty of other seats, all of them beside strangers who have nothing against me. But, in my current bipsy state, I don't want any of those seats. I want *that one*. So, instead of doing the easy, not-weird thing, I squeeze by a few people sitting at the end of the row and sit down right beside Faye.

"Vaporize," the chubby kid says, looking nervous. "May I have the definition?"

At first, Faye doesn't notice me. She's paying attention to Brandon. But as I settle back she glances over. She's smiling at first, but then, when she sees it's me, her smile falters, only to recover a second later. "Hello, Skye."

"Oh," I say. "Faye. Wow. I didn't even realize that was you sitting there. Hello."

"Vicky didn't mention you were coming."

"Is it a problem?"

She hesitates. Then: "No. It's fine."

"Vaporize," Brandon says. "V-a-p-e-r-i-z-e. Vaporize."

"No, I'm sorry, that's incorrect," the moderator says.

For a second, the kid looks like he's going to cry. Then he takes a deep breath, like he's grounding himself, and walks off the stage to the sound of pity applause.

I feel eyes on me and realize two of the people I squeezed by on the way to my seat are looking at me. Now I'm super paranoid that they can tell I've been drinking. When I glance over, one of them, a man, looks away. The other one, a woman, keeps staring until the man nudges her and she turns her attention back to the stage.

"Vicky," the moderator says.

Vicky stands up.

"Your word is 'aviation.'"

"Aviation," says Vicky. "A-v-i-a-t-i-o-n. Aviation."

"Correct."

There's a round of applause, with me and Faye clapping the loudest. The man sitting next to me yells "Yes!" and it's then that I realize he must be Vicky's father. I look down the row and, sure enough, there's Vicky's stepsister at the end. I didn't notice her before but now I recognize her from the fancy hot dog shop. The woman sitting between the stepsister and the father must be Vicky's stepmother. Now it's my turn to stare, and then smile awkwardly when they catch me staring, and look away.

"Angel," says the moderator. "Your word is 'disingenuous.'"

"Disingenuous," Angel says. "May I have the definition?"

"Not straightforward or candid."

"D-i-s-i-n-g-e-n-u-o-u-s. Disingenuous."

"Correct."

"Shit," I say, a little louder than I mean to.

A few parents turn to look disapprovingly in my direction.

Faye peers at me. "What's the matter with you?"

I peer back at her. "What's the matter with *you*?"

She stares at me for a long moment. I try to look normal as I stare back at her. It's hard because my eyelids feel heavy. To keep them open, I raise my eyebrows.

"Are you drunk?" Faye whispers.

"Ummmmm, I don't know if I'd use the word 'drunk,'" I say, raising my eyebrows a little bit higher. "More like bipsy."

She takes a deep breath. "Why would you show up drunk to a spelling bee?"

"Not drunk. Bipsy."

She blinks at me. "What the hell is 'bipsy'?"

Someone shushes us from the row behind. Which: Rude much? Jesus.

Faye glares at me for another couple of seconds before turning her attention back to the stage.

Ten minutes later, there are only two kids left in the bee. That Angel brat. And Vicky!

"Angel, your word is 'interrogative.'"

"May I have the definition?"

"Relating to verbs that ask for a reply."

Angel closes her eyes. "Interrogative. I-n-t-e-r-r-o-g-a-t-i-v-e. Interrogative."

"That's correct," says the moderator.

The audience applauds. Angel pumps the air with her fist, then sits back down.

"Vicky, your word is 'reflection.'"

"Reflection," Vicky says. "R-e-f-l-e-c-t-i-o-n. Reflection."

Are you really that lacking in self-reflection? I hear Tasha ask. *Still?*

I close my eyes and think about freshman year of college, about coming back to my dorm room after class every day and before even taking off my shoes, checking my voicemail to see if Tasha had called. I remember how abandoned I felt when there was no message, how sad, how angry. I feel that sadness and anger rising up in my belly now, swirling around with the bourbon. But then my brain stutters in this weird way, almost like a skipping record. Suddenly, I see myself standing in my dorm room, the wall phone to my ear, listening to a message from Tasha. When the message ends, instead of calling her back, I make a mark on a little chalkboard I have hung up by the phone.

I don't recall having a chalkboard in my room. At first. But the more I sit there thinking about it, the more clear the memory becomes. The marks were for keeping track of Tasha's calls. Once she'd left me five messages, I'd call her back. But not before.

The sound of a sharp intake of breath pulls me back to the present.

"What happened?" I ask Faye.

She gives me a look like, *really?* and then turns back to the stage without answering.

I see Vicky take her seat. She's frowning but she's not leaving the stage, so I figure she missed a word but isn't out of the game yet. If I remember right—and it's very possible I don't—when it's down to two people and one person misses a word, the other person has to spell two words right in a row to win.

"Angel," the moderator says, "your word is 'hallucinations.'"

Angel takes a deep breath. "Hallucinations. H-a-l-l-u-c-i-n-a-t-i-o-n-s. Hallucinations."

"Correct."

"Boo!" I call out, before I can stop myself.

"Skye!" Faye scolds as every single person in the auditorium turns to stare at me. Two people, who I guess are Angel's parents, shoot me particularly angry looks.

"Parents," calls the moderator, "please refrain from booing the seventh-graders!"

"I'm not technically a parent!" I call back.

The moderator shakes his head and turns back to Angel. "If you spell this next word correctly," he says, "you'll be West Philadelphia Montessori All-Grade Spelling Champ and move on to represent us in the citywide bee."

Angel nods, looking nervous.

"Your word is 'grotesque.'"

I see Vicky roll her eyes and I know she's thinking what an easy word this is.

Angel closes her eyes, all dramatic. "Grotesque. G-r-o-t-e-s-q-u-e. Grotesque."

"That's correct!"

There's a big round of applause and Angel's parents stand up and cheer. Vicky and Angel shake hands. The moderator presents Angel with a trophy, silver-plated and maybe twelve inches tall. Angel beams, while Vicky stands there holding a second-place certificate, sporting a smile I think is fake because she's showing all of her teeth and she never usually smiles like that. The moderator announces the date of the citywide bee, tells us all to come out and support Angel and the school, and then thanks us all for coming.

People start getting up and moving into the aisles. As soon as Vicky's dad and stepmother are out of the way, I beeline it out of our row, before Faye can say anything to me. I'm moving so fast that I trip over my own feet and almost take an L right in the middle of the auditorium. I'm bipsy, but not bipsy enough to allow myself to fall down in a room full of middle-schoolers. I HAVEN'T FORGOTTEN ABOUT THE PEACOCK EPISODE. I have to engage every muscle in my upper body—muscles I'm pretty sure I haven't used since that one time I tried yoga—to keep from hitting the floor face-first, but I somehow manage it. I straighten up and catch Vicky just as she's coming off the stage.

"You were amazing," I tell her.

"I lost."

"Yeah, but barely. And that Angel kid got all the easy words."

"What's wrong with you?" she asks. "You're all sweaty."

"It's hot in here," I say, wiping my brow.

"No, it's not."

"It is. A little bit."

"It's cold in here," she says. "Everybody's wearing sweaters."

"I run hot, okay?"

"Oh," she says, "because of menopause or something?"

WOOOOOOOOOW.

Faye comes over, followed by Vicky's father, stepmother, and stepsister.

"Great job, baby girl," her father says, reaching out and hugging her.

Vicky just stands there, her arms at her sides, looking annoyed.

When he releases her, he extends his hand to me. He looks like Vicky, or, I guess, she looks like him. Her russet-colored eyes and heart-shaped lips are his. He's tall and thin, with wire-rimmed glasses and a no-fade line-up, graying at his temples. He's wearing khakis, a pink golf shirt, and loafers. He has sort of a Barack Obama vibe but without the big ears or the swagger. "You must be Skye. I'm Kenny. It's nice to finally meet you."

"*Charmed*," I say, like I'm suddenly a floozie masquerading as a socialite in a Marilyn Monroe movie.

"We would have met a long time ago if it had been up to me," he says.

I don't know what he means by that. I remember Faye saying that Cynthia probably would've even kept the egg donor thing a secret from her husband if she could have, so maybe this is some kind of shade toward his dead ex-wife. Which: Really, Barack No-Bama? Gross.

Beside Kenny, his wife clears her throat.

"Oh," he says, like he legit forgot she was there. "This is my wife, Charlotte. And my stepdaughter, Sabrina."

"It's nice to meet you," Sabrina says.

I almost remind her that we've met before, but then I think maybe she doesn't want her parents to know she helped Vicky find me. Also, we didn't *technically* meet, she mostly just hovered nearby while I blew chunks.

"So, you're the egg donor," Charlotte says. "How fascinating."

Kenny frowns at her. "Char."

Char is very thin, with eyes I'd describe as "light" without having any particular color to them. She looks older than Kenny. "Well, it *is* fascinating," she insists. "Isn't it? I've never met an egg donor."

"How could you possibly know that?" I ask.

"Well," she says, thinking about it, "I guess you're right. I should say I've never personally *known* one. Unless my friends are keeping secrets from me."

"They probably are," Vicky says. "Because you're such a judgmental witch."

OH SHIIIIIIT.

"Vicky!" her father exclaims. "I told you not to talk to your step-mother like that!"

Charlotte gives Faye a wounded look, as if *she's* the one who called her a judgmental witch. "Is this what she's learning under your roof?"

"Vicky," Faye says, gently placing a hand on the kid's shoulder. "Say goodbye to your friends, so we can go."

Vicky shoots looks of thinly veiled hatred at her father and step-mother and walks off down the aisle, Sabrina following behind her.

"You told me her behavior was improving, Faye," Kenny says. "It doesn't look like it."

"You know Cynthia was the one who got Vicky interested in spelling bees," Faye says. "She's probably feeling bad right now on a lot of levels, so let's give her a break."

"Maybe you're giving her too many breaks."

"Meaning what, Kenny?"

"Meaning you're too easy on her," he says.

"Her mother *died*."

"That was two years ago! Look: We all miss Cynthia—"

Faye smirks. "Really, Kenny? We all do?"

"—but Vicky needs to get back on track."

"She will. In her own time."

"What if her own time is too late?" he asks. "What if she gets so far off track that in a few years she's where you were at sixteen? I'm not going to let that happen."

"Where were you at sixteen?" I ask.

They both ignore me. Which is rude, frankly.

Kenny shakes his head. "She's out of control. I never should have let you take her."

"She was out of control *before* I took her," Faye says. "Neither of you could handle it, which is why she's with me."

"That's not true."

"Fine," Faye says. "Then why don't you tell everyone why you *actually* sent her to live with me."

Kenny's eye twitches.

"What are you talking about?" Charlotte asks. She looks at her husband. "Kenneth? What is she talking about?"

Kenny laughs and shakes his head. "I have no idea," he says. He grabs his wife's arm. "Let's go, Char."

They walk together toward the exit just as Vicky and Sabrina are coming back up the aisle. Kenny kneels down to say something to Vicky. Whatever it is, she looks annoyed by it. I see her glance in our direction, maybe at Faye, then turn back to her father and shrug. Kenny stands up straight, grabs Charlotte's arm again, and they leave as Vicky and Sabrina continue toward us up the aisle.

"Aunt Faye, can Sabrina sleep over?"

"Sure."

Vicky looks at me. "Are you coming back to our house?"

"No," Faye says before I can answer. "She's not."

Oh. Okay, then.

Vicky looks like she's about to protest.

"I have some work to get done this afternoon," I tell her. "I'll call you later."

"Wait for me in the car," Faye says.

The girls leave and now it's just Faye and me.

"Skye," she says, her voice measured. "I'm going to make this short, because my patience is already running thin today. If you can't act responsibly around Vicky, I can't allow you to see her."

Which is totally fair.

"Jesus, Faye," I say. "Why are you being so dramatic?"

She frowns. "You booed a child at a spelling bee."

Which is true.

"I got a little overzealous. It's not that big of a deal."

"It is to me."

Which is reasonable.

"It's not like I'm falling down drunk or something."

"You *did* almost fall down."

Oh, she saw that? Wow.

"Falling down and *almost* falling down are two very different things," I tell her. Which is technically true. But also stupid.

Faye looks like she's about to scream. "Just don't drink *at all* before a school function," she says, exasperated. "Is that really so much to ask?"

It's really not. And I know I should just tell her that I forgot the bee was today and then I didn't want to let Vicky down. That I've been the kid who was let down and I know how much that shit sucks. That I won't be that person, even if I'm not really Vicky's parent. I know I should say all of that, but then I remember how Faye hasn't even invited me into her goddamn house and, instead of saying any of that, I say, "Okay, Faye. Whatever."

She sighs, shakes her head, and walks away from me.

Which is understandable.

12

I DO EVERYTHING I CAN TO NOT THINK ABOUT VIVA'S PARTY AND the things Tasha said. It goes okay at first. I spend the rest of Saturday in my room, eating fries and watching television on the wide-screen concealed inside the antique armoire. Did you know there is a whole-ass TV show where celebrities tell ghost stories? I'm not making that up! On Sunday morning, I work on my taxes, organizing my paperwork to send to my CPA, pausing every now and again when Vicky texts me links to hilarious baby and/or cat videos. At eleven, I go to the hairdresser to get my locs tended to. When I get back to the B and B, I work on my taxes again. Then, just when it seems like I'm fine, like I'm not even pressed about Tasha and her bullshit anymore, I find myself on her Facebook page. I'm staring at her profile picture. It smiles at me like we're still friends. I start scrolling.

I see the usual social media stuff—a photo of Tasha and some woman on a hike; a post asking for realtor recommendations; an art show she's RSVP'd to as "going"—all representations of a good, fun life. There are no pictures of bad hair days or crippling depression or uncertainty about a life misspent. Ain't no emojis for that type of shit.

A few scrolls down the page, there's a photo, posted yesterday, of Tasha and Viva at fifteen years old, with the hashtag #stillhomies. Tasha has the same hairstyle Salt sported on the beach in the "Shoop" video and Viva is wearing overalls with one of the straps undone, like Will Smith in ninety out of one hundred episodes of *The Fresh Prince of Bel-Air*. Their arms are around each other's shoulders, their faces frozen in the too-cool-to-smile, duck-lipped expression of teenagers trying to seem badass. The photo has sixty likes, including one from Viva. I know this photo. Viva has one just like it framed on a corner table in her suite at the B and B. Only *that* photo also has *me* in it. Sure enough, peering closer at the Facebook post, I see, resting on Tasha's other shoulder, a dark-skinned hand that is definitely mine. The rest of me is cropped out. I feel something rising in my chest, part anger, part sadness, at the thought that Tasha chose a photo with me in it to make me feel bad, to make me feel cut out of our past, like an amputated gangrenous limb. But then I think that's probably my own narcissism, like why would she even think I'd visit her Facebook page? It's possible, maybe even probable, that all of the photos she has of herself and Viva at that age include me. I was always there. We were always there together.

I think back on that year, on us as we were then, always leaned into one another, shoulder to shoulder, always touching, always connected. Now, she's pretending I was never there.

But whatevs. Who cares? Forget Tasha. Etc. Why am I even on this stupid app right now? I move my thumb to close it, but right before I do, I see another post, also made on the day of Viva's party, and a little farther down the page, that reads: *Don't trust a bitch who rewrites the past to make herself the victim.*

Hold. The. Fuck. Up.

I check the time stamp: 1:07 P.M. Which means she posted this soon after I left the party.

Without allowing myself a second to think about it, I click in the comment box under the post. There are a few ways I can go with this:

1. The diplomatic route: *Hi. Hello. Good morning. I was wondering if this post is about me? If so, I'd just like you to know that I find it grossly inaccurate. Good day.*
2. The reverse psychology route: *Totally agree! Bitches who make themselves the victim, when they were, in fact, the villain all along, are the worst!* **100**
3. The all-caps clapback route: *NEVER TRUST A BITCH WHO DOESN'T REALIZE SHE'S THE BITCH WHO CAN'T BE TRUSTED. ALSO: WHO ARE YOU CALLING BITCH, BITCH???*

All good, mature options, obviously, but I choose the last. I'm halfway through my all-caps reply when a text alert pops up on my phone. It's from Vicky.

Chu doin?

I stare at it for a second, trying to decide whether to reply now or wait until I finish this perfectly reasonable, totally well-thought-out Facebook comment. *Having a shitty day*, I write back, then I put down the phone and go back to the comment.

Another text pops up. *Steven Universe marathon is on. Wanna come over? I have snacks.*

I stare at the message for a long moment, then at my all-caps clap-back, my cursor hovering over the send button. I delete the message. I close Facebook and text Vicky back. *What kind of snacks?*

WHEN I GET TO VICKY'S, Faye answers the door in bare feet. Her toes are painted red. She's rocking a green camo sweatshirt with the collar cut off, revealing her delicate clavicles, and a long, flowy skirt. Her dark skin is agleam with some kind of oil, her hair is pinned up on top of her head in a pile of woolly magnificence, and she's wearing her glasses. I want to kiss her. Like, there's a pain in my chest that's partly everything that's happened over the last couple of days and partly an overwhelming desire to kiss her. And also possibly suck her toes if she was into it. "Hello, Skye," she says. "Vicky's not ready yet."

"Ready? For what? I thought we're supposed to be watching cartoons."

"I think she has a new plan," Faye says. "Would you . . . like to come inside and wait or . . ."

Would I like to come inside and wait? As opposed to hanging out on the porch like a Jehovah's Witness?

"I could go wait in the middle of the street and try not to get hit by a garbage truck, if that works best for you."

She stares at me for a moment, probably trying to figure out whether she's for or against me getting hit by a garbage truck. Then she takes a step away from the door and says, "Come on in."

I walk past her into the house.

Inside, it's very West Philly row house chic, part old-school, part remodel. The walls that separate the rooms in most row houses in this neighborhood have been taken down here, so, standing at the front door, I can see the whole first floor straight back through the kitchen. The walls that remain are painted an unconventional but very sharp gray with bright white trim. The decorative wood mantelpiece and ornate front window trim are classic West Philly accents, though, as is the thick, polished wood banister leading to the second floor. The place is decorated in what seems exactly Faye's style: flowy, cream-colored linen throws next to pillows with edgy camo shams; a comfy-looking, overstuffed sofa beside a very mod, bare wood Parsons chair, positioned beneath a leopard-print tapestry; and the Blackest of Black art on the walls, including a painting over the sofa of little girls in cornrows jumping double Dutch. The house is basically what you'd get if a Maya Angelou poem fucked a '90s Supreme streetwear catalog and I'm not one bit surprised.

"Can I get you something to drink?" Faye asks me, heading for the kitchen. "We have coffee, juice, water—bubbly or flat—and Vicky has a lot of root beer."

"I'm good," I say. I'm actually thirsty as fuck, though.

She continues toward the kitchen. I follow, because I'm not really sure what else to do.

The kitchen is cute: updated but not over the top. There's a large pot of water heating up on the stove and a colander full of wet collard leaves in the sink. A counter island in the middle of the room is covered with stacks of manila folders.

"Excuse the mess," Faye says. "Midterm papers."

"You're a teacher?"

She nods. "Honors English at CAPA."

CAPA: the Philadelphia High School for Creative and Performing Arts. I went to school there myself. For some reason, I don't mention it.

Faye takes a seat and starts marking up one of the papers with red pen.

Now I wish I'd said yes to that drink, so I'd have something to do other than awkwardly hover. I could tell her I've changed my mind, that I'd love a bubbly water, but she already seems to be engrossed in the midterm papers. So I just stand there, shifting my weight from one foot to the other, until she looks up and says, "Feel free to sit."

"I'm good." WHUUUUUUT.

"Okay," she says, and goes back to marking papers.

I shift my weight again and think seriously about killing myself.

"Hey, Skye." It's Vicky. Thank God.

"What's up?" I ask her. "I thought we were watching Cosmic Steven or whatever his name is."

"There's a festival at Clark Park," she says. "There's live music and a lot of records and stuff on sale. Can we go?"

"Okay," I say. I mean, I *was* low-key looking forward to putting my head under the covers and escaping into cartoons for the rest of the day, but sure. "You ready?"

She shakes her head. "My jeans are still in the dryer."

"You're already wearing jeans."

"Yeah," she says, "but I haven't worn *purple* jeans at all this week."

"You have to wear purple jeans every week? Like, as a rule?"

She nods. "Yeah."

"Why?"

"Because Prince," she says. "Duh."

"She's very into Prince this month," Faye says, glancing up from her work. "Next month, who knows?"

"No," Vicky says, super seriously. "It'll be Prince *forever*."

"You said that about Etta James last month," Faye says. "And you haven't even listened to that record I bought you."

Without another word, Vicky leaves the kitchen. About half a minute later, Etta James's "If I Can't Have You" starts to play. Faye looks at me, and I know we're both remembering that day at the record store when she rejected me. Cool cool cool.

"See!" Vicky calls from the next room. "I'm listening to it right now!"

Etta sings, *I-I-I-I-I don't want nobody, if I can't have you . . .*

I shift my weight from one foot to the other and die a thousand deaths inside.

Faye clears her throat. "Are you sure you don't want something to dri—"

"Bubbly water sounds great."

I watch her open a cupboard and take out a glass. When she opens the refrigerator to get the seltzer, I notice a photo on the door, of Faye and Cynthia as kids. It's the Cynthia I remember best: young, bright-eyed, smiling. Next to her, there's Faye, a few years older, not smiling, her dark eyes intense even then. Cynthia's arm is around Faye's shoulders, and their heads are touching. I think about what Faye said, about how they didn't like each other, and I wonder when that started.

Just before she closes the fridge, I notice a second photo, of Faye and another woman holding hands on a beach, with a younger Vicky skipping along behind them.

Faye pours the seltzer and holds the glass out to me, but as I reach over to take it, my arm swipes a stack of folders and some of them tumble to the floor.

"Shit. Sorry." I bend down and pick up the folders and see a book there on the floor, too, with a bunch of Post-it notes sticking out of it. I pick it up.

"Are you teaching *The Color Purple*?" I ask her, putting the folders back on the counter but not the book.

She nods. "To my twelfth-graders."

I turn the book over in my hands. It's the cover with the sunflower. Its corners and spine are worn. "I used to carry this book with me everywhere. I think I lost it in Nicaragua a couple of years ago."

I open it, to one of the Post-it-marked pages, and see notes written in the margins in neat handwriting. One note says: *This is how it feels to be shamed.* I close the book.

"Most books I got assigned in high school were by Black men or white people," I tell her. "I didn't even really know Black women writers existed. I mean, I did, but I didn't. And definitely not queer ones. I can't even imagine reading *this* in high school."

"At the high school I went to in Georgia," Faye says, "all the good books were banned. I didn't read this until sophomore year of college."

I discovered *The Color Purple* the summer after graduation, when I was eighteen. I remember almost running the three blocks to Tasha's house, sitting on her bed, reading passages out loud to each other for *hours*. It was the first time I saw my Black queer girl self in a book and it changed my life. I consider telling Faye all of this. But then I remember, again, how she barely says a word to me when I pick up Vicky, and how she gave me a hard time at the spelling bee, and how she *just now* almost made me stand out on the porch, and I suddenly feel super self-conscious and unliked, and instead of saying, "I love *The Color Purple*, it changed my life," I say, "That sucks for you."

That.

Sucks.

For.

You.

Faye holds out her hand for the book. I give it to her and she hands me the glass of bubbly water. I take a sip, as awkward silence opens up like a hellmouth around us.

I-I-I-I-I can't talk to nobody . . .

"So, you went to high school in Georgia, huh?" I ask loudly, trying to drown out the song.

She nods. "Jenkins. Which you've probably never heard of. But only for two years."

"How'd you end up there?"

"When I was fourteen, and my sister was eleven," she says, "our mother died. Our father was mentally ill—they just called it 'crazy' back then—and he was always disappearing, for weeks or months or years at a time. We didn't know where he was by then. Our grandparents were already gone. We were bounced around from foster home to foster home for a year, until the state located two relatives who could each take one of us in. Cynthia went to live with our father's cousin in Newark and I went to Georgia to live with a great-aunt I'd never met. I lived with her for a year. Then she died and I got passed around between her relatives, who were barely related to me, for another year after that."

See, this is why I don't ask questions. A perfectly innocent *so, you went to high school in Georgia, huh?* and here we are, smack in the middle of a Gloria Naylor novel. Don't get me wrong: It's not that I don't have compassion for orphaned children. I have tons. I swear! I'm just not any good at showing it. But we're at a pause in the conversation where I'm supposed to say something. And that something isn't supposed to be *wow*. I try to imagine what a normal person, who was good at human-people stuff, would say, and I come up with the following: "That must have been hard."

Faye looks at me, nods. "Yes, it was."

NAILED IT!

Etta is still singing, about hugging and squeezing and kissing, her voice getting real low and sexy and suggestive.

"Then you came back?" I ask Faye. "To Philly?"

"Yes." She gets up from the table and goes to the counter, where she starts de-stemming collards. "What about you?"

"What about me?"

"You're from here, too, right? Larchwood, around Fifty-seventh?"

I frown. "I'm starting to feel like Miss Newsome has an unhealthy amount of information about me."

"Vicky told me," she says.

"Ah."

"You still have family over there?"

"My mother and brother."

"What about your father?" she asks.

I shrug, which is my default answer to *what about your father?*

"Grandparents?"

"Nope."

The song is somehow still going. I sit there wishing it would end. Then it finally does and the room fills with heavy, awkward silence again. It creeps into my brain, it gets under my skin. My face feels hot. My armpits are sweaty. My ass itches!

"I went to CAPA!" I blurt out, all of a sudden and way too loud.

"Oh," Faye says, a little startled, almost as if she wasn't expecting me to start shouting. "Why didn't you say so before?"

"I forgot."

"You *forgot* where you went to high school?"

"Just for a few minutes. Then I remembered."

She's squinting at me, with her head tilted slightly to one side, like she's confused. Or like she doesn't know what to make of me. I can't imagine why. She goes back to de-stemming her collards. After a moment, she asks, "What was your major? At CAPA?"

"Writing."

She looks up at me, interested. "What kind of writing did you do?"

"Poetry. I wanted to be a poet."

She smiles at me. It's a real smile, the first one she's ever given me. A sudden spark of fire, it lights up her face, the room, my entire miserable being, and for a second, I don't feel like a Jehovah's Witness standing on the porch anymore.

"I need a new phone," Vicky says, finally returning to the kitchen.

"Why?" Faye asks.

"My camera's acting janky."

"Janky how?"

"Videos are all dark and, like, fuzzy."

"So, you don't need a new phone," Faye says. "You just need your camera fixed."

Vicky rolls her eyes. "Fine. When can it get fixed, then?"

"I'll make an appointment at the geek bar, or whatever it's called."

"When?"

"When I have time. Maybe next week."

"But what if I need to video something important?" the kid asks.

"Such as what?"

"I don't know. Just . . . something."

Faye peers at her. "Vicky, we already discussed this," she says, pointing a collard stem at the kid. "You're *not* recording the cops."

"But why?"

"You know why. Because you're too young."

"No, I'm not!"

"You are," Faye insists. "The *adults* on the block will look after the reverend. I don't want you interacting with the police. In any way."

"That's not fair! I'm not a little kid!"

"I didn't say you're a little kid. I said you're too young to—"

Vicky slams her fist hard on the counter. It's the first time I've seen her get angry and it's startling, like the unanticipated eruption of a tiny volcano. Her brow is tight; her fists are clenched. There's a vein throbbing at her right temple as she yells, "This is bullshit!"

Faye takes a long, deep breath, like she's trying really hard not to lose her shit. Then she says, in an impressively measured tone, "Vicky. Please lower your voice. And watch your language."

Vicky glares at her, but doesn't say anything.

"I understand you're upset," Faye continues. "But can you please try to understand where I'm coming from?"

The kid folds her arms tight across her chest, which I take as a *no*.

"I know you're not a little kid. I know you want to help the reverend. But I promised your mother I would keep you safe and that's all I'm trying to do," Faye says, and here her voice trembles the littlest bit. "Can you understand that?"

I watch her reach out and touch one of Vicky's braids. She rubs it between her thumb and fingers. I feel things threatening to break open inside me, things I'm not sure I can precisely name, my own volcanic earthquakes beneath the surface. Vicky's sitting there shooting eye daggers at Faye and part of me wants to scream at her: *Don't you know how lucky you are, you ungrateful little shit, to be seen and loved and protected like this?*

The dryer buzzes loudly from a nearby room. "Whatever," Vicky says, yanking her braid out of Faye's fingers. She gets up and disappears down a stairwell to the basement.

Faye sighs.

I take another sip of bubbly water. Clear my throat. "She's still having a hard time about her mom, huh?"

"She's been suspended from school three times in the last three months," Faye says.

"Shit."

"Some of that is the school and their horrible track record with Black students and suspension," she says. "That's a battle we're constantly fighting. And then some of it is Vicky acting out. Last time she got suspended because she was upset with one of her teachers and wrote 'white devil' on the blackboard."

"Ha!"

Faye frowns at me.

"Oh, am I not supposed to laugh at that?"

"It won't be funny when she can't get into a good high school because of her disciplinary record."

"Right," I say, nodding thoughtfully. It's still funny, though.

There's a loud bang from the basement. Faye rubs her temples.

"It must be challenging for you," I say. "Dealing with . . . all of that."

She sighs. "I pray to my ancestors every day to make me worthy of the job of parenting such a terrific kid. And to please, please keep me from throttling her."

I laugh and she does, too.

"It's gotten better," she says, "since she came to live with me. But in the last few months, since she found out about the eggs, and that I knew and didn't tell her . . ." She shakes her head.

"You knew before she did?"

She hesitates, like she's not sure she wants to be talking to me about it. Then, she says, "I found the papers in Cynthia's things, after she died. I locked them in a safe place, or what I thought was a safe place, until I could figure out how to handle it. I didn't really know what else to do."

There's another bang from the basement.

"Excuse me," Faye says, and goes downstairs.

A couple of minutes later, they come up from the basement together. Vicky's wearing purple jeans that, I gotta say, were worth the wait.

"I'm ready." She heads for the door.

"Thanks for the water."

Faye smiles a tired smile. "Have fun, you two."

13

CLARK PARK IS LIKE A MILE AWAY, SO OBVIOUSLY I START ORDERING a Lyft.

"We can walk," Vicky says. "It's just right down Cedar."

"Ugh. Fine."

It's a little bit cloudy today but still pretty okay weather. There are a lot of people out on the kid's block, sitting on their porches or front steps. Vicky says hi to almost all of them as we pass. She stops in front of a tiny yard filled with tiny, newly planted yellow and pink flowers and waves to the Mary J. Blige–wigged woman drinking coffee out of an enormous mug.

"Hi, Miss Vena."

"That you, Vicky?" the woman asks, squinting over the porch railing through dark glasses.

"Yes, ma'am."

"How'd Faye like those zinnias I sent over for your yard?"

"She likes them. We're planting them tomorrow."

Miss Vena smiles at me. "How you doing, baby?"

"Fine. And yourself?"

"Well, my gout is acting up," she says, rubbing her left knee. "And

I'm more blind every day. But otherwise, I'm feeling happy, thank the good Lord."

"The Lord?" asks the old man who has just come out of the house onto the porch. "You *should* be thanking the Jim Beam you got in that cup."

Miss Vena looks scandalized. "This is coffee I'm drinking!"

"Two splashes of Folgers in a double shot of whiskey."

"Oh, shut up, Mitch," she says, waving a dismissive hand at him.

"Hey, lil' Vicky," says Mr. Mitch. "Who this chocolate drop you got with you?"

"This is Skye."

"The sky, the sun, and the stars, too!" he says, grinning at me. "You got a man, pretty lady?"

I nod. "His name's Nino." I always call my fake boyfriend Nino. He sounds like a dude you don't want to upset by trying to pick up his girlfriend, because he's definitely been to jail.

We keep moving and, at the corner, we turn onto Cedar Ave and head east toward the park.

Philadelphia is a city of murals, and nowhere more so than West Philly. There are murals on almost every other corner here, painted on the sides of buildings, depicting famous Black Philadelphians, or iconic civil rights leaders, or just regular Black people hugging their kids or planting flowers. To me, the murals *are* West Philly. They capture the mood of the neighborhood and its people—colorful, loud, Black. They're one of the things I miss most when I'm not here.

"So, what happened?" the kid asks me as we pass a huge mural of girls jumping rope. "What made your day s-h-i-t?"

I don't know if it's appropriate to share my adult dramas with a twelve-year-old. But the weight of what went down with Tasha feels so heavy on my mind that I relish the thought of laying it down for a moment, even at the feet of a seventh-grader. Plus, I figure the drama started when I was eighteen, just a handful of years older than Vicky is now, so it's probably fine. Or at least defensible.

"I saw someone I used to be friends with a long time ago. Best friends, actually. We don't get along now."

"How come you stopped being friends?" she asks.

"She went to a different college. And didn't keep in touch."

"Even though you were besties?"

"Yep."

She shakes her head. "That's messed up."

"Yeah. She seems to remember it differently, though. She said I was pissed at her, so I was testing her to see if she really cared about me."

"I don't get it. Like testing her how?"

I shrug. "I didn't ask."

"Were you?"

"Testing her?"

"Uh-huh."

"No," I say. "I mean, I *was* pissed. I felt abandoned. I probably did wonder if she gave a shit about me." I sigh. "It was more than twenty years ago. Who the hell knows?"

"I used to be friends with this boy, Marco," Vicky says, "but not anymore. I still have to see him at school, like, every day. It sucks."

"Why aren't you friends anymore?"

"He had a crush on me. But I didn't like him like that. I still wanted to be friends, though. But he didn't."

"Ugh," I say. "Boys."

"Yeah. Then last year at sleepover camp, he held me down and tried to kiss me." She delivers it so matter-of-factly that it takes me a second to realize the full fucked-up-ness of what she's said.

"He . . . held you down?"

"Uh-huh. I had to knee him really hard in the balls to get him off," she says, demonstrating kneeing someone in the balls.

"Jesus," is all I can think of to say, even though I know more is probably required. "What happened? Did he get in trouble?"

"No," she says. "I didn't tell anybody."

"Why not?"

She shrugs. "I don't know. I guess I felt, like, weird about it."

"Did you tell your aunt?"

"No," she says. "I didn't tell anybody."

I'm not sure what I should say here. I'm not even sure it's my responsibility to say *anything*. But it feels wrong to just let that go, right? I ask myself: *What would Oprah say?* But all I can think of is, *You get a car! You get a car! You get a car!* Which really isn't helpful.

"Are you okay?" Vicky asks me.

"Sure. Why?"

"You just have a weird look on your face."

I sigh. "Sometimes being here feels like a lot."

"I thought you come back to Philly all the time," she says.

"I do. But I mostly just sleep for two weeks and then head out again."

We're at Fifty-second Street now. Fifty-second is the main commercial strip in this part of West Philly, starting way up at Market Street, where the el runs. The first two or three blocks from the el, there are some big brand stores, like McDonald's and Foot Locker, interspersed with small bookshops and clothing boutiques, street vendors, and the West Philadelphia branch of the public library. Farther down, where we are now, out of easy reach of the foot traffic off the el, it's mostly hair and nail salons, tiny laundromats, take-out spots, and bars.

"Where would you be if you weren't here?" the kid asks me.

"Right now? Rio."

"De Janeiro? That's in Brazil, right?" She smiles. "I got an A in geography."

I smile, too. "Geography was my favorite subject when I was your age." I was obsessed with other places. I daydreamed about a life as a painter or a poet, living in France like James Baldwin and Eartha Kitt—whose lives abroad I read about in an *Ebony* magazine article about Black Americans in Paris—traipsing the continent and beyond.

"English is my favorite subject," she says. "Then science. Then geography, third. I like reading about Australia. Do you know the Great Barrier Reef is there?"

"What's left of it, anyway."

"Have you been to it?" she asks.

"I've snorkeled there twice. Scuba dived once, a long time ago."

"That's so decent," she says, looking impressed, which makes me feel good about myself. "I think I might live there one day."

"In the reef? You want to be a shark when you grow up?"

She giggles. "*On land* in Australia. But not until I'm thirty-five. I want to live in Philly for a long time first."

"Why?"

She makes a face like that's a silly question. "Because all my friends and family are here. Duh."

I wonder what it must be like to be happy where you are.

The light turns green and we continue east down Cedar Avenue, past Fifty-first and Fiftieth and Forty-ninth. We talk about geography for a while, then Vicky tells me about the butterfly and moth science project she's working on at school. I listen with interest, as the houses around us get wider, the streets become tree-lined, and, eventually, the people get whiter. This is the part of West Philly you find in Zagat's, with its cafés, breweries, and overpriced, gluten-free donut shops.

The festival at Clark Park seems less a festival and more a gathering of randomness. There are people selling everything from used clothing to used books to used bikes. There's a DJ spinning old-school hip-hop, a stage set up with amps and microphones, and a sign announcing a NEIGHBORHOOD DOG SHOW at three. There's a Southern BBQ food cart, a vegan Middle Eastern food cart, and an Asian fusion food cart. There's a face-painting booth and two professional clowns. Despite the haphazardness of it all, there are tons of mofos in attendance. And not just any mofos. *Hipster* mofos. We've only been here fifteen minutes and I've already spotted three handlebar mustaches and seven pairs of ironic socks. It's awful.

"Your face looks weird again," Vicky says, standing among crates and crates and crates of used records, peering at me over a *Sign o' the Times*.

"Sorry." I point to the Prince record. "You buying that?"

"Yeah," she says, handing a few bucks to the bearded man selling it.

She wants to buy purple things to wear, so we move on to the used clothing section. I watch while she finds and rejects a purple T-shirt with a kitten on it, a long purple skirt, and a purple knit sweater. "I give up," she says. "Let's go look at books."

The used books area of the "festival" is at the other end of the park. On our way there, we get water ices from a guy selling them out of a little pushcart.

"Do you have interns at your job?" Vicky asks me through a mouthful of blue raspberry slush.

I tell her yes, I do, usually two for every trip.

"Can I be one?"

"Sure, when you're a little older."

"How much older?"

"College?"

She groans. "You sound like my aunt. She treats me like a little kid."

"You *are* a kid."

"Yeah, but not a *little* kid. I'll be a teenager in a year. I can do things. I can help with stuff. I'm not a baby."

"Is this about the cop thing?" I ask her. "Because I think Faye's just trying to protect you. The police are dangerous."

"She *over*protects me," Vicky says. "All the time. I think she's worried I'll be like she was."

"What do you mean?"

"She used to get in a lot of trouble. She was really wild."

"Wild how?"

"She did lots of drugs and stuff. When she was a teenager."

"What, like weed?" I ask.

Vicky shakes her head, no. "Like blow."

I stare at her. "You're using the word '*blow*' post 1984?"

She shrugs. "I heard it on TV."

"Blow is cocaine," I tell her, because she's obviously confused.

"Yeah," she says. "I know."

I shake my head. "No way Faye did coke."

"Yes way. She had this boyfriend down south who sold drugs to college kids. He gave it to her. And he got her pregnant. She was, like, sixteen. She had an abortion. Then she got pregnant by some other guy when she was seventeen. And she had another abortion."

Shit. "How do you even know all that?"

"I heard my dad talking to Charlotte about it," she says. "I think I heard my mom and dad arguing about it one time, too. When my mom was sick. My dad was mad that she wanted me to live with Aunt Faye."

"I thought they didn't get along. Faye and your mom."

"They didn't 'not get along,'" she says, doing air quotes. "They didn't fight or anything. They just weren't, like, besties."

This doesn't exactly mesh with what Faye said about her relationship with Cynthia. But maybe they didn't want the kid to see their mutual dislike. I think about the photo on the refrigerator: of Faye and Cynthia holding tight to each other. I think about Slade: how close we were as little kids; how as teenagers we moved in and out of closeness in waves; how as adults we hardly speak. Thinking about my brother makes me uneasy, though, so I stop.

"Who's that woman your aunt's holding hands with on the fridge?" I ask Vicky, mostly to get off the subject of siblings, but also because I'm dying to know. "I thought she was engaged to some man."

"She is. But she used to be with this woman, Sydette."

"What was she like?"

"Nice," Vicky says. "Butchy. People called her 'sir' sometimes."

"So, your aunt is super into masculinity or whatever, huh?" I ask, trying not to sound disappointed.

The kid shrugs. "I don't think so. Why do you care, anyway?"

"I don't. I'm just making conversation."

So as not to arouse further suspicion, I drop it.

When we finally get to the books, we split up. Vicky goes looking for YA while I search for literary fiction, for *The Color Purple*, specifically. Talking to Faye reminded me how much I like having the books I love around me, even when I'm constantly moving from place to place. I rummage through two dozen boxes before I finally find a copy in good shape.

"You gonna buy that?" Vicky asks, reappearing quite suddenly beside me.

I nod. "I think so."

"You shouldn't."

"Why not?"

"It's kind of expensive."

I point to the price that's scrawled inside the cover. "It's two-fifty."

She frowns.

"What?" I ask.

"I'm not supposed to tell you."

"Tell me what, Vicky? Jesus."

"Aunt Faye wants me to get that book for you."

I look at the book, then back at Vicky. "Faye wants to buy me a present?"

"Yeah. I think it's, like, a peace offering or something."

"That's sort of nice of her."

"So, you can't buy it," she says. "Because I'm supposed to buy it."

"Okay," I say, handing her the book.

"Just act s-u-r-p-r-i-s-e-d when she gives it to you."

"Got it."

When we're done buying books, we grab seats in front of the stage, where a bluegrass band is playing. We let some of the afternoon slip away on the twangy wings of the five-string banjo. Then, when the light begins to take on the ochre tinge of late day, we start making our way back to Vicky's house.

When we get to her block, loaded up with books, our bellies full of water ice and soft pretzels, I feel a whole universe better than I did after seeing Tasha's Facebook page. I'm also sleepy, in that good, fun weekend way, and all I want to do is go back to my room, crawl into bed, and close my eyes. Then Vicky spots a black car that's parked out front of her house and says, "Uncle Nick's here!" And I perk right up.

14

I MOVE TO FOLLOW VICKY UP THE FRONT STEPS.

"You're coming in?" she asks, surprised, since I already said I was going home to nap.

"I think I left my, um . . . room key in there earlier," I say. "I'ma just get it."

"Vicky!" a voice calls from up the block. We both turn and see Reverend Seymour hurrying toward us. "Are Faye and Nick around?" she asks the kid. "I rang your bell but there was no answer."

"Uncle Nick's car is here," Vicky says. "Maybe they're having sex or something."

"Jesus, Vicky!"

The reverend frowns at me, as if she's way more offended by me taking the name of her lord in vain. Then a look flashes across her face, something worried but low-key. That's when I notice she's wearing sneakers and the laces are only halfway tied, like she did them in a rush. She glances down the block toward her house, then back at me.

"What's your name, sister?" she asks me.

"Skye."

"Sister Skye! You're a friend of Vicky and Faye's, right?"

"Yes, that's right." A friend of Vicky's, anyway.

"Sister Skye," the reverend says, "I wonder if I could trouble you for some help."

"Um. Sure. I mean, I guess. What kind of help?"

She looks like she's not sure whether or not she wants to tell me. Which sort of piques my interest. "I have a little situation," she says finally. "At my house. I'd handle it myself, but I can't lift more than a few pounds. I had back surgery earlier this year."

Manual labor? Absolutely not, ma'am. Has she not noticed that I'm practically a comic-strip rendering of a bookish girl, with my thick-framed glasses and skinny arms? My whole persona screams *DON'T ASK ME TO HELP YOU MOVE* and that's not by accident. I don't even like to sweat during sex and that's *fun*.

I start to shake my head, no. "I actually need to—"

"We can help!" Vicky says, excited, like somebody just asked us to finish off some cake.

The reverend clasps her hands together. "Good neighbors," she says, smiling at the kid and then at me. "Thank you."

INSIDE, REVEREND SEYMOUR'S HOUSE LOOKS like the houses of my childhood, like the houses of my grandparents and great-grandparents, especially, with its floral wallpaper, small grandfather clock in a corner, and painting of a skinny, long-haired Jesus hanging on the dining room wall, although this Jesus is Black, which the Jesuses of my childhood never were. We follow the reverend upstairs to the second floor and down a short hallway to some more stairs, which lead up to a door. The door is closed, and at first she just stands there looking at it, not saying anything.

After a few seconds, I'm like, "What are we doing?"

"The door is locked," she says.

"Where's the key?"

"Inside."

"Okay," I say. "Is there . . . a spare?"

"Sister Skye," she says, looking amused, "if there was a spare, I wouldn't have had to bring you all the way down here." She doesn't say it like she thinks I'm dumb, but she doesn't say it like she thinks I'm smart, either.

"I thought I came down here to help you lift a heavy box."

She shakes her head. "I never said anything about lifting a box."

I don't remember exactly what she said, but I'm pretty sure there was lifting involved. Now I don't know what's going on. I look at Vicky, who just kind of shrugs.

"Do you want me to kick the door in?"

"Can you?" the reverend asks me, sounding unsure.

"Probably not."

There's a butter knife sitting on a small table near the closed door. She picks it up and holds it out to me. "I thought you could jimmy it. I tried, but my arthritis . . ."

I peer at her. "You don't have a dead body in there, do you?"

"No! Of course not! Sister Skye, how could you even—"

"Okay, okay, I'm just making sure."

Vicky giggles.

I take the knife and try to slide the tip of it into the doorjamb. It's not easy, even without arthritis.

"Jiggle it upward," Vicky says.

"I *am* jiggling it upward."

Reverend Seymour is just standing there watching me. This would normally make me feel uneasy, the way people of the cloth tend to, with their oppressive come-to-Jesus vibes, but it doesn't, because her energy is super chill. "I've noticed you coming and going a lot lately," she says. "But I've never had a chance to talk with you. You usually look like you'd rather be left alone."

That's accurate.

"Do you live close by?" she asks. It strikes me as a question you ask when you really want to ask something more pointed—like, *Why are you suddenly here all the time?*—but you don't want to seem rude.

"I stay close by," I tell her. "When I'm in town."

"You don't live in Philadelphia?"

"Nope."

"But you're from here, aren't you?" she asks. "You don't have much of the accent, but there's . . ." She thinks about it. "Philadelphian energy about you."

I sort of know what she means. I can usually identify a Philadelphian if I run into one out in the world.

She asks where I live now, where I travel, if I still have family here, if I still have a lot of friends in the area. I tell her I live everywhere, or nowhere, depending how you look at it, that I travel all over the world, that I have family here but I don't see much of them, that no, I don't have a lot of friends in the area. "What about a church?" she asks. "Do you have a church you go to when you're here?"

"No."

The reverend's eyebrows draw close together. She peers at me. "Well, what do you have?"

Wow. Okay. Up in my business much?

"Who are your people?" she asks me. "Where is your community?"

I shrug. "I don't really believe in community."

"You think it's a trick of the light?" she asks. "Like the Loch Ness Monster?"

El oh el.

"It's just been my experience that people don't actually care as much as they pretend to," I tell her.

"About what?"

"About everything. About other people."

"About other people? Who, specifically?" she asks.

"No one specifically. Just people. In general."

She smiles at me. It's a kind smile.

The butter knife slips down against the lock and, with a click, the door swings open. When it does, I almost shit. There is a nearly naked elderly Asian man, sprawled tighty-whitey-clad-ass-side-up, on the floor.

"He fell," Reverend Seymour says anxiously, hurrying into the room. "When he tried to get up, his back gave out."

The man, who is mid-sixties, chubby, and very balding, eyes me suspiciously as I enter, then says to the reverend, "Where's Nick?"

"You know Uncle Nick?" Vicky asks.

"He and Faye helped us out the last time Phil fell down," the reverend tells her. Then, to Phil, "Brother Nick, uh . . . isn't available."

He frowns.

"This is Sister Vicky and Sister Skye. Sisters, this Brother Philip Michael Nguyen. He's a good friend of mine."

Ya, he seems to be.

"She doesn't look strong, LaVonda," he says, studying my physique. "She's very skinny."

"Oh, she's stronger than she looks," Reverend Seymour says, looking at me. "Right?"

"I think I'm probably exactly as strong as I look."

Reverend Seymour laughs. Brother Philip Michael Nguyen does not.

"We can just go," I tell the reverend.

"No, no," she says. "Brother Nguyen is just embarrassed. Seeming ungrateful is his defense mechanism. Isn't that right, Phil?"

Brother Nguyen frowns, sighs. "Maybe so," he says. "No one wants to be found like this by strangers. It's humiliating, you know? And a kid, too?"

"I see my pop-pop in his underwear all the time," Vicky says reassuringly. "He just walks around like that."

"Do you think you can get him up?" the reverend asks me.

"I can try. Should we, um, get him dressed first?"

"Up first," says Brother Nguyen. "Please."

I move closer to him, examining his position on the floor, trying to decide how best to proceed. When I was about twelve, I lived with my grandparents for a few months, because home didn't feel good or safe, and one night my great-grandfather, who lived there, too, fell down on his way into the bathroom. My grandfather wasn't home, so I had to help my grandmother get her father-in-law up off the cold tile floor. I remember how frail my great-grandfather looked, and how guilty I felt, because I was the one who had turned the light off in the hallway, which made it hard for him to see where he was going. To ease the guilt, I decided it was my great-grandfather's fault, really, because if he had been a better parent, he'd have raised better kids, and then my grandfather would have been a better parent, who, in turn, raised better kids, and then my mother would have been a better parent and I'd have been at home where I should have been that night, instead of turning off lights in other people's houses.

I can tell from looking at him that Brother Nguyen is too heavy for me to lift on my own. He's not overweight so much as he's what I'd call "meaty." He has thick limbs and a torso like a small, fleshy tree trunk. Good news is, there's a bed at the other end of the room and it's in a wooden frame with a lip at the foot of it. Maybe Brother Nguyen can use it for leverage.

"Can you crawl to the bed?" I ask him.

He frowns, shakes his head. "Tried already."

"Okay, then. I'm going to have to try to drag you over there. Is that cool with you?"

He nods.

I hook the crooks of my elbows under his armpits and give a tug. He doesn't move a single centimeter.

"Use your core, Sister Skye," Reverend Seymour says.

Thanks for the tip, but also: My core doesn't work like that!

"Put your feet flat against the floor," I tell Brother Nguyen. "And try to push yourself back, while I pull."

He nods. He bends his knees and pushes against the floor with the bottoms of his feet. I pull, and his body moves a fraction of an inch. I pull harder and he moves just a little bit more. Ugh, this is going to take forever! I take a deep breath and put my best effort into it, pulling with all my might. Brother Nguyen starts moving a little faster across the floor and this is when I notice that the rug is bunching up underneath him, and his underwear, caught on the fold, is starting to slip down.

Oh, no. Oh, God, no.

"Wait," I say, just as he pushes with his feet again.

This is the moment when I should look away. But for some reason? I CAN'T. I watch as his underwear slips down just enough that his penis shaft pops out of the top, like a bald, colorless sea snake poking up out of the sandy seabed.

Reverend Seymour hurries over, and in one quick movement she hikes her boyfriend's tighty-whiteys up over his wrinkly peen. But it's too late, because *I can never unsee it*. It's burned into my memory like . . . well, *like an old man's dick*, quite frankly. I look over at Vicky. She's at the window with her phone camera held up to the glass, pointing down toward the street. On the one hand, this is highly suspicious. On the other hand, she seems to be completely distracted. Which is good because I'm pretty sure elderly prick isn't on the list of things I should be exposing her to.

Two trillion minutes later, Brother Nguyen and I reach the bed. He puts one arm around my shoulder, places his other forearm on the lip of wooden bed frame, and pushes himself up, while I pull. It works. In a minute, he's up, sitting on the edge of the bed.

Reverend Seymour grabs a blanket and wraps it around his shoulders.

I wipe sweat off my forehead.

Brother Nguyen takes my hand in both of his. "LaVonda was right," he says. "You are strong."

"Can I have this?"

We all turn to look at Vicky. She's left the window and is pointing to a dusty purple hat that's stashed on a shelf in a corner.

"That was my late husband's," Reverend Seymour says.

"Oh," the kid replies. "Never mind. Sorry."

The reverend walks over to the shelf, takes the hat down. "It's not doing anybody any good up here, is it?" She hands the hat to Vicky.

The kid takes it, beaming, and thanks her.

While Reverend Seymour helps Brother Nguyen put on a shirt, I cross the room to examine the hat more closely. It's a purple felt fedora with a pheasant feather in it, old school, like something my granddad would have worn whilst seeking out a woman to commit adultery with. "You're seriously going to wear this?"

Vicky shrugs. "Prince would've."

"He wasn't in seventh grade."

"Everybody was in seventh grade at some point." She puts on the hat and examines her reflection in a full-length mirror that's propped up against a wall.

And, you know what? She looks cool as hell. I watch her turning her head from side to side, admiring herself, and suddenly I'm smiling from ear to ear because here is a twelve-year-old girl who knows exactly how to wear a purple fedora with a pheasant feather in it.

But then, there's a moment. I see something flash in Vicky's eyes, something familiar: self-doubt. It appears in an instant, like a crocodile coming out of the murky water, jaws open, to snap a baby wildebeest and pull it under. I watch her move to take off the hat, and I am overwhelmed with the memory of being a twelve-year-old girl in constant battle, over what *I* saw when I looked in the mirror and what I feared *other people* would see. Other people, whose opinions of me always seemed to matter more than my own.

Sometimes, even what I *knew* to be true about myself was vulnerable to other people's revision. When I was thirteen, I failed algebra because I was so depressed that I missed a whole bunch of school days that year. My father said I'd failed because I was stupid. I was smart; I knew that for certain. But I remember wondering, in that moment, *Am I stupid?* I looked at my mother, who was standing nearby and had to have heard what he said, and waited for her to say he was wrong, to reaffirm what I *knew*. But she just kept on seasoning chicken thighs and said nothing. This memory, which I haven't conjured in years, cuts through me now like a hot blade, and I feel a seared breath catch in my lungs.

Vicky has turned and is staring at me like she's trying to see inside me again. I don't know why, but this time I let her. I don't look away or make a joke. I just stand there. It's just a few seconds, but it feels like eons. When I can't take it anymore, I nod at the purple hat, which is still on her head, and say, "You were right. It looks perfect on you, Vick."

She grins at me, then turns around to face the mirror again.

As I stand there watching her adore her reflection, I want to hug her and protect her from all the things in the world that will try to crush this self-love out of her. But I don't want to be weird about it, kna'mean?

"Vicky?"

"Huh?"

"Do you know where that Marco kid lives?"

She stops modeling the hat and looks at me. "Yeah. Why?"

"I could go kick his ass if you want."

"You're a grown-up," she says. "He's a kid."

If he's old enough to hold a girl down, he's old enough to get his ass beat, in my opinion. "No one will even know it was me. I'll punch him super hard in the kidneys six or seven times and then disappear into the night. Gimme his address."

She giggles. Then she looks like she's thinking for a second and says, "I kneed him in the balls real hard. He was walking kinda funny for a while. I think he got the message or whatever."

I nod. "Okay."

"But thanks," she says, smiling at me. "That's real ride or die."

15

TO THANK US FOR THE HELP, BROTHER NGUYEN INSISTS WE STAY for bánh bò. "I made it last night," he says. "So, it's nice and fresh."

My belly's still full of water ice and soft pretzels. Plus, I'm eager to get to Vicky's house and steal a look at Faye's fiancé. But I already know Vicky well enough to know that she's not about to turn down cake under any circumstances. So, I relent.

We sit on the reverend's back porch, looking out at her little flower garden, which is full of orange marigolds, purple morning glories, and pink-and-cream snapdragons. The bánh bò is chewy and soft. Brother Nguyen watches us eat it, looking pleased.

"Have you ever been to Ethiopia?" Reverend Seymour asks me.

"No, ma'am," I say. "I have not."

"I haven't, either, unfortunately. But Brother Nguyen and I saw an amazing documentary a few nights ago, about hyenas in . . . where was it, Phil?"

"Harar."

"Yes, that's it," she says. "Harar. The hyenas come right into the city and the people feed them. They think the hyenas are spirits. They pet the animals and even feed them by hand. And the hyenas let them. Isn't that fascinating?"

"Yes, it is," I say, making a mental note to go to Ethiopia.

"This world the Lord made is a wonder," she says.

Brother Nguyen nods his agreement.

There's the sound of a screen door creaking open and a woman steps out onto a back porch a few houses away. She's white, in her mid-thirties, and holding an infant in one of those carriers that's all fabric and a few well-placed knots. I remember red-faced Ethan, and figure this must be his wife. When she spots us, she hesitates for a second, then smiles sheepishly and waves at the reverend.

"Good morning, Amanda," the reverend calls. "How's that sweet baby doing?"

I'm surprised at her friendliness but I guess I shouldn't be, considering she's a reverend. That's kind of their thing. You can't bring souls to Jesus with a funky attitude. I notice she didn't call the woman *sister*, though.

"She's a little fussy this morning," Amanda replies, rubbing the baby's head. "But otherwise good."

With pleasantries out of the way, Amanda looks like she really wants to turn around and go back inside now. Instead, she sits down on her porch swing and begins to sway back and forth with her baby, staring out at the sunflowers in her backyard. It's so awkward.

"Sister Skye," Reverend Seymour says, turning back to us. "Tell us about your favorite place to travel."

"Yeah, tell us!" Vicky says.

"Um. I don't really have a favorite."

"Oh, you must."

I think about it. "Everywhere's so different. It's hard to pick one place. I like how the people in Denver are kind of weird at first, but once you get to know them, they're really welcoming. I like how familiar Gaborone feels. Whenever I go back, no matter how long it's been, I still know it. I like how high and chill everybody is in Oakland. I like how Black Brazil is. And how easygoing the people are about sex—" I stop.

Vicky giggles.

Brother Nguyen glances at Reverend Seymour and they share a little smile.

I haven't asked what their deal is because, despite what just happened upstairs, I don't feel like it's my business. But I'm dying to know.

We hear the sound of the screen door creaking again and Ethan comes out onto his back porch. When he sees us, he doesn't smile or wave like his wife did.

At the sight of him, Vicky blows a gigantic, bánh bò–flecked raspberry.

"Vick."

She shrugs. "What?"

Ethan whispers something to his wife, and she gets up off the swing and follows him back inside.

Brother Nguyen shakes his head, frowning. "That was uncomfortable."

"It always is," Reverend Seymour replies.

"You seem friendly with the woman," I say.

She nods. "I try to be. I know it's what God expects of me."

"I sense a 'but.'"

"But I've never had an easy time with women who stand by watching their men treat people badly. And think they, themselves, are not culpable. White women have a long history of that."

Not just white women.

When we're done with our bánh bò, Brother Nguyen returns to the attic and Reverend Seymour walks Vicky and me around the side of the house to the front. She thanks us again for our help with Brother Nguyen.

"Is he your boyfriend?" Vicky asks.

The reverend looks a little bit embarrassed. "'Boyfriend' isn't the term I'd use," she says. "We're . . . well, I'm not sure what to call us. But I've known Philip Michael for thirty years. He and his wife used to run the corner store. Folks called it the 'Chinese store' back then, even though Phil and his wife, Linh, were Vietnamese."

The corner store I frequented as a child was also run by Vietnamese people. We also called it "the Chinese store."

"I used to buy loose cigarettes there, when I still smoked," the reverend continues. "We struck up a good friendship. My late husband and I used to have Philip Michael and Linh over for dinner, and vice versa. People always assumed that Linh and I were friends. And I did like her, she was very nice. But Phil and I had so much in common."

"Like what?" I ask, interested.

"We both love baseball. We watched games together on TV and went to a few over the years. We both love to bake. And theology. We used to talk for hours about religion." She gets quiet for a moment. Then she says, "When Linh died, Phil . . . well, he couldn't handle it. He couldn't even get out of bed. He ended up losing the store. Then, one day, he was gone."

"Gone where?"

"Just gone. Vanished off the face of the earth. Even his grown children didn't know where he was. I didn't see him for fifteen years. Then, a couple of weeks ago, I was in Center City and I saw him sleeping on a park bench. I brought him home with me. He's been here ever since. No one knows, except Faye and Nick. My kids and grandkids would worry about it if they knew. I'm not going to turn him out onto the street. So, he just stays in the spare room. Nobody goes up there. He can stay until I get it figured out."

"Philip Michael is kind of an . . . unexpected name for an older Vietnamese man," I say.

"He named himself that when he opened the corner store. You remember that show *Miami Vice*?"

"Mmm-hmm."

"He thought if he gave himself the name of a well-known Black actor, the Black people in the neighborhood would embrace him."

I laugh. Partly because it's funny but also because I've never heard of an Asian immigrant who wanted to be embraced by Black people.

"Did they?" I ask. "Embrace him?"

She thinks about it, smiles. "I did."

We're in front of her house now and the reverend turns to me and opens her arms for a hug. I take two steps back and offer my hand for a shake instead. Don't get me wrong: She's a nice woman. But hugging strangers is not how I do life.

VICKY'S HOUSE SMELLS LIKE COLLARD greens and the hint of a man's cologne. I don't like it. From the front door, I can see Faye's dude in the kitchen, getting something out of the refrigerator. His back is to us, so I haven't yet ascertained exactly how ugly he is.

"Hi, Uncle Nick," Vicky says, skipping toward him.

He turns, just as we enter the kitchen and I stop walking, mid-step, because guess who the fuck it is? The guy I got drunk with a couple of weeks ago. The guy who slept naked in my bed. Mister "that's cold-blooded" himself. Ain't this a bitch?

He greets Vicky with a smile, avoiding eye contact with me. "Hey, Vicky. How was school?"

"It's Sunday," she says.

"Oh. Right." He looks nervous and he should.

"This is Skye," Vicky says.

Finally, he looks at me. "Skye. Faye was just telling me about you. Nick Ruffin," he says, extending his hand. "Good to meet you."

I just stare at him. Like, what in the entire hell?

"Vicky?" Faye calls from the basement.

"Yes?" Vicky yells back.

"Come down here, please."

Vicky disappears down the basement stairs.

"Wow," I say to him when she's gone. "You're *engaged*? To be *married*?"

"You can't tell Faye we know each other," he whispers.

"You expect me *not to tell her* she's engaged to a cheater?"

"Shhh!" He comes closer to me, takes my arm, and steers me out of the kitchen into the dining room. "It's not like that," he whispers. "I don't cheat. I never have sex with other women. I just like to go out and . . . have fun."

"Naked fun," I remind him.

"That was an unusual night. Most of the time I just *talk* to women. Maybe dance. That's it."

"If it's so innocent, why don't you want me to tell her? Why are you whispering?"

"Faye isn't as easygoing as you or me," he replies. "She wouldn't get it."

"*I* don't get it."

"Look," he says. "I know things between you two aren't great."

"How do you know that?"

"She told me."

"When?"

"Just a few minutes ago," he says. "She told me the whole story about how Vicky tracked you down and how she chased you and all of it."

"Just now?" I ask him. "You know all of that happened like two weeks ago, right? Why'd she wait so long to tell you? Does she sense that she can't fully trust you for some reason?"

He frowns. "If you tell her, it'll only make things weirder between you."

We hear footsteps on the basement stairs. Nick goes back into the kitchen. I follow him.

"Hi again, Skye," Faye says when she sees me. "Vicky said you left something behind earlier?"

"My room key," I say. "I don't see it, though. I must have just forgot it in my room. I'm going to go now."

"Nice meeting you," Nick says.

I ignore him. "Bye, Faye. See you later, Vicky."

And then I beeline it to the door.

I'm almost down the front steps when I hear, "Skye, hold on a second."

I turn and there's Faye holding the copy of *The Color Purple* Vicky got at the festival. I totally forgot this was going to happen.

"I wanted to give you this," she says.

I try my best to look s-u-r-p-r-i-s-e-d. "Oh, wow, what's this?"

"I asked Vicky to look for a copy for you at the festival."

"Oh, wow."

"It's important to have books around that are meaningful to you," she says, "even when you're . . . unsettled."

It's weird that she kind of read my mind.

"Think of it as a peace offering."

And I want to. I really do. But I'm conflicted. Because, on the one hand, I'm not a barbarian. I like peace. Also, if my goal is to have a good enough relationship with Vicky that she'll be willing to change my adult diapers in my old age, or at least put me in a pretty good nursing home, then peace with Faye is probably a good thing. But on the other hand, I don't trust people very easily.

Faye notices my hesitation and says, "I'm sorry I chased you down the street."

"Oh, riiiiight," I reply, laughing. "I totally forgot about that."

"And that I took so long to invite you into our home."

"Did you?" I ask, legit like Meryl Streep up in this bitch. "I didn't really notice."

"Okay," she says. "Well, I'm glad no slight was felt, then."

Oh, noooooooo, not at all.

I open the front cover of the book and see she's written something inside. *For Skye. From Faye.* Not exactly sentimental but still nice.

"Thanks," I say. "Really. I appreciate this."

She smiles and goes back up the steps.

"Faye?"

"Mmm-hmm?" She turns around to face me again.

I think about what Nick said, that telling her how I know him will only make the weirdness between us worse. I'm pretty sure that's bullshit. I'm pretty sure she'd thank me for exposing his ass. But another part of me doesn't want to risk ruining the peace when it's so fragile and new. At the last second, I decide I *will* tell her. But not now. Later.

Trouble is, she's looking at me, waiting for me to say something. Come on, brain, don't fail me n—

"I like your toes." REALLY, BRAIN? REALLY?

She looks down at her feet.

"The polish," I say, trying to sound less creepy. "It's nice."

"Oh. Thank you."

"What's it called?"

"A Oui Bit of Red. Like, French 'oui.'"

And we both smile, because that's actually really cute.

"Bye," Faye says, heading back inside.

"Peace out," I reply, ruining it.

16

EVERY OTHER FRIDAY EVENING, VICKY'S DAD PICKS HER UP AND TAKES her to Bala Cynwyd for the weekend. Spoiler alert: She hates that shit. "It's so boring over there when Sabrina's at college. My dad's always working. His dumb wife just bugs me about watching too much TV, but what am I supposed to do? Talk to *her* or something? I don't even know why I have to go over there at all."

It's a chilly day. For the last couple of hours, since school let out, we've been hanging out by the fire at the B and B, eating leftover pastelillos de guayaba Viva saved us from breakfast, and watching YouTube videos of stupid dogs, while Vicky waits to be hauled off to the suburbs.

"*Do* you have to go?" I ask her.

"My dad gets mad at Aunt Faye when I don't."

Kenny arrives, a blaze of horn-honking and bad new-school hip-hop announcing him before his beamer even pulls up to the curb. Through the parlor window, I can see the car idling, Kenny concealed behind dark-tinted windows.

Vicky's still watching dog vids, giggling through a mouth full of Puerto Rican pastry.

"Your dad's here."

She shrugs just as her phone rings in her hand. I watch her dismiss the call with a bored swipe of her forefinger.

Kenny honks again.

Viva comes out of her office, pops her head into the parlor. "Vicky, it sounds like your father's outside."

Vicky looks up from her phone. "Viva," she says, holding up her half-eaten pastelillo, "did you make this?"

"Sí," Viva says. "It's a twist on my abuelita's recipe."

"It's, like, the best thing I ever tasted."

"Gracias, cariño."

Vicky looks at me, then back at Viva. "What does 'cariño' mean?"

"Sweetie," Viva says.

Vicky smiles. I can tell she likes Viva. I'm not sure if it's an admiration thing or a crush thing or both, but it's cute. "Cariño," Vicky repeats, before taking another bite of pastry and returning to her phone.

Kenny turns off his shitty music, then gets out of his car and stands there, frowning up at the B and B. I shift a little to the left of the window, so he can't see me but I can still peek out at him. After a moment, he leans down and says something to someone inside the car, and I realize Charlotte must be with him. Sure enough, a moment later, the passenger door opens and she gets out, too, also frowning. I shift all the way out of view as they start walking up the front steps.

When the bell rings, Vicky doesn't move to answer it, or even acknowledge it in any way.

"They're not gonna go away, Vick."

She looks at me and frowns, looking a lot like her father frowning up at the B and B, then groans. "Fine." She puts her phone in her pocket and walks extra slowly to the door.

Kenny and Charlotte are dressed alike, in matching purple running clothes and pristine white Nikes with purple swooshes. It's gross. I half-smile a hello and introduce them to Viva anyway, because that is what you do when you stay in the same place long enough to have to see people you don't like on a semi-regular basis. If I'd met these fools in Brazil or Malaysia, I'd never have had to speak to them again.

"What took you so long?" Kenny asks Vicky.

"I was changing my tampon."

"Oh. Yeah. Okay."

Charlotte shakes her head at her husband. "She doesn't even have her period yet, Kenneth."

Vicky scowls at her. "You don't know my life, *Charlotte*."

Charlotte presses her lips tight together and takes a deep breath. "I don't have the emotional capacity to handle your attitude right now, Victoria," she says. "I just had a very stressful experience at a red light."

Neither Vicky, nor Viva, nor I ask what she's talking about. This doesn't stop her from continuing.

"A woman was so rude to me on the way over here. She was *glaring* at me, just because I'm a Caucasian woman with an African American man. Can you believe that? In this day and age?"

Viva glances at me with a look that asks: *Why did you let this woman into my house?*

"How do you know that's why she was frowning?" I ask Charlotte.

"Glaring," she says. "Not frowning. And trust me. I've seen it before. Plenty. Right, Kenneth?"

Kenny nods. "It's just silly and backward. It's the twenty-first century, for Christ's sake."

"Exactly," says Charlotte. "It's just flat-out unfair to look at me with such violence over something as trivial as skin color."

Okay, first of all: She looked at you "with violence"? That's some white nonsense. That's the type of shit white women say about Black women who don't bend over backward to make them feel comfortable in every imaginable situation. Maybe that Black woman was frowning because

1. you were breaking the unspoken rule of not making eye contact with other drivers unless it's to scowl at them for cutting you off a ways back;

2. she didn't like the mumbly, misogynist music Kenny was blasting from your obnoxious car; or

3. she'd just remembered how Judy Winslow disappeared from *Family Matters* with no explanation at all!

Or maybe she just had resting bitch face. I don't know and it doesn't even matter because—newsflash: It's not a Black woman's job to smile at you so you can feel comfortable about your life choices, *Char*.

But, honestly? There's no way I'm putting in the time to explain any of this to her, so I just say, "Caucasian is a racist term."

"Sí," Viva says. "*Muy* racista."

Charlotte blinks at us, looking confused.

Kenny says, "Um, we really need to get going. You ready, baby girl?"

"Dad. You promised not to call me that."

"I would never make that promise," he says. "Where's your stuff?"

"At home."

Charlotte's lips go tight again. "What do you mean, 'at home'?"

Vicky gives her a look that can only be interpreted as: *Bitch, are you deaf?* "I mean, my stuff is at home. *Like I just said.*"

Charlotte's mouth opens, but no words come out. She looks at Kenny.

"Vicky, stop it," he says, half-interested at best. Then he's like, "We can swing by Faye's house and get your stuff. But we have to be quick about it."

"It's my house, too," Vicky says. "I literally live there."

"Okay, Vicky," Kenny says. "Fine. Jesus. Let's just go, please. I have to drop you off in Bala Cynwyd and get back to Center City by eight for a dinner thing."

Vicky looks at me, like, *See?*

I give her my best look of solidarity. "You can call me if you need anything."

I follow them outside and watch Vicky get into the back of the beamer, looking more miserable than I have ever seen her. Charlotte waves goodbye to me, cheerfully, like we're homies or some shit. The mumbly hip-hop blasts on once again, and they drive off.

Five minutes later, I get a text from the kid: *Remember u said u'd punch Marco in the kidneys? Can u do that to Charlotte?*

I only have enuf upper body strength to beat up children. Sorry.

17

IT'S BEEN A MONTH SINCE I CLIMBED OUT A WINDOW TO ESCAPE Vicky, and now I kick it with her several times a week. Some days, I pick her up from school, after spelling club or activist club—which is also a thing—and we grab fries or smoothies on our way back to her house. On weekends when she's not in Bala Cynwyd, we take the el downtown and walk to the parkway, hit up the art museum, or take the bus to Rittenhouse Square and eat Froyo in the park. Sometimes we just kick it at Vicky's house, with snacks and card games or *Steven Universe*. A couple of times, Faye invites me to stay for dinner, but I don't, because Nick is always there. For the last couple of weeks, since I found out who he is, he's been with Faye every time I've seen her. I'd rather keep my distance from that whole thing. Whatever desire I had to put my hands and mouth on all of Faye's everything is mostly buried under the weight of that potential drama, hanging in the air like humidity before a thunderstorm every time the three of us are in the same room. Except Faye doesn't even seem to notice it, and I don't know if that makes it better or worse. In any case, I'm still planning to tell her about Nick. At some point. Soon.

"You like Nick, huh?" I ask Vicky one Sunday afternoon. It's early

May, warm and rainy, and thunder has been rumbling in the distance for hours. We're playing Uno on the porch.

"Yeah," she says. "He's cool. Why? You don't like him?"

"He seems like a creep."

"How?" she asks, throwing down a Skip card.

"I don't know. I just think Faye could do better."

"Nick's cool," Vicky says again. "Plus, he helps people."

"What do you mean?"

"He's a lawyer," she says. "He goes to court with people for free sometimes. And he coaches youth hoops at Baobab."

"What's that?"

"The community center," she says. "He helps a lot of kids who have crappy parents and stuff. He let this boy, Brian, live with him for like two weeks 'cause his mom and dad were high all the time."

"That was nice of him. *I guess*."

Vicky changes the color and then asks, "How come you don't like anybody?"

Who, me? "I like tons of people."

She twists her lips and tilts her head in an expression that says, *Oh really?*

"Okay, maybe not 'tons,'" I concede. "But some. I like some people."

"Who?"

"You want me to list all the people I like? Is alphabetical order okay?"

She shrugs. "I just think maybe you have trust issues or something like that."

"What are you, my shrink now?"

"Your . . . what?"

"Shrink. It's another word for therapist."

"Why?"

"Because some Amazonian tribes used to shrink the heads of their enemies."

She looks confused. "What does that have to do with therapy?"

"I have no idea. Point is, if I have trust issues, it's for good reason."

"What reason?"

"That I can't trust people. That's the reason. People don't show up."

"Show up where?" she asks, looking even more confused.

"I just mean people can't be counted on when it matters," I tell her.

"Counted on for what, though?"

"Whatever a person needs in that moment."

Vicky chews her lip very slowly, like she's thinking it over. Then she says, "How are you supposed to know what somebody needs?"

"They tell you."

"But what if they don't?"

"Then you figure it out. If you really give a shit."

I usually try not to curse in front of the kid, and she looks at me now with surprise. Then she says, "Well, how do *you* figure it out?"

The truth is that I *don't* figure it out. Because I *don't* really give a shit anymore. I stopped giving a shit a long time ago. But it occurs to me now that these are all messed-up things to say to a twelve-year-old—that people don't show up; that I no longer care enough to figure out how to show up myself. Especially because it seems like people do show up for Vicky. I shouldn't dump all *my* shit on this kid; I shouldn't weigh her down with my cynical view of the world and everyone in it. It's gross and weird to do that to a child. So, I don't. Instead, I tell her what is true about *me*. "I'm afraid to get close enough to know what people need."

"How come?"

I sigh a very long sigh. "Because people have let me down and I don't like the way that feels. So now, I mostly try not to expect people to show up in the first place, so I'm not hurt when they don't."

I have never admitted this to anyone. It feels like a pretty big moment. If this were a movie, there would be a long silence between us, during which an emotionally intense score would play, low and heart-wrenching, in the background. But this is real life and twelve-year-olds don't appreciate therapeutic pauses, so Vicky just shakes her head and says, "That's wild."

And I burst out laughing.

"What?"

I shake my head. "Nothing, kid."

Vicky plays a Reverse card and says, "Well, what about me?"

"What about you?"

"You can't trust me to show up?"

"You're a kid."

She shrugs. "So what?"

"So, it's not a kid's job to show up for an adult," I tell her, realizing that this is, in fact, why I *do* kinda trust her, in a way; why letting her see my raw, bloody innards doesn't feel as risky: I have no expectations of her in the first place. Because she's freaking twelve.

I play a *Draw Four* and Vicky groans, just as her bestie, Jaz, arrives. Jaz is chubby and light-skinned, and she stutters, especially when she talks about boys. I like her because she always laughs at my jokes.

"Where's your stuff?" Vicky asks her.

"I can't stay over because it's a school night."

"Ugh, that sucks. Your mom's worse than Aunt Faye."

Jaz nods. "Yeah, she's such a bitch."

"Jesus," I say. "Is this how twelve-year-olds talk about their parents now? I didn't start calling my mother a bitch until I was at least thirteen-and-a-half."

Jaz laughs.

"You don't even talk to your mom," Vicky says.

"Okay, but I'm not twelve. I've had many more years to build legitimate resentment."

"You don't have to be forty-five," Vicky says, "to have problems with your parents. Don't be so ageist."

I roll my eyes. "Fine. Hate your parents to your heart's content. But you know I'm not *forty-five*, right?"

She looks surprised. "You're not?"

"No!"

"How old are you?"

"Thirty-eight."

She shrugs. "That's almost forty-five."

OH, BIIIIIITCH.

"You don't talk to your mom?" Jaz asks. "Why not?"

"I talk to her. I just saw her like a month ago."

"Wait," Vicky says. "You didn't tell me that."

"Am I supposed to tell you everything?"

She frowns at me, like I'm being obtuse. "Um . . . yeah."

"Well, my brother tricked me into going to the hospital to see my mother. Now you know."

"Is she sick?"

"No," I say, realizing I probably shouldn't be telling her that, considering.

"Then why's she in there?" Jaz asks.

"She's out now. It was nothing," I tell them. "She's fine." Besides the whole traumatic brain injury thing.

"When am I going to meet her?" Vicky asks.

Wait, whut? "I . . . haven't really thought about it. Is that something you want to do?"

"Yeah," she says.

"Why?"

"To know who I come from."

"You come from your mother. Like, she literally birthed you. And your father, too. Half your genes are from Barack No-Bama."

Jaz guffaws at that, doubling over.

I smile at her. "Good one, right?"

She nods through the tears that have sprung to her eyes, holding her belly as it shakes with laughter. Wow, this kid really appreciates comedic genius. Good for her.

"You know what I mean," Vicky says.

I guess I do. But honestly, the people she "comes from" on this end aren't that great.

"Does she know about me?"

"No."

"How come?"

"Because I don't talk to her. Remember?"

Vicky frowns. "You could have told her about me when you saw her in the hospital."

"There was kind of a lot going on, Vick. And it's probably something I should build up to."

Faye comes up the front steps, carrying bags, with Nick following close behind her.

"Who wants bagels?" she asks.

Vicky jumps up like the little kid she swears she's not. "I do!"

"Me, too!" says Jaz.

Faye looks at me. "Skye?"

"Thanks. But I have a thing with Viva."

"Next time, then," she says.

"Yeah."

NEXT TIME COMES JUST A few days later, when Faye texts and invites me over for dinner. This is the third invitation she's extended since we buried the hatchet or whatever, and I'm starting to feel like it's rude to keep saying, "I have a thing with Viva." So, I text Vicky and ask her to find out if Nick is going to be there, but discreetly. An hour later, Vicky texts me back and says he's working late and won't be around. I text Faye and tell her yes and thanks and should I bring anything? She replies, *A nice bread that's good with soup.* I Lyft all the way down to Woodland Ave to get the chewiest, most delish French bread I know of, from a little bakery that's on the corner of the block I lived on when I was in elementary school. Back then, the block was all poor and working-class Black families, but now it's mostly college kids spilling out from Penn. Directly across from the bakery is the corner where, during one go-cart-racing afternoon when I was seven, Lakeisha Moore whispered in my ear, "I *like* like you," and then ran away. I chased her down the alley and over the fence into her family's back-yard and she kissed me against the back wall of her house. Her breath smelled like cherry Now and Laters. It's my earliest memory of doing gay shit, though I'd felt gay shit pretty much in the womb. The bakery wasn't here then. It replaced a barber shop where my brother and father got their hair cut for years. But it's Black-owned and has the best baked goods this side of the Schuylkill, so it's worth the detour before I double back to West Philly.

"Vicky's not here yet," Faye says when I get to their house. "She's at Jasmine's. She should be on her way back."

I hand over the bread.

She smiles, thanks me. "Would you like a drink? I was told bourbon is your thing, so I picked some up."

I'm pretty sure Nick didn't tell her that, so she must be talking about Vicky. She's not pissed, though, so I'm guessing the kid didn't mention the circumstances under which she learned this fun fact about me.

I say yes to the bourbon, then watch her open a cabinet and take out a tumbler. Her movements are slower and easier these days, with less of the tense stiffness present in the olden days of a couple of weeks ago, before the truce was called.

"You're not one of those people who doesn't drink, are you?" I ask, eyeing the single tumbler and realizing I've never seen liquor or even wine in this house.

She looks at me and frowns a little and I'm like: oh no. She's probably a whole-ass recovering alcoholic and here I am undermining her sobriety, on some *you're not one of those people, are you?* type shit. UGH. But then she says, "I don't like the taste."

"Of bourbon?" I ask.

"Of any of it."

"Any of it? At all? Not even . . . in cocktails?"

She shakes her head. "I have a drink occasionally, when I'm out with people who are doing that. But it's never really been my thing."

I think back to what Vicky said about Faye's wild teenage years and I figure maybe you don't really need liquor when you have cocaine? I probably shouldn't ask, right?

For dinner, Faye has made a butternut squash and kale soup, in a slow cooker. It smells heavenly. "It's Vicky's favorite. Considering how hard it is to get her to eat vegetables, I've been cooking it almost every week."

Considering how hard it is to get *me* to eat vegetables, I'm quite looking forward to it. "You cook a lot?"

She shakes the top of the slow cooker over the sink, and the condensation falls in droplets onto the stainless steel. "With a kid, you really have to. But I probably cooked at least a couple of times a week when I lived alone, too."

"Did you live alone before Vicky?" I ask, trying to sound casual, not like I'm trying to get all up in her business, which I definitely am.

"Yes," she says, stirring the soup. "For a while, after my divorce."

"You were married before?"

She nods. "Twice, actually."

"To men?"

She stops stirring and looks up at me. She shakes her head. "Not exclusively."

Not. Exclusively. Well, okay, then.

Now I want to ask who she was married to. I want to ask why she's so into marriage, which she must be, considering she's on the precipice of her third one. I want to ask why, with that many marriages, she doesn't have her own kids. Can she not have kids? Does she just not like kids that much? I want to ask so many things.

"What about you?" she asks. "Do you cook? It's probably hard to do while traveling so much."

The boomerang back to the cooking conversation is jolting. I want to be like, *Wait, hold up, let's talk more about your failed relationships*, but that would be pushy, right? So, I just follow her lead and let the moment pass. "I used to have a rule," I tell her, "that I had to cook for myself whenever I was staying somewhere with a kitchen."

"Used to?"

"I haven't really been on top of it lately. Which isn't great for my wallet. Or for squeezing my ass into my jeans."

"Exactly how much do you travel?" she asks.

"I lead groups ten months a year."

She looks at me with surprise, like she didn't expect it to be that much. I think she's going to ask me how I manage it logistically, like everyone else does, but instead she asks, "Why?" It's not a judgmental, *what's wrong with you* type of "why" but it still makes me a little bit uncomfortable.

"I . . . like it," I say.

"What do you like about it?"

For a few seconds, I can't remember anything I like about it. I sit there staring at her with my mouth open, waiting for reasons to come flying out, and she stares curiously back at me. Then, finally, my brain kicks in, like an engine rolling over, and I'm like, "I like seeing new places. Trying new foods. Experiencing different cultures. Meeting new people. Getting laid by women with foreign accents. The usual stuff." Nice work, brain!

"Well, if I traveled half as much as you do," she says, grabbing a knife in one hand and the French loaf in the other, "I'd go crazy. I'm too much of a homebody to handle anything more than the occasional trip."

"To where?"

"When I was in college," she says, "I studied art for a year in

Florence, and I developed a real affection for that city. I used to go back every year or so."

"Florence is great."

She nods. "Vicky loves the ocean, so we spend part of our summer break in Virginia Beach. Kenny has family down there, so she gets to see her cousins."

Faye's phone buzzes on the counter and she glances at it, then frowns.

"What's wrong?"

"Vicky is . . . dawdling." She sighs. "She's always been difficult to wrangle home. Ever since she was little."

"Has she?" I ask, my ears perking up. I haven't heard much about little Vicky yet.

"Cynthia and Kenny used to have such a hard time getting her to leave the playground," Faye says, "that they started telling her Santa and every single one of his reindeer were waiting for her at home."

"Did that work?"

"Three or four times, I think, before she caught on."

I think about a smaller version of Vicky, standing by the slide with her arms folded, and it makes me smile. "Do you have pictures? From when she was little?"

Faye walks into the living room and I follow her. There's a built-in cabinet in one corner of the room and she opens its small doors and takes out a brightly colored photo album. On its front cover there's a photo of baby Vicky, all cheeks and bright brown eyes, smiling toothlessly at the camera. I feel a little flutter in my chest.

Faye sits down on the sofa and I sit beside her. She opens the album and points to a photo of baby Vicky sitting in a high chair, with what looks like sweet potato all over her face. She's wearing a bib that reads: I'M FAMOUS AROUND HERE.

"She's about six months old," Faye says. "This was her first solid food, so she hadn't exactly learned how to eat it yet."

I've never been around babies much. Their ways are very much a mystery to me. The idea that a baby has to *learn* how to eat food is kind of mind-blowing, right?

Farther down the page, there's a picture of Vicky on Kenny's lap. She's holding her dad's fingers in her chubby little hands. Kenny is looking at her with tired eyes that are nonetheless brimming with affection. In the background, Cynthia is sprawled on the couch, her head back and her mouth slightly open. Her right tit is dangerously close to escaping her bra. She looks like every new mom I've ever seen: exhausted. For a second, I imagine myself in her place, imagine what it might have been like if I had given birth to Vicky, if I had been her mother. It's silly, because even if I'd had a kid, that kid wouldn't have been Vicky. Cynthia's doctors chose that one egg and it was fertilized by Kenny's sperm, and it became Vicky, under those very specific circumstances. But still. I imagine what it might have been like if I had nursed her and sniffed her little head and soothed her when she cried. It's kind of a nice thing to think about. Until I realize I also would have had to get up eleventy times a night to feed her, and change her poopy diapers, and listen to her scream for I-wouldn't-know-what-reason until my ears bled. That would be *me*, passed out on the couch with a rogue titty, without a good night's sleep in months. Which: Nah. I'm good.

On the next page, there's a photo of Vicky sleeping with her head on Faye's shoulder. Faye is looking directly at the camera, her dark eyes bright, half a smile on her face. She looks very much the same, except for her hair, which, in the photo, is shaved almost bald.

"Very nice look," I say.

She smiles. Then sighs. "This photo makes me feel so old."

"You're not, though. I mean, what are you? Like, forty?"

"Forty-two," she says. "Forty. Fucking. Two."

I shake my head. "That's not old. Old is like . . . forty-three."

She punches me in the shoulder. Playfully, but also kind of hard. I like it *so much*.

"I'm just messing with you," I say, laughing.

"Well, how old are *you*?"

"Ask Miss Newsome. I'm sure she has my date of birth and Social Security number."

She punches me again.

"Okay, okay. I'm almost thirty-nine. Which, according to Vicky, is actually forty-five, so."

Faye laughs and I feel like I'm winning.

She turns the page again and there's a picture of Vicky around a year old, standing up on her own and looking so very thrilled about it.

"Is this what you looked like when you were tiny?" Faye asks me.

I nod. "There's a resemblance. But Vicky was way cuter than I was."

"I'm sure you were cute," she says. "All babies are cute."

"You really think that?"

"Yes," she says. "Of course."

"Even white babies?"

She thinks about it. "In their own way."

Ha.

"Well, I was definitely one of those 'cute in their own way' babies," I tell her. "Honestly, it took like thirty years to grow into this face. And I'm still only barely managing it."

"I like your face," she says.

I look at her. "You like my face?"

She nods. "Yes."

Okay, remember when I said that thing about how my desire to put my hands and mouth on Faye's parts is now buried under the weight of all the potential drama, and something about humidity and thunderstorms and blah blah blah? Bitch, I lied. It's not buried. It's right here where it always was, pulsing like a heartbeat from the depths of my clitoris. THIS IS THE MOMENT IN WHICH I SHOULD LEAN OVER AND KISS HER. Isn't it? Or, like, at least try? If I don't, I could look back and regret it for years to come. It's been my experience that you don't always get another chance to kiss someone you really want to kiss. Sometimes the universe just doesn't ever line up that way again.

But I don't try to kiss her. Not because I'm not sure I should but because, right then, I hear a key in the door and the next second, Vicky is standing there.

"What are y'all doing?"

"Looking at your baby pictures," Faye says.

Vicky drops her backpack with a thud and bounces over to us, squeezes herself between us on the sofa. COCKBLOCK MUCH?

My phone vibrates in my pocket. I glance at it and see the beginning of a text from my brother. *Come see Mom tomorrow* . . . Jesus, he's *relentless*. I put the phone away without opening the message.

Faye flips to the next page and points to a photo of Vicky around three years old, sitting between Cynthia's knees, getting her hair done in plaits. Her little face is twisted into a frown.

"That's a familiar expression," Faye says, smiling at me.

I smile back, deciding to just accept the passing of the moment, and nod. "That's the look of every Black girl getting her hair done since the dawn of Black girls."

"Your mom did your hair like that?" Vicky asks me.

I touch my head with the tips of my fingers. "I can feel the tightness in my scalp just thinking about it."

"I actually miss it a little," Faye says.

"Why on earth?" I ask.

"It was done in love," she says, reaching out and touching one of Vicky's braids, rubbing it gently between her fingers, the way she often does. It's such a tender touch, and suddenly I feel a longing, almost a jealousy, though I'm not sure which of them, Vicky or Faye, I want to be in that moment. Either of them, I guess. The longing is for the closeness itself.

I remember myself, at seven or eight, sitting on sofa cushions on the floor between my mother's knees, while she parts my hair with a large comb, then gently rubs oil on my scalp all along the part. I feel her fingers in my hair. I hear her laugh and then my kid self is laughing, too. I feel happy and cared for.

"Our mothers just wanted us to look nice," Faye is saying. "Think how bad it must have been for them. Sitting there for hours, their backs and arms and fingers aching, and us complaining the whole time. I never appreciated how much work it was until"—she points at Vicky—"*this one*."

"Me?" Vicky asks, incredulous. "What did I do?"

"You told me I was 'child abusing' you the last time I put cornrows in your hair."

Vicky laughs. "Oh, yeah. That was funny."

Faye pushes her and she falls on the floor in a fit of giggles.

My phone vibrates again. For a second, I think about texting my brother back. But only for a second.

18

THE NEXT MORNING, I WAKE UP AT THE ASS CRACK OF DAWN. I'M talking seven A.M., y'all. An ungodly hour. If I'm not working, I don't get up before ten and, in this case, it's worse because I only fell asleep in the first place around four, after tossing and turning for hours. I finally drifted off and was dreaming an excellent dream about getting my head massaged and then—BAM—I'm suddenly awake again, staring at the bedside clock.

I lie there with my eyes closed, refusing to even entertain the notion of getting up. I think hard about head massages, hoping I can get my dream going again and settle back into sleep that way. The massage I was dreaming about was being done by my Philly hairdresser, Rhonda, who always rubs my scalp when she's tidying up my locs. I have this dream about once a month, no matter where in the world I am, when I'm overdue for a trip to the hairdresser. It's how my subconscious reminds me to keep my edges tight, so I'm not out here looking raggedy. Only, this time, I'm not overdue. I just had my locs tended to a couple of weeks ago. So, I don't know why I'm dreaming about it now. But whatever. It still feels good. So, I sink farther down into the covers and try to concentrate on Rhonda's fingers on my scalp, rub rub rubbing. It works. At first. I start to feel myself being pulled back into dreamland. But then the image changes. I'm eight, sitting between my mother's knees, and she's braiding my hair.

I open my eyes. It's now seven-ten. I sigh and get up.

FIFTEEN MINUTES LATER, I'M SHOWERED and dressed and standing in the dining room. There are other guests already there, enjoying breakfast. At one table, a couple that's staying in the Julia de Burgos room sits eating pancakes. At another, three pretty flaming gays I haven't seen before sip Bloody Marys. I grab a seat by a window and peruse the little paper menu. Viva comes out of the kitchen with a cappuccino, which she sets in front of one of the gays. When she spots me, she looks surprised, then suspicious. "What are you doing down here?" she asks me, coming over to my table.

I hold up the menu. "I came down for breakfast."

"Pero you *never* come down for breakfast."

"Sí. Pero I felt like company this morning."

She looks around at the other guests.

"Not them," I say. Ew. As if. "You."

"Oh. Well, that's nice. ¿Quieres café?"

"Espresso, por favor."

"And to eat?"

"Grits. And this frittata sounds good."

She takes out her phone and starts thumbing the keyboard. "I'm texting your order to the kitchen. Jason's on chef duty this morning." When she's done, she sits down across from me. She's fully dressed, in a matching skirt and top, yellow with tiny red flowers all over. Her hair is bouncy and lustrous. She's wearing makeup. It's impressive, considering I barely brushed my teeth.

"How do you look this good at seven-something in the morning? You get up at, like, four-fifteen?"

"I still do yoga at five, most mornings."

"Five . . . o'clock? Girl, is that even a real time? That sounds made up."

"You know I love mornings."

"Yeah, you always have," I say. "I remember you used to get up early to meditate before school. Which was weird."

"It wasn't weird. It was the closest thing I had to therapy back then. I had to do *something* to prepare myself for a school day surrounded by cis people."

"Fair enough."

"But only morning persons really understand other morning persons," she says. "Which begs the question . . ."

"What am *I* doing up at this hour?"

"Equelecuá."

"I couldn't sleep. Also, I'm considering visiting my mother today and I feel like I need a buffer of several hours, some strong coffee, and possibly a little bourbon first."

"Well, you're full of surprises this morning. What brought that on?"

I sigh. "I don't know. Looking over other people's fences, I guess. Which I have a hard and fast rule to *never* do. I guess I'm becoming less diligent in my old age. I had a disturbing memory, too."

"¿De qué?"

"My mother caring for me."

Viva draws her eyebrows together. "Why is that disturbing?"

"Because nostalgia is a lie, Veev. Obviously."

She frowns. "All of it?"

"Yes. I mean, that's the nature of nostalgia, isn't it? The scene I remembered was incomplete, it was pulled from my cerebral cortex without context. It's just the good stuff, without the traumatizing bits."

"If the scene was incomplete," she says, "how do you know there *were* traumatizing bits?"

"There were always traumatizing bits."

"That's not true, Skye. You know I was there, ¿verdá? We have shared history, remember?"

"Yeah. So?"

"So, nostalgia is good for us. You could use a little more nostalgia in your life."

"What does that even mean?"

"Why do you pretend tu madre es *toda* mala? Isn't it important to see the full picture of a person? If I were going to pick and choose only the worst angles, and ignore the rest, I would've stopped talking to *your* self-centered ass years ago."

"I'm self-centered now?"

"Now?" Viva laughs. "*Chica*."

Jason arrives with my espresso and a hot tea for his wife. "Hi, Skye. Frittata will be out in five." Then, to Viva, "The espresso machine's being weird again."

"Did you jiggle the thing?" she asks, sounding annoyed.

"Of course," he says. "Why are you snapping at me?"

Viva gets up. "I'll be right back."

They disappear into the kitchen.

While she's gone, I think about that shared history. Viva transitioned sophomore year of college, and the following summer, when we were twenty, she was working at the front desk of one of those super swank hotels in Rittenhouse Square. She got the job by being charming, and also by pretending to be her sister, Val, who'd given Viva her ID and Social Security number to use, because Val had a doctor husband and no kids and, thus, could spend her days getting manicures and shopping for housewares, not nine-to-fiving like some chump. I spent most of that summer at school, taking extra classes, but when my classes and summer job ended, I had to come home for a week to bridge a gap in housing. My father, who had been gone for six years, was back living with my mother temporarily, and I couldn't stand being in that house. Viva, who comes from a family of nurturers, of caregivers, and has always been those things herself, used her employee perks to get a free room at the hotel and let me stay there with her. We stayed up late watching home improvement shows—Viva fantasizing out loud about buying an old house to renovate and turn into a bed-and-breakfast—and travel shows that helped me push Philly far from my mind.

We told each other everything back then. Cried on each other's shoulders. Defended each other. Viva was the reason I came out to my mother, sort of. It was Thanksgiving 2003. I was twenty-three. My whole extended family was over for turkey dinner and games. During a break in Scattergories, Viva, Slade, and I slipped away to smoke some weed on the back porch. Somehow Viva and I got reminiscing about high school. About our junior prom, specifically, and how much fun we'd had in the back of our limo, sipping vodka miniatures we'd stolen from Viva's dad's liquor shelf. When we went back in the house, high and ready for more Scattergories, my mother took one look at Viva and started screaming. She'd been eavesdropping on our prom nostalgia and she remembered that night. She remembered me and my friends getting into the limo together and she connected the dots.

"Oh, Lord, it's a man!" she shrieked. "Oh, Lord! Oh, Jesus!"

I looked at my brother, who was dating Viva at the time, and we exchanged *oh shit* glances.

"I should go," Viva said, looking mortified.

"You don't have to go," I told her. "Mom, please chill."

Slade, disloyal jackass that he is, didn't say shit.

Before then, our mother had loved Viva. Like the daughter she never had, you might even say. She didn't recognize Viva from my high school days—she was pretty unrecognizable after her transition, and I'd never brought my friends around my house much, anyway, since I didn't even want to be there myself—but she always said Viva looked familiar, that she was sure she'd seen her before, she just couldn't put her finger on where. Our mother had been happy when Slade started dating this smart, considerate girl who brought her homemade arroz con gandules and tembleque. But in that moment on the back porch, things changed. Our mother assumed Viva had tricked Slade while he was minding his normal, non-deviant business. When Slade—after much prompting from me—told her he'd known all along, she pretended to faint and our grandparents, aunts, and uncles—who were watching the whole thing play out over second helpings of stuffing and candied yams—collectively gasped like a live television audience. It was then that I decided to come out to my mother. Like, right then. I figured

1. it would take some of the heat off Viva;
2. it would save me the trouble of doing it later and having to endure another fake fainting scene; and
3. lesbianism would seem ho-hum in comparison.

I was wrong on all counts. As soon as the words "I'm gay" came out of my mouth, my mother started screaming about Viva being the devil come to corrupt her children, and pretended to faint a second time. Viva left, swearing she'd never set foot in my mother's house again. My mother spent the entire next week in bed, only getting up to go to church, where I assume she prayed for my brother and me at length. When I came home a few months later, for spring break—which I only did because I didn't have money to go anywhere else—and was holed up in my room, depressed over some white girl I'd fallen for at school, I called Viva. She brought over butterfly shrimp and the first two seasons of *Sanford and Son* on DVD to cheer me up. She knew my mother might come home any minute and freak out on her. She risked further humiliation for me. Luckily, when my mother did arrive home, she didn't freak out. She knocked on my closed door and said, "I ordered some buffalo wings for y'all. Those ones Viva likes. I'll holler when they get here."

I haven't thought about this in years. Or, to be honest, I've only thought about the part where my mother acted a whole-ass lunatic. I haven't thought about her saucy peace offering.

I lean back in my chair and rub my eyes. I think about the ways good and not-so-good times fold together and overlap, the ways a memory of stress and one of reparation can sleep like lovers in the same bed, touching fingertips in the quiet, and I question myself. Why *do* I pretend it was all bad?

"What are you thinking about?" Viva asks, sitting back down across the table a minute later. She seems more relaxed now, not annoyed anymore. "Your face is all scrunched up."

What I'm thinking feels too new to talk about, so I say, "You remember that Thanksgiving when my mother—"

"Sí," she says before I can finish. "Girl. How could I forget it?" She places the back of her hand on her forehead in a fake-swooning gesture. "Oh, Lord! Sweet Jesus!"

I burst out laughing and Viva does, too.

I don't ask her if she really thinks I'm self-centered. Hearing the ways I suck sounds like a terrible way to spend breakfast. Also, despite what Tasha said, I'm not totally lacking in self-reflection. There's probably not much Viva could tell me about myself that I don't already know. The knowing is the easy part. It's the shaking it loose that's hard.

19

MY MOTHER STILL LIVES IN THE HOUSE WE MOVED INTO WHEN I WAS
eleven, in the Cobbs Creek section of West Philly, on a mostly treeless
block. Back then, when many of the homes were owned or rented by
people in their thirties who had school-aged kids, like my parents, the
block was kept up. People swept the sidewalks in front of their houses
and threw away litter that blew into their yards—or, more often, made
their kids do it. Not so much now. Many of the houses on the street
still look fairly well cared for—their tiny front yards either planted
with flowers or neatly paved over with concrete; their front steps
intact; their trims repainted within the last ten years. But others look
less well maintained—their yards overgrown; their front steps crumbling; the paint on their trims blistered and peeling. My mother's
house falls somewhere in the middle. The hedges in the front yard
look to have been recently cut and the front steps have sections of new
cement, like they've been recently repaired. But the house hasn't been
painted in what looks like decades. Coming up the steps, I see old
supermarket circulars in the front yard, still in their plastic sleeves,
thrown there by someone with bad aim and never retrieved by my
mother or brother. On the porch, there's a rusty rocking chair and,

beside it, a tiny plastic folding table with an overflowing ashtray on top of it. Before her accident, my mother was actively trying to quit her forty-five-year smoking habit and, according to my brother, was having a good amount of success. She was down to three cigarettes a day right before her fall. After her fall, when she woke up after the surgery they had to do to relieve the pressure on her brain, the first thing she asked for was a cigarette. With her memory shot, she couldn't remember that she'd been trying to quit and, with the stress of being newly disabled, she was no longer interested in giving up cigarettes.

I ring the doorbell. After about fifteen seconds, I see my mother peek through the blinds that hang behind the glass door pane. She sees me and looks confused. I hear the dead bolt click as she opens the door.

"Skye?" she asks, peering at me through the screen door that still separates us. "What are you doing here? Was I expecting you?"

"Slade asked me to come by and check up on you."

"Oh. I wish you would've called first. I'm catching up on my shows."

"I can go if this is a bad time," I say, wondering why I ever thought this was a good idea.

"No, it's alright," says my mother, opening the screen door. "I'm glad to see you. Come on in."

When I step into the house, the first thing I notice is how dark it is inside. All the curtains are drawn and the only light is from the television. My eyes actually have to adjust. Once they do, I kind of wish they hadn't. The house is a mess. The end tables are strewn with half-eaten plates of food, half-drunk mugs of coffee, and empty soda cans. A bunch of old *Ebony* magazines lie scattered on the floor in front of the bookshelf. The carpet looks like it hasn't been vacuumed in months. Since her accident, my mother either can't remember, or just doesn't care, to clean. The last time I was in this house, which was about a year ago, there were cockroaches everywhere.

"This is disgusting," I told my brother then.

"She won't clean up after herself," he said.

"Why don't you clean up, then?"

"I don't have time."

"You don't even have a job, nigga!"

I called an exterminator, then Rosa, the woman who cleans the B and B, and booked them both. I told my brother that if I ever saw the house like that again, I'd put our mother in a home and he could live under the el for all I cared.

Looking around now, it's not nearly as bad as it was that day. I don't see any cockroaches. But it's still not good.

"Where's Slade?" I ask my mother.

"At his girlfriend's," she says, taking a seat in the recliner in front of the television and grabbing the remote. "I think. He doesn't really stay here that much anymore."

"What do you mean? He doesn't live here?"

My mother isn't able to live on her own, because we can never be sure she'll remember important safety things like turning off the stove or locking the doors at night. She needs help and supervision, both of which Slade is supposed to be providing.

"I didn't say that," she replies a little defensively. "I said he's at his girlfriend's sometimes, that's all."

That's not what she said. But okay.

"As a matter of fact, he's supposed to come home later to take me to the grocery store. We're out of food."

I walk to the back of the house, to the kitchen, and open the fridge. It's almost completely empty.

"When's the last time you bought groceries?" I call out to my mother.

"I'm not sure," she calls back.

I come back into the front room. "Well, what have you been eating?"

"I had a couple of Lean Cuisines in the freezer," she says. "I think there's one left. Are you hungry? I can pop it in the microwave for you."

I'm going to murder Slade with my bare hands.

"I'll take you to the grocery store," I tell my mother. "If you want."

She looks like she's thinking hard about it, like it's a tough decision she needs to mull over or some shit.

"Or not," I say. "Whatever. I don't really care either way."

"Do you have a car?" she asks.

"No. We can just take a Lyft."

"What's that?"

"It's like a cab."

"Oh," she says, sounding disappointed.

"Slade doesn't have a car, either, Mom."

"He drives his girlfriend's car sometimes," she says.

Why. Does. It. Even. Matter. How. We. Get. There. Though?

"I don't like cabs," my mother says. "They smell bad."

"Okay, but it's not actually a—" I stop myself. Because why am I even having this conversation? If my mother wants to sit here and starve to death waiting for her fucknugget of a son to come through, that's her business.

"Okay, Mom," I say. "Just wait for Slade, then. It's fine. I'm gonna go now."

"Alright," my mother says, turning back to the television.

I head for the door. My hand is on the knob when I hear my mother say, "I don't know what time he's going to get back, though."

SOMEBODY SHOOT ME IN THE FACE.

I turn and look at my mother. "So . . . do you want me to take you to the grocery store? Or not?"

"Oh, yes, that's a good idea," she says, like this is the very first time she's hearing it.

* * *

WHEN WE GET TO THE grocery store, which is about half a mile from my mother's house, I ask her if she has her grocery list.

"I think so," she says, rummaging through her purse. After about half a minute, she says, "Oh, I can't find it. I guess I forgot to put it in my bag."

"Do you remember what was on it?"

She thinks about it, then shakes her head. "Not really."

I take out my phone. "I'll text your son and ask him what you need."

"That's a good idea."

Since we can't stand around all day waiting for Slade to exit the vagina of whatever poor sucker of a woman he's currently inside of and text me back, I tell my mother, "In the meantime, we can just walk down all the aisles and, if you see things you need, you can grab them."

The produce aisle is right near the front entrance, so we grab a cart and start there.

"What kind of vegetables do you want? Broccoli? Green beans? These collards look good."

My mother picks up a bunch of garlic scapes, examines them at length, then puts them in the cart.

I have never, not once in thirty-eight years of life on this earth, seen my mother eat a garlic scape. "You sure you need these?"

She nods. "Yes."

"For . . . ?"

She thinks about it for a second. "I'm not sure."

"Is it possible you . . . don't need them, then?"

"I'm pretty sure I do need them," she says. "I don't want to get home and remember why I need them and not have them."

I shrug. "Okay."

I push the shopping cart as my mother walks ahead of it, picking up different vegetables, deciding she doesn't want them, and putting them down again.

"So, where are you staying now?" she asks me, holding a green pepper up to her ear and shaking it.

"At Viva's." I'm surprised by the question. I'm pretty sure she's never asked it before.

"Oh, right," she says, nodding. "I think she told me that."

"You talked to Viva?"

"She calls me every now and then," she says, "to check on me."

I think maybe my mother is confused. She sometimes mixes up the present with the past. "She calls you every now and then?" I ask. *"Currently?"*

"Yes," she says, putting the green pepper back and picking up a bunch of asparagus. "I spoke to her last Sunday. I remember because she offered to drive me to church. She told me you stay over there when you're in town."

Hmm.

"Did you know she's a man?" my mother asks. "Slade just told me."

I frown. "She's not a man, Mom. She's a trans woman. And yes, of course I know. We've all known for like twenty years."

My mother looks at me, confused. "I knew?"

"Yes. You heard us talking about prom."

"When?"

"Like 2003."

She stares at me for a few seconds, then narrows her eyes. "Are you messing with me?"

"I'm not messing with you."

She frowns.

I think about Viva, how awful that whole situation was for her then, and how terrible it would be for her to have to go through it all again all these years later, because my mother can't remember any of it, including the part where she got over it.

"You were totally okay with it, too," I say.

"No, I wasn't." Then, sounding unsure, "Was I?"

"You were," I say. "We couldn't believe it, either. But you were really open-minded. Way ahead of your time. We were all super impressed."

"Oh," she says, slowly nodding, as if she's starting to remember now, as if it's all coming back to her, how ahead of her time and open-minded she was. "That does sound like me."

Mmm-hmm. Totes.

She puts down the asparagus and I follow her into the next aisle.

"What kind of bread do you want?"

"I don't need bread," she says.

"Are you sure? It's a staple."

"No," she says. "I don't remember that being on the list."

"That doesn't mean it *wasn't* on the list. And even if it wasn't, it's still a pretty safe bet you'll eat it, right?"

But she's already walking past the bread. At the other end of the aisle, she picks up a bottle of fish sauce and puts it in the cart.

I start to argue but then I realize there's no point. This is just how my mother's brain works now.

"Where's Slade?" she asks all of a sudden.

"At his girlfriend's. That's what you told me."

"Oh, right," she says. "I'm sorry. I forget things sometimes. Ever since I fell and hit my head last year."

"I know, Mom."

"Pop-Tarts!" she says. "That was on the list. Slade likes them for breakfast."

We spend a couple of minutes looking for the Pop-Tarts and finally find them in the cereal aisle. My mother grabs eight boxes and dumps them into the cart.

"Speaking of Viva, when are *you* going to find somebody to marry?" she asks, as if we were just now talking about Viva and her marriage, which we weren't.

"I'm mostly a lesbian," I say. "Did you forget?"

"No, I didn't forget," she says, incredulous, as if she's never forgotten anything in her life, as if her mind is a motherfucking steel trap. "Did *you* forget lesbians can get married now? You didn't fall and hit your head, too, did you?" She laughs.

"No, Mom."

"You can thank Obama for that," she says, nodding thoughtfully.

Okay, this is weird. Seriously. My mother has *never* voluntarily engaged in a conversation involving my queerness. She accepted it a long time ago, in the way you accept something you know you can't change, but it's always been a Thing We Don't Talk About Directly. Now here she is telling me lesbians can get married like it's the most ordinary of discussions, like what's on sale at Target.

"Well, then?" she asks, looking quite seriously at me.

"I'm . . . not looking for anybody to marry."

"Don't you still want a family? Children?" she asks, adding two more boxes of Pop-Tarts to the cart, bringing the total—in case you're bad at math—to TEN. "I need some grandbabies. I thought Slade was going to give me some but . . ." She shrugs.

Now that I think about it, it's actually kind of crazy that Slade doesn't have any kids. He's not exactly a responsible dude. I really can't see him rushing out for condoms in the middle of the night. Or paying for some unfortunate girl's abortion.

"I've never wanted kids," I tell my mother.

"You wanted four," she says.

"That must've been Slade. *I* decided I didn't want kids when Penny Pee-Pee peed on me."

She looks at me very seriously again. "It wasn't Slade. It was you. You wanted four girls. You even had names picked out. You were going to call one of them Grace, after Grace Jones."

Holy.

Shit.

She's right. There *was* a time when I wanted kids, when I was about sixteen. I spent an entire year or so obsessed with it, picking out names for each child, imagining the family activities we'd do together, the cookouts and birthday parties, the school plays I'd attend. I fantasized about how I'd drop them all off and pick them all up from school in our green minivan with its SUPERMOM bumper sticker. I even cut out pictures, from magazines and catalogs, of the few child models who had enough melanin to pass for my children-to-be, and pasted them into a Trapper Keeper labeled "My Future" that also had pictures of fancy houses I cut out of celebrity magazines. I'm not sure exactly when I stopped having those fantasies. But I did.

"I forgot all about that."

"You only remember what you want to," my mother replies. "You forget whatever doesn't fit your agenda."

"I don't have an *agenda*. What does that even mean?"

"Everyone has an agenda," she says. "I always thought Grace was a pretty name, though. I had a great-aunt Grace on my father's side. I think? Who knows?" Then she laughs, shaking her head, like an old woman who forgets things in a way that's funny, and not like a not-so-old woman who forgets things in a way that's tragic.

"I think I'm done," she says.

I look down into the cart. "Garlic scapes, ten boxes of Pop-Tarts, and a bottle of fish sauce? That's your groceries, Mom?"

She frowns. "That doesn't seem right, does it?"

"Why don't you just let me get your food? I think I have a good sense of what you eat."

"Maybe we should wait and see what Slade says."

"Slade isn't the only person capable of buying groceries."

"I know."

It doesn't seem like she knows!

Feeling my patience disintegrating, I take out my phone and pretend to check it. "Slade just texted me back," I lie. "He sent me a grocery list."

"Oh, good," she says.

I spend the next twenty minutes filling the cart with the groceries I know she needs.

WHEN WE GET BACK TO her house, my mother takes her seat in front of the television. "You wanna watch Ellen? I think she had Denzel on."

"You go ahead," I tell her. "I'll put your groceries away."

When I'm done, I consider cleaning up the dirty dishes in the kitchen sink, some of them crusted with days-old food, and then possibly tackling the mess of dirty plates and mugs and soda cans in the living room, and maybe even vacuuming. But, honestly, that's more work than I want to do. So, instead, I just wash the dishes and put the soda cans in a paper bag and leave the rest of it.

"I have to get going, Mom," I say, putting on my jacket.

"You sure you don't want to stay and say hello to your brother when he gets home?"

"I have a thing with Viva."

"Alright, baby," she says.

I grab the bag of recycling and move toward the door.

"Tasha!" my mother says all of a sudden.

I turn to look at her. "What?"

"That was another name you were going to give one of your daughters," she says. "After your friend Tasha. Remember her?"

Hmm, lemme think. Yeah, vaguely.

20

THE NEXT DAY, FRIDAY, I SPEND MUCH OF THE MORNING IN A VIR-
tual meeting with Toni. Our Cuba trip is halfway done, which means
there's about eight weeks left before I'm scheduled to lead the trip to
Bali.

"My flight to Ngurah Rai lands on the twentieth," I tell her, from
my perch in Viva's courtyard. I've taken to working out here sometimes, now that it's warm and sunny most days.

"Are you excited?" Toni asks me.

I'm not sure how to answer. On one hand, all this time with Vicky
has been great. On the other hand, there's a heaviness to Philly, a
weight made up of memories, good and bad, that feels unmanageable,
volatile, liable to overwhelm me at any moment.

"Yeah," I tell Toni. "I'm excited for the arts festival. I haven't been
there in a few years."

THIS NIGHT, VIVA INVITES ME to Floetic, a club and live music spot
downtown, for an exclusive twenty-fifth-anniversary party that she's managed to finagle tickets to. I haven't been to a club in probably ten years

and I don't necessarily think that needs to change. But I've been turning over what she said about nostalgia, about needing more of it in my life. Which: maybe. I'm willing to consider it, at least. And Floetic is part of our shared history. We used to go there when we were teenagers. So, I say okay, I'll go, but just for a couple of drinks. I dress myself in proper aggressive femme club attire—black V-neck, black leather skinny pants, black boots, and gold hoop earrings—and submit to a little nostalgia.

Traffic is terrible. We should've taken the el. Instead, we're in Viva's tiny car, creeping down Chestnut Street at an absurdly slow pace. It's warm out, almost summery, and the night air kisses my bare arms through the rolled-down windows. I may not like Philly any other time, but I love it on a Friday night in early summer, when the lights of Center City beckon revelers from every neighborhood and, from Old City to the Gayborhood to Rittenhouse Square, restaurants and bars and sidewalks vibrate with people who are in the best moods they've been in since last summer ended. I swear, I hear raucous laughter rising into the air six or seven times on the way to the club and soon I start to feel in a pretty good mood myself.

When we get to Floetic, there's a big guy at the door handing out party hats with glittery twenty-fives on them.

"There's no way I'm wearing this," I tell Viva, who's already putting hers on.

It's still early enough that the place isn't super packed yet. Everyone's moving their hips, looking halfway to buzzed and satisfied with life, as a singer sways from side to side onstage, delivering an impressive cover of the Roots' "You Got Me."

"Naima's in traffic," Viva tells me, scrolling her phone. "Let's get a drink."

I get the attention of one of the bartenders, a Persian-looking woman with thick, curly hair and large, dark eyes. She comes over smiling, saying, "What can I get you, cutie?" Which, first of all: What am I, seven? Also: I'm not dumb enough to take a compliment from a bartender seriously, even if I haven't had sex in six months.

The last time someone touched my vagina was in Mozambique. A friend who was hosting me there invited some of her friends over for a cocktail gathering and one of those people, a tall, thin librarian, made eyes at me across the coffee table for hours before finally approaching me on my way back from the bathroom and whispering, "Una macho mazuri." She smelled like cocoa butter and clove cigarettes. The day after our tryst, she called me, but I made excuses. The fucking had been nice but, during a quiet moment, I had sensed in her a need for intimacy beyond sex that I already knew I couldn't meet.

"Knob, please," I say to the bartender. "Neat. And a White Russian for my homie."

Not too far from the stage, there's one empty table. We snag it. The singer, who is tall and rail thin and dressed all in green, reminding me of an asparagus stalk, has finished her Roots cover and is now belting out an early-in-the-evening-style soul number, probably something she wrote herself because I haven't heard it before. It's a little heavy on the *ooo-ooo*s and *oh bay-bee*s but, all in all, it's pretty good.

I sip my bourbon and look around at the crowd. Back in the nineties, Floetic was the jawn where all the cool kids wanted to go, because the live music was the best in the city. Not only was the stage graced by many of the biggest acts in hip-hop and neo-soul, but the local talent featured was often even better than the big names. We came here a lot over the courses of our fifteenth and sixteenth summers. Our first time, I remember showing the front door dude my cousin's ID with shaky hands. He barely looked at it before taking my fifteen dollars and waving me in, behind Viva and Tasha and some of our other friends who'd finagled IDs from their older siblings or cousins, too. Back then, as now, the club was unique in that all sorts of Black people showed up and most were welcome, including baby dykes and gays like us. I remember Tasha putting her arm around my shoulders. "Why don't we come here every weekend?"

"We don't have enough money," I reminded her.

"Oh shit. Yeah. You right."

Applause plunks me back in the present as the rail-thin singer is ending one song and starting another. These days, Floetic is less the jawn where all the cool kids want to go and more the jawn where the cool kids who got pregnant there in the nineties go on date nights now that their kids are in college. The music is still the same old-school hip-hop and neo-soul from back then, with some jazz, reggae, blues, and soul to round it out, and the crowd is loving it, as the singer's band follows the soul number with a bluesy arrangement.

Viva and I sip our drinks and talk about the old days. About seeing De La Soul and Tony Rich and J Kelly Biz on this very stage.

"Remember we snuck backstage for Blackstreet?" she asks. "What was that, ninety-five?"

"Ninety-six. I remember because Teddy Riley smiled at me and asked me how old I was. When I said I was sixteen, he walked away without another word. Which I guess is a point in his favor?"

Naima arrives with a few of her other friends in tow, women I haven't seen since high school, who, even then, I barely talked to, and who I definitely don't want to talk to now. One of them, Tamika, a light-skinned jawn with a questionable blond weave, asks Viva if she went to our high school, too.

"Yes," Viva says. "Class of ninety-eight."

Tamika shakes her head. "I can't believe I don't remember you. You're so pretty, I feel like I would remember."

"I looked different then," Viva says. She's only out in queer community, and to family and close friends, and I can tell she's uncomfortable.

"I like your hair," I say to Tamika. I don't, but it's something to say.

Tamika smiles, flips the weave over her shoulder. "It's *just* like Beyoncé in *Homecoming*, right?"

Mmm. Yeah. Okay.

What follows is ten minutes of Tamika talking to me about her hair: where she gets it done, which of the stylists she likes best. I don't catch half of what she says because . . . well, because I'm not really listening. But looking directly at her seems to pass for listening well enough. When she finally stops talking to go order more drinks, I turn to Viva and whisper, "It's *just* like Beyoncé in *Homecoming*. Right?"

She laughs so hard that tears gather at the corners of her eyes.

The skinny singer has just begun to sing one of my favorite songs: "Trust In Me." The slow Etta James arrangement, which is by far the best arrangement of the song. The singer's voice is low and sweet. I settle back in my chair and sip my drink.

The song reminds me of London, where I studied during my junior year of college. It was my first time abroad. I was twenty-one and I'd decided beforehand that I would come out there, in this new, exciting place where no one knew me, where my gayness wouldn't have to compete with whatever ideas anyone already held about my sexuality because no one held any at all. There, I could be queer from the start, and I was. The music I chose to be the soundtrack of my queer semester abroad included Etta's iconic *At Last!* I'd listen to it almost every day on my tube ride from my homestay in Wimbledon to class at King's College. Now, whenever I hear "Trust In Me," or any of the songs from that album, I remember my first lesbian lovers, the first Caravaggio I ever saw in real life, and my first time feeling truly, deeply out of place. I returned to Philadelphia the summer after that semester and felt so disappointed to be back after the excitements of London. But at the same time, I was surprised by how comforting the familiarity of my city was, how suddenly, unexpectedly at home I felt, a Philly girl back in Philly.

"*Why don't you trust in me?*" the singer croons, the same way Philly did that summer, with its soft pretzels and familiar twangs and Black people saying hello to one another on the street. "*Oh and love, love will see us through . . .*"

When the song ends, a dude in a Kangol takes the stage to thank us all for a quarter-century of love and support. Then he introduces Schoolly D. The crowd goes crazy.

For their twenty-fifth, Floetic has landed some of the Philly-born icons of old-school hip-hop and neo-soul, class of 1994 through 2000. Besides Schoolly, Bahamadia is in the house. Black Thought. Even North Philly's own Jill Scott comes through for a minute. There are whispers about a surprise Will Smith appearance, but it seems far-fetched and doesn't pan out. Which is fine by me because by the time Jilly from Philly is done giving us our lives, I'm ready for bed. My obligations to nostalgia well-fulfilled, Viva releases me.

I'm ordering a Lyft and heading for the exit when I feel a hand on my arm and hear someone call my name, and when I turn around, Faye is there.

"Oh, hey. What are you doing here? Date night with Nick or something?" I look around for him, trying not to puke at the idea.

"I'm here with friends," she says loudly over the music. "Well, I *was*. I'm actually heading out. You?"

"Same."

"Need a ride?" she asks.

"I can just take a Lyft," I say, holding up my phone.

She peers at me, shakes her head. "Why would you do that when I'm standing right here offering you a ride?"

Because I've had two bourbons and I'm feeling a teensy bit goofy and I don't like feeling a teensy bit goofy in the company of women I want to sleep with. I like playing it cool around women I want to sleep with, or as cool as it is possible for me to play it, which actually isn't very cool, but is cooler than I am after two bourbons.

"Let me give you a ride," Faye says. "We're going the same way."

"Okay," I say, closing the app and putting the phone in my pocket. "Yeah. Thanks."

We make our way together through the growing crowd, toward the door. There are enough people in the club now that it's hard not getting separated as we move through them, so I reach out and take Faye's hand. It's not a move, I swear. It's what I've always done with my friends, to keep from losing one another in a swarm of bodies. I do it almost unconsciously, but once Faye's hand is in mine, it occurs to me that she might not like it. I mean, we're cool now I guess, but maybe not *that* cool. And I don't want her to think I'm trying something. So, half a second after I take her hand, I let it go, pretending to accidentally drop it when some dude pushes past us. A few seconds after that, I feel fingertips grazing my palm and I realize she's reaching for my hand again. I let her grab it. We weave through the crowd, fingers intertwined.

As we're passing the bar, the large, light-skinned brother in the Kangol, who was onstage thanking us earlier, reaches out, touches Faye's arm, and says, "Lucas! You came!"

Faye stops and smiles at him. "Hey, Win."

"Damn, girl," he says, getting up from his barstool. "How long has it been since I've seen you?"

"Seventy-five years," she says, letting go of my hand and hugging him. "Maybe eighty."

"Feels like it," he replies. "Especially in my knees."

Faye laughs and I notice how different it sounds from the times I've heard it: It's bigger and louder; the kind of laugh we laugh with people who knew us when we were young. It makes me smile when I hear it.

The large man notices me smiling and asks, "This your lady?"

"This is my friend Skye," Faye says. "Skye, this is Winston. He used to be a DJ here back in the day. He's one of the owners now."

Winston and I exchange "nice to meet yous." Then he says, "I was just thinking about you a couple weeks ago, Lucas. J Kelly Biz was up in here."

"I haven't seen Kelly in years," Faye says.

"You know J Kelly Biz?" I ask her.

J Kelly Biz was a rapper on the Philly scene back in the nineties, one of only a few women to garner any real respect in the local rap game.

"Yes," Faye says.

I want to ask how but she's already turning back to Winston.

"How is Kelly?" she asks.

"Good," he says. "Better than good, according to the crowd."

"She performed?"

"Oh, yes. Two jawns off *Big Biz*, from ninety-five. Took us all way, way back."

"I would've loved to see that."

"I woulda loved to see *you* up there," says Winston.

Faye shakes her head. "You know I don't rap anymore, Win."

Hold up. "You don't rap *anymore*?" I ask. "Meaning you . . . rapped at one time?"

Winston gives me a look like maybe he thinks I'm slow or something. "You don't know who you kicking it with?"

I look from him to Faye and back. I shrug.

"This is MC Faye Malice," he says.

Which: WHUT? MC Faye Malice? The most decent girl in the game? The illest rapper in the two-one-five? Nigga, is you drunk?

"No, it isn't," I say, laughing a little because who could even make such a ridiculous mistake?

Winston smiles at Faye and she smiles back at him. I peer at her and think back to 1994, when I was fourteen and my whole neighborhood was hype because "Rock This Jawn," by West Philly's own MC Faye Malice, was the hit song of the summer. Power 99 played it eleventy-thousand times a day. Every house party bumped it. Tasha and I dubbed it off the radio onto a cassette tape and played it nearly nonstop for like a month, until we couldn't stand the sound of it anymore, which is what you do with a record that slaps that hard. Only once did we ever see the face of MC Faye Malice—for about three seconds in a two-minute news story about the local music scene. I remember being surprised because she was so young. She still had braces on her teeth and I'd never seen a rapper with braces before. I don't remember anything else about her face, but still. There's no way *that* Faye is *this* Faye.

"Why are you lying to me like this?"

"I'm not lying," Winston says, chuckling. "This dime right here was once one of the baddest female MCs outta Philly—"

"Don't call me a dime," Faye says. "And since when are we qualifying it?"

"You right," he says. "I stand corrected. One of the baddest MCs outta Philly period. End of sentence."

"Wait," I say, because what the hell is even happening right now? "You're *really* MC Faye Malice?"

"Yes."

"Woulda been *the* best, probably," Winston continues. "If you hadn't quit so early."

"Okay, now you're taking it a bit far," says Faye.

"No, I'm not. I was there. I remember every bar you spit, girl. Your shit was fire." He looks over at the stage, where Jaguar Wright is singing. "Why don't you get up there?" he asks. "I can squeeze you in right after Jag."

"That's cute," Faye says.

"I'm serious. If Kelly killed, I *know* you'll kill."

"I won't kill. Because I'm not getting up there."

"One song," he says.

"Zero songs. Seriously, Win. I haven't been on a stage in twenty years. I don't even remember how to rhyme."

"Now I know you're lying," he says. "You *never* forget how to rhyme."

"You should do it," I tell her. Because I want to see this more than I have ever wanted to see anything in the history of my life.

"You gotta do it," Winston says.

Faye looks from him to me and smiles. "No."

Damn it!

"But it's nice seeing you, Winston."

Defeated, he opens his arms. "It's good seeing you, Lucas. Thanks for coming out." They hug goodbye.

As we head for the exit once more, the soulful sounds of Jaguar Wright are filling up the place, but all I hear is the hook off "Rock This Jawn," playing over and over in my head, as MC Faye Malice reaches for my hand again.

21

WE DON'T TALK MUCH ON THE RIDE BACK TO WEST PHILLY. THERE'S
something in the air. I might call it sexual tension, but that's maybe
just me. Faye seems far away, in her own head, even when she's asking
me which performance I liked best. For long stretches, we say nothing
at all. But it's not awkward silence this time. It's just silence. And it's
comforting. It's hard to find people you can be silent with.

When we're a few blocks from the B and B, Faye asks, "Are you
ready to go home?"

I look at her. "Do you have another idea?"

"I feel like being outside," she says. "Do you want to sit on my
porch—"

"Yes."

WHEN WE GET TO FAYE'S house, I have to pee, so we go inside. The
TV is on in the living room. Vicky is at a sleepover at Jaz's, so it must
be Nick. Sure enough, he comes out of the kitchen, eating a sandwich
and looking infuriatingly comfortable in a T-shirt and boxers. "Hey,

Skye," he says, smiling with a mouth full of pb and j. "I didn't know you were coming over. Good to see you."

I somehow resist the overwhelming urge to punch him in the dick.

When I get back from the bathroom, he's still there. No bears broke in and mauled him to death while I was pissing, unfortunately.

Faye is in the kitchen. I join her there. "Do you want a drink?" she asks.

Listen: I pretty much always want a drink. Much more than that, I want an excuse to spend more time with her, so I can figure out how to get her to hold my hand again. But the presence of Nick and his penis feels disruptive of the energy that moved between us at the club and in the car, and I'm not sure if we can get it back tonight, which makes me want to quit while I'm ahead. Also, I don't want to feel like I'm in a contest with Nick for Faye's time. Competing with men for the attention of women is not how I do life, y'all.

"I'm pretty tired," I tell her. "I think maybe I should just go to bed."

She looks disappointed. "Are you sure?"

NO, I AM NOT SURE.

"One really small drink," I say. "And then I should go."

She pours me a drink that isn't all that small, then grabs a bottle of Belgian beer from the fridge for herself.

"I thought you don't like the taste of alcohol."

She shrugs. "My friend Angie left this here. I'm in the mood."

We head for the porch.

"You coming to bed soon?" Nick asks Faye from his seat on the couch.

She nods. "In a bit."

"I'll be there," he says with a little smile.

I already regret not punching him in the dick.

*   *   *

THERE'S A NICE SET OF porch furniture, including a rocker and a chaise, but Faye bypasses all of that and takes a seat on the front steps. Which is so Philly, I can't even deal. Some people describe this city as having "porch culture" but what it really has is "step culture." My adolescence was chock full of neglected chaise lounges, my friends and I always preferring to perch on steps or stoops, which offered a better view of the block and whatever was happening on it that day.

I sit down beside Faye and sip my bourbon while she sips her beer and we both scan the goings-on around us. The block is pretty popping tonight, music wafting toward us from several different directions—some hip-hop, some R&B, and even, from farther down, some jazz. I can smell weed smoke coming from a porch a few houses up and hear kids who should definitely be in bed already screaming for no good reason from a porch a few houses down.

Faye takes off her shoes and places them neatly on the porch. I try to make out the color of her toes in the dark, but I can't. I watch her place her feet flat on the concrete step below and wiggle her toes in the warmish night air.

In the distance, sirens wail. When they go silent, their sound is replaced by the laughter of a group of girls walking by. One of them smiles at us. It seems almost like a summer night, even though it's only May.

"It feels a little like summer tonight," Faye says.

I nod. "I was just thinking that."

It's been a very long time since I sat on a porch and listened to—and watched and smelled—Philly at night. The familiarity of it is almost overwhelming, in the way nostalgia can be. I think again about Tasha and that summer when we were fourteen, when our entire world was somebody's front steps and the secrets we whispered to each other across them.

"Are you okay?" Faye asks me.

I come out of my head to find her watching me, a look of curiosity on her face.

"I was just thinking how crazy it is that you're MC Faye Malice. I can't believe Vicky didn't tell me."

"Vicky doesn't know. I swore her parents to secrecy."

"Why?"

She takes a long moment to think about it, then says, "That time in my life wasn't all good. Rhyming was fun. Being Faye Malice was fun. But other things were very hard. For a while, I put it all away. The bad, and the good along with it. You know what I mean?"

This is normally the point in a conversation where I'd start to get uncomfortable. We're veering into "difficult human feelings" territory and y'all know that's not my jam. But for some reason, I don't get awkward. Instead, I think about what my mother said the other day: *You only remember what you want to.* And I think maybe I do know what Faye means.

"Is that why you didn't get onstage tonight?"

"No," she says. "I didn't get onstage because if I'd bombed, it would've gone viral and my students never would've let me hear the end of it."

"What if you hadn't bombed?"

She smiles. "I guess we'll never know," she says, and takes another sip of beer.

"You can rap for me if you want," I tell her. "I promise to love every moment of it."

She laughs. It's a lovely laugh but it's not the laugh she laughed with Winston, and I find myself wishing it was, wishing I knew her when she was MC Faye Malice, and long before then, and after then, too.

"Why'd you stop rapping?"

"I didn't have time for it once I started college and had a full class load and a job."

"Do you miss it? Being onstage? Dropping the dopest of the dope rhymes?"

"Oh, God."

"Being the illest rapper in the two-one-five?"

"Stop."

"I'm not making fun of you!" I tell her. "I swear! I loved those albums!"

She eyes me like she's trying to decide if she believes me or not. Then she nods and says, "Sometimes I miss it. Mostly when I accidentally turn to the BET Awards and see today's rappers running around onstage, mumbling nonsensically."

"Right? Who even *are* those people?"

She laughs and sips her beer and is quiet for a few moments. Then she says, "What I really miss, more than rhyming, is just . . . being young in Philly. On a night like tonight, when I was seventeen or eighteen, I'd have been with my friends on South Street, probably high, talking to guys who were too old for me, never imagining that one day I'd be forty-two. You just never conceive that there will come a time when you're not young anymore, when your whole life won't be in front of you. You know?"

I nod and sip my drink. "I never hung out on South Street, though."

"Never?" she asks, like that's unheard of.

"Never felt cool enough to go there."

"So, where would you have been?" she asks. "On a warm Friday at"—she checks her phone—"eleven-thirty, when you were seventeen?"

"Probably on my friend Tasha's front steps. Drinking her mom's liquor mixed with blue raspberry Kool-Aid, out of a red Solo cup. Talking about gay shit, but quietly, so nobody would hear us. While *The Score* played in the background."

"That is *very* specific."

I laugh. I don't tell her how much I've been thinking about that time in my life lately.

"I envy you having gay friends at that age. I probably would have gotten into less trouble if I had."

"You think gay friends are *less* trouble?"

"I just mean . . . I think some of the trouble I got into was because I was trying to resist 'gay shit,'" she says. "Queer feelings."

"What kind of trouble are we talking about?"

"Drugs. Sex with boys," she says, "and its many consequences."

"I hardly did drugs," I tell her. "Not that I was morally opposed or anything. My friends just weren't cool enough to know any drug dealers. We only got weed when we could talk someone's older sibling into getting it for us or steal it from their room when they weren't paying attention. Which wasn't that often."

"Sex?" she asks me.

I resist the urge to say something corny like, *Yes, please.* "I never got laid in high school."

"What about your gay friends?" she asks. "You weren't . . . ?"

"Ugh. No. I knew Tasha since first grade. She was like a sister to me, except with better parents. The couple of times we tried to make out, it felt wrong on a deep, deep level. I did fool around with a couple of girls junior and senior year, but it was mostly above the waist."

"Okay," Faye says. "Boys must have tried below the waist, though."

I sip my bourbon and nod. "They always do. But none of the boys I knew were sophisticated enough to balance out my awkwardness to the point that actual sex was possible. It was a lot of fumbling and early ejaculations. Really early. Like, before I even took my shirt off. Tyrone Edmonds came in his pants while offering me a can of grape soda. What even is that?"

She laughs.

"It's funny now. It wasn't then. I wanted to be having sex so badly," I say, sighing. "I envy you."

"No one envies a pregnant teenager."

"Okay," I say. "Yeah. I don't envy that part. That sounds hard. But I think sex—not its consequences, but the act itself—can only ever be a temporary regret. Do you think there are ninety-year-old ladies on their deathbeds thinking, *Wow I shouldn't have got laid so many times*?

Probably not. In fact, I'd guess most of them are like, *Damn, I really shoulda had more orgasms.*" I say that last part in my best ninety-year-old-woman voice.

Faye makes a sound like "hmmm," like she's thinking about that. Then she nods slowly and says, "You might be onto something."

"Oh, I definitely am."

"I wish you'd been around when I was being called a ho by my social worker," she says.

"So do I."

She looks at me like she did in the record store that day, with that same intense gaze. I watch her eyes travel from my eyes down my face to my lips and linger there. I can think of no reason why a woman would stare at another woman's lips with this level of interest other than that she wants to be kissed. So, I kiss her.

The moment our lips touch, a sound escapes her. It's part moan, part sigh. All yes. Her mouth opens. Her eyes close. She leans her body into mine. All of this I take as a sign that I made the exact right decision and should keep going, which I do, eagerly. I put my left hand on her left thigh, for leverage, and also because I really want to touch her thighs, and I wrap my other arm around her waist and pull her closer. She slips her tongue into my mouth. She tastes like fancy Belgian beer in all the right ways. We kiss for what somehow feels like both a long time and no time at all; it's maybe half a minute. And then I feel Faye's hands on my shoulders, pushing me away.

"Stop."

"Okay," I say, leaning away from her, breathless. "Why?"

"I'm getting really turned on."

Which, not gonna lie, doesn't make me want to stop.

"That's bad?"

"It is when I'm in a monogamous relationship with someone other than the person currently making me wet."

Again: DOESN'T MAKE ME WANT TO STOP.

She stands up, adjusting her blouse, which has become a little disheveled in the heaviness of our making out. She looks suddenly worried and tense. I consider telling her that she's engaged to a cheater and that being faithful to him is the last thing she needs to concern herself with. But something tells me that, of all the wrong moments to do that, this is the wrongest. For a lot of reasons, one being that even if knowing the truth makes her more likely to let me see her naked, it wouldn't be purely out of desire for me. It would be tainted with anger at Nick. And fuck that. If I ever do get the pleasure of Faye's mouth on my most sensitive regions, I don't want Nick to have anything to do with it.

Suddenly, out of nowhere, a question occurs to me: "Do you love Nick?" I ask Faye.

"That's irrelevant."

OH, IS IT?

"It seems pretty relevant to me."

"Of course I do."

This answer catches me completely off guard. Because, honestly, it's never before occurred to me that she might. I don't know why. Maybe because she's smart and sexy and interesting and he's a liar pretending to be a good guy.

"If you love Nick, why'd you kiss me?"

"My kissing or not kissing you has nothing to do with Nick," she says. "Besides, you kissed me."

"You kissed me back!"

"Okay," she says, holding her hands out, palms down, like she's trying to push down the rising tension levels. "You're right, Skye."

I know I'm right!

"I'm attracted to you," she says.

I'M LISTENING.

"I thought I could ignore it. I tried to. But then when you started coming over so much . . ." Her voice trails off. She shakes her head, sighs. "I don't know. I guess I thought if we became friends I could somehow . . . manage my attraction to you."

"How's that going?"

"It was going okay until just now," she says, sounding almost defeated, like kissing me was a failure. Which I sort of get, considering the situation. But also: Wow, that doesn't feel good at all.

"Skye," she says quietly, gently, "I like that you're here. I like it for Vicky. And for myself. I like our friendship. I don't want one kiss to complicate all of that. It has to be platonic between us."

I think about São Paulo. And Paris. And Atlanta. And Shanghai. And all of the places this wouldn't be happening right now.

"Because of our friendship?" I ask. "Because of Vicky? Or because of Nick?"

She doesn't answer, just shakes her head.

Here's the thing: She's right. If I know anything about sex and romance, it's that they complicate *everything*. I have avoided meaningful romantic relationships for a decade because they're just so goddamn extra. Who wants to have to deal with all of those feelings? Not this girl. So, I get it. It's a lot. It's too much to manage, especially when there's also a possessive kid and a dead sister you didn't like and a fiancé who's cheating on you but you don't even know that yet. It's emotionally exhausting to think about! And also: I still want her.

"It's late," Faye says. "I should go to bed."

I nod and start down the steps.

"I can take you home," she says.

I want that. I want to get in her silver SUV and spend the two minutes it'll take to get to the B and B with her. But I know that when we get there, I'll just want her to stay. And if, by some unforeseen turn of events, she does stay, and we talk and make out until morning, I still won't want her to leave. And even if she doesn't leave right then, even if I can talk her into eating breakfast with me first, she'll still have to go at some point, to make Vicky's breakfast or suck Nick's dick or whatever. What I'm saying is: I can't make her want me by just drawing this moment out as long as I can. So I tell her, "It's okay, it's only six blocks." And I fucking walk.

22

"IF YOU HAD TO DIE FROM AN ANIMAL ATTACK," VICKY ASKS ME, "BUT you got to choose what kind of animal, which animal would you choose?"

It's around eleven the morning after I kissed Faye. I got up "early" to kick it with Vicky for a bit before she's dragged off to Bala Cynwyd for the rest of the weekend. We just finished buying lipglosses and Tastykakes at the corner store. On our way back, Miss Vena gave us some tomato starts to give to Faye, and Vicky and I each carry one as we walk back to her house.

"Hippo," I tell the kid, adjusting one of the plants in the crook of my elbow.

She stops walking and looks up at me. "Why?"

"Well, hippos don't have claws. So there wouldn't be any tearing of flesh. It'd probably just trample me. It's super heavy and has really big feet, so it would be over in, what? One or two stomps? That's pretty quick. I'd rather not suffer. Also, 'she was killed by a hippo' is a really cool obit ending. Amirite?"

She stares at me for a few seconds, wide-eyed, then says, "That's the best answer EVER!"

Her phone plays a tune and she looks at it and frowns. "It's my stupid dad. He's on his way."

Kenny was supposed to pick Vicky up yesterday, but he called last minute and said he couldn't because he had a work thing out in Cherry Hill, and that he was sending Charlotte in his stead. Vicky refused, said she wouldn't go with Charlotte, and Kenny relented, agreeing to pick her up today instead, although Vicky's preferred pickup day was never.

We get there before Kenny and Charlotte. Faye's not home, which, on a Saturday, usually means she's out with Nick or Angie of the Belgian beer. I'm relieved not to have to face her yet. After I got back to my room and rubbed one out, I realized kissing Faye was a mistake. I'm in Philly for Vicky, not for romance. I need to stay focused.

"You want a snack?" Vicky asks me, after we put the tomato plants by the back door.

"Shouldn't you be packing?"

She shrugs.

When Kenny's beamer pulls up out front twenty minutes later, we're on the sofa eating Butterscotch Krimpets and, once again, Vicky doesn't move a muscle to respond to the honking. When the bell finally rings, she rolls her eyes and trudges miserably to the door.

Kenny and Charlotte are all matchy again, in sea-green golf shirts and aviator sunglasses. Kenny is already on his phone and barely looks up to say hello. Charlotte is bouncy and cheerful. "Good morning, ladies," she says. "I brought flowers from our garden." She holds a vase filled with spring blossoms out to Vicky, who just stares at them.

"What am I gonna do with these?"

"I thought you and Faye might enjoy them."

"Aunt Faye doesn't like flowers."

Which is a total lie. There are no less than three flower-filled vases in the house at this moment.

"No one doesn't like flowers, Victoria," Charlotte says.

Vicky shrugs and puts the vase on the coffee table.

"What's going on with your hair?" Charlotte asks, after eyeing the kid for a moment.

Vicky frowns. "What do you mean 'going on with' it?"

"I just mean, you have a different hairstyle every time we see you," she says. "What are these? Some sort of cornrolls?"

Corn*WHAT*?

"They're Bantu knots," the kid says.

Charlotte examines Vicky's hairdo at length, then says, "I kind of like it. It's quirky."

Vicky glares at Charlotte, then looks at her father. "Can you please tell your wife to stop giving me her racist opinions about my hair?"

Kenny doesn't even look up from his phone.

Charlotte looks confused, then exasperated. "I said I *like it*. It was a *compliment*. How is that racist?"

"You said you *kind of* like it," Vicky corrects her. "That's not a compliment. And it's *my* hair. I'm sick of having to hear what you think about it. You're not Black."

"Only Black people can have opinions about hairstyles?" Charlotte asks. "Isn't *that* rac—"

Skreech. Nope. Nuh-uh. "No," I say before she can get the word out. "It's really not."

The sound of my voice seems to get Kenny's attention. He looks up from his phone. When he sees all of our faces, he frowns. "What's wrong? What's happening?"

Charlotte is looking at me, and I think she's trying to decide if she wants to argue with me about this. I can almost hear the *I CAN'T BE RACIST, I'M MARRIED TO A BLACK MAN* on the tip of her tongue. But, finally, she sighs and says, "Fine. Sorry. Forget I said anything."

"Said anything about what?" Kenny asks.

This nigga. Ugh.

"About my hair," Vicky says. "She's always complaining about it. Ever since I chopped out that relaxer she made me get."

"*Made you?*" Charlotte asks, incredulous. "I seem to remember you saying you liked it because it made you look more like your mother."

"I never said that!"

"You did so!" She looks at her husband. "Didn't she, Kenneth?"

Kenny shrugs. "I don't know."

Charlotte looks like she wants to grab him and shake him hard. She turns back to Vicky. "I guess it's just easier to blame me for everything."

"I only blame you for stuff that's your fault."

"Nothing is ever *your* fault, is it, Victoria?" She shakes her head. "Your mother wouldn't be pleased with the way you've been acting lately."

Vicky turns as red as a Black girl can. "Don't talk about my mother," she says through clenched teeth.

I look at Kenny, like, *Are you really just going to stand there not saying shit?* He frowns, like, *Yeah, I was, but I guess I won't if you're going to look at me like that about it.*

"Let it go, Char," he says.

"She's the one who—"

"Jesus Christ, Charlotte. She's twelve. Just let it go, alright?"

Charlotte looks like she can't believe the words that are coming out of his mouth, which makes me think he probably never checks her ass. I think about my mother and how she never checked my father. Charlotte's nowhere near as bad as he was, but still. If you're not going to have your kid's back, maybe don't have a kid in the first place?

"Where's your stuff, Vicky?" Kenny asks.

"Upstairs."

"Upstairs, packed? Or not packed?"

"Not," Vicky says.

Charlotte throws her hands up in the air. "Great. That's just great. So, now we have to wait for her to pack? Again?"

"If you don't want to wait, just go to the car," Kenny suggests.

"Waiting in the car is still waiting, Kenneth!"

I follow Vicky upstairs to her room.

"Ugh!" she says, shutting the door loudly behind us. "I hate her so much!"

Honestly? I feel the teensiest bit bad for Charlotte. Yes, she's sort of terrible. We can all agree on that. But Vicky's maybe harder on her than is absolutely necessary. On the other hand: Our people have endured enslavement, Jim Crow, redlining, and police brutality, and Charlotte's people have not. So. She'll be aight.

Vicky opens her closet and pulls out the oversized backpack she always takes to Bala Cynwyd. She refuses to leave anything but the barest essentials at her father's house, even though she has her own room there, so she always has to haul everything else she needs back and forth. It seems like a huge hassle, but I guess whatever point she's making matters more to her than convenience.

"I swear to God," she says, opening the backpack, "I'm going to wait until no one's looking and trip her down the stairs."

I'm sure she doesn't mean it, but—not gonna lie—she sounds a teensy bit serious. I wait for her to say psych or something, but she doesn't. She just grabs her laptop and slips it into her bag.

"You're not really going to do that, right?" I ask.

She shrugs. "I'm just kidding." But she doesn't laugh.

So . . . this might be the moment in the After School Special when the viewer realizes there is a capital P problem. Because for all her talk about the helpfulness of therapy, this is the second time she's "joked" with a straight face about injuring her stepmother. Which: I get it. I really do. I've only been around Charlotte maybe an hour total and I've already fantasized at least half a dozen times about karate-chopping her in the neck. But still. I don't want Vicky to do anything crazy. Like, what if the kid just snaps one day and tosses a hairdryer into Charlotte's bubble bath, becoming one of those tween murderers they make bad TV movies about, thanks to a neglectful pseudo-parent who didn't take the signs seriously enough? I don't want to be that person! On the other hand, what if I go all Danny Tanner at the end of a *Full House* episode in which D.J. has done something irresponsible, cue up some "very important lesson" music, and end up coming off as a bummer for no reason, because Vicky really *was* just joking? I don't want to be that person, either! But, like . . . I have to say *something*, right?

I watch Vicky pack her things, nodding and agreeing while she calls Charlotte everything but her Christian name. Once she's all packed, she sits on the end of the bed with her arms folded. "I'm not going to go down for a few more minutes. Just to annoy them."

"Aight, cool," I say. "Um, listen, Vicky. About that whole tripping-Charlotte-down-the-stairs thing? I know you were just joking, but . . . is there something we should talk about?"

"Like what?"

OH, I DON'T KNOW, YOUR SEETHING ANGER, PERHAPS?

"I just want to make sure you're okay."

"With what?"

"Just . . . generally."

She looks like she's thinking about it. After a long moment, she says, "I'm as okay as I can be."

And, honestly, I don't know if that's good or bad.

We hear Faye's voice downstairs. I feel a flutter of nerves in my stomach.

"I guess we better go back down," Vicky says.

Faye is in the kitchen with Kenny and he's whispering something to her before we come in. When he sees us, he smiles. "Ready, baby girl?"

"No."

He frowns. "Charlotte's in the car. Let's hit it."

Vicky groans.

"Call me if you need anything, Vicky," Faye tells her.

"Same," I say.

Vicky trudges out, her father trailing behind.

When they're gone, Faye says, "I give it an hour before she calls one of us asking to be picked up."

"It sucks she has to go over there. She really hates it."

"I know," Faye says, sighing. "But Kenny's her father. There's nothing I can do about that."

We stand there in silence for a few seconds. It's not the comfortable silence of last night in the car. It's that awkward shit again. Finally, I'm like: "I better get going."

"Fun plans for the day?" she asks.

"Um, yeah," I say. "Super fun plans. With some cool friends of mine. You know how it is."

"Great," she says. "Well. Enjoy."

I start walking toward the door. I'm halfway there when I realize I want to stay. Yes, kissing Faye was a mistake. I would undo it if I could. But I wouldn't undo holding her hand as we moved through the club. I wouldn't undo sharing memories of being young in Philly. I don't want to go back to awkward! So, I decide to do something I rarely do: behave like a well-adjusted adult. I turn back to her. I say: "Actually, I don't have any fun plans. I was just gonna go back to my room and read magazines and maybe take a nap. I'd be willing to forego all that if you wanted to hang out and do platonic stuff."

She smiles. "Okay. Maybe you can help me with something?"

WE'RE SITTING IN THE BACKYARD, in the soil beside the little vegetable garden. The afternoon sun is warming the bare skin of our forearms and casting a glow in Faye's hair as we dig holes for the tomato plants that Vicky and I brought over from Miss Vena. I'm not dressed for gardening. My jeans are too tight, and they're getting really dirty from the knees down. But I barely notice, because Faye is telling me that Cynthia liked Charlotte, that they were "almost what you'd call friends."

"You're messing with me."

"I'm not."

"But why?"

"Cynthia had a higher tolerance for white lady nonsense," she says. "So, I think she was able to see and appreciate things about Charlotte that maybe you and I can't."

"For instance?"

"Charlotte is very outgoing. Very open to friendship. She's the kind of person who invites people to Thanksgiving dinner after meeting them only once, because she knows they don't have anywhere else to go. She's generous and welcoming and she really likes people. Cynthia appreciated that, for some reason, even though she wasn't very into people herself. Charlotte visited Cynthia a lot when she was sick. Much more than Kenny did."

I think about what Slade said, about how Cynthia only had one or two visitors near the end, and I start to doubt the accuracy of his intel.

"How'd you get Kenny to give you joint custody of Vicky?" I ask, suddenly realizing I've never asked her or Vicky that before.

"Blackmail."

I look up from the hole I'm digging. "I'm going to need you to say more."

She's quiet for a moment, her eyes thoughtful. I think she's trying to decide whether or not she really wants to tell me. I wasn't expecting the answer to be anything juicy, but now I'm thinking it might be.

"Just between us," she says. "You can't tell Vicky."

"Okay."

"It's kind of a long story."

"We already established I don't have anything else to do, right?"

She smiles. I watch her place a tomato plant in a deep hole and start covering the roots with soil. "Kenny had a huge crush on me when we were kids. He used to send me love notes in junior high. I always thought he was . . . well . . . how he is: dull. Even when he was thirteen, he was dull."

"I can see that."

"Cynthia and Kenny ended up at Carnegie Mellon at the same time and that's when they first got together. My sister liked boring men, so they were a perfect match."

"All men are boring," I interject.

"Maybe," says Faye, "when compared to women. Compared to one another, some men are less boring than others."

I want to ask her if she thinks Nick is less boring than other men. I don't, though.

"They broke up after college, and Cynthia married someone else. Then, after her divorce, she and Kenny got together again. And eventually got married. Over the years, I had reason to think Kenny's crush on me never went away."

"What reason?"

"He always found a way to seat himself next to me at gatherings. Sometimes I'd catch him gazing at me, when no one was paying attention. But he never said anything or did anything. And he did seem to love Cynthia. So, I ignored it." She smooths the soil around the tomato plant, pats it gently. "When my sister was sick, when she knew she wasn't going to beat the cancer, she told Kenny that she wanted me to have custody of Vicky. They'd been divorced for years by then and Kenny was already remarried. He works constantly and Cynthia realized that it wasn't a good idea to have Charlotte raising her child. She liked Charlotte, but not *that* much."

"That's a relief, at least."

She nods. "Right. But Kenny wouldn't agree. So, after Cynthia died, Vicky went to live with them. A few months later, I was at my apartment, wasting time on Facebook, when I saw an ad for one of those realtor websites. I clicked on it randomly, and ended up looking at houses for sale, for no other reason than to pass the time on a Sunday morning. That's when I saw this house and recognized the address. My mother and sister and I lived in this house for three years. It was the only time in our lives we had something that felt like stability. We had community when we were here. Safety. Consistency. For a while, anyway."

As she talks, I look back at the house and out at the yard and try to imagine her and Cynthia running around, screaming and laughing and feeling safe. I think about Cynthia at ten and eleven, when I knew her, how grown up she always acted, how independent. She made money babysitting some of the younger kids after camp and on weekends. I thought it was so cool to be paid to babysit, especially since I was almost the same age as her and still got baby*sat*. Now, I wonder if she wasn't *acting* grown up, if she was one of those kids who had to *be* grown up, for real, because being a kid wasn't an option. I think about myself at eleven, independent in the ways I had to be as an underprotected child, and I feel a connection to Cynthia again, and to Faye.

"So, you bought this house because of . . . nostalgia?"

"I guess that's one way of putting it," she says. "Unfortunately, nostalgia isn't a very sound financial consideration. You can't pay for updated plumbing or lead abatement with memories. But owning this house felt right then. And it still does most of the time."

"Because you're happy here?"

"Yes. I have Vicky and our little vegetable patch. I have Angie right up the street. I have plant sharing with Vena. A relatively short commute to work with students I like, for the most part."

I notice she doesn't mention Nick. I resist the urge to make it mean something.

"And now you, too," she adds, "just a few blocks away and willing to help me plant tomatoes." She smiles at me. I smile back. We sit there smiling at each other for what feels like a long moment and then she looks away, patting the dirt around an already-planted tomato vine that doesn't really need any more attention.

I think about Vicky and Faye in this house and, for a brief moment, I imagine myself here with them. Not just visiting. Living here, belonging with them. It's sort of a nice thought, at first, but then I feel this weird pain in my chest, like a stabbing, so I stop.

"So, what happened?" I ask Faye. "With Kenny?"

"Right. Kenny. Well, one evening, a couple of months after I moved in, Kenny came by. Vicky had left one of her textbooks here when she was sleeping over and he came to pick it up on his way home from work. I was looking for the textbook when I caught him gazing at me again, the way he always used to. This time he did not look away." She glances at me, and there's a look in her eyes.

"No," I say. "You didn't. Oh my God."

"I did."

"You *slept with Kenny*?"

"Yes."

"So you could blackmail him into giving you custody?"

"Not exactly," she says. "I mean, yes, it occurred to me that I could have sex with him and then threaten to tell his wife. That's mostly why I did it. But I'd also just broken up with Nick. It wasn't permanent, obviously, but I didn't know that then. And I was missing a certain kind of closeness."

"You were lonely."

"In a particular way, yes. And I've known Kenny since I was in seventh grade. He was familiar in a way that felt comforting at that moment. So." She shrugs. "I fucked him."

This is maybe the moment I start to fall in love with Faye. Because here is a woman who would smash the boringest nigga on earth, who happens to be the ex-husband of her dead sister, in order to blackmail him into giving her what she wants, which isn't money or a bigger house, but custody of her troubled adolescent niece, and it's so wrong and, at the same time, so perfectly right, that I almost can't even deal.

"So, then what happened? You threatened to tell Charlotte unless he shared custody of Vicky?"

"Yes."

"And he gave in?"

"Yes. But by that time Vicky had been living with them for half a year, and she was miserable. I think Kenny was already starting to see that it wasn't a great idea. He's not as oblivious to Charlotte's nonsense as he seems to be. I think he'd figured out Vicky would be better off here. He's not a perfect father. But he has his good moments."

A question remains, though, and it must be asked: "How bad was the sex?"

Faye thinks about it for a second. "It depends on what you value in a sexual encounter."

LOOOOOOOOOL. "Wow. *That* bad?"

She laughs. "It wasn't bad, really. I mean, yes, his technique left quite a bit to be desired—"

"I bet it did!"

"—but he was actually very sweet. He was tender. Loving. That's what I needed the most right then."

"Okay," I say. "I get that. You probably wouldn't have turned down an orgasm, though, would you?"

"I would have welcomed an orgasm with open arms and a cold glass of lemonade," she says, and we both laugh until actual tears roll down our faces.

We stay in the vegetable patch for a while, planting tomatoes—then weeding, then watering—and talking. A few times, my mind wanders again to images of myself here, belonging with Vicky and Faye. Each time it does, I feel the same stabbing pain in my chest. And I push the thoughts away as fast as I can.

23

THE FOLLOWING SATURDAY, THERE'S A COOKOUT AT REVEREND SEY-
mour's and Vicky asks me to go.

"Is Nick gonna—"

"Maybe," she says, rolling her eyes. "But who cares? Geez. You're
so weird about him."

"No, I'm not."

"Yes, you are. Anyway, there's probably going to be a ton of people
there. It's not like you have to hang with him if you don't want to."

The cookout is in the reverend's backyard. There's a big folding
table with a spread of standard cookout foods: potato salad; macaroni
salad; a green salad that's just lettuce, tomatoes, and cucumber placed
next to a couple of bottles of ranch dressing; corn on the cob; baked
beans; and meats of all sorts, with accompanying buns. There's a smoking grill, one of those old charcoal jawns, and it's being tended by a very
tall man who looks a lot like Reverend Seymour. There's a Bluetooth
speaker wafting the sounds of contemporary gospel through the air.
Vicky was right: There are lots of people here, including many of their
neighbors, and people I've seen going into the reverend's basement for
church on Wednesdays and Sundays. Brother Philip Michael Nguyen is

sitting with Miss Vena near the folding table, eating a gigantic plate of potato salad. I haven't seen him outside since we ate bánh bò.

"Hey, lil' Vicky! Hey, chocolate lady!" Mr. Mitch says, walking by us on his way to the food.

"Skye. My name is Skye."

He's already out of earshot.

Vicky spots the reverend's granddaughter, Keisha, and runs off before I can stop her. Now I'm standing here alone, looking friendless, probably. Awesome.

"Sister Skye!" Reverend Seymour calls, heading toward me.

I smile at her, relieved.

"You're still in Philadelphia," she says. "I'm so glad. I guess you want to spend as much time as you can with your daughter?"

Wayment. "My . . . what?"

"Oh," she says, sounding uncertain. "I thought . . . well . . . Faye mentioned . . ."

"Did she?" I ask, surprised.

"Well, she didn't use the word 'daughter,'" the reverend says, "now that I think about it. That's my word. I'm old, so I'm not up on all the lingo. Is there lingo? For that?"

"Donor kid, I guess? Although, our relationship is less donor-offspring and more like an older cousin–younger cousin type of vibe."

The reverend nods. "Oh. Alright."

"I see Brother Nguyen has broken free of the attic."

"Well, don't make it sound like I had him chained to the radiator up there."

I laugh. "Sorry. What did your kids say about it?"

"Nothing yet," she replies. "I still haven't mentioned he's staying here. But I knew Phil could only tolerate being up there for so long. He's lived on the streets for years now; he's not used to being cooped up anymore. Besides, nobody wants to feel they have to hide, do they? Everyone wants to feel welcome, wherever they are. Everyone wants to feel they belong."

I guess.

"I don't get why it's such a big secret," I tell the reverend.

"Because I don't know yet how my family, or my congregation, will handle it," she says. "With Phil's time on the street, our ages, his Asian-ness. It's a complicated situation to manage."

"So, why are you doing it?"

She looks at me curiously, almost amused. "Because I'm not so old that I don't want love in my life, Sister Skye. *That kind* of love. Romance. Companionship. Even sex. I want it all, the same as you."

"I'm not sure I do want it," I say.

"I find that hard to believe," she replies, "at your age."

"I want sex, sure. But the rest . . ." I shrug.

"Oh," the reverend says, nodding, like she gets it now. "You mean, you don't want to get attached."

"Yes."

"Because people don't really care as much as they pretend to?"

"That's right."

She laughs.

"Wow, Reverend. Wow."

"I'm sorry," she says, grabbing my hand and holding it. "I'm not laughing at you."

"You definitely are, though."

"I'm more laughing at the parts of my younger self I see in you. When I think of all the time I spent keeping folks at a distance, trying to avoid being let down . . ." She sighs, shakes her head. "It was a waste of the precious time the Lord gave me. People let us down. We let them down. Letdown is inevitable, Sister Skye."

Which doesn't make me feel better.

"But, you know what else is inevitable? If you allow yourself to close that distance? Connection. Joy."

"Maybe."

She laughs again, louder this time.

When she heads to the grill to check on the ribs, I look around for

Vicky. She and Keisha have disappeared. I could hunt for the kid. Or I could start eating. When Faye's friend Angie and her husband, Giancarlo, wave to me from the food table, I decide Jesus wants me to have a hot dog first.

I've chatted with Angie and Giancarlo a few times now, and although they've never said anything about the egg donation thing, I know they know. Because even though they're always super friendly and seriously chatty, asking me a thousand questions about my travels, neither of them has ever asked who the hell I am. A few times, I've caught Angie staring, and when our eyes met, she smiled.

"We brought the potato salad," Angie says to me now. "It's my grandmother's recipe. We eat it every day in the summer, don't we, hon?"

Giancarlo nods. "I eat it twice a day sometimes."

"It's good!" Mr. Mitch calls out to me from the spot he, Brother Nguyen, and Miss Vena have staked out at the end of the table.

I put some on my plate.

"Are you off again soon?" Angie asks, offering me mustard for a hot dog I'm about to scarf down.

"Not soon," I tell her. "I'm here for six more weeks."

"Oh, good," she says, sounding relieved. "I know Vicky loves having you around."

When she's not disappearing on me, sure.

"Do you know she got suspended three times this past winter? Faye was at her wit's end. These last . . . what's it been since she met you, a month or so?"

"Five weeks, six days." Not that I'm counting.

"Well, all that school trouble has stopped completely," she says.

"I'm not sure I can take credit for that."

"You can. And you should."

Two hot dogs and some pretty good potato salad later, I go looking for Vicky. I find her alone by the side of the house, tucked next to a bush, holding her phone up in front of her.

"What are you doing?"

She jumps, startled, and I know she's up to something. When I peek out on the other side of the bush, there's the reverend's troublesome white neighbor, Ethan. He's on his porch, a few houses down, fixing a bike. He's crouched, and his ass crack is peeking out of his shorts.

"What's going on?" I ask Vicky.

"I'm keeping an eye on him," she says.

"He's . . . not doing anything?"

"Yet."

Ethan looks around, like he heard something, then scratches his ass crack and goes back to bike-fixing.

"I'm not sure this is a great idea, Vick. Especially since Faye told you not to do it."

"She told me not to video *the police*."

"I doubt that's a technicality she'll appreciate."

"Well, she's wrong," the kid says. "I don't think I should have to listen to someone when they're wrong just because they're an adult. That's, like, ageism."

"I'm one hundred percent sure that's not what ageism is."

She groans, super dramatically. "I *have* to do this."

"Why?"

"Because!"

"Not a reason."

"It just makes me feel better," she says.

"About what?"

"Everything! All the bad stuff that happens that you can't do anything about!"

Wait. Is this about Cynthia somehow? Because if it is: SHIT. I'm not prepared for this.

Ethan stands, pulls up his sagging shorts, and peers in our direction. We're at ground level, below him, three houses away and pretty well tucked behind this bush, but I'm still worried he'll see Vicky pointing a camera at him and go white people crazy. Which is like regular people crazy but with help from the cops. So, I take Vicky's arm and slowly pull her away from the bush, until we're in the back-yard once again.

"Hey, you two."

We both jump this time. It's Faye.

"Why are you skulking?" she asks.

"We're not," Vicky says.

"You are," Faye insists.

Vicky looks at me. I know she's waiting to see if I'm gonna narc on her.

"I came over here to . . . fart," I tell Faye. "I didn't want to do it around the food."

She's speechless, as you might imagine.

"Yeah," Vicky says, nodding. "It was super stinky."

Okay, let's not go nuts.

Faye looks from Vicky to me and back again. "Did you come to smell the fart? Or to add your own to the mix?" she asks, in a tone that suggests she may not be completely convinced of our story.

"Where's Nick?" I ask, to throw her off our super stinky scent.

"I don't keep track of Nick's every move."

Mkay. You probably should, though.

"I'm gonna get a burger," Vicky says, and hurries off.

"Sorry," Faye says after a moment. "I didn't mean to be snippy just then." She rubs her right temple.

"Everything okay?"

"Everything's fine. I'm just hangry probably."

We follow Vicky to the food.

Despite the fact that I just ate, I decide to eat more. It's a cookout, so overeating is pretty much expected, right? I'm eyeing the burgers when Faye asks me if I'll be around next Friday.

"I'm having surgery," she says.

"For what?"

"I'm getting new tits."

"Oh. Okay. Cool," I say, like that's totes run-of-the-mill and shit. "Um, just out of curiosity—and please feel free to tell me to mind my own beeswax—is there . . . something wrong with the tits you have now?" BECAUSE THEY LOOK GREAT TO ME.

"They're wearing out," Vicky says through a mouthful of corn on the cob.

Faye frowns at her.

"What? They *are*."

"But you don't have to put it like that."

I look from Vicky to Faye, and back. "I'm missing something, aren't I?"

Faye hands me a paper plate. "I had a double mastectomy. And breast reconstruction. About fourteen years ago."

"Holy shit," I say. "Cancer?"

She nods. "There were two lumps, one in each breast. Given my family history and high risk of re-occurrence with lumpectomy, I opted to—"

"Chop 'em off," Vicky says, making a hacking motion with her left hand.

We both frown at her.

"She's right, though," Faye tells me. "I opted to chop them off."

"Wow."

"It was actually a relief," she says. "I mean, eventually it was. After worrying my whole life about when—not if—I'd get breast cancer."

I load food onto my paper plate and think about Cynthia dying of cancer at thirty-seven. It's an intense, depressing thought. Then I remember that Vicky has my genes, not Cynthia's or Faye's, and I feel a little guilty for feeling extremely glad about that.

"So those are . . ." I gesture vaguely toward Faye's rack.

"Implants," she says, nodding. "Which only last ten to twenty years. These are fourteen now and the silicone is starting to show signs of wear, so . . ."

"So, you're getting new tits," I say, nodding.

"Recovery won't be bad. I just have to take it easy for a few days. Angie can keep an eye on Vicky, too, but her mother's been ill, so a lot of her time is taken up with that."

"I'll help any way I can."

She reaches out and touches my arm, squeezes it.

We hang in Reverend Seymour's backyard all day. We eat. Faye brought deviled eggs and they're the best I've ever had. We listen to gospel music. When Keisha cues up the Electric Slide, we dance—we all know the steps, even Vicky—before it's back to gospel again. Miss Vena brought watermelon and cantaloupe, so we eat more. When it's near-dusky, and the air begins to cool, we say our goodbyes and start making our way up the block.

The sun is setting and the sky is lavender and orange, dramatic and striking. It does what sunsets always do: instills a sense of wonder at the natural world. Which can be particularly poignant when walking down an inner-city street. I've watched the sun set from so many places around the world that I can't even name them all. What I remember right now, though, is that when I was young, I made sure to watch every summer sunset over Philly. Usually posted up on Tasha's porch after a long, hot day of not doing shit. I remember the color of the sky, just like it is now, the orange-saturated clouds and purple-tinted edges, the consistency and familiarity of it, day after day after day.

Vicky is walking close beside me and she reaches out and puts both her arms around my waist, so she's encircling me. She's never done this before, never physically attached herself to me. I like it, even though it makes it really hard to walk. I drape my arm around her shoulders, where I feel like maybe it belongs.

24

ON SUNDAY, MY MOTHER CALLS TO ASK IF I CAN TAKE HER TO CHURCH in one of those "cabs that aren't cabs." I start to ask why Slade can't take her in his girlfriend's car but then I don't. I just tell her yes. I know that the main reason my mother never makes it to church—even when she really wants to go—is that she simply can't remember to get ready, so I tell her I'll come early to help.

When I get there, Slade is on the couch eating Pop-Tarts right out of the box. He smiles at me with crumbs and blue goo in his teeth. The house looks somewhat cleaner today, most of the dirty cups and plates gone from the living room.

My mother is upstairs in her bedroom, staring at the small TV on her dresser, which isn't even turned on. When she sees me, she looks like she forgot I was coming.

"I'm here to help you get ready for church."

"I remember," she says. She's still in her pajamas and her hair is in plaits that look several days old.

"Do you know what you want to wear?" I ask her.

"I have some dress clothes in that closet," she says, pointing.

I open the closet. There are a bunch of churchy outfits: a blue dress; a beige suit; a lavender skirt with a matching floral blouse. The suit looks too small to accommodate the weight my mother has put on since her fall, so I leave it there and pull out some of the other options, holding them up for my mother's review.

She points to the dress. "That one."

I lay it on the bed beside her.

She fingers the material. "This reminds me of a dress I used to have."

"You wear pantyhose with this?" I ask.

She nods, points to the dresser.

I open the top, right-side drawer, where there are pantyhose and socks.

"Your father bought it for me," she says.

I look at her. "What?"

"The dress I used to have. Your father bought it for me. A long time ago. When we were first married."

I take a pair of pantyhose out of the drawer, hold them up to the light to check for runs.

"It was the same color as this one and the same fabric," my mother continues, still fingering the material. "But it was a young woman's dress. You know what I mean? I used to wear it out dancing."

I hold the pantyhose out to her.

She takes them. "Your father loved to take me out dancing on Saturday nights," she says, and her eyes are bright with the memory.

I make a face at her.

"What's wrong?"

"Nothing," I say, shaking my head. "I just don't get what you ever saw in him."

"Well, he could dance, for one—"

"I'm not asking," I interrupt. "I don't actually want to know."

"He was handsome, too," she says as if she didn't even hear me. "He had good taste in music. His record collection was exceptional. And he had good dick."

"Ugh! Mom! Can you not? Jesus!"

"Alright, alright. Calm down," she says. "I didn't know you were such a prude. The truth is, I liked him because he could be really sweet."

"I find that hard to believe."

She nods. "Well, he could be mean, too. Over the years, the mean overtook the sweet. Once it did, I had to divorce him."

Which isn't true. She divorced him, sure, but it wasn't "once the mean took over the sweet." He was mean my entire life. Whatever sweet he'd been was long gone by the time she finally divorced him.

"What shoes do you want to wear?" I ask, hoping she'll just stop talking about him.

"I have some nice white flats in there, on the right side by the boots, I think."

I find the shoes and put them on the floor by the bed.

"Some things were easier for me after he was gone," she says. "And some things were harder. Raising two kids on my own wasn't easy. But I think I did a great job."

I feel heat rising in my chest. I want to scream at her that she didn't do a great job. At least not for me. That the damage had already been done by then.

"What about jewelry?" I ask her. "You planning on accessorizing?"

She gets up off the bed and goes over to her dresser. There's a jewelry box on top of it and she sifts through it. After about a minute, she's still sifting.

"Mom?"

She looks at me, confused, and I know she's forgotten what she's supposed to be doing.

I pull a necklace from the box—silver with a pink stone—and hold it up. "What about this one? To go with the dress."

She smiles, nods her head. "That works."

I help my mother get dressed. The hardest part is getting her shoes on, because her feet are so swollen. Once she's dressed, I help her choose a wig. Then we go downstairs to wait for the church van, which I arranged to pick her up instead of a Lyft.

Slade is still eating Pop-Tarts on the couch. I tell him he has to be here when the van drops our mother off after church. "Don't forget."

"I won't," he says, looking offended at the notion of me questioning his unfaltering reliability. Then he peers at me. "What's wrong? You look upset."

I shake my head. "I'm fine."

He frowns. "Mom talking about Dad again? She's been talking about that nigga all day."

"Yeah, she was. Why?"

"I don't know. Something reminded her of him this morning. Now he's stuck in her head. I had to tell her to stop but I don't think she can turn it off like that, when her brain starts fixating. It's not her fault."

"Yeah," I say. "I guess."

"You want to go get a drink?"

I look at him. "What?"

"A drink. It's usually something that comes in a glass."

"No. I can't. I have plans." I turn to leave.

"You know we grew up in the same house, right?" he asks. "We're carrying the same shit. It might help sometimes to carry it together."

I never really think about the shit my brother is carrying. I certainly never think of it as the same as mine. I want to ask him if our father ever locked him in a closet for talking back. I think I'd remember if he did. But maybe not. *You only remember what fits your agenda.*

"I have to go," I tell Slade. "Maybe I'll call you later."

"You should," he says.

Or, at least, that's what I think he says. I'm already out the door.

25

I WASN'T LYING WHEN I SAID I HAD PLANS. I'M TAKING VICKY TO ONE of my fave spots in Philly. When I get to her house, I find her sitting on the porch, scrolling on her phone.

"Hey, kid," I say, coming up the front steps just as Faye is coming out of the house, followed close behind by Nick.

"We're off," Faye says. "Have fun, you two."

They head for Faye's car.

"Where are they going?"

"North Philly," Vicky says.

"Ew. Why?"

"Uncle Nick's dad lives there. I think he has cancer."

"You think?"

"Aunt Faye said he's sick, but when I asked her what's wrong with him, she changed the subject. So, yeah, probably cancer."

I nod. "Probably."

"I guess she thinks I can't handle the C word at all now. But I can. I'm not like a basket case or something, you know?"

"I know."

"Anyway," she says, shrugging, "where are *we* going?"

"To June's. It's a pool hall I used to frequent when I was a kid. It's low-key seedy but the games are cheap. If you need to pee, go now, because you definitely don't want to use the bathroom there."

"I peed a few minutes ago," she says. "Pooped, too."

"Oh, I was positively dying to know when you last took a shit, so thanks for sharing that."

She giggles.

June's is down Forty-seventh, so we hop on the bus.

"By the way: I told Faye we're going to the arcade, so don't tell her where we're really going." There used to be a Pac-Man machine at the pool hall, so it's not a total lie.

"Okay."

Then I'm like, "Wait. Maybe I shouldn't be asking you to keep secrets from her."

"She keeps secrets," Vicky says, "so why shouldn't I?"

I frown at her. "Are you still giving your aunt a hard time because she didn't tell you about the egg donor thing?"

"I'm not giving her a hard time. And she's not even my real aunt, anyway."

Woooooooow.

"Of course she is. Just because you're not genetically related doesn't mean she's not your family. She obviously loves you. A lot."

"If she loves me so much, she should've told me where I really came from."

"So, you're planning to hold it against her forever? Wow, that's immature."

"I'm twelve."

Solid point.

"You know Faye isn't the only one who kept the egg donor thing a secret from you, right? You mad at your mother, too?"

"No."

"Why not?"

"Because she died," Vicky says. "Being mad at dead people is dumb. They can't even be sorry."

"What about your dad, then?" I ask. "You mad at him?"

"I'm always mad at him. It doesn't matter, though. He never says he's wrong about anything."

So that just leaves Faye, I guess, to face the kid's wrath. It doesn't seem fair.

I watch Vicky staring out the bus window, her brow tightly furrowed now. I try to imagine what it must be like to just be going about your twelve-year-old business and then suddenly discover you're not genetically related to half the people you thought you were genetically related to. SOUNDS AWESOME, ACTUALLY. WHERE DO I SIGN UP? But that's me. Vicky actually *liked* her mother.

"I guess it's hard, huh?"

"It's just weird. I used to know this girl, Lainey, at my old school, who came from her mom's eggs and some rando sperm. Out of a catalog or whatever. When she told me about it, I was like, 'That's cray.' Not out loud, just in my head. But now *I'm* the one whose, like . . . *existence* . . . is cray. Except it's worse."

"Worse why?"

"Because my mom *died*. And then I found out she *wasn't* my mom. So she kinda died again. Like, metaphorically."

I start to tell her again that Cynthia *was* her mom. In literally every way that matters. That genes don't mean shit. That, a lot of the time, genes just tie you to people you'd never choose to be tied to if you had a choice. That the fact that she *would* choose Cynthia means more than any DNA could ever mean. But something tells me none of that will help. And I don't know what will.

We ride the rest of the way in silence. When we get to our stop, when we get off the bus and walk the half-block to the spot where June's should be, it's not there. In its place is a coffee shop. An actual coffee shop, packed to the brim with gentrifying hipsters.

"No fucking way," I say. "You've got to be fucking kidding me. Could this be any more of a fucking cliché?"

"That's a lot of F-bombs," Vicky says. "Are you okay?"

"What? Yeah. I'm . . . fine. I'm just surprised."

It doesn't even look like the same building, with its floor-to-ceiling windows and bright green paint with no graffiti on it.

"Why do white people like coffee shops so much?" Vicky asks.

I shake my head. "Let's just go."

"Where?"

"Anywhere but here."

WE WALK TO A WATER ice stand a few blocks away and get mango ices and soft pretzels. We sit outside and Vicky talks a bunch—about gentrification and white supremacy and capitalism—but I'm distracted. I wish I'd gone into the coffee shop and asked questions, like how long it's been in business, so I'd know how long it's been since the pool hall closed. I try to remember the last time I walked or rode by it and saw it open, but I can't. That makes me sad, then annoyed with myself, because why does it even matter? Nostalgia aside, it was a dive I hadn't even stepped foot in, in twenty years. Its sudden absence—or my sudden awareness of its absence—shouldn't be a big deal.

After we eat, Vicky says she wants to head home to watch a movie. We walk back to the bus stop.

The ride is kind of a blur.

When we get back to Vicky's house, I'm still so distracted that I don't even look for Nick's car, I just follow Vicky inside. Which is my bad, because—you guessed it—Nick is there. He's stretched out on the sofa, one arm behind his head, staring up at the ceiling with a tight brow, when we enter. He doesn't seem to notice us.

"You're back already?" Faye asks, looking up from the papers she's grading at the dining room table.

The question pulls Nick out of his own distracted state and he sits up quickly and smiles. "How was the arcade?"

"It's gone," Vicky says. "There's a coffee shop there now."

I feel a lump swelling in my throat, the kind of thing that happens when one is about to cry. But I never cry, so I know it can't be that. Gotta be acid reflux. I swallow it down hard.

"A coffee shop?" Nick asks, standing up and smoothing out his jeans. "Could that be any more of a cliché?"

Vicky looks at me. "That's the same thing you said."

Yeah, but that shit sounded way smarter when I said it.

"I thought you were going to North Philly."

"We did," Nick says. "But my dad wasn't feeling up to company much."

"We decided to watch a movie," Vicky says, "since the arcade is closed."

The lump in my throat swells again, bigger this time.

"I have to pee," I tell the kid, before taking the stairs two at a time and locking myself in the bathroom.

I'm standing in front of the mirror, the glow of the bulbs casting an amber-ish light on my skin, wondering what is wrong with my throat, when I start to cry. Like, legit. Actual, factual tears start squeezing their way out of my eyeballs. At first, I try to hold them back, but I quickly find that I'm no match for them. Before I can take a deep breath to try to get my emotions in check, the tears overwhelm me and I'm ugly-crying, complete with guttural sobs and full-on snot. It's gross. But I can't stop. My shoulders shake. My knees buckle. I sink to the floor, holding myself and bawling. My whole body trembles. As my sobs intensify, I feel something hot and angry rising in my chest, something I'm pretty sure is a scream.

Q: How batshit would it be if I started screaming on this bathroom floor right now?

A: PRETTY. FUCKING. BATSHIT.

Just as I'm deciding whether or not "pretty fucking" is a level of batshit I'm comfortable with, there's a knock on the bathroom door. I put my hands over my mouth to muffle my sobs.

Faye calls my name. "Skye? Are you okay?"

Shit.

I get up off the floor and slap myself hard on both sides of my face. The crying stops just long enough for me to say, "I'm fine. I'm just . . . changing my tampon. I'll be out in a minute."

After a pause, I hear Faye's footsteps moving away from the door. When I'm sure she's gone, I start sobbing again. I cry and cry, for two or three minutes straight, and then I wipe my eyes, blow my nose in a wad of toilet paper, and whisper to my mirror reflection: *Get it the fuck together*.

When I open the door, Vicky's standing right there, looking at me, and I almost jump out of my skin. "Jesus! You scared the shit out of me!"

"Your eyes are all red," she says. "What's wrong?"

"It's allergies."

She gives me a look.

"What? It's allergies! Jesus, kid!"

"Don't get mad at me!"

"I'm not," I tell her.

"Okay," she says, "well, I set up the movie in my room. We just need snacks."

All I want to do is go home. But the movie is *Ninotchka*, the Garbo jawn she used to watch with her mother, and I know how much it means that she wants to show it to me. So, I suck it up and say okay and follow her back downstairs.

Nick's no longer in the living room. Faye's back at the dining room table, grading papers. Her eyes follow us as we walk past her into the kitchen. I smile like nothing weird just happened.

"I want chips," Vicky says, opening a cabinet. "And Oreos. Oh! Aunt Faye? Where's the popcorn?"

"Basement."

Without another word, Vicky skips to the basement door and disappears down the stairs. I take the chips out of the cabinet and pour some into a bowl. When I turn around to look for the Oreos, Faye is standing right there.

"Jesus! Why's everybody so lurky today?"

"I just wanted to make sure you're alright."

"I'm fine. Why wouldn't I be?"

She gives me a look, like, *Really, girl?* "Because you were crying in the bathroom."

I don't know why, but being reminded of the crying makes me want to cry again. I feel a lump swelling in my throat. Which: no way. I don't cry in front of people. I WILL RUN SCREAMING FROM THIS HOUSE BEFORE I LET THAT HAPPEN.

"Crying?" I ask with a chuckle. "No, I wasn't."

"I could hear you through the door."

"That wasn't me."

Okay, listen: I'm crazy, but I'm not so crazy that I don't know when I *sound* crazy. And right now? I sound crazy. I know that. And I know I should just stop. But I can't. Because as long as I don't confess to the crying, as long as there are no credible eyewitnesses, maybe it didn't really happen. Maybe I didn't really fall all the way apart over some shitty pool hall in a city I don't even like.

Faye's not looking at me like I'm crazy, though. Her eyes are soft and full of concern, not judgment. She reaches out and puts one hand on my arm.

The lump in my throat gets larger. "It's okay," I tell her, feeling tears tingling at the corners of my eyes. "It's not a big deal."

I can't adequately express how desperately I don't want to cry. But I can't stop it. It's like I've come apart at all the places where my threads were already loose, and I'm spilling out.

Faye puts her other hand on my other arm.

I shake my head, feel tears fall on my shirt. "It's stupid."

"Why is it stupid?"

"Aunt Faye!" Vicky yells up the basement steps. "I can't find the popcorn!"

"It's on the second shelf!" Faye yells back.

"It's not there!"

"It is there! You have to actually look for it!"

"I am looking!"

Faye rolls her eyes, then turns back to me. "Why is it stupid?"

"Because it was just a pool hall. With dirty bathrooms and sketchy dudes. It wasn't something to cry about. I haven't cried in three years; it doesn't make sense for me to cry about this."

There's a flash of a frown on her face and I realize I slipped and said pool hall instead of arcade. But she lets it go.

"I lost a place a few years ago," she says. "Not to gentrification. It burned down and the owners couldn't rebuild."

I pull up the hem of my shirt and use it to wipe my eyes. "What kind of place was it?"

"Hoagie shop," she says, laughing a little. "I used to go there with my girls after school, in eighth grade. It wasn't anything special. Nothing to cry about, either. It probably failed every surprise inspection it ever had. But we shared a lot of shit in those booths, you know?"

I do know.

When I was thirteen, I would go right home most days after school because my parents were still at work. Sometimes, Tasha came with me. We'd do our homework and get a snack and then, a few minutes before my father was due home, we'd leave. Sometimes, we'd take the bus to June's to shoot pool. It was fifty cents a game. The old heads who hung around there would give us quarters and watch us play, or challenge us to a game. LeRoy, the manager, always stayed close by, making sure no one got out of line with us. Besides leering, and an occasional *you got a boyfriend yet, sweet thing?* they mostly didn't. Tasha and I would hang there for three or four hours sometimes, playing game after game, talking shit to your uncles and granddads, and then, when it was late enough that I could be pretty sure my father was snoring loudly in front of the TV, I'd go home, grab whatever cold dinner my mother had left for me in the kitchen, and take it to my room. For years, even after my parents split up and I didn't need to avoid home as much, Tasha and I—and eventually Viva—went to June's, to shoot pool and talk shit. It was our spot. Now it's gone. Now it's a goddamn coffee shop.

Faye is watching me, waiting patiently for me to tell her what I'm feeling, the way Viva always does, the way Tasha used to do.

"I shot pool with my friends at June's sometimes," I say, "when I didn't want to be at home. It was kind of a refuge for me. Losing it feels devastating in a way I didn't expect."

"This is the wrong popcorn!" Vicky yells from the basement.

Faye ignores the kid. Her hands are still on my arms and she rubs them, gently squeezing. The warmth of her palms on my skin is deeply comforting.

My tears have stopped. I lean back against the counter. Faye leans beside me. We stand there like that, our shoulders touching. After a couple of minutes, she asks, "Have you really not cried in three years?"

I sigh a long sigh. "Yes."

Nick walks in through the back door. Ugh, I thought he went home already. "Grill's clean," he says to Faye.

"Thank you."

When he sees my face, which I'm sure is a mess from crying, he looks worried. "What are you two whispering about?"

"We're not whispering," I say.

"We were just talking about gentrification," Faye tells him.

"Oh. Yeah. I can't believe how bad it's getting in some parts of the city."

"Whatever," I say, shrugging. "It was just a pool hall. I mean, arcade. It was just an arcade."

Vicky comes trudging up the steps, a big bag of popcorn and another of chips in her arms.

"It's never just an arcade," Nick says. "Places like that provide something to a community."

Yeah, drugs, usually.

"Even places that don't seem like much end up meaning more to a neighborhood than places that look like a bigger deal on paper. Arcades. Candy stores. The corner cheesesteak spot. Those places are part of the fabric of the community. Without them, it starts to fall apart. And without community, you have nothing."

Why is this nigga talking so much, all of a sudden?

"What?" he asks, seeing the look on my face, I guess. "You disagree?"

"That's just not my experience, is all."

He frowns. "Well, it's definitely ours." He looks at Faye. "Community is the most important thing. Right, babe?"

"Sure," she says. "Top three, anyway."

"Exactly! And *Philly* community is the best. But I was born here," he says, as if everyone in the room wasn't, "so maybe I'm biased. I grew up in these streets. But it wasn't until I went to college out West that I realized how special Philly is."

I really wish he'd shut up.

"What's special about it?" Vicky asks, looking interested.

"The people. They're real."

I smirk. "As opposed to pretend people?"

"You know what I mean. As opposed to fake. As opposed to putting on airs, pretending to be somebody they're not. We're also the friendliest people in the urban northeast. Maybe the friendliest anywhere outside the South."

Well, Nick is certainly "friendly." I'll give him that.

"You can meet somebody at a bus stop in Philly," he continues, "bond over the twenty-one always being late, and be best friends by the time it finally shows up. Real friends, too, not that fake shit they do out in Cali."

"I love California," I say, even though I'm actually pretty meh about it.

"Me, too!" Vicky chimes in.

"You've never been to California, Vicky," Faye says.

Vicky takes a six-pack of root beer out of the fridge. "I know but I think I'd like it."

"You wouldn't," Nick says. "The people are fake and passive-aggressive. I hate California. So does Faye. Don't you, babe?"

Faye shrugs. "It's not my favorite place. But lots of people love it."

"With all the places you've traveled," Nick says to me, *still talking*, "you don't think Philly is the best city in America?"

I don't, but it doesn't matter because he doesn't wait for an answer.

"I wouldn't want to live anywhere else." Then, looking at Faye, "Would *you*, babe?"

"Probably not."

"*Probably* not? You always say you wouldn't want to live anywhere else. Why you frontin'?"

"I'm not," she says. "I just think you're laying it on a bit thick."

He frowns. Then he puts his hands up in a yielding gesture. "Okay," he says, smiling now. "I do get carried away sometimes. Sorry if I'm coming off like a dick, Skye."

"Language, please," Faye says, nodding toward Vicky.

Vicky shrugs. "I like 'dick.'"

"Vicky."

"What? It's a funny word!"

Nick takes Faye's hand and kisses it. He pulls her close to him, wrapping her arms around his waist. Before now, I've never felt envious of him. I've always felt better than him because, whatever I am, I'm not a cheater and a liar. But watching them now, I'm jealous.

Jealousy is yet another intense emotion on top of the sadness and grief I already feel over losing June's, and for a second, I think I might start spilling out again. To stop that from happening, I squeeze my butthole closed. Because tears are like farts, I guess? To my surprise—and yours, no doubt—it works.

"You ready?" Vicky asks.

I look over at her. She's holding up the snacks and cold sodas. She's happy, excited.

"Yeah. Let's do it," I say, and follow her out of the kitchen.

26

I MAKE IT THROUGH *NINOTCHKA* WITHOUT CRYING AGAIN. I ACCOM-plish this by not letting myself think about June's. At all. Not for a second. I let myself be immersed in the undeniable charms of Greta Garbo and her surprisingly convincing Russian accent. The second the credits start to roll, I tell Vicky how great it was, how psyched I am that she shared it with me, and how I ate too many snacks and have a stomachache and now have to bounce.

I walk to the B and B in a kind of stupor, my brain heavy, weighed down by memories of June's, and places and times now far out of reach. At some point, I almost get hit by a bright yellow bike that's covered in I HEART PHILLY stickers. "Watch it!" the cyclist yells at me as he comes to a hard stop a foot away from me in the bike lane.

"YOU watch it!" I yell back, because fuck him and his bike.

I spend the evening eating mini powdered donuts and sipping bourbon straight out of the bottle while watching a TV show about the worst cooks in America. I fall asleep with the TV on. I dream I'm on a cooking-type show, coming in last in the simplest challenges, like spreading butter on sliced bread and cracking eggs.

Around seven the next morning, I go down to the dining room, still in the clothes I fell asleep in. I can't remember if I brushed my teeth. Probably not, considering how my mouth tastes.

When Viva sees me, sitting in her pristine dining area with my powdered-donut-flecked sweatpants and wayward hair, she looks low-key horrified for a second. She recovers quickly, though, her horror replaced with a look of worry. She points a finger at my general person and asks, "What's all this about?"

I tell her that June's closed. That there's a coffee shop there now.

She sits down. "That was our spot," she says, sounding sad.

A lump is swelling in my throat. I feel my threads coming loose again. Tears tingle at the corners of my eyes. I will myself not to cry. Not to spill out all over this dining room. It's no use.

"I miss us," I say, quick and sudden, like a sneeze.

Viva looks surprised. Then her eyes soften and she reaches over and grabs my hand.

And I sob. Right there at the table.

Viva comes over and puts her arm around my shoulders. "You don't have to miss us," she says. "We're both still here."

I shake my head. "It's not the same."

"Claro que no," she says. "It was twenty years ago. It can't be the same. But it can still be good. It can still be what we need it to be."

Which is a nice idea. But the unnamed person here is Tasha and I doubt she feels the same.

I take a deep breath and pull myself back together. "I can't believe I'm melting down over this damn pool hall again. I already cried about it at Vicky's."

"In front of la nena?"

"In front of Faye."

"Wow."

"Yeah," I say, nodding. Then, "It was actually okay, though. She was . . . comforting."

Viva smiles. "Eso es bueno."

"It was. For a minute."

"And then?"

"And then I realized Faye and her meat stick are soulmates."

Viva sits back down in her chair and sighs. "What are you talking about?" She sounds a little bit annoyed now.

"I'm talking about shared values, Veev."

"Girl," she says, *what does that mean?*"

"It means Nick belongs with Faye and Vicky, and I don't," I tell her, shrugging.

Her jaw tightens. After a long moment of silence, she says, "You still haven't told Faye about Nick. ¿Por qué?"

"I'm going to."

"¿Cuándo?"

"Soon, probably."

"Do you *want* her to marry that pendejo?"

"Of course not."

"Then why don't you stop her from marrying him?" she asks, more annoyed, almost angry. "It might make things awkward, pero at least she won't be married to a man she can't trust. Isn't that more important?"

"Yeah, but . . ."

"But what?"

"Why do you care so much about this all of a sudden?" I ask her, annoyed myself now.

She doesn't answer. Instead, she says, "Maybe you *do* want her to marry him."

"Okay. Um . . . any idea why?"

"No sé. Maybe if Nick were out of the picture, you'd have to rethink your policy about serious relationships."

"Why?" I ask. "It's not like if she broke up with him, or he suddenly dropped dead—fingers crossed—I'd have to marry her in his place. She and I could still just fuck."

"You're really going to sit there and pretend that sex is the only thing you want from Faye?"

"No. But there are many levels between sex and a serious relationship, Viva. There's friends with benefits. Love affairs. Situationships."

"*Situationships?*" She looks horrified.

"It's a thing," I tell her. "Ask the millennials."

"That sounds like some cishet nonsense. But, as usual, you have an answer for everything. Which is how I know que estás hablando mierda."

"Why do you care so much about Faye all of a sudden?" I ask again.

"I care about *you*. You, who was just sitting here, *five minutes ago*, crying about not having any friends."

"That's not exactly—"

"I'm tired of watching you live this disconnected life. I'm tired of you showing up here, more of a shell of your former self every time, more self-centered and . . ." She searches for the right word. ". . . *foreign* to me with each visit. And all the time you're pretending that everything's melaza, no hay problema, and you're not completely fucked up."

Well, shit.

"If you don't want me here, you could have said so, Viva."

"Ay bendito, you know that's not what I mean."

"I'll leave today," I say, getting up from the table. "Checkout's at noon, right?"

"And go where?" she asks. "¿Pa' donde tu madre? Maybe you can have your old room. Maybe Slade will save you some of those damn Pop-Tarts he's always eating."

"Okay, Viva."

"Or why not Faye's? Maybe you can sleep between her and Nick. Take turns sucking his bicho."

"Okay, Viva! You made your point. I have nowhere else to go. Here. In Philly. But, guess what? Philly isn't the only place that exists."

"So, just leave?" she asks. "What was the point of staying in the first place, then? What was all that shit about not dying alone?"

"All that shit was about *Vicky*. She's the one who's going to rub arthritis cream on my knees when I get old and probably even cry at my funeral. My relationship with *Vicky* is the reason I canceled my trip to Brazil. Remember?"

Viva nods. "Sí. I do remember."

"So why are you busting my balls about Faye?"

"Porque I think you're in love with her."

"Ugh," I say incredulously, standing up. "Whatever. I'm going back to bed."

"It's seven-thirty. You've only been up half an hour."

"Half an hour too long," I tell her and take the back stairs two at a time to my room.

FOR THE NEXT FEW DAYS, I try really hard to hold my shit together. I avoid Viva. I communicate with Vicky only via text, so I can steer clear of Faye and Nick. I work on the smallest details of the Bali and Sydney trips, and the New Zealand, Indonesia, and Malaysia trips that will follow it. I do not cry. About June's or anything else. Mid-week, I find myself at Philadelphia International for the third time in as many days.

PHL isn't the worst of major U.S. airports, but it's bottom five, easily. It's ugly and dirty and the customer service is like if drunk Mel Gibson had angry sex with drunk Russell Crowe and they had a baby who worked in customer service at the Philadelphia airport. And yet, here I am, sitting in a faux-leather seat in terminal F, watching through fingerprint-and-possibly-snot-smudged windows as anonymous international flights take off. Late, probably.

I used to come to this shitty airport when I was a teenager. I sat in seats like this for hours sometimes, watching planes, daydreaming about being anywhere but Philly. Back then, buying a ticket and boarding a plane to wherever I wanted to go wasn't an option. Now, if I wanted to, I could whip out my passport and my credit card and disappear. I think about doing just that. About meeting up with Toni and our Nicaragua group, which is in Granada right now. Or flying somewhere else entirely, somewhere I can be alone for a few weeks—or months or years—somewhere I don't have to self-reflect or show up or belong because I'm a foreigner, a stranger.

An Airbus A321, an Aer Lingus, is taxiing down the runway. I hear a boarding call for a flight to London. I could do it, I think. I could just . . . go.

But then I remember how crushing the loneliness can be. How that crushingness sometimes sneaks up on me, at night in my hotel room, or smack in the middle of the day, at Callejon de Hamel or the Arc de Triomphe, surrounded by hundreds or thousands of people, pulling me at my loose threads.

I'm tired of watching you live this disconnected life. I guess I'm tired of it, too, because I don't buy a ticket. I don't get on a plane. I watch a few more flights take off and then I leave to pick up Vicky from therapy.

VICKY'S SHRINK HAS AN OFFICE a few blocks from where June's used to be, near Penn, on the second floor above a florist. The stairwell smells of flowers. At the top of it, there's a door leading to a small waiting area with bright yellow walls, chairs upholstered in colorful patterns, and, in the center of the room, one of those toddler activity centers with blocks and shapes and buttons that light up. There's a shelf full of toys and, higher up on the wall, out of a little kid's reach, another shelf full of pamphlets about depression, anxiety, abuse, and other mental-health-related issues. On one wall, there's a small painting of a Black child eating a mango.

The waiting room is empty and quiet, which I didn't anticipate. I guess I expected the muffled cries of traumatized children confronting their demons, or whatever. But there's none of that. Just a handful of closed doors. A big clock on the wall tells me it's quarter to four. I sit in one of the colorful chairs and wait for Vicky to appear.

I can't help but think about the therapist waiting rooms I've been in before. In college, the counseling center's waiting area had been awash in fluorescent lighting. That's all I really remember about it. The other time I went to therapy, the time I didn't tell Vicky about, when I was fourteen, the waiting area was bright and colorful like this one, but still somehow depressing. Our family had mental healthcare coverage through Medicaid, like the rest of the poors, ever since my parents broke up and my father refused to pay child support, so our options for therapists weren't exactly stellar. Spoiler alert: Nobody really cares that much if poor kids go crazy. Least of all the Commonwealth of Pennsylvania. Anyhoo, I remember sitting there, staring at the bright orange walls and feeling depressed despite them, and also a little bit enraged, which was the norm for me then, waiting for my name to be called. Every time it was—by my therapist, who was medium-brown and skinny, with a high-pitched voice, short, kinky hair, and bangle bracelets that looked too heavy for her thin wrists—it took every ounce of self-control I had not to scream. I remember holding the sound in the back of my throat, tight, like it was a mad dog on a too-short leash, telling myself that if I let it go there in that waiting room, they'd drag me off to one of those nut joints like in the movies. What I *don't* remember is any of the actual sessions, of which I think there were four or five total before I stopped going. But I probably talked a shit ton about my father and how deeply I despised him. The therapist, whose name I don't remember, probably asked me why I hated my father so much. I probably said, "He's a dick." I mean, that sounds like something I'd say.

"When you say 'dick,' what exactly are you trying to say?" she probably asked me.

"That he's a dick. A penis walking on two legs. He's even bald."

The therapist's bangle bracelets probably jangled as she tilted her head to one side and stared at me.

I probably conceded that he wasn't an actual penis, just a raging asshole. By which I would have meant "a terrible person who treats his kids like shit."

"When you say 'like shit' . . . "

"When I was seven, he hit me in the head with a shoe, five times, 'cause I didn't clean up my room. My mom just stood there."

The therapist probably looked at me sympathetically, maybe even put a hand on my shoulder. I probably cried. Or maybe not. Maybe I refused to cry. That sounds like me.

I feel a hand on my shoulder, but it's not my old shrink, it's Vicky.

"Hey, kid," I say, working to keep my voice from cracking. "How was therapy?"

"Therapeutic," she says, giggling.

THERE'S A VERY GOOD HOAGIE shop on the way to the bus stop, so Vicky and I stop there to get dinner for later. Our bus is arriving as we're coming out of the hoagie shop and we have to run to catch it. It's nearing rush hour, so there aren't many seats, but we manage to snag a couple by the back door. I hate sitting in the back of the bus on principle, because Rosa Parks, but it's better than standing up, so.

I'm supposed to take Vicky home and stay over tonight so I can take her to school tomorrow morning while Faye is having surgery. I haven't seen Faye since the day of the June's incident and, now that we're en route to their house, I start to feel anxious. What if Nick is there and I have to watch them belonging with each other again? Ugh.

"Is Nick going to be at your house?" I ask Vicky.

"I doubt it," she says, "since they broke up."

Wait. Whut? "Faye and Nick broke up?"

"Yeah. Like a few days ago."

"She told you this?"

"Yeah. And I heard some of it, too. Some crying."

"Faye was crying?"

"Uncle Nick was crying."

Oh, really? "So, *she* broke up with *him*?"

"Probably," Vicky says. "That's what it sounded like."

In this moment, I experience a number of feelings: curiosity about what led to this breakup; happiness for Faye to be rid of Nick; and also—as Viva predicted—a little unease at the thought of Faye being suddenly single. I don't have time to sort out these feelings, though, because Vicky is staring at me like she's trying to see into me again.

"You don't *like* like Aunt Faye, do you?" she asks.

With some effort, I feign shock. "What? No! Of course not. Ew. What? No!" Etc.

She chews her lip.

"But . . . just for the sake of argument," I say, ". . . hypothetically . . . what if I did? Would that be bad?"

"Yes!"

"Why?"

"Cuz you're mine. I didn't find you just to give you to Aunt Faye." Find me? *Give* me?

"You know I'm not a stray dog, right?" I ask, annoyed.

"Sorry. You know what I mean."

"I sort of don't, though."

She shrugs. "Well, since you don't *like* like her, it doesn't matter anyway, right?"

"Yeah. Right. It doesn't matter."

The bus sighs and lurches as it moves. Vicky leans her head on my shoulder, slips her hand into mine. My annoyance quickly gives way to a vibration under my ribs, like I felt that first day in the hot dog shop when she laughed.

We sit like this for a while, the movement of the bus jostling us gently from side to side. I feel something weird. Something like contentment. Maybe even happiness, whatever that is. It's nice. For about twenty seconds. Then the bus stops again, opens its doors, and Tasha gets on.

Motherfucking.

Tasha.

I watch her put money into the money thingamajig, then start making her way farther into the crowded bus. She doesn't notice me; the bus lurches forward and she grabs a pole for stability.

I feel suddenly nauseated. I take a deep breath but the stale air inside the bus doesn't help. At all. Seriously, never take a deep breath on a city bus.

"What's wrong?" Vicky asks.

I shake my head. "Nothing."

We ride for a few more stops before I realize I'm staring a hole into the back of Tasha's head, silently willing her to turn around and see me. I don't know what I hope will happen if she does. Maybe I think if she sees me with the kid, she'll realize she was wrong about me and that I'm plenty good at relationships. Or, even if I'm not, that I'm trying, that I'm not a total lost cause.

But she doesn't turn around.

I cough.

She doesn't turn around.

I clear my throat loudly, like your uncle who smokes five packs of Newports a day.

She still doesn't turn around.

Vicky reaches over me and pulls the cord for our stop, then bounces toward the rear doors. I follow her, and now I'm standing like two feet behind Tasha. I could reach out and grab her. But that would be weird, right? Instead, I pretend to be jostled by the motion of the bus and "accidentally" bump my shoulder into her back. She turns, frowning.

"Oh. Tasha. I didn't see you."

She knows I'm lying. I can tell by the look she gives me. I should have expected as much, considering she's known me since second grade and has witnessed me lying in a hundred different situations, from being caught skipping school to missing curfew to telling my sixth-grade boyfriend that yes, I did indeed *want* to touch his penis but that I simply *couldn't*, on account of my devotion to Christ.

"I think you probably did see me," she says. "If you have

something to say to me, say it. I'm too old for this bullshit, Skye. We both are."

Well, shit. When did everybody become so damn direct? I don't even know how to respond. I open my mouth and nothing comes out. For a few seconds, I stand there gaping at her. Then I feel a familiar lump swelling in my throat.

Oh, no.

OH, GOD, NO.

I quickly clench my butthole tight and start frantically considering what other orifices I might be able to squeeze shut to hold back the tears. But then I stop. Because I realize

1. holding in tears all the time is exhausting;
2. it's been exhausting for a really long time; and
3. I can't do it. Like, I can no longer muster the energy to *not* cry.

So, if coming apart on this bus is what's about to happen? I'M JUST GOING TO LET IT.

But it doesn't happen. Because this is when I hear Vicky call my name, and when I look, I see she's already off the bus, peering up at me from the sidewalk, as the doors begin to close.

Why me, Jesus?

I make a quick move to get off, thrusting my arm out in front of me. I'm holding my jacket in my hand and the door closes on it. It's half in and half out as the bus sighs and starts to pull away from the curb. Vicky just looks at me, confused, through the closed doors.

"I'll meet you at the next stop!" I shout. She probably can't even hear me.

So, now I'm standing there, clutching my jacket as it flaps against the outside of the bus, pretending I don't notice everybody is staring at me.

"Her jacket stuck in the door!" I hear somebody yell.

Then somebody else says, "Hey, bus driver! This lady's jacket is stuck in the door!"

The bus driver looks concerned. He quickly pulls over in the middle of the block and opens the doors, rushing back to make sure I'm not hurt. Just kidding! This is Philly. He doesn't even glance in the rearview to see what's going on!

It takes fifty-seven-million years to get to the next corner. It's the longest fifty-seven-million years of my life. During these fifty-seven mega-annum, I think about myself at eighteen, in my dorm room, listening to Tasha's messages and making marks on a chalkboard. I feel sorry for my younger self. But also annoyed. It was college. I could have been at a party. I could have been having a life. Instead of setting Tasha up to fail at friendship.

When the bus finally reaches the next stop, when it finally pulls to the curb, when the doors finally open and my jacket is dislodged, I want to run away screaming from the scene. But, somehow, I muster the composure to say to Tasha, "I'm sorry I tested you. I don't think I really knew I was doing it. Or, maybe I knew but I didn't know why."

Her eyes soften a little and I realize she's probably been waiting a long time for this apology. "Do you know why now?" she asks.

A dude behind me sucks his teeth, annoyed. "Yo, you getting off the bus or not, sis?"

I can see Vicky skipping up the street toward the bus. I look at Tasha. There's really nothing I can say, in this half-second, that will give me back twenty years of missed connection with this person I once loved so much. So, I hop off the bus. The annoyed dude and some other people get off behind me and then the doors close and the bus pulls away.

27

THAT NIGHT, I'M LYING AWAKE IN FAYE'S GUEST BEDROOM, STARING UP at the ceiling for hours, thinking about all the tests I've given over the years, and all the people who failed them; not just friends, like Tasha, but also every girlfriend who ever got close enough to trip the alarm in my crazy-lady brain. DANGER! YOU CAN'T COUNT ON ANYONE! EVACUATE RELATIONSHIP IMMEDIATELY! I could give you a list of all those people and how many weeks or days or just hours it took me to get on a plane and put a city or a country or even a continent between myself and them. But it's a long list and it's already three in the morning.

I get up to pee.

On my way back to bed, I notice that the door of Faye's room, at the other end of the hallway, is ajar, and there's a light on inside, even though there's still three hours before she needs to leave for the hospital. I knock softly. I hear a shuffling movement, and then Faye appears.

"Skye," she says, buttoning the top buttons of her pajama shirt.

"I saw your light on. I just wanted to check everything's alright? Sorry if I—"

"It's okay," she says. "Come in."

I've never been inside Faye's bedroom before. I've peeked in a couple of times, to satisfy my curiosity, and to see if there were any interesting sex toys lying around, which there weren't.

"How are you feeling?" I ask her.

"I'm fine." She sits down at the end of the bed. "I mean, I've *been* fine, all this time, knowing the surgery was coming. And I still am fine. Probably."

"But?"

"But suddenly, I'm feeling really attached to these breasts."

"Well, that's—"

"Don't make a joke."

"I wasn't going to!" I was going to.

"Can I tell you something?" she asks.

I sit down next to her on the bed.

She chews her bottom lip for a moment, the way Vicky does. Then she says, "Losing my breasts was very hard. Harder than I'd ever imagined it would be. I know breasts don't make us women. But when parts of you are cut away, it's hard to feel whole."

"Yeah," I say. "I get that."

"But I did feel whole again. Eventually. And relieved. But now . . ." She sighs. "It's strange to have those same fears again this time. I didn't expect it. It doesn't really make sense to have them. These aren't my real breasts any more or less than the next ones will be. But it still feels like a loss."

Question: Do you have any idea how difficult it is to listen to someone talk this much about their breasts and not look at said breasts? I'm trying so hard to keep my eyes on her face. But every time she says the word "breasts," my eyes drop there.

"These aren't my real breasts," she says again, "but they've been with me through quite a bit, this last decade and a half. I feel like I should have thrown them a going-away party or something."

"That would have been amazing." My eyes once again drift downward against my will. I drag them back up.

"Anyway," Faye says, shrugging. "It's very late. I guess I should try to stop thinking about it and get some sleep."

"I'm sorry you lost your first boobs," I blurt out. Which: ugh. Why was I even born with vocal cords? "I mean . . . sorry about the cancer." Which is only maybe twenty to thirty percent better than SORRY ABOUT YOUR FIRST BOOBS. "I mean . . ."

"I know what you mean," she says.

"I'm sorry about Cynthia's cancer, too. I'm sorry she died." Then I say the thing I've been thinking since I first heard about the new tits: "I'm glad you didn't die."

Faye reaches out and takes one of my hands in both of hers. She looks pensive, and a teensy bit sad.

You know what would be the worst possible moment for my gaze to drift downward again? THIS MOMENT, FAM! But guess what? That's exactly what my gaze does. And in the fraction of a second before I can pull it back up, I hear Faye say, "My eyes are up here, Skye."

NOOOOOOOOOOOOOOOO!

"I'm so sorry!" I say, wondering if I should kill myself by belt-hanging or a clean gunshot to the face.

She smiles. "I'm just messing with you. It's probably not possible to talk this much about someone's breasts and not look at them."

"Oh, thank God." I won't have to commit the suicide now.

Then she says: "Do you want to see them?"

Do I what the what now?

"Do you . . . want me to see them?"

She nods. "It's not a going-away party. But I think I'd like them to at least be looked at one last time. I was looking before you knocked, but it's not really the same, you know?"

"Sure," I reply, nodding.

"You can say no," she tells me, "if it feels inappropriate."

I know what you're thinking. But it's not like I haven't looked at my friends' breasts before. Women and girls undress in front of one another all the time and it's not sexy or weird. Plus, this seems to mean something to Faye and I want to be a comfort to her if I can be, that's all. I'M BEING A GOOD FRIEND, OKAY?

"I'm happy to help."

Faye smiles, and her dark eyes twinkle. She takes a deep breath. And starts to unbutton her top.

I don't think I can adequately describe my excitement. I don't even breathe as her buttons come undone. When she opens her top, and her breasts are exposed, I am almost light-headed with longing for her. This is when I realize this was a bad idea. Because now I want to touch her. But I'm not sure she wants that, and I don't want to ask and potentially turn this moment of super-platonic breast-appreciation into something awkward. So, I ignore the wetness in my panties.

It occurs to me that I should say something. Something like, *these are great* or *excellent rack, friend*. But I understand that it's not my opinion of her breasts that she wants, so I shut up and just . . . sit there. Staring. At her breasts. For like two entire minutes. They are two of the very best minutes of my entire wasted life.

She

has

a

tiny

mole

near

her

right

nipple

that

I

would

murder

you

over

if

I

had

to.

As it turns out, two is the precise number of minutes of her bare breasts that I can take without having a full-strength orgasm where I sit, so then I reach over and start buttoning her top, slowly, feeling her eyes on me the entire time.

When I finally look up at her, there are tears in the corners of her eyes, but she's smiling. "Thanks, Skye." Her raspy voice is almost a whisper.

"You're welcome, Faye," I say, smiling, too.

28

AFTER I DROP VICKY OFF AT SCHOOL, I GET A TEXT FROM ANGIE THAT Faye's surgery went perfectly well, and that Angie is taking her home after an hour of recovery at the hospital. "I planned to be with Faye all day," Angie tells me. "I took the day off work. But my father just called, in a state, so I need to go and take care of some things in Germantown. Can you come look after Faye for a couple of hours? She doesn't need much. She'll probably just sleep."

When I turn onto Faye's street, I hear a siren—not the wailing kind, but the woop-woop you hear when a cop car pulls you over—coming from up the block. A cop car is stopping in front of Reverend Seymour's. I watch two cops get out. Without thinking, I start walking toward them.

When I get near Reverend Seymour's house, I linger by some bushes and watch the cops as they head for the basement door. I can hear church music coming from the piano, which is unexpected because there's usually no service on Monday afternoons.

One of the cops, the bigger, meatier one of the two, knocks on the basement door. Then he and the skinnier cop both walk to the front of the house and start looking around. For what, I don't know. They don't seem to notice me. I take out my phone and start recording, just as Reverend Seymour comes out of the basement and walks around to the front of the house. She's dressed in a white kaftan and she's carrying her Bible. The music is still playing, the sounds of praise song filling the air. With all that, plus her kind smile and calm demeanor, she looks absolutely saintly. I see her notice me, giving me an almost imperceptible nod, and then she greets the cops. "Good afternoon, officers," she says. "How can I help you?"

"We got a complaint about the noise," the skinny cop says, "from one of your neighbors."

"We're singing the gospel," the reverend says. "It's choir practice. My granddaughter is playing piano. You're both welcome to come inside and listen if you like."

"Are you aware that this block is residentially zoned?" the meaty cop asks.

"I've lived here for forty years."

"Is that a 'yes'?"

The music stops. I look toward the basement door and see a few people poking their heads out, trying to see what's going on.

"Yes," the reverend says. "I'm aware of the zoning. Churches are exempt from noise ordinances."

"*Official* churches," says Meaty. "*Actual* churches. Not a bunch of people singing in the basement of your run-down house."

Reverend Seymour looks down at her hands, clasps them together, unclasps them.

People begin coming up out of the basement, but they hang back, away from the cops. Brother Nguyen comes out of the house and walks down the front steps to stand near the reverend.

"Unless you've registered this 'church' somewhere?" Skinny is asking.

"It's just a small gathering of neighbors," the reverend replies. "There's never been a reason to—"

"Well, now there's a reason," Skinny says.

"Unless you want to get fined. Do you want to get fined? Because we can do that."

Reverend Seymour stares directly at the cop and says, "How much is the fine?" I can see anger behind her eyes. But also fear.

The cops glance at each other and smirk. "Up to three hundred dollars for an initial violation," one of them says.

The reverend sighs. "I can't pay that. I'm on a fixed income."

"You could take it out of the collection plate."

"We don't take an offering," says the reverend. "One of the reasons people come to worship with us is they don't have to feel ashamed of what they can't give when a collection plate comes around."

The meaty cop snickers. "Why even have church if you're not going to ask for money? I thought taking people's hard-earned cash was the whole point of church."

Both of the cops laugh.

I glance down at Ethan's house and see him standing at his door, his head poking out, watching what's going on.

"We're gonna let you off with a warning this time," one of the cops says. "Next time, we'll fine you. Keep the noise down. Got it?"

"Have a blessed day, officers," Reverend Seymour says.

As the cops head back to their car, the rest of the churchgoers emerge from the basement. They gather around the reverend, talking in hushed voices.

Both cops spot me as they approach their vehicle. One of them glares. I'm not gonna lie: It's intimidating. I know it's my legal right to film them; Vicky has reminded me of that a hundred times. BUT DID I MENTION THEY HAVE GUNS AND IMPUNITY? My hand starts shaking a teensy bit. I consider putting my phone away. Like, why am I even here right now? I don't know Reverend Seymour *that* well. I like her, sure, but not enough to get my ass beat, or worse, by the cops. We still don't know what happened to Sandra Bland. Besides, I don't even live on this block. This is none of my damn business!

I don't put my phone away, though. I take another deep breath and keep recording. Through the rectangle of my screen, I watch the cops get into their car and drive away.

Brother Nguyen looks over at Ethan's porch, where Ethan is still peeking out of the front door. "Hey!" he calls, moving toward Ethan's house. "Excuse me!"

At first, I think Ethan's going to duck back inside. But he pushes the door open wider, steps out onto the porch, and glares down at Brother Nguyen. "Yeah?"

"Did you call the police on my friend's church?"

"It's not a church!" Ethan yells. "I called the police on *the noise*. Just like I warned her I would if she kept this up."

"My friend, *the reverend*," Brother Nguyen says, pointing at Reverend Seymour, "has been living on this block longer than you've been alive."

"So, what? Does that mean my baby isn't supposed to sleep?"

"No, it—"

"You have kids?" Ethan asks.

"Yes. Four children."

"Then you know how hard it is to get a baby back to sleep," Ethan says. "Or maybe you don't. I don't know how involved men were with their kids back in your day, in your culture."

Brother Nguyen frowns. "Calling the police on Black people can be dangerous for them. Don't you watch the news?"

Ethan rolls his eyes, like he couldn't possibly give less of a damn.

"This isn't how you solve problems with your neighbors," Brother Nguyen says, "if you want to be part of a community."

"That's right!" someone yells.

"Tell him, Asian brother!" yells someone else.

"Gentrification is hard enough on Black people already," Brother Nguyen says.

Ethan smirks. "Your people don't have a great reputation when it comes to Black neighborhoods, either, do they?"

Brother Nguyen frowns again. "No. But I always respected my neighbors."

"Why don't you just mind your own business, man?"

"It is my business when my friend is put in harm's way."

"You better tell that fool!" someone yells.

Ethan laughs. "Who are you supposed to be? Their Asian savior? That's a new one."

"Just a good neighbor," Brother Nguyen says. "Which is what we *all* should be."

"Tell that to *her*!" Ethan says, pointing at the reverend.

"It's alright, Phil," Reverend Seymour says. "You tried. That's all you can do."

Brother Nguyen shakes his head at Ethan and walks back up onto the reverend's porch.

I suddenly realize I'm still watching all of this through my phone camera, still recording. I turn the camera off just as Reverend Seymour starts walking toward me.

"Sister Skye!"

"Hello, Reverend."

"Are you familiar with Romans 8:16?"

"Can't say I am."

" 'The Spirit himself bears witness with our spirit that we are children of God,' " the reverend says. "The Lord calls upon us to bear witness for one another, in the name of Jesus. Thank you for bearing witness for me today. Amen?"

"Totes."

She opens her arms for a hug. I let it happen this time.

"Would you like to join us for the rest of choir practice?" she asks. "I bet you have a lovely voice."

"The rest? You're not shutting things down after . . . the cops came?"

"Oh, no. We'll reduce the volume on the next song. But we're not going anywhere," she says loudly over her shoulder.

Ethan frowns and goes back inside, slamming his door shut behind him.

"I'm on my way to Faye's, to help her with something," I tell the reverend. But, honestly, even if I wasn't, I still wouldn't say yes to joining them. I'm glad to have been a witness, in the name of Jesus and all that fun stuff. It actually feels good to have done it. But not good enough to take my ass to church.

FAYE IS ASLEEP ON THE couch when I get there. Angie thanks me and slips out. I have my period and I'm a little crampy, so I take some Advil. Then I get a root beer from the fridge and sit on the floor by the couch, reading the news on my phone, until I hear Faye stirring. She smiles when she sees me. I move to sit beside her on the couch and ask how she's feeling.

"Groggy. Sore. But otherwise fine. I was dreaming about Wildwood. Did you ever go there when you were a kid?"

"Sure." Wildwood is a boardwalk, amusement park, and beach in New Jersey.

"Good memories?" Faye asks.

"We used to go there on the last day of camp every summer," I tell her. "A lot of my memories are of running down the boardwalk with Cynthia, eating funnel cake."

Faye makes a little sound, like she's ruminating on that. Then she says, "We used to go sometimes with our mother. We screamed our heads off riding the Sea Serpent. That's what I was dreaming about just now."

She's smiling at the memory. I'm not sure post-surgery is the right time to talk about *acrimonious kinship*, but I can't help but ask. "What happened between you and Cynthia? Why weren't you close as adults?"

Faye is quiet for such a long moment that I think maybe she's not going to answer. But then she starts talking. "When our mother died and we got separated, Cynthia and I had a plan. On my eighteenth birthday, I was going to get on a bus and collect my sister from Newark. I was going to petition to become her legal guardian."

"What happened?"

"Nothing," she says. "I turned eighteen. And I didn't do it."

Of all the stories I could have imagined about what happened between Faye and Cynthia, one in which Faye failed to show up would not have been among them. "Why didn't you?" I ask her.

"Because those two years in Jenkins had been very bad."

I remember the drugs and the abortions and it all starts to make sense.

"I ran away from Georgia when I was seventeen and came back to Philly," Faye says. "I got a job at night, studied for the SAT during the day, and started rhyming in front of people. But I was still doing drugs. I was still making lots of bad decisions. By the time I turned eighteen, I had barely figured out how to take care of myself. I didn't think I could take care of anyone else. And I didn't want to try. I was selfish." There's anguish on her face and in her voice when she says this.

"You were only eighteen, Faye," I remind her.

She nods. "But Cynthia was only fifteen. And not as understanding. When I told her I couldn't do it, she stopped talking to me. Completely. I didn't hear from her again until twelve years later, when Vicky was born."

"Why did she reach out to you then?"

"Because I was the only blood family she had left. I think she wanted Vicky to know where she came from."

I think about Vicky's *she's not even my real aunt* shenanigans and I wish she were here so I could shake my head in disappointment at her.

"But it didn't mean all was forgiven," Faye says. "Cynthia still resented me. Her resentment manifested as judgment most of the time. She had *lots* of opinions about how I lived my life then. And I still felt guilty. Regretful. And probably angry at her for not being able to forgive me. We could never really get past it."

I think about my own sibling. I've resented Slade our entire adult lives. He never left me. *I* left, the very day I turned eighteen. He stayed. His staying is what I resent.

Faye yawns and rubs her eyes. I can see she's tired, so I drop acrimonious kinship for now. I fluff her pillows.

"We should go to Wildwood," she says, settling back against them. "You and me and Vicky. Before you leave for Bali."

"Okay," I say. "Yeah. That sounds fun."

"I HEAR YOU'RE AN ACTIVIST now," my mother says.

I'm crouched beside her bed, guiding her left leg into a sheer knee-high stocking. It's Wednesday evening and I'm helping her get ready for the weekly vespers service at her church.

"Where'd you hear that?" I ask.

"Viva told me."

I only told Viva about recording the cops as a way to break up some of the tension that had been lingering between us since our argument.

I shrug. "I just took some video of the cops, that's all."

"We've always had problems with the police in this neighborhood," my mother says. "Either they were beating somebody up for *nothing*, or you called them for *something* and they never came."

"Well, they come now. As long as the right people call."

She nods. "I'm proud of you for the work you're doing for the community."

"Thanks," I say, feeling pretty proud of myself, even though I'm not actually doing any work for the community.

"I was never that big into activism," she says. "I was working since I was fifteen, so I never had time for that *plus* school. And once I had kids? Forget about it. I was lucky if I had time to take a shower, let alone get myself involved in a demonstration."

I get up from my crouching position, stretch, hear things pop and crack in my lower back. I go to the closet and push aside clothes, looking for something for my mother to wear.

"I think I did join a protest once, though," she says, her face scrunched up trying to remember. "What was it for? Oh, I remember! We marched against the boys at my high school."

"Really? Why?" I ask, trying not to sound as shocked as I am. I can imagine a thousand different reasons to protest high school boys. But I can't imagine my mother doing it for any of them. She's more the kind of woman who lets men get away with anything.

"They were dogs," she says. "They were always grabbing at us and saying crude things when the teachers weren't around. And sometimes when the teachers *were* around. Not that the teachers did anything about it. Nobody did anything about it. So, my best friend, Maureen—you remember Maureen?"

"Yes."

"Well, this was 1971 or 1972 and everybody was rallying around Angela Davis, trying to get her out of jail. A lot of high school students were doing walkouts, even in Philly. So, Maureen got the idea to do a walkout, too. Not for Angela, but for us. To put pressure on the teachers to get those boys in line."

"Did it work?"

She shakes her head. "Not that first time. Most of the girls who said they'd do it chickened out. It ended up being only me and Maureen and a couple of others. Everybody pretty much ignored us."

"That's depressing."

"Well, we didn't really know what we were doing," she says. "As far as organizing. It took us a while to figure out we hadn't been loud enough. We hadn't shocked them. So, the next time, we came up with a slogan: 'Kick 'em where it hurts!'"

"You mean . . . in the dick?"

"That's right!" she says, slapping her knee and laughing. "We made signs showing girls kicking boys in the privates. And we went all through the halls shouting, 'Kick 'em where it hurts!' That got everybody's attention."

I imagine my mother at fifteen, shouting down sexual assault and harassment in the halls. I think about Vicky, kneeing Marco in the dick, some fifty years later.

My mother is still laughing. "I need to call Maureen," she says, wiping tears of laughter from her eyes. "It's been too long since we spoke. I wonder how she's doing."

"Maureen died, Mom. Like, ten years ago."

"Oh, yes," my mother says quickly, nodding. "That's right. I do remember that."

I'm not sure she does, though.

I pull a plain-ish beige dress from the closet. "You want to wear this?"

She eyes it, then shakes her head, no. "I have a pretty green one in there somewhere."

I hang up the beige dress and look for the green one.

"You coming with me to church this time?" my mother asks.

I give her a look.

"No harm in asking," she says, shrugging. "I was just remembering you when you were little, in your pink pantyhose with the hearts on them that you loved so much. And your patent-leather shoes. Singing with the other little ones in the choir. You were adorable. People used to say, 'You got a smart girl there, Amaryllis.' And I'd say, 'Who you telling? That's my baby.'"

She's smiling at the memory and it makes me smile, too.

I find the green dress and hold it up. My mother nods approvingly. I lay the dress out on the bed.

"Mom, do you know what egg donation is?"

She nods. "I think so."

"Okay, well, I did that. I donated eggs to someone. A friend of mine."

She squints at me. "Who?"

"Cynthia. From camp. You wouldn't—"

"The one you used to match outfits with?"

I stare at her for a second. Then, I'm like: "How could you possibly remember that?"

She shrugs. "Sometimes I remember the strangest things. My neighbor down the street used to have a cat named Stevie Wonder. I remember that, even though I was only seven at the time. I can't remember what I had for breakfast most mornings, but I remember that. The cat wasn't even blind. Isn't that absurd?"

Frankly, yes.

"Anyway . . . I donated my eggs to Cynthia and she had a kid."

My mother sits forward on the edge of the bed and peers at me. "You mean, I have a grandbaby?"

"No. I mean, I guess. Sort of. Not a baby, though. A twelve-year-old."

"When do I get to meet him?" she asks with an eagerness in her voice that I didn't expect.

"*Her*. And . . . I don't know. Do you *want* to meet her?"

She frowns. "What kind of a question is that? Of course I want to meet my own grandchild. That's why you're telling me, isn't it? So I can meet her?"

"Not exactly."

"Well, why else?"

"To see if you care, I guess?"

Her frown intensifies. "Why do you say things like that? Of course I care. And of course I want to meet her."

"Okay," I say.

She nods, smiling, looking content.

"You need a slip with this dress," I tell her.

She points to the underwear drawer of the dresser. I look in there for a slip but don't find one. She tells me there's one in the dryer downstairs, so I go and get it. When I get back to her room, I find her crying. She looks me right in the eyes and says, "Why'd this have to happen to me?"

Shit.

"I've never done anything bad to anybody," she says. "As a matter of fact, I did everything I could for everybody else my whole life."

Which is almost true. She did everything for my father when they were married. Everything for Slade. Everything for her parents when they were aging. Everything for her church. I'm probably the only person she didn't do everything for, as a matter of fact. Which makes me exactly the wrong person for her to be having this conversation with.

"I thought God was looking out for me," she says. "I read my Bible and prayed every day and I thought the Lord was listening. But now I don't know."

This isn't the first time I've heard this. When I visited her in the hospital after her surgery, she said the same things to me. I didn't have any answers then, and I still don't. Back then, she'd seemed angry more than sad. I sat beside her hospital bed as she cried and cried. I felt sympathy for her and the terrible thing that had changed her existence so drastically, but I also felt disconnected. Because how do you comfort someone you resent? How do you show up for someone who didn't show up for you? I didn't know. All I *did* know was that I couldn't hold my mother's anger because I had no room for it, with all the space my own anger was taking up.

Now, I sit down beside her on the bed. I think about Vicky, how she held my hand on the bus. I think about how easy the love is between me and her, how unencumbered. There are no regrets between us, and no resentments, because we have no history. History is where shit gets messy.

I don't take my mother's hand. I can't. I don't even really want to. But I remember what Reverend Seymour said, about bearing witness, and I think maybe I can do that. So, I sit and wait, in case she wants to say anything else. She mostly just shakes her head from side to side and sniffles. I pat her back a couple of times. We exist there for a while, like that.

"Look at me," she says finally, "acting like the child instead of the mother. I should be taking care of you, not the other way around."

You have never taken care of me. Not like you should have, anyway.

After a while, I ask, "Do you still want to go to church?"

"If it's not too late."

"We have time," I say. It's not a metaphor. I'm only talking about church. The rest of it, I still don't know.

29

ON SATURDAY, I PICK UP VICKY AND JAZ AND TAKE THEM TO MAL-
colm X Park to meet up with a bunch of other kids from activist club
at a big protest rally against police brutality. Vicky screams "What do
we want? Justice! When do we want it? Now!" and "Whose streets?
Our streets!" so loudly and with so much guttural rage that I worry
her throat is going to bleed. After the rally, we get cheesesteaks.
Around one, we drop Jaz off at her house and head back to Vicky's.

Faye's in the kitchen, on her phone, when we come in. She does
not look happy.

There's a pizza on the kitchen table. Vicky makes a beeline for it,
even though she just snarfed down an entire sandwich and fries.

"Okay," Faye is saying into the phone. "Thanks for letting me
know."

"What's wrong?" I ask when she hangs up.

Faye looks at the kid. "Vicky, have you been taking video of the
white man down the street?"

OH. SHIT.

"No," Vicky says, with as straight a face as a person can have with
a mouth full of cheese.

Faye peers at her. She's torn. I can see it in her face. She wants to believe Vicky. She wants the kid to be telling her the truth, to not be lying right to her face. "Okay," Faye says. "Well, someone said they saw you doing it. Several times. Are they mistaken?"

"Yup," Vick says without a moment's hesitation. "It must have been someone else."

Faye's mouth twitches at the corners. She looks over at me.

I have a flash of a moment to make a choice here. I can hold Vicky down and pretend to know nothing, ride-or-die style. Or I can give Faye the information she needs to parent Vicky, who we both love and want the best for. It feels like a shitty decision to have to make, but I realize that I've brought it on myself. If I had stepped up when I saw Vicky stalking Ethan at the reverend's cookout, and figured out then and there how to parent the kid, we might not be here now. Still, I cannot bring myself to betray Vicky. So, I try to keep my face as blank as possible, feigning complete ignorance.

It doesn't work. Faye takes one look at me and knows everything. She moves toward Vicky, holding out her hand. "Vicky, give me your phone."

Vicky glares at her. "No."

"It's my fault," I say, stepping forward, almost between them. "I wanted to keep an eye on Ethan. To help the reverend. I asked Vicky to do it, too."

Faye ignores me. "Vicky," she says. "Give me your phone."

"No."

"I explicitly said not to take video of Ethan."

"No, you didn't," Vicky insists. "You said not to take video of the cops."

"I said not to get involved!"

"I told you, it was my idea," I say helplessly.

"I'm sure it was *not* your idea, Skye," Faye says, finally looking at me. "But the fact that you obviously know about it and went along with it is *astounding*."

"It's not a big deal," Vicky says. "Nothing bad happened."

Faye looks at the kid and in her eyes there is a kind of anger I have never seen there. "Vicky, leave your phone on the table and go to your room," Faye says. "You're grounded."

"No!"

"Um, Vick?" I say. "Maybe you should—"

"It's not fair!"

"It's not fair?" Faye asks, her voice shaking with anger. "You went behind my back and did something I explicitly told you not to do and you just now stood here and lied about it to my face. But it's *not fair* to ground you?" She points a shaking finger at the stairs. "Go to your room *right now*."

"I'm not going!" Vicky screams.

Faye takes a few more quick steps toward her, grabs her arm, and steers her toward the stairs. Vicky pulls her arm out of Faye's grasp and pushes her hard into the wall. Faye looks stunned. Vicky grabs the bookshelf with both hands and knocks it over, sending the books in it, along with the potted plants and framed photos on top of it, crashing to the floor.

"Shit!" I jump back out of the way of flying glass and soil.

"Vicky," Faye yells, "you need to calm down!"

Fuming, Vicky throws her phone on the floor, and then turns and stomps up the stairs. We hear her go into her room and slam the door so hard that the floors shake.

Silence—the kind that hangs heavy in the air after a fight—fills the house.

Faye stares at the bookshelf, rubbing her shoulder where it hit the wall.

"Are you okay?"

She doesn't answer. She picks up Vicky's phone, which, thanks to a bulky case, looks undamaged, and starts toward the mess. I move to follow her but she puts her hand out in a *stop* gesture.

"You've done enough," she says.

I frown at her. "You seriously don't want help with all this? There's dirt and glass everywhere."

"How long have you known she was taking video of Ethan?"

"I don't know. Maybe two weeks?"

She shakes her head in disbelief.

"I only saw her doing it *once,*" I tell her in my defense. "I didn't know it was a regular thing."

"Did you tell her to stop?" she asks.

"Yes. Kind of."

"Kind of?"

"What was I going to do, Faye? Forbid her? She would have just kept doing it anyway. She doesn't listen to you; why would she listen to me?"

"'She would have done it anyway' isn't a reason to ignore it," Faye says, bristling. "She's a child. She needs rules. She needs boundaries. You have to say no sometimes, Skye."

"I know."

"Do you?"

"Yeah."

"When have you ever said no to her?"

I think about it. "The other day. She wanted cheesesteaks and I was like, 'Nah, let's get burgers.'"

She just stares at me, like she's trying to figure out how one becomes such an idiot. Then, she's like, "Do you really not understand why pointing a camera at a 911-happy white man is a dangerous thing for Vicky to be doing?"

"I do understand."

"Then why didn't you put a stop to it?"

I don't answer because *I didn't want Vicky to be mad at me* sounds pathetic.

"I know it's great being Vicky's favorite," Faye says. "Being the only cool grown-up in her life. When Cynthia was alive, I was the cool aunt who let Vicky eat ice cream for dinner and stay up too late. But now I'm the one raising her and that requires saying no sometimes. It's not fun. It's not cool. But I have to do it. Because she's twelve and she makes very bad decisions. Like eating an entire box of Little Debbie Oatmeal Creme Pies, getting horrible diarrhea, and sitting on the toilet crying and shitting for an hour."

"Wow."

"Yeah," she says. "That happened."

"Okay. I get it. But it's not just about being her favorite. It's more . . . egg donor specific than that."

"Meaning what?"

"Meaning Vicky's my genetic offspring, right? But I didn't give birth to her and then give her up for adoption. Or, like, abandon her on the front steps of a nunnery or some shit. I didn't give her away."

"Okay."

"But I also didn't raise her," I say. "Which would have resulted in screwing her up in any number of ways, I assure you. So . . . it's kind of ideal, as far as parent-child narratives go."

She peers at me. "I don't think I'm following you."

"There's nothing for me to regret," I tell her. "And there's nothing for Vicky to resent. How many family relationships can you say that about?"

She nods slowly, and I know she's thinking about herself and Cynthia. "Not many."

"It makes the love between us easy," I say. "*That's* what I don't want to risk."

"Easy love is hard to come by," she says.

Truer words, y'all.

"And I also just want Vicky to know that I'm always on her side. That I have her back. My mother didn't have mine and it sucked." I sigh. "And I know I'm not her mother. I know that. But still."

"How did your mother not have your back?"

I consider not telling her about my childhood traumas. Maybe I don't want her to know the things that messed me up. But then she comes and stands close to me, looks at me—into me—with eyes full of care and affection, and I want to tell her everything that matters.

"When I was a kid, my dad was really shitty. He liked to lock me in the closet when I didn't behave. He called me names, told me I was stupid. He knocked me around sometimes. My mother didn't stop him. She didn't protect me from him."

When I feel the sting of tears, I just let them happen.

Faye puts her arms around me. I bury my face in her shoulder. She rubs my back as my tears fall onto her shoulder.

After a couple of minutes, I detach myself from her. "I'm getting snot all over you."

"I don't mind."

I look at the mess on the floor. "I think we should clean this up."

Together, we lift the bookshelf and stand it upright again. Then Faye starts cleaning up the dirt and broken pot pieces while I start putting books back on shelves.

We hear stomping upstairs, then a thud, then silence again.

"Do you want me to go talk to her?" I ask.

"No," she says. "I've found it's better to just let her settle down on her own."

I go back to the books. After a minute, I ask, "Do you think settling down is what she needs?"

Faye stops sweeping and looks at me. "What does that mean?"

I'm not totally sure what it means. I think about the way Vicky talks about Charlotte. The way she screamed at the protest rally. I think about myself at twelve, holding back a scream of rage until my throat was sore. "I just think maybe the kid has a lot of anger in there that needs to get out."

"It got out," Faye says, gesturing toward the bookshelf and its decimated contents.

"It didn't, though. It started to. And then you told her to calm down. Like you've done before. Like Kenny and Charlotte always do. Like her teachers and principal probably do. So, she did. For now. Until all that anger boils to the surface again. And again. And again."

I suddenly feel very tired. I take a seat on the floor, against the wall, away from the broken glass and smashed pots. I lean my head back. I say, "I think if we keep trying to push it back down, Vicky's anger is going to turn into something worse."

"What?"

"Depression. Disconnection."

"You're saying we should just let her explode," Faye says. "And then what?"

"Then she moves through it," I say. "Past it."

Faye looks like she's thinking about that. After a long moment, she says, "No."

"No?"

She shakes her head. "No."

"Why not?"

"Because I don't know how bad that could get and if I'd be able to handle it," she says. "And considering you can't even say no to Vicky about anything more important than cheesesteaks, you're not really in a position to criticize me for that."

"I'm not criticizing you. Honestly. I know parenting is hard. I mean, I assume it is. But you're a great parent."

"I'm not."

"You *are*."

She shakes her head again. "Vicky hates me."

"She doesn't hate you," I say. "Trust me. If she hated you, I'd know. She hates Kenny. She *really* hates Charlotte. She's not shy about expressing hatred for people."

"She's never said she hates me?"

"Never."

"You swear?"

"I swear. Not even once."

She sits down beside me on the floor, very close, so our shoulders and knees are touching.

"You really think I'm a great parent?"

"You're a thousand times better than my parents were, in every way," I tell her. "I think Vicky's super lucky you fucked her dad to get custody of her."

She smiles and punches me in the shoulder.

"Really, though," I say. "Jokes aside. You're wonderful, Faye."

She reaches over and takes my hand, interlocks her fingers with mine. Her nails are painted A Oui Bit of Red. She leans her head back against the wall and closes her eyes. We sit there for a couple of minutes in silence. Then she says, "I broke up with Nick."

She says it almost casually, the way you might tell someone that you don't like Adele anymore. *Actually, I stopped listening to her music when she accepted the Grammy after she admitted Beyoncé deserved it more.* But when I look over at her, she's watching me, and there's nothing casual in those intense, dark eyes of hers.

I don't tell her I already know. "What happened?" I ask.

"Nothing really happened," she says. "But the closer I got to my surgery date, the more my thoughts were consumed with cancer and loss and life and death, the more I just wasn't sure I wanted to marry Nick. And he wasn't okay with that."

To hell with him, is what I want to say. Instead, I ask, "Are you okay?"

"Yes."

I can feel the change in her energy now, from stressed-out parent to something else entirely. If there have been moments when I wasn't sure what Faye wanted, this is not one of them. Something has shifted and, as I feel her red-tipped fingers intertwined with mine, there's no doubt in my mind that she wants something to happen right now.

The thing is: I lied. I don't want to be Faye's friend with benefits. I don't want a situationship. Viva was right: That *is* some cishet nonsense! But I'm also terrified of the idea of something more. I'm terrified of loving Faye; of counting on her; of wanting to belong with her.

I feel the slightest movement, a shift in the position of her body, and I know she's going to kiss me any second. I take my hand out of hers and pat her knee, the way your grandma does when you do something cute, and say, "I'm glad we're friends."

There's a flash of surprise on her face, as though, of all the things I could have said right now, she didn't think it'd be that. She recovers quickly, nodding and smiling and saying, "I'm glad, too."

BEFORE I LEAVE, I GO up to check on Vicky. I knock on her door but she doesn't answer. "It's Skye," I say, hoping that matters.

"Come in."

She's sitting on the bed with a book in her lap; one of those fantasy series with teenage witches or demigods.

"You okay, kid?"

"I'm fine," she says. "We don't have to talk about it."

I feel like we should probably talk about it. But I can't force her. And also: I'm a little talked-out right now.

"I'll call you tomorrow," I tell her.

"I don't have a phone."

"I'll call you on Faye's phone. Or send a carrier pigeon. Whichev."

She doesn't look amused in the least.

30

MY THIRTY-NINTH BIRTHDAY FALLS ON A SATURDAY. WHEN I WAS young, this fact would have had me psyched. But I haven't really celebrated my birthday in like ten years. Don't feel bad for me, okay? It's not like I put my head under the covers and lament the cruel passing of time; I just don't make a big deal out of it. I don't even shower this morning. I just rub a wet washcloth on the important parts and call it done. I don't have any clean underwear, so I go commando. I'm almost out of clean bras, too, so I put on my emergency bra. Y'all know the kind of bra I'm talking about. It's white, it's more than ten years old, and it looks like something your grandmother would have worn under her church clothes. Pretty sure I got it at JCPenney. But whatever.

Usually, I'm traveling when my birthday rolls around, without actual friends to throw me a party or even just buy me drinks. Today, I'm right here in Philly, where I've been for almost two months now, and there are people in my life who know it's my birthday. Thus, there is a candle in my pancakes.

"You shouldn't have," I say to Viva across the table.

"You only turn thirty-nine once," she replies.

"You only turn every age once."

"You know what I mean. It's the last year of your thirties. Es importante."

"Why?"

She frowns. "Girl, just blow out the candle."

I blow.

"Are you excited about your party tonight?" Viva asks me.

"You might want to lower your expectations," I tell her. "Three women and a twelve-year-old isn't really a party."

"So, you're not excited, then?"

I sigh. It's an unintentionally long sigh.

Viva squints at me. "Why do you sound like you're going to the electric chair and not to a birthday dinner with your loved ones?"

I chuckle. And shrug.

I invited Viva to Faye's for birthday festivities because she's my closest friend and that is the kind of thing you do. But I haven't told Viva that Faye and Nick broke up. In fact, we haven't talked about Faye since Viva accused me of being in love with her. I don't want to tell her she's right, and that I'm too damaged to do anything about it, even though I'm pretty sure Faye is in love with me, too, or, at least, that she *like* likes me. The idea of dinner with the two of them makes me a little anxious.

I spend most of the day working in the courtyard. There's still a ton to get done for the Bali-Sydney trip, which is now in five weeks. I get distracted a few times, thinking about Faye. About her breasts. The smell of her hair when I cried on her shoulder. And the heat of her body when she's close to me. When I can't take it anymore, I run up to my room to rub one out and then get back to work. A little before seven, Viva and I walk the six blocks to Faye's house.

It's been a week since Vicky knocked over the bookcase. As penance, she was confined to the house and backyard for the whole week, allowed to leave only to go to school. We've only chatted a couple of times, via landline. The first call, Vicky was mostly quiet, perking up only when complaining about what a raging bitch Faye is. By the second call, a couple of days ago, she was her normal, chatty self, like the whole fight never happened. Now, with her grounding completed, she bounces up to me and Viva as we enter the house, looking excited to see us. "Happy birthday!" she says, throwing her arms around me.

"Thanks, kid."

Viva and Faye have met but they've never spent time together. Still, like most Black women from Philly, even those meeting for the first time, they hug like homies. Nick was right. Philadelphians really are friendly people.

"I love your house," Viva tells Faye. "It's so pretty and warm. I sense good energy."

Faye thanks her. "I'm really glad you're here," she says.

Birthday dinner is hot sausages, sweet potatoes, onions, peppers, and corn on the grill. We eat together with the fading sun on our shoulders. Faye asks me what my goals are for my fortieth year on earth.

"I'll just be glad if everything doesn't fall apart."

She smiles. Whatever worries I had about things being weird between her and me disappear. She's the same as always: warm, curious, open. It's almost as if that whole awkward *I'm glad we're friends* moment never happened. So much so that I start to think maybe it *didn't* happen. Maybe she wasn't about to kiss me; maybe I just made the whole thing up in my head. Which is fine. Really.

"Viva," Faye says. "Tell us what Skye was like in high school."

"Ooh, yeah, tell us!" Vicky says.

"She was a goofball," Viva replies. "She was always making us laugh. When she wasn't being moody. Emocional. Like most poetisas. She used to like to read Lucille Clifton out loud to us and cry."

"*Really?*" Faye asks, interested.

"Don't let the walls she's built up fool you. She's a real crier underneath all that."

"Oh my God, Veev."

"*You are,*" she says. "Remember how mad you used to get when

Tasha and I didn't cry, too?" Then, to Faye, "She told us we didn't have the souls of poets. She called us *barbarians*."

They share a laugh at that. I shake my head at Viva, but I feel happy. I think about Tasha. I wonder if we'll ever be friends again, if we'll ever be close the way Viva and I are.

Faye asks Viva what her major was at CAPA. Viva tells her it was dance and we reminisce about our junior year collab, when I wrote a poem about our enslaved ancestors breaking their chains and read it aloud while Viva performed a dance she choreographed for it.

"That sounds so cool," Vicky says.

"It was probably very corny," I reply.

"Sí," Viva agrees, putting her arm around my shoulders. "But we had a good time."

Viva brought a bomba y plena mix and we listen to it, dancing in our chairs while we eat, until we can't stay seated anymore and the music pulls us onto our feet. We dance and eat and dance and eat, talking and laughing until moonlight and streetlight replace sunlight on our shoulders.

"Can we eat cake now?" Vicky asks. "I have to go soon."

"Vicky," Faye says, giving her an annoyed look.

"Wait, where are you going?" I ask.

"Jaz's. It's her birthday, too, remember? She's having a sleepover." Then, to Faye, "What? Everybody knows there's cake on their birthday. It's not a surprise."

"I did suspect there would be cake," I say in Vicky's defense.

"Fine. I'll get the cake."

The cake is all chocolate everything, with candles shaped like a three and a nine. Faye starts to sing that Stevie Wonder "Happy Birthday to Ya" song and Vicky and Viva quickly join in.

When the kid leaves for Jaz's, Viva says, "I have to go, too. I have guests checking in late this evening."

"I'll walk back with you."

"You will not," she says. She gives Faye and me each a kiss on the cheek, Puerto Rican style, and bounces.

When it's just us, Faye says, "I'd offer you a drink, but I'm out of bourbon."

"No worries."

"Let's go out?"

I'm already full of cake and sausages, but a little bourbon to end the evening doesn't sound bad.

Faye changes out of shorts and flip-flops into something more bar-friendly—black sweater, white denim capris, and strappy white sandals.

"You look nice." She looks *incredible*.

The Swank is only a few blocks away but Faye wants to take me to a new jawn she went to with Angie last week. She thinks I'll like it because they have a hundred different bourbons and they do flights. It's in Cedar Park, on Baltimore Ave, which is pretty much gentrification station at this point. "But it's Black-owned," she says. "So, we're good."

The spot, which opened just a few weeks ago, is called Tender and it's already busy when we arrive. There's a jazzy band playing on a small stage. I see two seats opening up at the bar and I head for them but then Faye takes my hand and leads me to a table.

"This is reserved." I point to the card in the middle of the table.

"It's reserved for us," Faye says.

I'm impressed that she called ahead but before I can say so, a server appears at my side with bourbon flights for me and a Belgian beer for Faye.

"I'm starting to think this wasn't really spur of the moment."

She smiles. "I'm not sure I'm a spur-of-the-moment person. But, even if I was, I'd still have a hard time playing it by ear on your thirty-ninth birthday. It's a big deal."

"It's not a big deal," I assure her. "On the other hand, I don't mind reserved tables and speedy drinks. So, cheers to you." I raise a tumbler of bourbon in her honor.

"To *you*," Faye corrects me, clinking her beer against my glass, "on your birthday."

We drink.

The jazzy band ends its set and is followed by the rail-thin singer from Floetic, who belts out a rendition of "A Song for You" that rivals Donny Hathaway's. When I look over at Faye, she's teary. "Cynthia loved this song," she says. "She used to sing it to Vicky when she was a baby."

I take her hand and squeeze it.

She looks at me. "I didn't tell you this before, but raising Vicky was my idea. I convinced Cynthia to let me do it. I thought if I could take care of my niece, it would make up for not taking care of her mother."

I let out a long breath. "That is *a lot* of pressure to put on yourself, Faye."

"And that's not even the half of it," she says. "When you first started spending time with Vicky, I felt like I was betraying Cynthia. It's been so hard to figure out how to let you into our family without feeling like I'm being a bad sister again."

"I know Cynthia didn't want anybody to know about the eggs. But do you really think she wouldn't want me here, in Vicky's life, now that she's gone?"

Faye shakes her head. "It's not just Vicky's life you're in. You're in my life, too. You're at our house almost every day. You cook with us and eat with us. You're part of our family."

When she says this, that I'm part of their family, I get that weird feeling of happiness again.

"And you think Cynthia wouldn't like that?" I ask.

"Maybe she would," Faye says. "Or maybe she would feel like she was being replaced. I don't know. I'll never know."

This is when I realize that it was never Nick between us. It was Cynthia all along.

"So, what?" I ask her. "You're just going to feel guilty forever?"

She shakes her head. "No," she says. "I'm not."

We stop talking and listen to the rest of the song. I imagine Cynthia singing to baby Vicky. It's a nice thing to imagine.

When the singer leaves the stage, a chubby brother in a porkpie hat and sagged jeans starts a jazz-hip-hop-fusion number.

"Bathroom," Faye says. "Back in a minute."

Porkpie has finished a couple of jazzy raps, but Faye is still not back. Another dude takes the stage. "How y'all doing tonight?" he asks the crowd. He looks familiar. But he has a shiny, bald head and graying goatee, like eleventy-thousand other Black dudes his age, so I can't place him. "I'm T. Winston Turner," he says. "Y'all can call me Win. I own this place. I want to thank y'all for coming out tonight and introduce a very, very special guest performer. I first met this dope sister back in ninety-four when 'Rock This Jawn' dropped."

There's whooping from the crowd.

I'm like: WAIT.

T. Winston Turner smiles, nods his head. "Yeah, I know y'all remember 'Rock This Jawn.'"

I stand up. I don't know why, I just can't stay in my seat. Because WHAT IS HAPPENING RIGHT NOW?

"She doesn't rap anymore," says T. Winston Turner. "But it's a special occasion. So, y'all give it up old-school style for MC Faye Malice."

I can't tell you whether or not the crowd gives it up old-school style, or even exactly what that means, because the moment Faye takes the stage, everything that exists in the universe that *isn't* Faye disappears.

She's taken off her sweater, so she's all in white now, and her hair, unpinned, falls in a thick, woolly cascade against her shoulders. There's an energy radiating from her that I have never seen, something more than her usual in-control-ness, something way past confidence. It's *swagger*. There's fire and hubris in her dark eyes as they find me in the crowd.

A drumbeat starts. It's instantly familiar, a whole memory in a few pulses of sound. For a few seconds, I'm fourteen again, on the stoop with Tasha, connected and happy. Then MC Faye Malice starts to rhyme.

> *Yo, I'm West Philly born*
> *'Bout to rock this jawn*
> *Get close, lend me your ear*
> *So I can put you on*
> *It's not a party 'til I get here*
> *Party's over when I'm gone*
> *So, yo, get you a drink*
> *We gon' be here 'til dawn*

And it's perfect. Her raspy voice. Her body language, all tough lady rapper, her shoulders and hands moving in rhythm with every verse, every beat.

> *It's Faye, the illest rapper in the two-one-five*
> *These niggas wanna sweat me cuz I'm fly and I'm live*
> *But you ain't got the gravitas for a girl like me*
> *I need somebody who reads*
> *Not somebody who just smokes weed*
> *I'm talking Baldwin, I'm talking Brooks*
> *Show me your Hansberry plays*
> *And your bell hooks books*

The crowd roars so loudly that I remember there *is* a crowd, and for a moment, their presence pushes in, and I can see people jumping up and down and waving their hands in rhythm with Faye, and I can hear them rapping along, loud and so happy, and I know this is a memory we share, we who came of age in Philly circa 1994, and for the first time in a very long time, I'm glad I'm from here.

MC Faye Malice absolutely brings down the house and when the song ends, Faye's eyes find mine and she grins at me and says, "Happy Birthday, Skye." It's barely audible over the din of the cheering crowd, but that's okay because it's all mine.

When she comes offstage—a little bit breathless, her skin glistening with sweat, her eyes twinkling—several people lean in to tell her how much they love that song, how it took them back, how good she looks after all these years, how she's still got it. She's smiling, confident and gracious. And then she's standing there in front of me, reaching for my hands, saying "happy birthday" again.

And I don't know. I just can't stop myself.

"I'm in love with you."

I say the words just as some annoying dude with terrible timing taps Faye on the shoulder and she turns to said dude as he begins to loudly explain that, while *Rock This Jawn* was his shit, his favorite album was actually *All the Way Faye*, which

1. he's wrong; *All the Way Faye* was ill but still second-best;
2. nobody cares what he thinks, and by that I mean *I* don't care; and
3. THIS IS NOT THE MOTHERFUCKING TIME.

But now Faye is distracted, thanking Captain Interruption Pants for his unsolicited opinion, affable and oozing charm, and I'm standing there with my metaphorical dick in my hand.

When this annoying dude finally goes away, Faye turns back to me.

"What did you say?" she asks me loudly, over the crowd and also the drummer who's beginning a set.

I shake my head. "Nothing."

She takes my hand and leads me away from the table, past the bar, to a door marked PRIVATE. The large man standing next to it moves aside without a word. Faye opens the door and leads me through it, up some stairs, then up some more stairs, and then through another door. We come out on the roof of the building.

The night is warm and very humid and the smell of rain hangs heavy and thick in the air. We stand at the edge of the roof. To the east of us, the Philly skyline winks and sparkles.

"This is nice," I say.

Faye takes a step closer to me. "What did you say?"

"I said 'this is nice.'"

She shakes her head. "Before. Downstairs."

I can tell by the way she's looking at me that she already knows.

"I said I'm in love with you."

She nods, a little smile spreading across her face. "That's what I thought you said."

"Are you in love with me?"

She gives me a look, like, *Really?* "I just got onstage in front of two hundred people and risked potentially humiliating myself, which I said I would not do, all for you on your birthday."

"Okay. Say it, though. So I'm sure."

She moves closer to me than she has ever been, pressing her body against mine, slipping her arms around my waist. "I'm in love with you," she says in her little-bit-raspy voice. And she kisses me. Her mouth is warm and tastes of beer with a hint of peppermint. Her breath is glorious. After we've been kissing for a minute, she says, "Do you want to take me to your room?"

"Yes."

She grabs my hand and starts leading me back to the door. This is when I remember there's something I have to tell her.

"Faye. Hold on."

She stops, turns to look at me.

"Nick was cheating on you."

For a second, I'm not sure she's comprehended what I've said. She stands there blinking at me. Then she's like: "What are you talking about? How do you know that?"

"I met him at a bar. Before I met you. We were drinking and some things happened. Not sex, but things an engaged-to-be-married person shouldn't be doing with a strange woman. When I confronted him later, after I knew he was your fiancé, it sounded like it was a regular thing for him."

"Why didn't you tell me this before?" she asks.

I don't want to say. Because the answer, *the honest answer*, makes me look like a selfish asshole. But I know I have to. "I didn't tell you because I didn't think I could handle you being single. Which is very weird. And very selfish. And I'm sorry."

Faye moves away from me, to the edge of the rooftop, and looks out over the city, saying nothing. I watch her, waiting.

"Do you want me to leave?" I ask her.

"No."

"Are you sure?"

"Yes," she says. "I just need a moment."

She stands there staring out at Philly for another full minute. Then she rubs her temples and says, almost to herself, "I really don't want to be thinking about Nick tonight." She turns back to me. "Why are you telling me this now, Skye?"

"Like I said, I didn't think I could handle—"

She shakes her head. "But why are you telling me *now*?"

It's a good question. For a second, I can't think of an answer. Why *am I* telling her now, in this moment, when we've just used the love word for the first time, when we're on our way to my room to finally do the sex? This is the absolute *worst moment*. I suddenly hear Tasha's voice at the back of my brain. *You test people to see if they really care about you.*

Now I start to panic. Maybe I'm testing Faye. Maybe I don't believe she really loves me and I'm telling her about Nick now to make her *prove her love* by forgiving me. Maybe I haven't grown or changed at all. Maybe I'm just as jaded and disconnected and messed up as I was when I landed in Philly two months ago. But then I look at Faye. She's watching me with those intense dark eyes. And I feel sure. Sure I love her. Sure she loves me. And it's such a relief.

"I think I'm telling you now because I want you to have all the information," I say, realizing it's the truth as I'm saying it. "So you can decide if you still want to sleep with me or not."

She's quiet for a moment, thinking about it. Then she sighs. "That's such a good answer."

NAILED IT.

"Please don't keep any more things from me," she says.

"I won't."

She comes and stands close to me again. She puts her hands on my face. "I still want to sleep with you."

Oh, thank God.

BACK IN MY ROOM, WE lie on the bed and kiss. And kiss. And kiss. I cannot get enough of Faye's mouth, of the taste and smell of it, of the way her lips feel against mine. I could lie here with her tongue in my mouth for the rest of my life. But after a few minutes of kissing, she climbs on top of me. She sits up, so she's straddling me, then she pulls me into a sitting position, too. She tugs at my shirt and, as I raise my arms, she pulls it over my head. This is when I realize I'm still wearing my emergency bra and begin to scream internally.

Faye looks at the bra and I can see the horror in her eyes, like: *WHY ARE YOU WEARING YOUR GRANDMOTHER'S BRASSIERE?*

"I . . . wasn't expecting this to happen today," I tell her.

"It's okay," she says. "It's coming off now anyway."

She reaches around to unhook the bra. Thing is: Grandma's bra has one hundred and seventeen clasps. Oh, you thought Meemaw was just going to be out here with a regular-ass bra with a regular-ass number of clasps? You thought Gam-Gam was going to risk her titties not staying perfectly still through a four-hour church service? What if she caught the spirit? You thought she was finna risk her bosoms just falling out all over the place while she was praising Jesus? You. Thought. Wrong.

Thirty seconds later, Faye has managed to unhook two, maybe three of the clasps. Sweat is starting to form on her brow.

"Um, you know what?" I say. "Just let me do it."

She lets go, looking relieved.

I take the straps off my shoulders, twist the bra around and unhook it, then hurl it across the room like I'm exorcising a demon.

I reach for Faye's top and she lets me pull it over her head. She's wearing the kind of bra you want to be wearing whilst getting laid. It's black and silky. When I take it off, there are her new breasts. They're different from her previous breasts, for sure. They're higher, bouncier, firmer. I like them exactly as much as I liked the old ones, which is a lot. I suck one nipple and then the other, and hear Faye's breath quicken.

She pushes me back on the bed again and kisses my stomach. She unbuckles my belt, unzips my jeans and pulls them off. Thankfully, I'm not wearing your grandmother's drawers. I'm not wearing underwear at all, in fact, which makes things easy. Faye pushes my thighs apart. I close my eyes and wait for more pleasure to wash over me. It . . . sort of does and it sort of doesn't. I mean, she's definitely down there doing stuff. But . . . to be quite honest . . .

Faye stops and looks up at me. "Is this okay?" she asks.

"Okay" is exactly what I'd call it.

"It's been a while," she continues. "I might be a little . . . rusty."

"I can talk you through it if you like."

She smiles.

So, I talk her through it. She goes back down and I tell her exactly what to do and how to do it, how slowly, how softly. Not like that. Yes, there. There. Yes. She listens, her tongue following my every instruction, until it feels as though she's got the hang of me, that she understands how I like it, and then I shut up and let her take over again. And it's wonderful. I come, thinking about how lucky I am, how safe and happy I feel.

And that's not even the best part. Because now it's my turn, now I get to go down on her. I get to feel her hands in my hair, her thighs against my cheeks. I get to see her back arch and her head fall back. I get to hear her little-bit-raspy voice wrap itself around my name when she comes.

31

THE NEXT COUPLE OF WEEKS ARE THE BEST OF MY ENTIRE WASTED life. I spend my days working on the final deets of the Bali-Sydney trip, which kicks off three weeks from now, and planning the New Zealand and Indonesia trips in late July. I tell Toni that I'd like her to lead the Malaysia trip in August, so I can get back to Philly in two months instead of three, and offer her a promotion and a raise.

Most days after school, and on the weekend, I hang with Vicky. Some nights, Faye comes to my bed. We agree not to tell Vicky about us just yet, what with the whole *I didn't find you to give you to Aunt Faye* thing.

"We'll figure it out," Faye assures me.

We make plans to go to Wildwood the week before I leave, which is also the first week of summer break for Vicky and Faye.

I give more thought to introducing Vicky to my mother, who asks about the kid when I take her to the grocery store and again when I help her get ready for church.

"You bringing the baby next time?"

"She's not a baby."

"She's my grandbaby. Baby or not."

Vicky is similarly eager for the intro, asking me to take her with, every time I mention I'm going to my mother's.

"What harm can it do?" Viva asks when I talk to her about it.

I figure she's right. My issues with my mother are mine. They aren't really relevant to Vicky, who will never need to depend on my mother for anything.

So I give in. I tell them both that I'll bring Vicky to visit next Sunday afternoon. I tell Slade to make sure the house is clean by then.

"Why?"

"I'm bringing someone to meet Mom."

"Who?"

I haven't mentioned anything about Vicky or the eggs to my brother. I'm not keeping it a secret or anything. I guess I just figured my mother would tell him. Which, apparently, she has not.

"Good for you," he says, smiling wide, when I tell him about the kid. "I'm glad you found something to stick around for." There's only a little bit of shade in his voice; he mostly sounds sincere, earnest even.

I never called him about that drink. I feel kind of shitty about it now.

"Can I meet her?" he asks. "Or just Mom?"

"You can meet her, if you want."

"Aight," he says. "Aight, cool."

ON THE LAST DAY OF school, there's an awards ceremony at West Philadelphia Montesssori. Faye has to be at her own last day of school across town, so I ask Viva to come along so I have someone to share shade-glances with when Kenny and Charlotte annoy me. Vicky gets certificates of excellence in English, science, and geography, and an extra special certificate with embossed gold print on it for outstanding achievement in spelling. I get teary every time she walks onstage.

"It's kind of crazy loving somebody this much, isn't it?" Kenny asks, and when I look at him he's a little teary, too. I decide he's not quite as annoying as I thought.

When the awards ceremony ends, I hurry over to Vicky, ready to tell her how proud I am of her, how smart and good at stuff she is, but when I open my mouth, what comes out is, "I love you so much, Vick."

She beams up at me. "Same."

I WAKE UP SUNDAY MORNING in Faye's bed. Vicky's at her dad's, so I slept over. We had a rough night. In a sexy way. My nipples are sore. And there's a visible bite on my right inner thigh. Faye is a ravenous lover, with an eclectic sexual appetite. Pretty confident every hole in my body has had her tongue in it. Even my nose, although I'm eighty percent sure that was an accident. Well. Seventy-five percent. She's kinky. Is what I'm saying.

The moment I open my eyes, she's wrapping her arms around me, pulling me on top of her, opening her legs. I slip my fingers inside her and she moans in my ear. We stay in bed for hours, fucking in different positions, with our hands, or our mouths, or my vibrator, or the strap-on Faye picked up for us at a toy shop on her way home from work. During breaks from all the sex, we talk.

I ask her why she doesn't have children of her own. She says she never thought she could handle kids. "My parents never really seemed to be able to handle us. I didn't think I could do much better." She's lying on her side, propped up on her elbow. Through the window, morning sun casts amber light on her face and in her hair.

I ask about her former spouses. She tells me about Nigel, the Jamaican boyfriend she married right out of college. "He was like my father in some ways. He'd disappear for days at a time and then show up bearing gifts. In the end, I realized that wasn't something I had to accept in a relationship. And I divorced him."

"But you got married again?"

She nods. "Five years ago."

"To a woman?" I ask, twisting a lock of her hair around my finger.

"Yes," she says. "Sydette."

"What was she like?"

"Smart. Ambitious. Obsessed with the idea that I was going to leave her for a man." She shakes her head, annoyed at the memory. "I've left men for women. I've *never* left a woman for a man."

"So, why'd you break up?"

"She left *me*, for a lesbian. Whose sexuality wouldn't aggravate her ulcer, I guess."

"Wow."

"We're still friends, though," she says. Then, "What about you, Skye? Who are your significant exes?"

"I had a long-term thing in my twenties," I tell her. "Mostly it's been short-term and *very* short-term things since then."

"Why?"

"It's what I've wanted."

She makes a little sound, like *hmm*. After a moment, she asks, "Is it still what you want?"

"No."

She kisses me. Softly at first, and then with an increasing passion. I grab fistfuls of her hair and slip my tongue in her mouth, and she reaches for the strap-on.

When it's nearly eleven, we disentangle our bodies and drag ourselves out of bed. We shower together and put our clothes on, and we're fully dressed when Kenny drops Vicky off.

"WHAT'S GOING ON?" VICKY ASKS me. "Why are you smiling so much?"

We're walking to my mother's house. It's a mile away, but it's a bright afternoon.

"Nothing's going on. Can't I just be in a good mood?"

"Yeah," she says. But she looks suspicious.

Faye isn't coming to meet my mother, because Vicky wants it to just be us. Which I'm fine with. Having Faye meet my mother feels like a lot, under the circumstances of all the sex we're currently having. And it's still nice to just kick it with Vicky, to be goofy with her, to talk about Grace Jones, and gossip about Jaz having a new boyfriend who looks like Gerald from *Hey Arnold!*

When we get to my mother's house, she's waiting for us on the front porch. I'm a little surprised she remembered we were coming. Her hair is done in fresh plaits and she's wearing a lavender tracksuit I've never seen before. When she spots us coming up the steps, she stands, nervously smoothing out her outfit, and I think she wants to look put together for the kid.

"Hey, Mom. This is Vicky."

Despite harassing me to introduce her to my mother, Vicky is silent now, bashfully waving hello. My mother's not having any of that. She wraps her arms around the kid and squeezes. After a few moments, she takes a step back and beams down at Vicky. "Look at this perfect child," she says, her hands on Vicky's face, examining it from every angle, while the kid smiles up at her. I'm smiling, too, watching them.

"I've been praying for you to come and see me," my mother says to Vicky. "I feel so blessed today."

"This is for you," Vicky says, reaching for the potted plant I'm holding. "Aunt Faye wanted us to get amaryllis but they didn't have that at the flower store. This is a red begonia." She hands it to my mother.

"I love begonias," my mother says.

I'm wondering if that's true or not when my brother hurries out onto the porch, looking stressed.

"Why didn't you answer my calls?" he asks me.

"I didn't get any," I tell him, taking my phone out of my pocket and realizing it's still on silent from last night.

Slade looks at Vicky and smiles, but there's something weird in his face.

"What's going on?"

"Skye?" a voice calls from inside the house.

A man's voice.

My father's voice.

"Is that Skye out there?"

I move away from the door.

"He showed up yesterday," Slade whispers. "I didn't know until I got home this morning."

Vicky and my mother are still talking about the begonia. I take the kid's hand and pull her away.

My mother looks at me. "What's wrong, Skye Beam?"

"What's Fred doing here?" I ask her.

"Oh," she says. "Well, your father doesn't have anywhere to stay right now—"

"He's staying here?"

"For a little while," she says.

I feel walls suddenly closing in on me.

"Skye?" my father calls again, his voice closer this time. And then there he is, standing in the doorway. His light skin is even lighter than it used to be, almost papery with age. He's wearing thick glasses that make his eyes look small. The twenty-five years since I've seen him have not softened him. He's still thin and relatively muscly, still stern-faced. Still menacing, at least to me. "I thought I heard your voice," he says, smiling.

I look at my mother, standing there holding the begonia, blinking at me as if she doesn't know why I'm upset, and I feel twelve again, unprotected and unloved.

"You not gonna say hello to your own father?" Fred asks me. He looks at the kid. "This my grandbaby?"

I start down the front steps, pulling Vicky along behind me.

"Where are we going?" she asks.

I don't answer. My face feels hot. My chest is tight. We start down the street.

"Where are we going?"

"Home." Only I don't actually know where we're going. Is the bed-and-breakfast this way? Is Vicky's house in the other direction?

Slade catches up to us near the corner. "I told her to make him leave," he says. "But it's not my house. *I* can't make him leave. I would if I could."

But I barely hear him. Because this is the corner where, when I was twelve, I stood in the rain trying to decide which direction to run, after my father hurled a pot of coffee across the room at me because I rolled my eyes at him, and all my mother said in response was, "Calm down, Fred. It's too early in the morning for all that."

I leave my brother standing there, on the spot where coffee dripped from my sneakers onto the pavement, and pull Vicky across the street. I don't look back.

"WHAT HAPPENED?" FAYE ASKS WHEN Vicky and I enter the house, less than an hour after we left. "Why are you back already?"

"Skye's dad was there," Vicky says. "She got all freaked out."

"She's exaggerating."

When we got to the other side of the street, I was reeling. A few blocks later, I was seething. By the time we got to Vicky's block, I'd pushed the past back down into the bowels of my psyche, where it belongs. And now I'm fine. Really. I'M FINE.

"What was your father doing there?" Faye asks.

I shrug. "He doesn't have a place to live, I guess. I didn't hang around to get all the details."

She peers at me, concerned. "Are you alright?"

"I'm fine. It's my fault, anyway."

"Your fault how?"

I let my guard down. I let myself forget for a minute that nobody actually gives a shit about me. "It doesn't matter," I tell her. "I don't even want to talk about it anymore."

"Skye—"

"I don't want to talk about it, Faye."

My phone buzzes in my pocket. I don't look at it.

"I have to go," I say.

"Now?" Vicky asks. "I thought we were gonna hang."

"I have work stuff," I tell her, turning and heading for the door.

I hear Faye saying, "Are you sure you're—"

But I'm already on the porch, then down the steps, then almost running down the block.

MY PLAN IS TO GO back to the bed-and-breakfast and bury myself in work. Really. I swear, I don't intend to leave the country. But then I cross Larchwood and walk past the beauty supply shop where I stood outside for an hour once when I was thirteen because, on the walk home from school, I suddenly realized I didn't want to go home, ever. Tasha had been picked up early from school by her grandparents and taken to Wilmington for the weekend, so I didn't know where to go. I just stood there. After an hour, the Asian store owner threatened to call the cops if I didn't move along, so I walked down to the next corner and sat in the bus shelter until finally deciding I might as well go home. The bus shelter is still there, too. I really hate this city.

By the time I get to the B and B, I'm reeling again, my mind cluttering with flashes of shitty memories, one after the other, that I can't push away no matter how loudly I scream internally. When I get to my room, I grab a suitcase without even thinking about it. I'm not even sure what I pack. I grab my passport and call a Lyft to take me to Thirtieth Street Station.

I'm on the train to New York when I open my airline app with shaking hands and pay a ridiculous amount of money to change my flight to Denpasar, which leaves in a week, to tomorrow.

32

Where are you? Can you pick up? Vicky's not handling it well.

I get this text six minutes after boarding my flight at JFK. It's eight in the morning, and I've been up all night, pacing the airport or slouched in a cramped seat. All I've had to eat is coffee.

I turned my phone off last night after changing my ticket. I only turned it on just now to text Toni that I'm on my way to Bali. When I turned it off, it was to forget that anything existed outside JFK. When I turn it back on, the world, my life, flood back in. There are THIR-TEEN voicemails. And this text.

I've done a pretty good job of not thinking about Vicky or Faye all night. That might be hard to believe, but I have spent years perfecting my ability to not think about people I don't want to think about. It's my superpower. Or evidence of my unresolved trauma. Whichev. Point is: When I get this text, when I let my brain kick on, after hours and hours without food or sleep, and remember that Vicky exists, back in Philly, where I'm not, I feel . . . well, not much, to be totally honest. Numbness, mostly. Emptiness. I tell myself I'll check in with Vicky when I get to Bali. And I turn off my phone again.

I lean my head back and close my eyes as the sounds of boarding continue around me. I start to doze off a little bit, but then I feel a tap on my shoulder. The other passengers in my row are boarding, so I have to get up from my aisle seat to let them in. They are a grown man and a tween-age boy. Ugh. I hate sitting next to dudes on flights. They fart SO. MUCH.

When they're finally in their seats, I retake mine. I lean my head back and close my eyes again. I think I fall asleep for I don't know how long, just a couple of minutes, probably. What wakes me up is the sound of familiar voices.

I open my eyes and squint hazily at the tween sitting next to me. Light plays across his face and I realize it's from the laptop he's holding, as are the familiar voices. The familiar cartoon voices. This kid is watching *Steven Universe*.

It's an episode I've seen six or seven times over the last couple of months, one of Vicky's favorites. There's a lot of pizza in it. I stare at the screen as Vicky floods in and I realize I've made a huge mistake.

"Sean," the dad or uncle or whoever says to the kid. "Earbuds, please."

Sean starts digging around in his backpack for earbuds.

I want to scream. Not internally. EXTERNALLY. But I'm Black, so I don't, because that kind of shit can get me killed by the airline cops. So instead? I grab the barf bag from my seatback and ralph up the last coffee I ate.

Sean is staring at me, wide-eyed and, I'm pretty sure, hella amused.

"Ma'am?" his father or uncle asks. "Are you okay?"

"I'm actually not," I say, suddenly standing up, my barf bag swinging wildly. "I need to get off this plane."

I grab my laptop bag from under the seat and sling it across my shoulder. People are still boarding, jamming the aisle. I step out of my row anyway, reaching for my carry-on in the overhead bin and almost dropping it on the head of an elderly woman who, if we're being real, doesn't look like she could survive this level of injury. I manage to catch it, but only by dropping the barf bag. Its coffee-puke contents splash onto my shoulder and against the side of my face. There is a collective UGH from everyone around me. The tween boy looks thrilled to death with the quality of entertainment on this aircraft.

A flight attendant I've never seen before is squeezing through the aisle toward me. "Miss, you have to get back in your seat, we're still boarding."

"I'm getting off," I tell her.

"You can't. You have to sit down."

I am *this close* to screaming in her face the African American proverb: I DON'T HAVE TO DO SHIT BUT STAY BLACK AND DIE. Luckily, another flight attendant, a brother named Lamont who I've flown with a dozen times, is hurrying from the other end of the aisle toward me, saying, "Skye? Are you okay? Are you sick?"

"Yes. I need to get off the plane."

Lamont tells everyone in the aisle to step to one side. He puts a glove on his right hand and picks up my barf bag. With the other hand, he takes my carry-on and leads me back to the front of the plane, and off onto the jet bridge. He dumps my puke into a trash can and rolls my luggage down the jet bridge behind me. At the end of the corridor, we dap, and Lamont hurries back to the flight.

When I emerge back at the gate and hurriedly turn on my phone, it starts ringing immediately. It's Faye. I pick up.

"What happened?"

"What do you mean?" she asks. "Didn't you get my messages?"

"My phone was off. *What happened?*"

"Ethan called the cops again," she says. "One of them hit Reverend Seymour. She fell and hit her head."

"She's . . . ?"

"She's in intensive care at Penn. Vicky is . . . not doing well, I think."

"She's breaking shit?"

"No. She's not doing anything. She's not talking."

A staticky voice on the PA system announces final boarding for my flight.

"Are you at the airport?" Faye asks.

"Oh. Um. Yeah."

"Are you going somewhere?"

"Bali. Actually."

She's silent, and for a second I think she's hung up. But then she's like: "You're leaving the country? *Now?*"

"I . . . needed to go," I say. "But I'll . . . come back. If Vicky—"

"No. Don't come back. I'll take care of Vicky."

This time, she definitely hangs up.

IT TAKES ME A COUPLE of hours to get back to West Philly, not including the fifteen minutes I spend in the airport bathroom cleaning puke off myself before I hop on the AirTrain. When I finally turn onto Vicky's block, there are people everywhere. It looks like nearly every neighbor is out, standing in small groups of three or more. Some of them look teary, some angry, some both. There's a huge, handmade poster in the reverend's front yard. GET WELL, REVEREND SEYMOUR. WE'RE PRAYING FOR YOU.

"Did you hear?" Miss Vena calls to me as I'm dragging my laptop bag and carry-on past her house.

I tell her yes, I heard, and ask how she's doing.

She shakes her head, and her lip trembles. "I've known LaVonda forty years. She's one of the best people I've ever met. She didn't deserve to be treated this way."

I look down the street at Ethan's house.

"Nobody's seen that white fool since it happened," Miss Vena says. "He took his family and drove off before the ambulance even got here."

"I'm surprised his house is still intact."

"Mmm-hmm, me too," she says. "But I think folks know LaVonda wouldn't want anything like that to go on, on her behalf. If it was me? I'd want y'all to burn this whole damn city down."

Same.

Faye answers the door with a look of complete disinterest on her face, like I'm—you guessed it—a random Jehovah's Witness come to call. And, honestly? It's a relief. Because I don't want to talk about it. Any of it. My father. My mother. My leaving. I came back for Vicky. That's all.

"Hello, Skye," Faye says, polite and cold. "Vicky's not here."

"Where is she? I've been calling and texting her."

"I took her phone to the geek bar this morning. She's at the library with Jasmine."

"Oh. Okay," I say. "Which lib—"

She's already closing the door.

I CONSIDER HEADING TO THE library to find Vicky. But there are three libraries nearby and searching them all will take forever. So I walk back to the B and B. I never told Viva I was leaving, so I figure my room and all the shit I left in it are unchanged. I can hang there and then . . . look for Vicky at Jasmine's later? Or go back to Faye's? Or just wait for her to call me? I'm not sure what to do. But then, when I get to the B and B, Vicky herself is sitting on the porch swing, watching her sneakered toes drag along the wood planks as she swings back and forth. When I see her, I feel that familiar vibration under my ribs. *I have never seen such a perfect human being.* I feel anger rising in my chest. Anger at myself. For almost not being here. For almost letting her down. I don't deserve to have her cry at my funeral.

"Where have you been?" she asks, jumping up off the swing. "I texted you a bunch."

"My phone was off. I'm sorry. I'm *so sorry* I wasn't here for you, Vicky."

She frowns. "Why are you being weird?"

"I'm not!"

"You kind of are."

I place my bags by the front door, sigh heavily and sit down on the swing. "I guess I'm just . . . out of whack. Because of the reverend."

"It's so messed up," she says, sitting beside me.

"How are you doing?"

"I was real mad at first. I thought I was going to lose it. But then . . ." She shrugs.

"Then what?"

"What's the point?" she asks.

"Of getting mad?"

"Yeah," she says. "It just gets me in trouble all the time. I'm over being in trouble. I just want to be normal again."

"What's normal?" I ask her.

"Just, like . . . not messed up."

Wow. You and me both, kid. But also: "You are normal, Vicky. Anger is normal."

She doesn't respond to that. "There's a vigil for the reverend tonight," she says. "To pray for her. Can you come?"

"Yeah."

"Are you going to the hospital?"

"No. Are you?"

"Aunt Faye won't let me. I would if I could. How come you're not?"

"It's not really my thing."

"I thought the reverend is your friend."

I sigh heavily again, and hold the top of my head in my hands.

"What's wrong?" Vicky asks.

"Nothing. I just fucking feel like fucking screaming my fucking head off."

"That's so many F-bombs."

"I've felt like screaming so much lately," I tell her. I take my hands off my head and look at the kid. "Do you feel like screaming?"

"I always feel like screaming," she says. "But, like, for real?"

"For real."

"Right now?"

"On the count of three. One. Two. Three."

We scream. It's kind of half-assed: the way you scream when you're frustrated about slow internet. But it's something. It feels good. It's a start.

"That was . . . okay," I tell Vicky. "But I think we can do better."

So, we scream again. This time, I think about Ethan. And the police. I think about Reverend Seymour. I feel myself letting go. My volume rises; my throat opens; my chest vibrates. Vicky looks wide-eyed at me, impressed, I think, and then her own scream kicks up a notch, into a shriek so loud that she covers her own ears. But she keeps screaming. I do, too. We both stop a second for a breath and then we scream some more.

I scream for my twelve-year-old self, locked in a dark closet. For myself at fourteen, in the therapist's waiting room, holding a scream in my throat. I scream at my mother. At my father. At my adult self, for not having yet figured out a way to get past it all, to not be so messed up, to be normal, to have a life. I *scream*.

There are people walking down the sidewalk and they stare. Miss Newsome comes out of her house and peers across the street at us. Vicky stands up straight, like a rocket about to blast off, her fists clenched, her eyes closed, her mouth open to the sky. We scream, over and over, louder and louder, until my throat is raw and there are tears streaming down my face, and Vicky's fists slowly unclench. This is when Viva appears, hurrying up the street with a yoga mat over her shoulder and grocery bags in her arms, yelling, "Chicas! Stop scream-ing, por el amor de Cristo!"

Shit.

"Sorry, Viva," I say, hurrying down the steps to help her with the bags.

"Dios mío, Skye. You know I'm running a business here, ¿verdá?" Then she sees my face. "¿Qué pasa?"

We tell her about the reverend.

She softens. "That's horrible," she says, sighing and shaking her head. "But come inside, por favor. Before my guests start leaving bad Yelp reviews."

WHEN I GET TO THE Hospital of the University of Pennsylvania, it occurs to me that they might not let me in to see Reverend Seymour because, according to reputable authorities on the matter, i.e. every TV show I've watched over the last thirty-nine years, you have to be a close family member to visit a patient in the ICU. Turns out, TV lied, though, and they don't ask me how I'm related at all. I just show my ID, sign in, and go up to the intensive care department. At the ICU desk, I have to sign in again. I notice the reverend's name on at least half of the lines of the clipboard sheet, under "Patient Being Visited." I stealthily flip back to the previous sheet and it's the same. She's had like a dozen visitors already today and it's only three in the afternoon.

When I get to the reverend's room, I hear voices, so I slow down and peek in from the hallway. Two men, including the one who was on grill duty at the cookout in the reverend's backyard, are sitting in chairs by the reverend's bedside. A woman is standing on the other side of the bed, fussing with the sheets and blankets. Keisha and another teenage girl are sitting on the windowsill, talking quietly to each other.

I expected half of Reverend Seymour's head to have been shaved, for some kind of emergency surgery, like my mother's was. But she still has a full head of hair. She's hooked up to a respirator, which is making a sighing sound that can be heard over the voices in the room. The reverend is asleep or unconscious. I don't know which.

I sense movement behind me and when I turn around, there's Nick. Ugh.

"Oh," he says. "Skye. Hey."

I don't hey him back. "Why are you here?"

"Because I care about the reverend," he says. "I'm also representing her and her family in a case against the police. Along with Brother Nguyen."

"What's Brother Nguyen got to do with it?"

"He was there. He tried to protect Reverend Seymour," Nick says. "Got a cop's elbow in the face for it. Broke his nose."

"Shit."

"Yeah."

For a second, he looks like he's going to turn around and go back the way he came. Which: Please do. But then he doesn't. "Listen," he says, "I'm glad I ran into you. I've been meaning to get in touch."

Ew. "Why?"

"To say sorry. I shouldn't have pressured you not to tell Faye."

"That you were cheating on her?"

"I wasn't cheat—" He stops, takes a breath. "*I* still wouldn't call it 'cheating.' But we can agree to disagree on that."

"I don't."

"You don't what?" he asks.

"Agree. To disagree."

He frowns. "Fine. Either way, I shouldn't have put you in that position."

"You shouldn't have."

"I know, Skye," he says. "That's literally what I'm saying."

I peer at him, trying to decide what his angle is. But he actually seems kind of sincere?

I shrug. "I also had my own reasons for not telling her. So."

"Oh." He looks interested in that. "Like what?"

I'm not sure what he knows about Faye and me, and I have no intention of giving him any information. So, I just sigh a big sigh and shake my head and say, "Like none of your damn business, nigga."

He puts his hands up, all mea culpa or whatev.

My phone vibrates. It's a text from my brother. Two words: *He left*.

"You going in?" Nick asks me.

"I don't think so."

"Why'd you come down here, then?"

Wow, he's really Questions B. McCurious today, isn't he?

I think about recording the cops outside the reverend's house that day. How she thanked me, hugged me. How it doesn't seem to have amounted to anything. I'm not sure showing up now amounts to anything, either. She probably won't ever know I was here. But Vicky was right. The reverend is my friend.

"I just wanted to see her, I guess." Which is true. But the strange thing is? I also came because every time I've talked to the reverend she's made me feel a little less broken; a little less like a failure at life, and I could use some of that right now. But that's ridiculous, because she's obviously in no condition to help me. So, all I can do is stand here, peering through the curtains at her and her loved ones.

Letdown is inevitable, Sister Skye, she told me. *But if you close that distance, so is connection. So is joy.*

The times I've felt happiest and most connected in the last couple of months have been when I closed the distance between myself and another human. Vicky. Faye. Viva. The reverend. Even Tasha, that time on the bus, even with that whole jacket-in-the-door situation. But you know what else? I closed some distance with my mother and that was a pretty big mistake.

So, what should I do? is what I want to ask Reverend Seymour, but can't.

It occurs to me, though, that there might be someone else I can ask.

33

MY BROTHER IS SITTING ON THE STOOP, SMOKING A BLUNT AND reading a book about Paul Robeson, like a proper West Philadelphian, when I walk up. When he sees me, he looks surprised as shit.

"I was sure you were going to leave town after . . ." His voice trails off.

I sit on the steps beside him. He takes a drag off his blunt and offers it to me. I haven't smoked weed in years. I had two consecutive marijuana-related panic attacks back in 2005, and the stuff just makes me feel anxious now. Anxious is not the feel I need at this particular moment in time. "You have bourbon?"

He shakes his head. "Nah. I have some scotch, though. It's not too peaty."

I agree to scotch. He goes inside and brings it out in a coffee mug. I take a drink. It's peaty as hell. Like licking the mossy side of a tree. Like what you'd expect a hobbit's butthole to taste like, if you happened to be part of the ass-eating community of the Shire. But I have a rule that I never complain about free liquor. So, I drink it while my brother smokes his blunt, and wonders why I came, probably.

"Why'd you stalk me and blow up my phone for weeks trying to get me to see our mother?" I ask him. "You never really seemed to care before."

He thinks about it. "A lot of reasons, I guess. Mostly, I was hoping if you visited more, you might want to help out more. It seemed to work, too, until Dad showed up."

I frown at the mention of Fred, and take several large sips of scotch. "How do you stay here," I ask Slade, "and not just be enraged all the time? Is it the weed?"

He laughs.

"It's the weed, right?"

"It wasn't all bad," he says. "There was a lot of good stuff, too, especially after he was gone. When I feel resentful, I try to remember that stuff."

You only remember what you want to remember. What fits your agenda.

"Do you know I went back to church a few years ago?" he asks.

"You go to church?"

"Nah. But I did for a little while. Most of it was whack. Sexist. Homophobic. But one idea I took from it really helped me."

"Vengeance?" I ask. Christian God is so dick-hard for vengeance.

"Mercy."

I squint at him. "What do you mean?"

"It means forgiving—"

I put a hand up. "You don't need to mansplain mercy to me, Slade. I know what *it* means. I'm asking what *you* mean. How it helped you."

"Sorry," he says. "Okay, so, I basically had it out with Mom a few months ago. After I lost my job at the tax place. I felt like it was her fault—their fault—that I couldn't get my life together. I asked her why she didn't protect us from our father, why she kept him around so long. You know what she said?"

I shrug.

"She couldn't remember."

"Remember what?" I ask him. "Why she kept him around?"

"Any of it. She said she thought she divorced him when I was five. I told her I was fifteen. She just sat there looking confused."

"You really believe she doesn't remember what actually happened?"

"Yes," he says, sounding very sure. "Skye, she can't remember half her life some days. She thinks people are alive who died in 1980. Sometimes she doesn't remember what her parents' names were. I wanted her to see how she jacked up my life and own up to it. I wanted some kind of . . . closure, I guess you'd call it? But closure is a joke even when people do remember. With Mom?" He shakes his head. "If that's what you're waiting on, you can forget it. It doesn't exist."

"So . . . what, then?" I ask. "You forgave them?"

"Not *them*. I'll never forgive *that nigga* as long as I live."

"But you forgave Mom?"

"I had *mercy* on her," he says. "Because she needs mercy. And because I needed to get on with my damn life."

"So, you think I should have mercy on our mother?" I ask.

"I think you should do whatever you need to do to be able to have the life you want."

"Do you?" I ask. "Have the life you want?"

"I'm working on it," he says. "I have a job I like. I have a girl I want to spend more time with, maybe even in a permanent way. It may not look like much progress to you, from the outside. But, yeah. I'm getting there."

I sip my scotch and we don't say anything for a while. It's the easy kind of silence. I forgot how easy Slade is to be silent with.

After a couple of minutes, he says, "Can I ask you something?"

"I guess."

"Why do you hate me?"

"I don't hate you. Jesus. Don't be so dramatic."

He frowns. "You literally told me you hate me. *I hate you so much.* That's what you said."

That does sound like me.

"Seriously, Skye," he says. "What did I do?" He looks young in this moment. Like a rejected kid. Like someone who loves you and can't figure out why you don't love them back. It low-key makes me feel like shit.

"I think I resented you for not leaving," I tell him. "It always felt like you were excusing it all by staying with Mom. I guess I decided you were disloyal."

He laughs. "*Disloyal?* Shit. You really are a lot sometimes, you know that?" He shakes his head. "I wasn't excusing anything. I ain't have nowhere else to go. I flunked out of college. I was nineteen and broke."

"That was twenty years ago."

"Okay," he says. "But I'm not like you, Skye."

"Meaning what?"

"Meaning . . . special. Not everybody can just go and do whatever they want with their life. I'm not young, gifted, and Black, on some Nina Simone shit. I'm a *regular* nigga."

It's my turn to laugh. Slade laughs, too. It feels familiar, in a good way.

He takes a long drag off his blunt.

I take another sip of scotch.

"Your kid's cute, by the way," he says. "She looks like us."

I start to say she's not my kid, but decide to skip it.

"I hope I get to meet her properly soon," he says.

"You heard about the elderly lady who got knocked down by the cops?" I ask. "The reverend?"

"Yeah, I was just watching that on the news. These violent-ass cops never stop with this shit. You know that lady?"

"Yes. There's a vigil for her tonight at dusk. You should come if you want. Vicky and I will be there."

"Okay," he says, smiling. "I will."

"Skye, is that you?" our mother calls from inside the house.

I get up off the step.

"You going in?" Slade asks.

I hand him the empty coffee mug. "Not today."

"Maybe next time?"

"Maybe next time," I say, going down the steps. "Or maybe never. We'll see."

34

THE VIGIL FOR REVEREND SEYMOUR IS PACKED. FROM VICKY'S PORCH, she and I watch hundreds of people gathering. There are two news vans at the corner. And there are cops. A dozen of them, at least, standing on the sidewalks and leaning against squad cars, looking menacing.

"Of course you pigs show up at a peaceful vigil!" Mr. Mitch yells at them from his porch. "Y'all ain't done enough already?"

Slade arrives, wearing a Malcolm X T-shirt and holding hands with a woman. "This is my girl, Elle," he says. Then, to her, "This is my little sister, Skye."

Elle hugs me. She's tall and curly-haired and looks a little bit like Viva.

Vicky walks up to Slade. "Vicky Valentine," she says, offering him her hand, all serious.

Slade shakes it. "Slade Ellison. Nice to meet you."

"I like your name. It sounds like a prehistoric vampire."

"Yeah," Slade replies. "It kind of does."

"Do you want some Oreos?"

"I'd love some," he says, sounding genuinely excited, almost as if she'd offered him Pop-Tarts.

I spot Viva and Jason in the crowd halfway down the block and wave. I warned her that Slade would be here, so I don't expect her to join us on the porch, but I'm glad she came. I see Nick in the crowd, too, in a shirt and tie, looking like a lawyer, which, considering there are cops at this peaceful vigil, I'm guessing is intentional. For a second, I think I spot Tasha down the block, but when I look again she's not there.

Faye comes out of the house with candles. She's still being cold and polite with me. I haven't apologized for leaving or tried to smooth things over at all because there hasn't really been space for it. But honestly? Three months ago I didn't even have Vicky. And now I do. Why get greedy? The kid is enough. She's plenty! The rest of it—my mother; this neighborhood where every corner is a potential traumatic setback; the idea of trying to reconnect with Tasha; and, maybe especially, a relationship with Faye—still all feels too risky. The safer thing is to go back to my old life with regular Vicky time when I'm back between trips, just like I planned when I canceled my flight to São Paulo.

Mr. Mitch is still yelling at the cops. Brother Nguyen walks by with Keisha. He has a splint on his nose and a black eye, but he waves at us.

Kenny, Charlotte, and Sabrina arrive. Sabrina's carrying a BLACK LIVES MATTER sign. Kenny looks somber. He's not even on his phone. "Hey, baby girl," he says to Vicky. She doesn't look annoyed when he hugs her.

At dusk, we come down off the porch and stand with the rest of the crowd and light our candles. One of Reverend Seymour's daughters leads a prayer for her recovery. I don't believe in prayer, but I bow my head and pray along anyway.

I feel someone brush past me. I look up and see a cop moving to my right, toward Slade. I feel a rush of panic. I didn't see my brother do anything. But I figure he probably has weed on him, which is decriminalized in Philly, but you can still get a citation and a fine, and are much more likely to if you're Black. But the cop moves past Slade.

"Sir? Are you intoxicated?"

Mr. Mitch, who has his head down and his eyes closed, PRAY-ING, looks up, startled. When he sees the cop, anger spreads across his face. "I don't drink. I leave that to my wife," he says. "Leave me the hell alone."

Some people have stopped praying and turned to see what's going on. "Leave him alone!" somebody says.

Then, at the top of her lungs, Vicky yells, "Leave us alone, pig!"

The cop looks over at her, takes three swift steps toward her, and grabs her arm. Which: OH, HELL NO.

I step between them, grabbing his arm in turn and wrenching it off of her. Looking surprised, and pissed, he takes a step back and reaches for his gun.

Shit slows down. Just like in the movies. There's a rush of sound, and I think people are screaming? But it's muffled, so I'm not sure. What I am sure about is that I can see his pale fingers touching his gun.

And then I can't. Because someone is standing between me and the cop. It's Faye.

The next fraction of a moment, Mr. Mitch, Miss Vena, Sabrina, and Slade are all there, standing in front of Faye, and other people, including Nick, Kenny, and Jason, are pushing in toward the cop, forcing him back. Other cops rush in, and one of them starts yelling at the first cop not to touch his weapon again. "You're going to start a riot! There's not enough of us!"

People are losing their shit now, screaming, "Leave us alone, pigs!" over and over until it becomes a rage-filled chant.

The cops yell back, telling people to dissipate. No one does. More and more people push in, forcing the cops back away from us. I look around for Vicky, but I don't see her. Suddenly, there's a soft bang and then a cloud of smoke. Faye grabs my hand.

"Where's Vicky?" I ask her, panicked.

"Viva got her away," she says, pulling me toward the sidewalk. And then we're running.

Y'ALL ALREADY KNOW HOW I FEEL ABOUT RUNNING.

It's all I can do to keep up with Faye. I've never heard her mention sports, but surely she's a professional athlete or something? I'm dragging along behind her, panting, wondering if I will have survived a dangerous encounter with the police only to perish by running-related lung failure, when Faye starts to slow down and I realize we're blocks away from where we started, halfway to the bed-and-breakfast.

I double over, holding my chest.

"We have to keep moving," Faye says. Despite the fact that she just put herself between me and a cop with a loaded firearm, she's resumed the coldly polite tone from earlier. "We have to get inside."

I shake my head. "Can't run no more."

"We can walk now," she says. "But we can't stop."

So, we walk.

While I catch my breath, I try to decide what to say to her, how to tell her that I'm sorry for leaving and that I love her so much. I know! It shouldn't have taken her jumping in front of a gun for me to believe that I can count on her, since she's already shown up for me in so many other ways, like

1. helping me when I had an actual factual meltdown over a grimy pool hall;
2. pretending it wasn't super gross when I got snot on her shoulder while crying about my childhood trauma; and
3. deciding to still love me even though I waited way too long to tell her about Nick.

My phone buzzes. It's a text from Viva: *V is safe.* I show it to Faye. She looks relieved.

She takes out her own phone and makes a call. I can hear Kenny yelling on the other end. "Where are you? Where's Vicky?"

"She's at Viva's. Meet us there."

He says okay and they hang up.

"Faye, listen," I say, stopping in the middle of the sidewalk.

"We have to keep moving, Skye."

"I know. But just listen for a minute."

She stops. She doesn't look happy about it.

"I decided to stay in Philly and get to know Vicky," I tell her, "so maybe there'd be someone in the world who'd give a shit if I dropped dead. I realize now that was stupid. Because does it even matter how I die if I don't have a life I want in the first place?"

She peers at me, blinks. "Are you asking me?"

"No. I don't know why I put that in the form of a question. Sorry."

A siren wails.

"Talk faster," Faye says.

"I'm sorry. For leaving. I did it because I didn't think it was safe to count on you. On anybody, I guess."

"I know why you left," she says. "It was obvious with the state you were in when you came back from your mother's. What I don't know is why you didn't tell me that. Why you just left *without a word*."

"I . . . didn't mean to." Which is sort of true. But is also stupid.

Faye starts walking again. I walk beside her, but I don't say anything else because what else can I say? I think about our trip to Wildwood, which was supposed to be today. Jesus, I really fucked this whole thing up. But then a question occurs to me.

"If you hate me, why did you jump in front of that cop?"

She stops, looks at me. *"To protect Vicky."*

Ohhhhhhhhh. Right. Yeah, that seems really obvious now, actually.

"And I never said I hate you. We're not in eighth grade, Skye. I can't fall out of love with you overnight."

"So, you love me?"

"Of course I do," she says, walking faster. "But that doesn't mean I can be with you."

We're almost at the bed-and-breakfast, turning onto Viva's street.

"So, when you jumped in front of that cop to protect Vicky, you weren't thinking about me at all?" I ask.

She doesn't answer, just keeps walking.

"Not even a teensy bit? As a side note, maybe?"

We're in front of the B and B now and she stops and turns to look at me. She looks like MC Faye Malice in this moment—tough; unfuckwithable—and I think she's not going to forgive me, she's not going to let me back in. But then she says, "Maybe as a side note."

I move closer to her. She lets me.

"I can't handle disappearances," she says.

"I know. I'm sorry. I won't disappear again. I promise."

The toughness slips away. Her shoulders relax, her eyes soften. She looks at my lips, in that way she has. So, I kiss her.

When we go inside, we find Vicky in the parlor with Viva and Jason. She's sitting by the front window, so I think she must have seen us kissing, but she doesn't say anything. She looks happy to see us both.

I expect Faye to scold the kid for yelling at the cops but she doesn't. She just grabs her and hugs her so tightly I think Vicky might pop. When she lets go, I grab the kid and hug her even tighter. I kiss her cheeks and the top of her head. Then we pass her back and forth between us, hugging and kissing her, until she gets annoyed and asks us to stop.

Epilogue

MY FLIGHTS FROM JAKARTA ARE TWENTY-FIVE HOURS LONG, NOT including a two-hour layover in Doha. By the time I touch down in Philly, I'm so tired that I'm not sure I can find my way off the plane. I drag my carry-on through the terminal, yawning every ten seconds, in a zombie-like stupor. All I can think about is sleep.

And then I see Vicky.

She's standing just on the other side of the security exit, waving to me, bouncing up and down with excitement. My exhausted brain and body are suddenly flooded with energy and I do something I swore I'd never do again unless my life was in danger, and maybe not even then. I run. Like a character at the end of a movie, sprinting toward her love, if said character was a janky-ass runner.

I've talked to Vicky every week since I left Philly. I've called her from Bali, texted her from New Zealand, facetimed her from Indonesia. But seeing her now, in the flesh, is something else entirely. *I have never seen such a perfect child.* I throw my arms around her and squeeze and feel like the luckiest person in the world when she squeezes back.

"I missed you, kid."

"Me, too," she says.

I breathe in the slightly stinky scent of her and feel happy tears at the corners of my eyes. Viva was right. I *am* a crier.

"What'd you bring me?" she asks when I finally let her go.

"Lots. But you have to wait until we get to the B and B."

She groans.

"Viva's saving us some pastelillos from breakfast," I tell her, and she's all smiles again.

"Where's Faye?" I ask, looking around for her.

"She's waiting in the car," Vicky says. "I wanted to come in by myself so I could see you first."

In the two months since I've been away, Vicky has not completely warmed to the idea of Faye and me. We talk and text about it a lot, and she's definitely getting there—she's stopped using the phrase *stole you from me*, which is something, right?—but she's taking her time about it, and Faye and I are both okay with that.

On our way to baggage claim, Vicky tells me we have to go visit Reverend Seymour after breakfast. She's back home, continuing her steady recovery. "I promised I'd bring you over when you got back," the kid says.

"Okay, but I'm definitely going to need a nap first."

She looks at me like I'm being ridiculous. "You can't *nap* on your first day home."

"Why not?"

"Because there's a hundred things we have to talk about!"

"Like what?"

"Like, do you know Aunt Faye took me and Jaz to a bunch of rallies downtown? We protested police brutality *and* prisons *and* sexual assault."

"Yes, I do know. You told me."

"But did I tell you I learned how to disable a tear gas canister?"

"You did?" I ask, impressed.

"Yes! And I did a street medic training!" She's literally bouncing up and down. "Activist club is gonna be so lit this year!"

It takes forever for the bags to start coming down the baggage carousel. While we wait, Vicky gives me details on her summer that I didn't get during our short calls, including "Jaz broke up with her boyfriend and now she goes with this girl, Trina," and "My stepsister dropped out of college and Charlotte is SO MAD," and "My dad stopped working on our weekends. We went to a Phillies game last Saturday. It was boring."

I listen with interest to every word, despite being only half awake.

My luggage finally appears and we stack it precariously on a push-cart and head for the exit.

A giant panoramic print of the Philadelphia skyline covers an entire wall on the way out. I've walked past it a hundred times and never cared. This time, I can't help smiling at it as Vicky tells me how Slade came over and showed her how to fix a bike chain.

I'm happy to be in Philly. The people I love live here, and so do I.

Acknowledgments

In the course of my writing this book, my partner and I had our first child. My grandmother died. We had our second child. We left the city and moved to the country. My mother died. A pandemic swept the globe. Through it all, there was this book to finish. I could never have done it without the support of my parenting partner and best friend, CarmenLeah McKenzie-Ascencio. Thank you for loving me, in all the big and small ways. Thank you for bringing me lunch and café Cubanos, and entertaining the kids for extra hours so I could get more writing done. Thank you for continuing to choose me. Thank you for putting up with me.

To my mother-in-law, Margarita Ascencio, thank you for always being willing to babysit extra so I could work on this book. I can't think of a better gift for a writing mom.

To Caitlin McKenna, the most perfect editor I could have hoped for, thank you for seeking me out and beginning this professional relationship, and also for the friendship that has followed.

To my friend Shaadi Devereaux, thank you for your always sharp analysis; Liliana Ortega, thank you for helping me get all the Spanish right; and my agent, Alexa Stark, thanks for many things but especially for calling me a "comedic genius."

And to my babies, Story and Rio, thank you for always finding me funny. Your laughter is my favorite sound. You make my life the life I want.

PHOTO © CARA BROSTROM

MIA MCKENZIE is the award-winning author of *The Summer We Got Free*. She grew up in West Philly and still uses the word "jawn" every day. She now lives in Massachusetts with her family.

@miamckenzie